Spire Publishing

www.spirepublishing.com

Haven

Shadow Lands: Book Three

by
Simon Lister

Spire Publishing
www.spirepublishing.com

Spire Publishing, January 2008

Second edition. This edition first published in Canada 2008 by Spire Publishing.

Spire Publishing is a trademark of Adlibbed Ltd.

Note to Librarians: A cataloguing record for this book is available from the Library and Archives Canada. Visit www.collectionscanada.ca/amicus/index-e.html

Printed and bound in the US or the UK by Lightningsource Ltd.
Cover photo/design © S Lister

ISBN: 1-897312-64-4

Simon Lister was born in Twyford and raised in Berkshire. He studied and lived in London for several years before travelling and working around the world. He now lives and writes on the North shore of Loch Tay. His Arthurian saga comprises of *Shadow Lands*, *Causeway* and *Haven*.

For information on ordering the books in this series please visit:
www.simonlister.co.uk

Haven

is for

Steve

- thanks for all the editorial work

Acknowledgements

Thanks to Rick who co-wrote the earlier Shadow Land stories when we were kids and who helped editorially in these later versions. Thanks also to: Anna and Stan for Loch Tay. Tish and Bren for all the support and encouragement, and Mark too, who was there with the original inspiration back when I was doing a primary school essay. Paul Biggs and Jenny Grewal for the valuable feedback, and Steve Forrow for the re-reading, critical assessments and editorial input. And a final thanks to the folks at PABD for all the effort and patience in getting these books to print. Any errors that remain are, of course, solely of my own doing.

Characters

The Wessex

Arthur – Warlord of Wessex
Merdynn – Counsellor to King Maldred
Ruadan – Arthur's second-in-command and brother to Ceinwen
Trevenna (f) – Arthur's sister, married to Cei and a warrior in the Anglian war band
Ceinwen (f) – healer and ex-tracker for the Wessex war band, sister to Ruadan
Morgund – Captain in the Wessex war band
Mar'h - Captain in the Wessex war band
Balor – Wessex warrior
Morveren (f) – Wessex warrior
Ethain – Wessex warrior
Cael – Wessex warrior
Tomas – Wessex warrior, married to Elowen
Elowen (f) – Wessex warrior, married to Tomas
Tamsyn (f) – Wessex warrior, sister to Talan
Talan – Wessex warrior, brother to Tamsyn
Llud – Wessex warrior
Laethrig – the Wessex Blacksmith
Kenwyn – Wessex Chieftain

The Anglians

Cei – Anglian Warlord, childhood friend to Arthur and married to Arthur's sister, Trevenna
Hengest – Cei's second-in-command, son to Aelfhelm
Cerdic – Anglian warrior
Aelfhelm – Anglian warrior, father to Hengest
Elwyn – Anglian warrior and boat captain
Aylydd (f) – Anglian warrior and boat captain
Lissa – Anglian warrior and boat captain
Leah (f) – Anglian warrior

Saewulf – Anglian warrior
Cuthwin – Anglian warrior
Berwyn – Anglian warrior
Roswitha (f) – Anglian warrior
Herewulf – Anglian warrior
Osla – Anglian warrior
Wolfestan – Anglian warrior, brother to Elfida
Elfida (f) – Anglian warrior, sister to Wolfestan
Godhelm – Anglian warrior
Thruidred – Anglian warrior
Wayland – Anglian warrior
Ranulf – Anglian warrior
Leofrun (f) – Anglian warrior
Aelfric – Anglian youth
Henna (f) – Anglian healer
Aelle – Anglian Chieftain

The Mercians

Maldred – King of the southern tribes
Gereint – Mercian Warlord, brother to Glore
Glore – Mercian warrior, brother to Gereint
Dystran – Mercian warrior
Unna (f) – Harbour master of the Haven

The Uathach

Ablach – Uathach Chieftain of the lands to the North of Anglia, father to Gwyna
Gwyna (f) – Uathach warrior, daughter to Ablach
Ruraidh – Uathach Captain
Hund – Uathach Chieftain of the lands to the North of Mercia
Benoc – Uathach Chieftain of the lands to the far north

The Cithol

Venning – Cithol Lord and ruler of the Veiled City, father to Fin Seren
Kane – Commander of the Veiled City
Fin Seren (f) – daughter and heir to Lord Venning
Terrill – Captain of the Cithol

The Bretons

Bran – Chieftain of the Bretons
Cardell (f) – Advisor to Bran
Charljenka (f) - Breton child
Nialgrada – Breton child

Chapter One

The Causeway had fallen to the invading Adren. Arthur and his warriors had held the enemy for as long as it was possible but the horde from the East had numbered too many and were it not for the arrival of Gwyna's Uathach, and Seren's warning of the Adren trap, then none of the Britons would now be making the retreat to the Veiled City.

It was Gereint, the Mercian Warlord, who led the column of warriors that made their way back on the Westway towards the Winter Wood. He rode alone and although several of the Mercians tried to engage him in conversation they soon fell back rebuffed by his grim silence. His brother, Glore, had fallen before the Adren swords as they held the last bridge on the Causeway. He felt the loss all the keener for the knowledge that an hour after Glore had died they had finally made it to the safety of the cliffs. He had not even been able to retrieve the body to send his spirit onwards through the cleansing flames of the funeral pyre. He felt that he had let his brother down in death as much as he had in life and the bitterness of the acknowledgement seeped through his thoughts and poisoned his mind. He could stomach no other company and could not escape his own. He rode in silence and stared straight ahead and he heard nothing of the world around him and saw nothing but the distant Westway winding through the rolling countryside.

Of the proud southern warriors who had ridden to the Causeway only half undertook the return journey. The contrast could hardly have been starker. The returning warriors were slumped in their saddles with exhaustion and many carried injuries that ranged in seriousness from cuts and bruises to broken bones and wounds that may yet prove fatal. Ceinwen rode slowly along the column helping to temporarily address the various injuries until more permanent action could be taken once they stopped at the camp above the Winter Wood. She wanted to keep her body busy and her mind occupied and away from the one truth that obsessively commandeered her thoughts; she had treated and healed countless warriors yet she had been unable to aid her brother, Ruadan. Not only had she not been able to save him but with Morveren's arms wrapped around her and dragging her backwards she could only watch as his body was butchered in a bloody fury of curved swords. She hadn't truly realised just how much she had depended upon him since the deaths of her own family. Even when they hadn't been together she had drawn strength from the knowledge that someone close to her was still alive and able to understand and support her in her loss. Over the months since Branque she had formed good friendships with Morveren and Morgund, and got on well with most of the other warriors, but none had been so close to her as Ruadan. The pain of losing her husband and daughter had barely begun to heal and now she had lost her brother too. Like many around her she rode in silence, unheeding of anything but the hollowness of her grief.

All the warriors had lost friends and comrades. The loss was all the harder to bear in defeat, and they had the look of a beaten army in retreat. Arthur rode at the rear of the column with Morgund and Balor. He thought the battle on the Causeway was anything but a defeat. It was impossible to assess with any accuracy but he guessed that they had destroyed between a quarter and a third of the enemy force as they had originally estimated it but having since seen the whole of the Adren army from the vantage point above the flats he felt it was more likely now that the Adren had only lost a fifth of their force in gaining the Causeway. More of them would die before Gwyna withdrew her Uathach warriors from the cliff tops. He had wanted to line his warriors alongside the Uathach but he knew they had fought beyond their limits and to throw them once more into battle would have been to sacrifice them for little gain. There had been no other option but to retreat from the fighting and rest.

While he did not regard the battle on the Causeway as a defeat, and despite the fact that the Adren had lost thousands of their soldiers, he could not bring himself to regard it as a victory either. He had lost almost half the total of warriors from Mercia, Anglia and Wessex and the latter two had already suffered greater losses than the Mercians had. The Adren, at best, had lost a fifth of their force and if the exchange continued at that rate then the outcome could only be complete defeat. The addition of the Uathach warriors would redress the balance to its former unequal footing, and there was still the hope that Mar'h could train an effective force from Caer Sulis, but it was an inescapable conclusion that the losses of the hardened and trained warriors of the southern war bands could only be replaced by wild, undisciplined warriors and hastily trained and untested soldiers. Added to this was the fact that they had just lost the most defendable position in the whole of Britain.

Once again Arthur's thoughts turned to Merdynn and Cei. So much rested upon their attempt to destroy the Adren source of supplies. Arthur knew that if he could delay the Adren advance long enough for Cei to permanently cut their supplies then the Adren would have to turn back. No army could keep going forward when the country around them was bare of food and no supplies were being delivered to them. Despite Arthur's best attempts to keep Cei's mission a secret the word had gradually crept out until all the southern warriors knew the truth of his and Merdynn's absence in the East and the importance of buying them as much time as possible. The memory of his dream returned unbidden and the image of Merdynn lying lifeless on a cold headland lingered in his thoughts.

Whether or not Cei had yet succeeded Arthur knew he had to make his stand in the Winter Wood. If Cei had already managed to destroy the Adren's source of supplies then they would need the Veiled City to replace it and if Cei had yet to succeed then the Adren's original aim of taking the Veiled City would still hold true.

His attention returned to the present and he noticed how silent Morgund and Balor were. He looked along the length of the column ahead of him and saw the same slouched silence. He cursed loudly and both Balor and Morgund looked across at him in surprise.

'What are you? Jilted milkmaids? Sulking farm hands? You're warriors! Warriors who have just killed thousands of the enemy! Act like this now and the next time you face the enemy will be the last time. You two can start acting like the warriors you are and set an example for this lot or slink off home now and get out of my sight!' He spurred his horse forward in disgust and started to work his way along the strung out line ahead of them. He shamed, praised or encouraged each group he passed through and gradually the visible despair of the worn warriors was replaced by a pride for what they had done and, while their obvious exhaustion remained, a grim determination steadily spread along the column, the battle hadn't been lost and neither had the war; they would make their stand in the Winter Wood.

After the initial shock of Arthur's scorn wore off Morgund watched as the subtle transformation took place ahead of him. No battle songs rang out, their pace did not increase and no boasts of combat sprang up but group by group their heads lifted to look forward and they sat straighter as they neared their destination. When they eventually reached Dunraven, the camp above the Winter Wood, they no longer had the appearance of a defeated army but the look of a battle-worn war band, exhausted and bloody, but proud of what they had done, proud of those who had fallen and determined to avenge them further.

Despite their weariness they set about the business of setting up camp. Much of what they required was already stored there and they soon had food cooking over fires. Some of the warriors decided to postpone their meals in favour of the desperate need to sleep and they slumped amongst the furs and blankets that were already laid in the makeshift sleeping quarters.

Ceinwen finished attending to the last of the injured and had them carried off to rest in the same lean-to shelters where others already slept. She wiped her face with a dirty cloth and tossed the last of her short knives and stitching needles into a pot of water that boiled over a low fire. She sat back on her heels and massaged her painful neck before opening a packet of powder and tipping it onto her tongue. She grimaced slightly at its bitter taste and felt her jaw as if expecting the pain there to be dulling already. She closed her eyes and felt herself slipping into sleep almost immediately but the image of Ruadan falling under the Adren swords sprang straight to her mind and slapped her back to wakefulness. She groaned softly and felt the weight of grief and despair settle deep within her chest until it filled her with a contradictory feeling of hollow emptiness. She ran her hands up the sides of her still dirty face and up into the roots of her tangled hair. She sensed someone standing by her side and fought back the bitter foretaste of tears.

'He died as a warrior defending the land he loved, the people he loved. Fighting for you, and me. It was quick and we can only hope for the same when it comes to our turn.'

She looked up at Arthur silhouetted by the rising sun behind him. She blinked in the brightness and saw that his hand was stretched out towards her. She took it and he lifted her to her feet. She linked her arm through his and leant against him as they walked to the edge of the copse where they stood overlooking the Winter Wood.

'This is where I sat with Leah. You stood here watching the Wood while we all slept.' She still spoke with a conscious effort not to move her healing jaw too much. She was silent for a while remembering the time she had sat here with Leah then asked quietly, 'Was it really only seven, eight months ago?'

'Yes. And Cei sat here with you both.'

'So much has happened since then. So many have died. So much has changed.'

'When we stood here the Belgae already lay dead in their valleys and the Branque villages had already been slaughtered.'

'And now they've come to slaughter the peoples of Britain.'

'And that's why Ruadan fought and died. To stop that happening.'

'Yet still it's happening.'

Arthur turned to look at her and took her by the elbows. 'Listen to me Ceinwen. I need you. We all do. Don't do Ruadan and your family the dishonour of giving up either in your heart or thoughts. We know the Adren won't stop until we are all dead but we haven't yet lost a single village in Britain. They want the Veiled City and they want all other peoples exterminated. They want the world to themselves and themselves alone. Ruadan and the others died attempting to stop that and stop them we will. We stood on the Causeway and they died in their thousands. We'll stand here and again they'll die in their thousands. We'll fight them until every last dog soldier of theirs lies dead. And when we've hacked the head off the last of the corpses of those who sought to defile our shores then we can grieve and lament our own dead. But now we have to carry on the battle and I need you to fight with all your strength. Use Ruadan's death to steel your resolve, don't let it rob you of everything that he fought for.'

She looked up at him and nodded despite the silent tears rolling down her face. He gently brushed them aside and the completely unexpected tenderness of the simple act broke her resolve not to weep for her dead friends and family. She wept for the brother she couldn't save. She wept for her daughter who had been so full of life. And she wept for her husband, Andala; good, steadfast Andala. Her sobbing tears racked her anew at the memory of her husband; the husband she had never truly loved. The marriage had been founded more on his love for her than on any reciprocated feelings and the guilt she felt about having been unable to equally return that love added remorse to her tears; she hadn't deserved his love and he hadn't deserved to die.

Arthur held her for long minutes as she sobbed without control or embarrassment. He needed her to be free from her grief because she was one of the few Britons who had been in the Veiled City and she would be important in helping to calm any fears the other warriors might have about entering the Winter Wood.

Finally she pulled away and rubbed the heels of her hands into her eyes and said with a shuddering voice and an attempted smile, 'Enough! Ruadan would be ashamed to see me weep before the battle ends!'

Arthur smiled sadly at her, 'A warrior has more right than anyone else to weep for their dead and the dead have every right to demand it. You have nothing to reproach yourself for.'

She smiled more genuinely and took a deep breath. As they returned to the sleeping shelters she said, 'I wonder where Cei and Leah are now.'

During Arthur's seemingly sincere attempt to comfort her his thoughts had been occupied by much the same question.

When he saw her bedded down and drifting quickly to sleep he looked around the camp and saw Gereint sitting alone with a hot drink clasped in both hands before him. He crossed the camp to go and sit silently beside him.

When he finally took his turn to get some rest he went to sleep thinking about Gwyna and the rearguard on the cliffs above the Causeway but it was the image of Seren that crept into his dreams.

Arthur awoke some hours later to the sounds of the camp around him. Half the warriors were still sleeping but those who were awake were feeding the horses, cleaning weapons and checking on what remained of their stores and provisions. He lay still for a minute listening to the rain fall on the canvas roof of the sleeping shelter. As the land warmed under the gradually rising sun it drew in the colder air from the East and while he had been sleeping heavy clouds had crept across the land bringing with them petulant showers of hail and cold rain.

He sat up and cast aside the cloak that had served as a blanket and watched as the hail bounced off the ground outside the shelter. Every muscle in his body seemed to be contracted in a knotting ache and he absently massaged the back of his thigh where he had been hit by an Adren arrow several months ago. The wound still troubled him, more so than the other various injuries he had received over the years and he put it down to no longer being young; his body was beginning to rebel against the demands he forced upon it. He ran a hand over the deep gash on his left forearm that Ceinwen had stitched together some days ago and struggled to his feet.

The warriors nearby called a greeting to him and he nodded in return as he surveyed the camp. Everything else was at it should be and he noted with satisfaction that the warriors seemed to be in better spirits now that they had slept and eaten. He saw Gereint standing with Morgund on the eastern edge of the copse. They seemed to be arguing and he frowned as Gereint turned angrily aside and stalked off alone. Morgund stood in the hail watching him for a while then made for the shelter where Arthur was standing. As he passed by, Arthur asked, 'What was that about?'

'Nothing really,' Morgund replied without catching Arthur's eye then added by way of an explanation, 'Glore died back on the Causeway.'

'I know. And he blames me?'

Morgund gave up on his attempt to avoid the conversation and faced Arthur with a shrug.

'Why?'

'He thinks that if we pulled back when he suggested then his brother would still be alive.'

'Does he?'

Morgund shrugged again to show that he did not agree with Gereint's opinion.

'Have you slept, eaten?' Arthur asked.

'Yes but not enough of either.'

'Spend some time with Ceinwen. I don't want her dwelling on Ruadan's death.'

Morgund agreed but he was thinking that he might spend some time with Morveren instead.

'Ceinwen,' Arthur reiterated and walked out into the hail in the direction Gereint had taken leaving Morgund to wonder if Arthur had just been repeating himself or correcting him about whom to spend some time with. He had the uneasy feeling that Arthur had indeed been correcting him and he groaned quietly to himself as he suddenly remembered who Morveren's father was rumoured to be. He went to find Ceinwen.

Arthur caught up with Gereint on the edge of the copse overlooking the Winter Wood. 'You blame me for your brother's death,' Arthur stated straight away.

Gereint looked warily at the warlord before turning away and saying bitterly, 'Yes.'

'Why?'

Gereint glanced quickly at Arthur trying to gauge the other's temper. 'We should have retreated when I told you to.'

'When you told me to,' Arthur repeated coldly.

'When I said we should pull back from the Gates,' Gereint said correcting himself.

'And you think your brother would be alive now if we had?'

'Yes,' Gereint said, turning to face Arthur directly.

'No. He would still be dead. You would be dead. I'd be dead and so would everyone else. But more than this Britain would be dead. We'd have been out on the flats before the Uathach arrived and caught between two Adren forces and there Britain would have died.'

'You didn't even know the Uathach were coming or about the Adren behind us when I said to pull back! You were just too blood-thirsty and too bloody-minded to retreat!'

'But the Adren were behind us and the Uathach did come. Many of our warriors died on the Causeway but Britain didn't.'

'Not yet.'

'So this is the Mercian way, is it? This is what makes a Mercian Warlord.'

'What?'

'Surrender. Giving up when your own blood is spilt. Finding someone or something to blame instead of seeking retribution.'

Gereint's anger threatened to break and it was all he could do to restrain himself from striking at Arthur. Arthur just stared at him.

'You don't blame me. You don't even blame the Adren. You blame yourself for Glore's death and you shouldn't. He was a warrior and warriors die. Britain must not.' Arthur turned away and left Gereint standing in the icy rain.

The last of the winter showers scurried westwards leaving the bright sun to inch higher in a clear blue sky. The first real warmth of the coming summer spread across the land and the warriors at the copse relaxed in the shade of the trees or lounged on the grassy slopes as they waited for word from the Uathach who were holding the cliffs against the Adren.

Three days after arriving at the camp above the Winter Wood Arthur sent out mounted patrols to the East to look for the returning Uathach. He feared they had been drawn into a full-blown battle against the Adren. He had expressly told Gwyna and Ruraidh that such a battle could only be lost and to avoid it at all costs but he was not there to order them when to abandon the cliffs and he paced the camp irritable and frustrated.

He had also expected the Cithol to have made contact with them by now. Both Seren and Terrill knew to keep a watch on the copse and Arthur was disturbed that not even a message had been sent to him.

When the patrols returned and there was still no news from either the Cithol or Uathach Arthur decided to ride east along the Westway until he came across either the Uathach or the Adren. He took Morgund and Morveren with him and left Ceinwen at the camp in case Seren or Terrill finally made contact. He had only been gone for four hours when a Cithol messenger emerged from the Winter Wood but Ceinwen could tell straight away that it was neither Terrill nor Seren who laboured up the steep hill.

The other warriors kept their distance but watched with curiosity as Ceinwen met the hooded Cithol. Even those who had previously kept alive the hope that the Cithol would send a force to help them had now given up any such expectations and they wondered what message the Cithol could have for Arthur.

Ceinwen led the messenger into the shade of one of the shelters and offered him food. The offer was declined and the Cithol kept his hood close about his face. Ceinwen sat opposite him and waited quietly for him to begin. The silence stretched to awkwardness and Ceinwen finally broke it. 'You have a message from Lord Venning to Arthur?'

The Cithol tilted his head slightly as if to hear better and Ceinwen realised that he probably had not understood her. She knew they spoke the same language but this was probably the first time the Cithol opposite her had spoken to anyone outside the city and she realised that her inability to move her jaw properly was hindering the process further. She held up a hand to indicate the Cithol should stay where he was and went to fetch Balor. She explained to him what she thought the problem was and they both returned to the waiting Cithol.

'What do you want then?' Balor asked and Ceinwen groaned quietly.

'Are you Arthur?'

Balor laughed and Ceinwen shook her head.

'I'm sorry.' The Cithol clasped his hands in front of him before continuing, 'You look much the same to us.'

Balor snorted derisively, 'He's about a foot and half taller – with hair. Not much the same if you ask me.'

'I meant no offence,' the Cithol said bowing his head.

'There is none taken,' Ceinwen enunciated carefully. She was wondering what had possessed her to choose Balor as a spokesman instead of Hengest or Gereint. Balor was looking at the Cithol's pale skinned hands and Ceinwen could see what he was about to say next so she quickly put a hand on his knee to silence him.

The Cithol noted the gesture and introduced himself, 'My name is Vosper. I am one of the Cithol and I come from the Veiled City.'

'Do you, by gods?' Balor asked sourly before Ceinwen could stop him.

'Yes,' the Cithol replied, either missing or ignoring Balor's scornful sarcasm.

'I'm Ceinwen and this is Balor. You have a message for Arthur from Lord Venning?'

'Yes and no.'

Balor snorted again and the Cithol turned to him, 'Yes; the message is for Arthur, but no; it is not from Lord Venning.'

'We're Arthur's, er, captains,' Ceinwen said for want of a better explanation.

'Yes, I have heard of you Ceinwen,' Vosper replied, then looked with studied silence at Balor who actually bristled with indignation.

'Is the message from Fin Seren?' Ceinwen asked desperately trying to keep the exchange on track.

'The message is from Captain Terrill. No one has spoken to or seen Seren. She is being held in the Palace as is Captain Terrill but he managed to get word to me to watch this place.'

'Why are they being held?'

'I am not on the council,' Vosper replied.

Ceinwen did not know if that meant he was unable to tell them or whether he was unwilling to tell them but clearly all was not as it should be in the Veiled City.

'What's the message then?' Balor asked bluntly.

'Is Arthur not here?'

'No. He's riding back to the Causeway,' Ceinwen explained.

'Does he still hold the Causeway against the Adren?'

'The Causeway fell a few days ago. The Uathach are now holding the cliffs.'

'Then the Adren will be here before long,' Vosper concluded.

'Ready to fight yet?' Balor's tone had lost none of its former antagonism.

'Yes.'

Ceinwen and Balor exchanged surprised glances at the Cithol's reply.

'You're going to need to be because there's thousands of the bastards,' Balor said but the wind had been taken from his sails.

'Terrill's message?' Ceinwen prompted.

'Many of us disagree with the council's decision not to have joined you in the battle for the Causeway even though we would have been of little use to you. Many of us agreed with Captain Terrill that we should have done more. He told me to gather together those that knew the Winter Wood and who felt the same as us. They are waiting below on the edge of the wood.'

'How many?' Balor asked.

'Fifty.'

'Fifty?'

'Yes.'

'Hardly an army is it?'

'We can't fight as you do. We are not warriors.'

'Then you're no bloody good to us are you?' Balor said in disgust ready to stand up and finish what he felt was a pointless meeting.

'I disagree. We have our crossbows and we know how to use them but the real benefit to you will be as guides through the Winter Wood. We know all the paths and tunnels while you don't, and nor does the enemy.'

'More prancing through woodland! I'm sick of forests, that's why I joined the Wessex war band – to get away from the bloody things!'

Vosper stared at Balor uncertainly, 'I do not understand. Are you unhappy that we want to fight to protect our city?'

Ceinwen turned angrily on Balor and told him to leave them alone. He stood up just as angrily and abruptly left.

'I apologise for his attitude,' Ceinwen said slowly and as clearly she could.

'Perhaps the wound on his head troubles him?' Vosper offered.

'Quite possibly,' Ceinwen said with a smile, 'Your offer to act as guides is greatly appreciated. I'm sure Arthur will accept it and be thankful for it. He probably won't be gone too long. Would you like to stay and wait for him here?'

The Cithol looked around the camp at Ceinwen's invitation.

'We can bring you some food,' Ceinwen offered and that stopped the Cithol's pretence at decorum immediately. He hastily stood.

'We will wait on the edge of the wood for Arthur's return,' he said and before Ceinwen could stand up he had turned and left the lean-to shelter.

Ceinwen remained where she was and took out another folded packet of powder from a pouch on her belt. Tilting her head back she emptied the packet onto her tongue and closed her eyes against the pain from her jaw and broken teeth. She wondered what was happening in the Veiled City. Seren and Terrill had been at the white cliffs expressly to warn Arthur of the Adren tunnel but why just the two of them and why Seren? Why had they returned to the city without waiting for Arthur and more importantly why were they now being held by Lord Venning? It seemed implied by Vosper's words that his detachment of fifty Cithol were not wholly acting with Lord Venning's sanction. She was still trying to make sense of the scant information she had gleaned when Hengest and Gereint approached the shelter and sat down. The powder she had taken was beginning to dull the pain and the last thing she wanted was a prolonged conversation but she saw that she had little choice.

'What did the Cithol want?' Hengest asked.

'He was offering his people's help as guides in the Winter Wood – and the tunnels.'

'So they expect us to help defend their homes after they left us to fend for ourselves?' Hengest asked in disgust. The withdrawal from the Causeway had effectively handed the Adren free access to most of Anglia.

'Let them defend their own lands. I say we pull back to Caer Cadarn,' Gereint said.

Ceinwen sighed and took a deep breath before beginning, 'You know why Cei and Merdynn went east? The Adren have a city something like the Cithol one. Whatever it is, they can produce food throughout the whole year like the Cithol do. It's why they're able to support such an army. Cei will destroy the source of that power. We can't let them replace their loss with the Veiled City. It's that simple.'

'Who's to say they can succeed in the East?' Hengest asked, quietly thinking of his father, Aelfhelm, who had gone with Cei.

'They have Merdynn with them,' Ceinwen pointed out desperate for the debate to end so that she could rest.

'That's no guarantee,' Gereint belligerently replied.

'Look, even if they don't succeed we still can't let them take the Veiled City and double their power.'

'You saw the Adren numbers from the cliffs, we all did. There's tens of thousands of them! We can't stop them with a few hundred warriors!' Gereint spoke bitterly but he was only saying aloud what many of the warriors had been thinking since the Causeway fell.

'I'm too tired and my jaw aches too much to argue with you. I suggest you prepare your surrender treaty for the Adren. You may want to put in a clause about how your families and property must be respected by the Adren.' She stood up and added just before leaving the shelter, 'I'm sure Arthur will want to look over it before you hand it to the Adren.'

They sat in silence for a few minutes after Ceinwen had gone thinking over what she had said.

'We can't surrender and there's nowhere in Britain where we can hide for long,' Hengest concluded.

'Not in Britain no. But we have the ships to take us west.' Gereint looked at the ground as he spoke, already half-regretting that he had voiced the thought.

Hengest was quiet for a moment as he considered Gereint's implied suggestion. He was thinking of Ruadan and the others who had died on the Causeway; to abandon Britain now seemed like a betrayal of those who had already fallen. He looked at Gereint and said quietly, 'I don't think you ought to suggest that to Arthur.'

Arthur returned to the camp a day later at the head of the Uathach riders. The warriors at the copse gathered to watch them cover the distance from the Westway to the camp. In the chaos on the flats and the hurried departure from the cliffs it had been difficult for the Britons to form an accurate assessment of how many Uathach horsemen there had been but the general consensus on the hill was that they had not lost many in the defence of the cliffs.

Arthur had been concerned that Gwyna may not have had the necessary control over the Uathach warriors to stop them becoming involved in an outright battle with the Adren but his fears had been groundless. The slaying of her father and replacing him as chieftain had been the most convincing way to demonstrate to them her worthiness as their leader in battle. No one else had dared to challenge Ablach in his long years as the leader of their tribe and to them it was only fitting that a son, or daughter, should claim their rights of inheritance in such a manner. As Gwyna pointed out to Arthur on the ride back from the cliffs, it was not so different from his slaying of the southern king, Maldred.

The defence of the white cliffs had gone well. At first the Adren had only sent probing attacks up to the headland as they organised their main forces on the flats. These had been repelled easily as had the more serious attempts that followed. When the Adren finally put their full force to assailing the full width of the cliffs Gwyna quickly realised the inevitability of being outflanked and ordered her warriors to mount up and withdraw.

The Adren seemed to have no desire to give chase and instead began setting up a staging camp where the abandoned Anglian village still stood. Arthur had met Gwyna about halfway between the cliffs and the copse and together they had set up patrols to watch the Adren army and report back on its movements. Arthur had put Morveren in charge of one of these patrols with orders to ride to the copse above the Winter Wood as soon as the Adren army formed up to march onwards into Britain.

When the Uathach horsemen rode into the camp one of the Mercian warriors began a loud chant and soon the hilltop rang to the noise of acclamation as the southern warriors voiced their praise of the Uathach's charge on the flats. Gwyna's warriors were surprised to be so welcomed by the Britons but the reception made them feel even prouder of their exploits and in an unexpected way made them feel prouder of the Britons who had stood on the Causeway and held back the Adren for so long. As the Uathach sought food and quarters to sleep in, many of them renewed acquaintances and friendships with the Britons they had first met in the Great Hall at Caer Sulis. If the Britons resented the lateness of the Uathach intervention then none of it showed in that initial meeting.

Arthur looked on with satisfaction; he had known that once they had fought in a battle together their old enmity would rapidly diminish but he was nonetheless relieved to see it actually happen. As he was watching the greetings Ceinwen came up to him and took to him one side to tell him about the visit from Vosper. They went to get something to eat and while Ceinwen mashed some food in a cup she told him what little news the Cithol had to impart to them. Arthur frowned when she mentioned that Seren and Terrill were being held in the Palace but she was unable to elaborate or provide any answers to his questions.

Arthur immediately left Dunraven and descended the hill to the edge of the Winter Wood in search of Vosper and his guides. He had not gone far into the fringes of the wood when he came across them sitting by a fire in a bower of latticed branches. He stood looking at them while they in turn studied him. His clothes were still caked in dried blood and mud from the marsh and he reeked of the battlefield. He was the embodiment of the Cithol view of an outsider; dangerous and barbaric. One of the

Cithol stood and took a step closer to the outsider.

'You are Arthur of the Britons?'

'Yes. Vosper?'

'Indeed. Please, join us by the fire.'

Arthur stepped into the circle of the Cithol and looked down at the fire noting with disappointment that there was no food cooking over it. He wondered why they had lit a fire when the day was already warm enough. He took a seat and stretched out his stiff leg.

'Your offer to act as guides through the woods and tunnels is gratefully accepted. As is your offer to stand alongside us against the Adren. But why do you sit out here in the open woodland? Are you unwelcome in the city?'

There were several nervous looks exchanged at Arthur's question.

'Lord Venning is still of the opinion that the Adren may not trouble us here. Like Captain Terrill we do not agree.'

'Is he still sending supplies and weapons to Caer Sulis?'

'I believe the last shipment left a few days ago.'

'The last?'

'Yes.'

'Why?'

'I do not know. Perhaps the council think they can stay hidden from the Adren?'

'What of Seren and Terrill?'

'Lord Venning is holding them at his Palace but again, I don't know why. Perhaps they strongly disagree with his decisions and he's concerned they may incite some unrest by openly questioning the council's stance. That certainly seems to be the case with Captain Terrill as he was the one who got word to us to meet you and offer our assistance.'

Arthur stood up and said, 'Then let's go and find out exactly whose side Lord Venning is on; the Cithol's or the Adren's.'

Vosper stood up quickly and held out a hand, 'Commander Kane has ordered the Guard to shoot any outsiders seen in the Veiled City. You can't go into the city.'

'Kane would order Britons to be killed?' Arthur's voice was level and his tone reasonable but Vosper and the others knew instinctively that the unpredictable barbarian before them was suddenly very dangerous.

'I'm sure that the order was given in case of any Adren incursions,' Vosper quickly said, desperately wanting to take a step away from the peril he faced.

'Was it Kane who placed Seren under guard?' Arthur asked staring at Vosper.

'I don't know, perhaps – he is the commander of security in the city but I don't know.'

Arthur took a step past Vosper clearly intent on going to the city. Vosper took a deep breath and abandoned himself to his fate. 'You must not enter the city, Arthur. To do so alone would certainly mean your death.'

Arthur turned to face him and Vosper saw the coldness in the barbarian's eyes and genuinely thought he was about to die but as he faced Arthur they all heard a horn being blown from the Briton camp on the hill. Arthur took his eyes from Vosper's and looked back into the depths of the wood before turning his gaze to the direction of the camp.

'The Adren army is on the move. They'll come directly to the Veiled City. Make what preparations you can and I'll meet you back here in a few days time.'

The Cithol watched with relief as the Warlord of Britain turned his back on the Veiled City and headed back through the trees to the encampment on the hill.

When he reached the copse he found that Morveren had ridden back into the camp and was standing surrounded by a small group that included Gwyna, Gereint and Hengest. He made his way over to them and Morveren saw him approaching.

'The Adren are beginning to move out from their camp.'

'You have patrols shadowing them?'

'Yes but it looks like they're heading straight for the Westway, and here.'

'How do they even know where the Westway is or where it leads?' Hengest asked, both relieved that the enemy seemed to have no interest in the abandoned Anglian villages to their north and aghast that it appeared they knew exactly where to go to find the Veiled City. No one answered his question.

'There's still no sign that they have any mounted soldiers?' Arthur asked.

'We haven't seen any yet, other than some of their captains. They're all on foot,' Morveren answered.

'Then it will take them a few days to reach here,' Gereint said as much to himself as the others.

'Gwyna, make sure the message gets to your people to make for Caer Sulis immediately and make sure they leave nothing behind them. Whatever food they can't carry must be burnt or spoiled. Ceinwen, send word to Caer Sulis and Caer Cadarn that the Adren will be attacking the Veiled City within a few days. Everyone at Caer Sulis must be prepared to make for the Haven. Then gather up the warriors and we'll show the Adren what happens to an army that marches on foot.'

Messengers left for the North and West with the news that the Causeway had fallen and to spread the word for those still in the country to make for Caer Sulis. The wounded had been laid out on the wains and Ceinwen had made them as comfortable as possible before they began their arduous journey back to Caer Sulis.

Gereint watched them leave then turned his attention to his Mercian warriors who were already donning their war gear and re-supplying themselves with fresh bags of arrows from the camp store. He had not issued any orders but he realised he had no need to now for they were automatically taking their orders from Arthur.

Hengest was standing nearby handing out the long ash spears that the Anglian riders carried into battle. Gereint made his way over to him and when there was a gap in the line said, 'So, we're going to ride back and launch ourselves at the Adren army again?'

'Looks like it,' Hengest replied, bending down to cut the tie around another bundle of spears.

'Madness.'

Hengest straightened up and with a quick glance at Gereint began handing out the spears again.

'It's madness. He's acting like the demented king he killed. He's under some illusion he's leading an army!' Gereint said looking around at the mounting warriors.

Hengest turned to face him with a smile, 'Someone's got to do it and as we're the only army hereabouts...' He shrugged and once more began handing out the long spears, 'Want one?'

Gereint snatched the offered weapon and briefly thought of breaking it over his knee but the ash pole was as thick as his wrist and the only likely outcome of such a gesture would be a bruised knee. Instead he spat in the grass to show his disgust and strode off to his horse.

Arthur was already mounted and trying to keep his horse under control as he led the first of the warriors out of the hilltop camp. Morveren was just behind him and watched Arthur's efforts with exasperation.

'I should give him riding lessons,' she said shaking her head and the warriors nearby laughed as Arthur turned and pointed a warning finger at her.

'You can give me riding lessons,' Morgund said wistfully and Morveren blushed as the others laughed again. Balor saw the blush and crowed. Before long he had started up a variation of an Anglian rowing song that revolved around the question of what should be done with a drunken woman. She took it with good grace and, much to Morgund's delight, even joined in the repetitive chorus despite its obscene references to herself. The singing lasted for a few miles before Arthur broke it up by sending Morveren off to find and round up the patrols and to ascertain exactly how far the Adren army had progressed along the Westway.

No one had seen the war band when it had left the Causeway and no one watched them now but if anyone had then they would not have recognised them as the same band of warriors.

Chapter Two

Arthur watched the Adren army from a belt of trees that crowned a rise to the North of the Westway. Morveren had gathered the scattered patrols that had kept an eye on the army's progress and brought them back to the main body of Arthur's warriors. The Adren had advanced fifty or so miles into Britain and they had kept to the Westway as it crossed the rolling countryside of the southeast. Their numbers darkened the broad roadway for as far as the eye could see and Morveren estimated that the column was over ten miles long and that there were at least forty thousand of the enemy advancing towards the Veiled City.

Arthur had called forward Gwyna, Gereint and Hengest and together they stood in the shade of the trees and discussed the best way to attack the column. Arthur had initially wanted to make straight for their supply train, which was situated towards the rear of the long line, but Morveren had already informed them that the enemy had anticipated such an attack and had concentrated a large part of their strength around the wagons that carried their food and supplies. She had also reported that the Adren still kept a base on the cliffs above the Causeway and that they had stationed another five thousand soldiers there to protect their supply lines.

Arthur discounted his plan to attack the Adren supplies on the basis that such an assault would result in a pitched battle on open ground and even with their advantage of being on horseback the possibility of being hemmed in and suffering heavy casualties was unacceptable. Hengest was still arguing in favour of launching an attack upon the rear of the column and Gwyna was tending to agree with him despite Gereint restating the inherent dangers of such a plan. Arthur let them discuss the issue for a few more minutes as he finalised the plan they would implement.

'Gereint's right. We have to destroy their supplies but now is not the right time. An opportunity will present itself later. Our advantage of speed and mobility will be lost if we are drawn into hand-to-hand fighting. This is what we'll do.' Arthur knelt down and outlined his plan in the dirt beneath the trees.

Ten minutes later he was leading the horsemen of the southern tribes westwards to cut across the Westway out of sight from the Adren. Once they had crossed the road they rode south for a few miles before wheeling around and stopping in a fold in the land that hid them from anyone travelling on the Westway. Arthur sent Morveren off to keep a watch on the Adren's progress and to report back when the first ranks had passed by their position.

Arthur knew they had about half an hour to wait so he went between the various groups of Mercians, Anglians and Wessex and told them all the same message: hit the Adren line at a full charge and to keep going. Most of the warriors carried the long handled Anglian spears, which were the ideal weapons for what was planned. A few, like Balor and Arthur, preferred to use their own weapons but all the warriors had been trained how to use the spears on horseback and many of them were now practising the routine that had been drummed into them; how to lower the spear and hold it so that the full power and speed of the horse's charge was transferred into the target and how to flick it free once it had struck the enemy.

Morgund was going through the same motions with an easy rhythm. He recalled one of his instructors from years ago acknowledging that sometimes the spear was wrenched from your grasp and that it was better to lose it rather than break your wrist or be dragged from your horse. He imparted his wisdom to Ceinwen who looked at him as if he was an idiot. Undeterred he turned to Balor and gave him the same advice. Balor pointed out he was not carrying a spear and swung his war axe in a full circle to emphasis he had no need for such refined additions or techniques. Morgund shrugged and nudged his horse onwards clearly committed to tell everyone what his instructor had once told him.

Finally Morveren rode back into the fold and told Arthur that the head of the Adren column had passed their position.

Arthur turned to the warriors, 'Mercians on the left, Anglians on the right. Charge straight through. Don't stop.'

He dug his heels into his horse's flanks and led the warriors out of the fold and onto the open grassland. Behind him the Mercians and Anglians spread out to the flanks and the horses picked up speed.

It was a clear day and the rising sun was already shining down brightly and warming the land. The Adren on the Westway could have seen them the second they left the fold but it was more likely to have been the thundering echo in the ground that first alerted them to the Britons' charge.

Arthur's horse, despite his minimal control over it, was one of the fastest and he stayed at the head of the charge as they rapidly covered the ground to the Westway. He could see the Adren directly ahead hastily trying to shape up into defensive positions and he urged his horse to go faster. Morveren was just behind him and out of the corner of his vision he could see horses to his left and right as they edged forward and backward in a tight charging line.

The nearer they got to the Westway the quicker they seemed to be covering the ground and Arthur studied the forming Adren line ahead of him as best as he could from the galloping horse. Taking one hand from the reins he drew his sword and leaned slightly to the right preparing for the moment of impact. His horse began to angle right too and he corrected the swerve as he charged up the slope to the roadway and seconds later he crashed into the unready Adren.

All along the Briton line the spears dipped at the last second and the battle cries were drowned out as the horses smashed into the Adren. Arthur's horse charged straight over two of the enemy and he hacked at the head of a third and suddenly he was on the downward slope on the other side of the Westway. He carried straight on and looked over his shoulder to see that the other riders were doing the same. Behind them was a gap in the Adren line about two hundred yards wide and filled with the broken bodies of the enemy.

Adren soldiers were streaming after them from either end of the smashed line and Arthur and the others slowed their pace as they veered off to the right of the tree-lined rise from which they had watched the Adren advance on the Westway.

When Arthur heard the war cries of the Uathach and felt the ground reverberating to their own charge he reined in his horse and turned about. The Uathach were streaming from the far side of the rise and wheeling around to charge into the flank of the pursuing Adren. Once they had passed through the Adren Arthur led the Britons on a last charge back through the carnage of those that had been chasing them.

The Adren captains had finally managed to stop their soldiers breaking ranks and as the Britons finished the slaughter in the fields off to their right they formed back into a column and marched onwards.

Over the next two days Arthur continually harried the flanks of the Adren column. Three more charges on different sections of the column resulted in the same slaughter but on the last of those charges the Adren had been better prepared to stand against the charging horses and a fourth attack would have resulted in more serious losses for the Britons.

Arthur decided to change tactics and brought his warriors to within two hundred yards of the enemy line where they dismounted to loose volleys from their longbows. Two hundred yards was beyond the Adren archers' range so their captains would organise a thousand strong contingent to break away from the column and advance upon the Britons who would simply mount up and ride a mile or two further along and repeat the process. All the time the Adren were losing soldiers to the Britons' spears and longbows but throughout each charge and throughout each attack from the hated bowmen they kept marching onwards and mile by mile they drew nearer to the Winter Wood.

Morgund likened the Adren army to a beast too intent upon its prey to be bothered by the hornet that stung its flanks and it surprised no one to see that the Adren were prepared to lose hundreds to the Briton attacks so long as they kept on moving towards their goal: the Veiled City.

Seren and Terrill sat opposite each other at the long table in Lord Venning's council room. They were alone and the guards who had brought them there now stood outside the barred double doors. It was the first time they had seen each other since being taken prisoner by Commander Kane's guards as they had approached the city.

'What have you told them?' Seren asked quietly, leaning forward across the table.

Terrill's eyes were drawn to her hands that fidgeted constantly on the tabletop.

'Nothing,' he replied, then leaned towards her and dropped his voice, 'but I managed to speak to Vosper briefly. He promised to watch the hill in case Arthur made it there.'

Seren cast her eyes downwards and stared at her hands. She seemed oblivious to their constant twitching. Neither she nor Terrill actually knew for sure if Arthur and the others had been able to escape from the Adren trap on the Causeway. Seren had left the cliff top convinced that the charge led by the wild Uathach girl would clear a path for Arthur and the Britons and make their retreat possible but doubt had stolen into her mind during the long hours of her solitary confinement and now she was far from certain that the escape was as inevitable as she had once thought it to be.

'Arthur and the others would have made it back up the cliffs,' Terrill said softly, correctly guessing her thoughts and trying to reassure her. He was alarmed by her appearance; wan, grey bands shadowed her eyes and her already slight frame seemed much thinner. He feared she might be in danger of losing her child and, before he could stop the thought, wondered if that might not be a good thing. He snapped his eyes away from her in guilt but Seren was staring vacantly at the table with her head bowed and guessed nothing of his thoughts.

They both turned their heads as the bolt slid from the door and it swung open. Seren moaned softly as Commander Kane stalked into the room followed by her father. The door shut behind them and Lord Venning took a seat at the table. Kane remained standing with his pale red eyes fixed on Seren.

'You went to the Causeway to warn the Britons about the tunnel,' Kane stated.

'Yes.' Seren's shoulders seemed to sag as she answered quietly still staring at the table.

'And did you warn them?'

'Yes,' she replied again.

'Fools! Both of you!' Kane turned away in disgust.

'Did you tell them all you know?' Lord Venning asked.

'We only told them of the tunnel,' Terrill replied.

'You realise that Arthur will only lead the Adren here?' Lord Venning asked in a tired voice.

'And that he'll fight them here and condemn the whole city and its people to destruction?' Kane was almost shouting at them.

'The Adren would have come here anyway. Lazure would have destroyed us. Now we have a chance to defend ourselves.' Seren said the words automatically and without any passion. She held her gaze on the surface of the table.

Kane stormed across to her and stood behind her, bending down so that his face was close to the back of her head. 'Defend ourselves? How? We had a pact with Lazure! He'll think we betrayed him and now we're doomed like every other race that has tried to stand against his armies and all because some stupid girl got pregnant with a barbarian's child and pregnant with stupid ideas of freedom and fighting. I should kill you now but I want to see your face as you watch the Adren slaughter the women and children of the Veiled City! And every grisly death and every tortuous moment of pain of every single Cithol will be because of you!'

Seren physically cringed under the assault and when Kane had finished and turned away once more she looked to her father. Terrill saw her face and it was the look of a child imploring a parent for help.

'You have damned us,' Lord Venning said. 'Our only hope is that Arthur and his warriors die and die quickly. We have one hope to persuade Lazure that we had nothing to do with Arthur's actions and that we still hold true to our word.'

Terrill shot to his feet, 'Lazure would destroy you whether or not you had a treaty! There is still time to fight, to organise a defence of the city!'

'Fool! Surrender is our only hope now!' Commander Kane shouted back at him and then called for the guards. Terrill was led away struggling and still shouting but Seren had to be helped up from her chair. As she walked slowly from the room between two guards she turned and said quietly, 'Arthur and the Britons will come. If you won't save the city, they will.'

Arthur's warriors had just arrived back at the copse above the Winter Wood. They had harried and attacked the column constantly over the last few days but the Adren had pressed on towards the Veiled City and there was nothing that the warriors could do to slow their advance. The Adren were only ten miles behind them.

In the centre of the camp Hengest, Gereint and Gwyna stood with Arthur as he outlined what they had to do next. About them the warriors of the southern tribes and the Uathach hurriedly ate quick meals and stowed away the last of the supplies. The word was spread that the horses were to be taken to the bridge over the Isis to the West of the Winter Wood and corralled there. They would fight in the woods on foot. The warriors quickly redistributed the supplies and war gear and the horses were led away in a long line between the last of the wains that headed off to skirt the southern edges of the woodland.

Most of the warriors had expected to have to enter the Winter Wood and few were now unduly concerned about doing so. Many of them had already met or seen the Cithol and those who had not had questioned Ceinwen and the others until their fears had been allayed.

Arthur thought that the Adren would attempt to penetrate the woods at dozens of different points. Once they had entered the woods proper the paths narrowed and most of them led nowhere near to the hidden entrances of the Veiled City. He decided to split his force into four bands so that they could cover most of the eastern sweep of the woodland. Vosper's Cithol would act as their guides and as runners between the different groups so that they could keep each other informed of the Adren's movement and co-ordinate their counter attacks.

They left the hill when Morveren brought word that the Adren had turned aside from the Westway and were making for the Winter Wood. No sooner had the warriors entered the wood than Vosper and his fifty Cithol met them. Arthur explained to him what their basic plan was and Vosper assigned various members of his band to the four groups of warriors. Gwyna had divided the Uathach into two separate groups; she would lead one and Ruraidh the other. Gereint led the Mercian band and Arthur the survivors of the combined Wessex and Anglian war bands with Hengest as his second-in-command.

The two Uathach bands headed northwards led by their Cithol guides while Gereint's warriors filed away to take up positions between the Uathach and Arthur's band. Within two hours the four groups were spread across ten miles covering the eastern side of the Winter Wood.

Vosper suggested that Arthur's band stay where it was for the time being while he and two companions ventured to the edge of the woodland in an effort to gauge where the Adren would make their first attempt. Once Vosper had gone the remaining Cithol retired some distance away and the warriors began to relax in the cool shade of the trees. The temperature had steadily risen since the aching cold of the fog on the Causeway and the spring sun was now warm enough for the warriors to be thankful to be in the cool forest and they spread out amongst the earth banks and moss-covered, half-buried ruins of a previous age.

Someone started a small fire to cook some meat and soon a thin haze of smoke drifted through the trees picking out the sunlight in gently swirling shafts. The Cithol watched the Britons curiously as some of the warriors began eating the half-cooked meat while others took the opportunity to sleep. Most of the warriors sat around in small groups and talked quietly. Arthur passed amongst them checking on individual supplies of arrows. He eventually joined Ceinwen and Balor who were sitting with the two Anglians, Hengest and Elwyn.

Hengest looked up as Arthur sat down holding his stiff leg out before him.

'The calm before the storm, eh?' Hengest said.

'The calm between storms you mean,' Balor corrected him.

'Is it still troubling you?' Ceinwen asked Arthur nodding to his leg.

Arthur dismissed the question with a wave of his hand.

'The arrow wound from Branque?' Hengest asked.

Arthur nodded his reply and Hengest fell silent as he recalled the village across the Causeway. He remembered a red headed girl there whom he had met once when he and Cei had escorted the villagers to Caer Sulis. Or perhaps it was escorting them from Caer Sulis back to Branque, he honestly could not remember, but he was sure her name had been Caja. He had heard that she had died during the attack and the thought still sickened him. Quite a few of the Anglian warriors had shown an interest in the lively girl but he seemed to recall that she had taken a shine to Cei and his thoughts inevitably turned to Cei and his father who were somewhere deep in the Shadow Lands. 'Do you think Cei and the others will succeed?' he asked Arthur.

'They have to. It's the only way to stop the Adren in the end.'

'Your father's with him, isn't he?' Elwyn asked suddenly remembering that Aelfhelm had been one of those to leave with Cei.

'Yes.'

'Well then, the old warhorse will keep Cei on the right path,' Elwyn said with a laugh.

'You ought to watch who you're calling an old warhorse,' Ceinwen said with an unsubtle glance at Balor and Arthur.

Balor began to bridle at the comment but was cut short when Arthur suddenly asked, 'Where are Morgund and Morveren?'

The question was met by silence and as he looked at them they all looked away either taking an interest in something near at hand or appearing to be lost in their own thoughts.

'Well?'

'I think they went for a walk, possibly,' Ceinwen answered in the embarrassed silence. Everyone was acutely aware of the rumour that suggested Morveren was his daughter and to make matters worse Elwyn had made his intentions towards her fairly clear over the winter months.

'A walk?'

'Possibly.'

'Together?'

'Well they left together,' Ceinwen said, hopefully implying that it was more than likely that they had soon split up and gone their separate ways.

'Bring them back. Vosper will return soon and I don't want to have to search for them,' Arthur said standing up.

'I'm not really sure which way they went,' Ceinwen said, also standing to show she was keen to help despite obviously being unable to.

'You're a tracker aren't you?'

'Yes.'

'Then track them,' Arthur said and strode away.

Ceinwen shrugged to the others and set off reluctantly through the trees. She found them soon after but could not face intruding upon them and so she sat behind a tree to wait, mortified and wishing she were anywhere else.

Vosper returned before Ceinwen did but he had little to report other than that the Adren were setting up a main base just on the southwest fringes of the Winter Wood.

Over the following days the Adren busied themselves with the various necessities of setting up a camp for so many soldiers. Arthur took patrols close to the Adren pickets but like the others he had to content himself with waiting for the enemy to make the first move. During this time the

Britons familiarised themselves with the paths through the woodland and sought out the best ambush points and then enhanced them.

Balor became increasingly irritable at finding himself once more in the woodland surroundings he had hoped to leave behind but the others welcomed the brief respite from the fighting and took the opportunity to eat and sleep as much as they could, knowing that once the battle started again they would have little time for either.

The Britons were surprised that the Winter Wood was so peaceful considering that there was an Adren army camped only a few miles away. The daunting winter darkness of the forest had been banished for a few months and the spring sun shone warmly on the sprouting leaves and cast dappled shadows on the new grass and saplings that grew in the few open spaces. The glades were hazed by bluebells and when the gentle breeze from the West breathed across these glades it seemed as if an indigo mist eddied across the woodland floor.

Morveren was reflecting upon the same strange contradiction as she lay in a patch of sunlight and listened to a wood pigeon softly calling from a nearby tree. Next to her lay Morgund and he twitched in his sleep as a fly landed on his face then instantly flew off. Morveren smiled and was trailing a strand of her long black hair across his face in an attempt to elicit the same response when she heard someone crashing through the undergrowth not far away.

She shoved Morgund awake and sprang to her feet quickly throwing some clothes around herself and reaching for her sword. Morgund was still half-asleep and struggling into his clothes when Ceinwen burst into the clearing. Ceinwen took one look at their dishevelled state and wished that she wasn't the one to have to keep track of the two of them. 'Get dressed the pair of you. The Adren are moving into the woods! Get back to the camp and for the gods' sake, make sure you arrive from different directions!'

They need not have worried about being noticed when they returned as the camp was a scene of frenzied activity with shelters being dismantled and war gear hurriedly collected. Arthur was still conferring with Vosper and two other Cithol who had arrived from the Uathach bands to the North but word had already spread that the Adren were probing the western fringes at eight different points and each force contained at least a thousand soldiers.

Morgund made straight for his longbow and set about re-stringing it; dozens around him were doing likewise. When he had finished he helped Morveren string her shorter bow. Arthur was shouting orders for everyone to form up and moments later they were running along a path that narrowed as the trees grew thicker to either side.

Vosper led them at a quickening pace and at the back of the line were more of the Cithol, stationed there to make sure no one at the rear mistook the path. They were moving northwards and the patches of sunlit ground lessened as the canopy above them became thicker. The woods around them were getting darker as the path descended into a sunken lane with steep banks covered by gorse and tangled bushes sloping upwards on either side to a narrow skyline that was mostly obscured by the overreaching branches.

Morgund was close to the front of the line and running behind the shorter Balor who was already finding the going hard. Suddenly they ran out into an open space and those ahead of him faltered. Behind him the other warriors from Wessex and Anglia spilled into the clearing.

Arthur was roaring out one word but Morgund's mind struggled to understand it; surely they were not prepared to launch an ambush yet? He looked around for the Cithol who had been leading them but they were nowhere to be seen and as he looked back to find those who had been bringing up the rear the first flight of arrows tore through the Britons. He struggled to release the shield on his back as the second flight flew at them from the opposite direction. He abandoned his efforts to release the shield and fought down the panic as he frantically looked for Arthur. He could not see him but he heard his voice raised above the chaos.

'To me! To me! Charge! Charge!'

Some of the warriors around him were sprinting to his left and he followed automatically as another volley of arrows decimated their ranks. He could see Arthur now. He was leading the charge to one side of the clearing. He was doing the only thing possible; attacking one of the flanks of the ambush that had caught them.

Morgund took his bow in his left hand and drew his sword as an arrow clattered into the shield strapped to his back. He was flung forward and as he scrambled in the dirt he felt another arrow scythe through the air above his head. He swore and felt a hand grip him under the armpit helping him to his feet.

'Bloody daft time to duck,' he heard Balor say as they sprinted onwards. Then they were in the tree line and fighting erupted all around them. He jabbed his bow into the face of an Adren and swung out at another.

Arthur was still roaring them onwards. To be trapped here with the other side of the ambush now racing across the clearing after them would be just as fatal as staying in the centre. Balor despatched the Adren Morgund had swung at and missed, and together they ran forward deflecting and parrying blows rather than stopping to fight.

The woods were thick but passable and they sprinted between trees and hurdled fallen boughs as arrows flew around them and cracked into nearby trunks. All about them other Britons were trying to fight their way out of the trap and gradually they drew together in loose bands as their embedded training took hold once more.

Morgund hoped their headlong flight was taking them westwards towards the city and not east to the main Adren army. He caught a glimpse of the sun above them and quietly thanked Arthur for choosing the right direction. Just when he thought they were free of the Adren line they crashed straight into a group running in the opposite direction. They were embroiled in a frenzied skirmish for a precious few minutes and by the time they had killed the last one they could hear the sounds of their pursuit dangerously close again.

There was nothing to be gained by pacing themselves; if they could not lose their pursuers in the next minute or two then they would be overhauled and cut down. They sprinted as fast as they could and with complete disregard for the roots and vines that waited to send them sprawling but the pursuit was dogged and did not fall far behind.

Suddenly there was the shattering clash of battle behind them and Morgund risked a glance over his shoulder. He drew up and shouted after Balor who slowed and turned around. Behind them a band of forty Britons had lain in wait as they passed and then sprang at their pursuers. The fighting was sudden, brief and vicious and when the last Adren was cut down Arthur ran across to them.

'Are there any others who got out?'

'Don't know. Didn't see,' Balor replied, taking great gulps of air.

'Morveren? Is she with you?' Morgund asked Arthur. Arthur shook his head and Morgund groaned.

'What happened back there?' Balor asked still wiping the sweat that poured down his face.

'The Cithol,' Arthur said and it suddenly dawned on Balor that the Cithol had betrayed them and led them into the Adren trap. He began to swear unholy retribution. Arthur did not say a word but those around him could feel his cold fury.

Hengest came running up and called out, 'There's more of us this way!'

The warriors set off again with Balor and Morgund lagging after them. They rounded up eleven more survivors from the ambush then had to hide themselves in a tumble of overgrown and concealed ruins while a large contingent of Adren swept through the area.

They drank what little water they had while they waited for the Adren to move further away. Morgund went among the group to see who had gotten out and to ask if anyone had seen Morveren. He was relieved to see that Ceinwen and Hengest were among those sheltering in the ruins but no one had seen Morveren since before the chaos of the ambush. Balor pointed out that no one had seen her fall either but Morgund was dwelling on the thought that perhaps she had been taken alive.

Ceinwen and Hengest cautiously approached Arthur, 'The other bands might have been led into an ambush as well,' Ceinwen tentatively pointed out.

'Should we try and get word to them?' Hengest added.

'We don't know the woods to the North of us. We don't know where they are and we're more likely to run into more Adren than we are to find the others. They'll get out as best they can and head for the base where our horses are. Then they'll make for Caer Cadarn.'

'Is that where we're heading?' Ceinwen asked warily, already knowing the answer.

'No.'

Hengest looked puzzled but before he could ask, Ceinwen quietly answered his question, 'We're going into the Veiled City.'

'But...' Hengest stopped as Arthur looked at him.

'Do you know where the entrances are?' Ceinwen asked.

'I know where one is. The Winter Garden.'

Ceinwen suddenly remembered the sculpted ice and frozen fountains of the wall-enclosed garden and she remembered the Cithol girl who had welcomed them there, Fin Seren, and knew that she was one of the reasons why Arthur must enter the Veiled City.

'Arthur, the woods are crawling with Adren and if the Cithol are against us then the city will be no better. Can we not return to the Veiled City at a later time?' Ceinwen said in a final appeal even though she knew it was pointless.

'No. We go there now.'

He told her to prepare the others to leave. They left the overgrown ruins in bands of four or five and followed each other as Arthur led them westwards and deeper into the Winter Wood which was eerily quiet after the running battles and clamouring pursuit. It seemed as if the woods had been shocked into silence and were now waiting in wary tension to see what would happen next.

They moved through the thicker parts of the wood as quickly as possible and through the more open stretches with as much caution as possible, all the time following Arthur as he picked his way from path to path. After an hour of silent progress and as they crouched and waited while Arthur and Ceinwen ranged ahead to find the right direction they heard the distant and unmistakable clash of weapons. Morgund swore he heard Uathach battle cries but no one else was willing or able to confirm his assertion.

When the sound of battle died away a lone crow broke the silence around them as it strutted on a branch overhead noisily trying to betray their position. Morgund unslung his longbow and fired an arrow at it. The crow gave a last outraged screech as it spied its attacker then disappeared in a swirl of black feathers as the arrow tore through it and sent it flying to land in a hollow over a hundred yards away.

'It's bad luck to do that,' Balor pointed out to him.

'It is for the crow,' Morgund answered.

Balor grunted in agreement.

'Are you sure they were Uathach battle cries?'

Morgund shrugged, 'I thought so but it was a long way away.'

'What a bloody mess,' Balor said. He spoke it quietly but with real anger.

Morgund nodded his agreement. Through the trees he could see Arthur and Ceinwen returning and he was glad to be moving again. He was desperately trying not to think of Morveren and it was easier to do so if he had to concentrate on moving quietly and quickly through the woods.

It took Arthur over six hours to lead them to the high walls of the Winter Garden. Only once did they come across a band of Adren, several hundred strong, and they quickly melted from the path and lay in concealment until the enemy had moved on. The only entrance to the Garden was through a stone gateway carved into one of the high walls and the remnants of the Wessex and Anglian war bands waited in the undergrowth while Ceinwen crept forward to investigate. Everyone suspected another trap and they freed their bows and fitted arrows to the strings. The only sound was the low roar of the westerly wind as it passed through the tall trees that surrounded and encroached upon the towering walls of the Winter Garden; it sounded like a distant sea crashing its surf on some far beach and had an oddly calming effect on their taut nerves.

Ceinwen reached the stone gateway and slid through to the more open space within the walls. The waiting warriors watched the entrance and listened intently for any indication that something was wrong but they heard nothing other than the wind-ruffled trees.

Morgund watched the empty gateway while beside him Balor was quietly urging Ceinwen to return. Suddenly she slipped back around the side of the archway and beckoned them forwards. At a crouching run the warriors left their cover and lined up against the side of the wall.

'Any signs of life?' Arthur asked as he joined Ceinwen.

'No. None.'

'Good.'

'Arthur?'

'What?'

'It's completely wrecked. Everything's been torn down – there's only one of the trees still standing.'

Arthur stared at her. They were both thinking the same thing; clearly the Cithol would not destroy their own Winter Garden which could only mean that the Adren had, but Vosper and the other Cithol had betrayed the Britons to the Adren and that in turn could only mean that the Cithol were in league with the Adren. So why would the Adren destroy the Winter Garden?

44

Arthur smiled.

'What?' Ceinwen asked.

'Perhaps the Cithol's new allies haven't turned out to be such welcome guests.'

'But this means the Adren are in the Veiled City already,' Ceinwen said, gesturing to the destruction through the gateway.

'Indeed it does,' Arthur replied and signalled the warriors to follow him.

As he ran to the centre of the garden and the domed entrance to the city he cast his eyes around at the ruins of the Winter Garden. He thought he spotted the rubble of the bower where he had slept with Seren in his arms. The thought of being so close to her now and the thought that the Adren were already in the city hurried his pace.

With the others following behind him he ran down the spiralling stone stairway that led into the Veiled City. When he reached the bottom he looked wildly around at the corridors that radiated out to different locations within the city and then set off down the one that Merdynn had taken so many months ago.

Their feet echoed dully on the pine-strewn floor and the warriors bunched together feeling out of their natural element so far underground and surrounded by stone. They passed the huddled shapes of four Cithol who had been hacked down by Adren swords but they saw no signs of life until they burst out into the Great Hall.

Arthur had always felt the Veiled City to be an alien place of cold stone, a place that contrasted too sharply with the homes of the Britons, nonetheless there had been no denying its magnificence or grandeur but the scene that greeted them as they ran into the hall stopped them dead. It looked more like a vision of hell with scattered stacks of burning wooden tables that filled the hall with wreathing smoke and cast a flickering red glow against the walls so that it looked like even the stone was burning. Everywhere lay the hacked and mutilated bodies of the Cithol who had been in the hall when the Adren had swept through. Here and there they could see the crawling form of someone they had left alive for later entertainment but the Adren had clearly moved on to slaughter elsewhere leaving only ruin behind them.

Arthur led them running across the hall and ordered them to ignore any cries for help. As they passed the raised dais he saw a grotesque heap of blood-drenched naked bodies piled around the High Table but they were mutilated beyond recognition and he knew there would be no point in stopping and searching among them.

They left the Great Hall and suddenly they were looking out over the sloping stone houses that led down to the lake. It seemed like fires were burning inside every house and the whole cavern that contained the city seemed to be twisting in fire. The normally dark lake was now alive with reflected flames and its wide waters carried and echoed the screams of the dying and tortured.

Every stone path and walkway seemed to have sporadic huddles of fleeing people too panicked to pay heed to anything other than what they fled from. Arthur scanned the valley side looking for Lord Venning's Palace. He saw it and it seemed to be one of the few buildings that was not lit from the inside by flames.

He led them towards the Palace and the Cithol who saw them coming fled down side paths thinking they were more of the dreaded attackers. Even some of the Adren they came across shouted their approval at them thinking they must be allies to be so boldly striding through the burning city. Arthur's warriors soon learned not to attack such groups and to pass them by as quickly as possible.

When they neared the Palace they saw a band of twenty to thirty Adren gathered outside the main gateway. The warriors thought at first that they were attacking the Palace but as they drew closer it became obvious that they were guarding it from other marauding bands.

The Adren saw them approach and waved them angrily away as they had others. They only realised their mistake when the warriors rushed at them with swords drawn. The brief battle at the gates only lasted a matter of minutes and seemed to have gone unnoticed amidst the slaughtering of the Cithol elsewhere in the city.

Arthur started dragging the Adren corpses into the courtyard and the others joined him then he left Hengest to command the defence of the Palace should it become necessary. He told them to wreck the courtyard and start a fire or two so that it looked much as any other house in the cavern and hoped that other Adren would just pass it by as having already been ransacked. Then he took Morgund and Ceinwen with him and made his way to the council room.

He found the double doors barred from the inside and sent Ceinwen back to fetch Balor who took one look at the doors and swung his axe down into the centre join. The wood splintered and he struck again cleaving straight through the bar on the inside. He stepped back and Arthur kicked the doors open.

There were five Cithol in the room and they had jumped to their feet at the first axe stroke. One of them called out his name and he found himself looking at Seren.

'Arthur! I knew you would come!' Seren cried out. At first she had not been sure if it was Arthur. The man before them holding the glistening and dripping sword could not have looked wilder; his clothes were torn and sweat stained, and covered in mud and fresh blood; his unshaven face was smoke-blackened and his hair was lank with sweat and clumped together in clots of dried blood. The other three who entered the room with him were no better and the stink of their sweat immediately filled the room.

Arthur stared at Seren. He had not seen her for long months but her image had always been close to his memory. His memory seemed to have lied to him. The Cithol woman before him was no more than a girl and although her face still held a beauty it looked more like a face composed in a desperate dignity laid over the knowledge of a fatal illness, and she looked very ill indeed. Her cheekbones were more pronounced, dark circles sunk her green eyes and her bare arms looked emaciated. Then he saw she was pregnant and immediately he saw once more the girl he had known before. He looked back to her eyes which gave him the answer even before he had time to frame the thought.

He tore his eyes from her and looked at the others in the room. Lord Venning was sitting back down heavily. Commander Kane was staring defiantly back at him. Terrill had moved to Seren's side and in the background stood Vosper.

Balor recognised the latter at the same time and surged forward with his axe.

'Balor!' Arthur's voice cut across the room and it became completely still. Balor stopped abruptly and hated himself for doing so but there was absolutely no future in crossing Arthur at a time like this. He stepped aside as Arthur walked slowly towards the table.

'Have you been mistreated in any way Seren?' he asked her calmly.

'No,' she answered with a sidelong glance at her father. Everything about this first meeting with Arthur was wrong; nothing was as she had expected it to be. She suddenly realised she was scared of the man now standing on the other side of the long table.

He turned his lifeless gray eyes to Terrill, 'You and Seren brought word to us about the Adren tunnel?'

Terrill nodded and Arthur considered this for a moment.

'Seren, stand over there with Ceinwen,' he said to the shaking girl.

'Arthur?'

'Do it!' He roared at her and everyone started at the violence in his voice.

Behind him Ceinwen groaned softly and Balor grinned. Seren took a faltering step around the table and then edged closer towards Ceinwen. Arthur watched her and then turned back to Captain Terrill.

'And how did you know about the tunnel?' Arthur's voice had reverted back to a reasonable tone and Terrill's eyes darted towards those still standing with him.

'Come to judge us have you? Like a barbarian king dispensing justice?' Commander Kane stared levelly at Arthur but a flicker of his upper lip betrayed his welling panic.

'Yes,' Arthur replied simply.

'They heard me speak of it,' Lord Venning said from his seat at the table.

'And you broke with your orders and came to warn us?' Arthur asked Terrill.

'Yes,' Terrill answered, looking at the floor as if he were shamed by the admission.

Arthur indicated for him to join Seren and he too edged around the table.

'How did you know about the tunnel?'

'We have ancient maps. We have knowledge of many things beyond your understanding,' Lord Venning answered wearily.

'Had. You have nothing now.'

'You can't defeat Lazure's Adren. No one can. We had to choose, Arthur.'

'Not 'we' Venning, you. You were your people's leader and you chose to side with the Adren. You chose to tell the Adren about the tunnel. These were the wrong choices.'

'It was the only way to preserve the Veiled City!' Kane defended himself automatically and Arthur turned his gaze upon him.

'Have you seen your city?' Arthur roared at him sending spittle flying across the table. In the next instant he stated in an even tone, 'And you told Vosper to lead us into an Adren trap.'

'You should be dead by now. You will be soon,' Kane snarled at him.

Arthur brought his sword crashing down on the table and it smashed in two. He stepped across the broken table and faced Commander Kane.

'You sought to silence the only two people who would speak for the Veiled City and you betrayed Britain.' Arthur spoke as if he were delivering a sentence and Kane took a step backward with his empty hands held out before him.

'I have no weapon!' he screeched in desperation.

'You lived with an empty heart, you can die with empty hands.' As he finished speaking Arthur thrust his sword into Kane's stomach. Kane screamed and Arthur twisted the sword that was still embedded there. He fell to the floor still screaming and Arthur slowly withdrew the sword and left him flailing on the floor in his own blood.

Vosper darted for the door but Balor grabbed him and threw him back towards Arthur with a laugh.

'Time you stopped running, Vosper,' Arthur said and swept his sword in a low arc. Vosper collapsed staring at his raised right leg that ended in a stump just below his knee. Arthur looked at him for a second then swung his sword down on the other leg. It clanged against the cold stone as it sliced straight through the muscle and bone. He too started to scream and behind Arthur Seren sank to her knees and retched. Terrill knelt between her and the bloodshed and held her face against his chest fearing what was going to come next.

'What do you plan to do after murdering me?' Lord Venning asked equably. It was difficult to hear him above the screams in the council room and Arthur signalled to Balor who stepped forward willingly and ended the screams with the unmistakable sound of an axe thudding into flesh.

'I'm going to destroy what has kept the Veiled City for so long.'

'No!'

'No! Arthur, you mustn't!'

Arthur turned at the second voice and saw the look of horror on Seren's face as she tried to claw herself free from Terrill's embrace.

'You can't Arthur! We can't live here without it!'

'And nor can the Adren Master.'

'But we can never replace it! It's the only relic of the old knowledge! You came to save the city, you can't destroy it!' Seren implored him in desperation.

'I came to destroy it. What use is there in Cei and Merdynn destroying the Shadow Land City if the Adren Master simply takes this one?'

Lord Venning laughed and Arthur turned back to him frowning. Lord Venning stood and stabbed a finger at Arthur, 'You're nothing but a blood-drenched barbarian. You only know about blood and how to spill it. You can't even grasp what's at stake here, can you? Kane was right all along! You've always meant to destroy the Veiled City! This is the knowledge from the old world – it's far greater than you're capable of understanding. All you can manage is to roll in blood, roll in muck and roll in bed!' Lord Venning was standing and screaming at him as he added, 'You're nothing but blood-thirsty barbarians!'

Arthur advanced on Lord Venning, 'I know enough to know what is worth fighting for and what is worth dying for. Can you say what you did was worth dying for? You led your people and you betrayed them: that's between you and your people. We offered you an alliance and you betrayed us: that's a matter for you and I.'

'Can you say what you've done was worth the deaths of Cei and Merdynn, and your sister too?' The room was suddenly very still and very quiet. 'That's right. They're dead and you sent them to their deaths!'

'Who told this?' Arthur asked coldly.

'Lazure trapped them on the Breton coast and the Adren slaughtered them just as they'll slaughter you.'

'Lazure lied to you.'

'They're dead. Their quest failed. At least one city still holds the old knowledge safe from barbarians like you!'

Ceinwen grabbed Seren and started to haul her from the room but she was too slow and Seren screamed soundlessly as Arthur cut her father down and hacked at his dead body.

Arthur turned away from the smashed body of the Cithol leader and stopped dead when he saw Seren staring at him in horror. He looked at Ceinwen who was still clutching the girl and said, 'Take her out of here to safety. You know where to go.'

'Arthur, you can't mean to destroy the old power? Everything we did was so that you could protect it!' Terrill said taking a step forward.

'I would have protected both the Cithol and the city but now it's too late to save either. Lazure cannot have the power that lies here.'

'But Arthur...'

'Take them both to safety.' Arthur stopped the entreaties and strode between the two stricken Cithol and back out to the courtyard.

'Any sign of the Adren yet?' he asked Hengest once he was outside.

'Not in here but there's plenty going on out there.'

Arthur turned to Balor who had followed him out and said, 'There's a building to the left of the gates, about four houses along where you'll find hammers and building tools. Take whatever you'll need to knock down a bridge and bring it all back here.'

Balor took five others with him and sidled out the main Palace gates. Arthur watched as Ceinwen selected three warriors and left, leading the two Cithol between them as they cautiously slipped through the gates.

'He was lying about Cei and the others wasn't he?' Morgund asked quietly by his side. Arthur continued cleaning his sword of the blood he had spilled and did not answer.

Balor returned shortly afterwards and Arthur strode out of the main gates and down towards the underground river that ran from the lake. As they neared the lake edge a group of fifty Adren raced wildly onto the roadway ahead of them. They stopped and stared at the warriors for a few seconds then Arthur just charged at them. The Britons raced to catch up with him. The Adren had met almost no resistance so far in the city and Arthur's sudden attack caught them entirely by surprise. Most of them died by the Britons' swords and only a few escaped back up one of the side paths.

Arthur raced on to the river.

'There! Take that aqueduct down or block it up but stop the water entering that tunnel there!' He pointed to the place he meant and Balor and the others jumped into the knee-high flow carrying sledgehammers and iron spikes. The rest of the warriors fanned out to form a protective ring around the bridge that carried the water down into the stone tunnel.

The city still burnt. Whatever the Adren found to burn they set alight and the roof of the cavern was hidden in smoke. Dim light still emanated from various points but it was the flames that lit the underground city in a flickering red glow.

The Adren came at them in sporadic bands and the warriors defended the bridge while Balor and his crew smashed at the stonework. Finally a large section of the walled bridge fell away and water cascaded over the edge. Balor went to work on the other side smashing a spike into the polished stone then driving it in like a wedge. The others joined him and all the time he was aware that the warriors were fighting increasingly frantic battles as more and more Adren realised that someone in the city was putting up a fight.

The second section gave way quicker than the first had and Balor clambered back onto the roadway. He took one look at the fight going on around him and called together the others he had been working alongside him. With a shouted warning to the warriors in front of him he led a charge into the Adren ranks. The sledgehammers crashed through the Adren lines and the Britons all followed the charging Balor up one of the side paths.

Arthur overtook him and took another narrow alleyway between the stone houses that were still billowing out smoke. After another few twists and turns they were racing across the Great Hall, which was still empty of the Adren soldiers. They sprinted up the spiral stairway without being pursued by the Adren; either they had lost them in the sideways and smoke or their pursuers had been distracted by easier and softer targets.

As they came out into the smoke-tinged air of the ruined Winter Garden the ground beneath them trembled. Arthur's instinctive reaction was to look for horsemen but he discounted it immediately; they were in the middle of woodland. The ground beneath them shuddered again and some of the warriors lost their balance.

'What's happening, Arthur?' Hengest shouted with a trace of panic in his voice.

One of the huge stone walls cracked and began to fall in on itself.

'Quick! Get away from here!' Arthur shouted at them and ran for the gap where the wall had stood.

They ran westwards as hard as they could and for as long as could. Each tremor only served to hasten their pace and lengthen their endurance. It took them four hours but eventually they reached the more open woodland on the western fringes where they stopped to rest and to drink from a stream that flowed into the woods.

The ground shuddered one last time and many of the warriors looked to Arthur.

'The Veiled City is gone. I want these woods burned.'

'What about the other bands? Gereint's and the Uathach?' Hengest asked.

'None of them would have gone into the Veiled City so if they could have got away then they would have done so by now.'

'There may still be Cithol in the woods,' Morgund pointed out.

'Burn it,' Arthur replied.

They set fires every hundred yards along a two-mile stretch of the western edge and left them to burn. From a distance they watched as the westerly wind carried the fires into the heart of the Winter Wood and they watched as the raging flames cut huge swathes through the forest.

The remnants of the Wessex and Anglian war bands watched until all that was left were the charred skeletons of ancient trees standing among the exposed bones of an ancient city.

Arthur turned away and began the journey back to Caer Cadarn.

Chapter Three

Morveren stumbled through the clawing undergrowth that grew in sprawling thickets beneath the close packed trees. She gritted her teeth against the pain in her side as she tugged her clothing free from the clutching thorns and briars. Her hands and forearms were scratched and bleeding from the constant struggle but she forced herself onwards. She had not seen or heard any sign of the Adren for many hours now but still she kept pushing herself northwards. It was no longer the Adren that she was trying to escape.

The tangled ivy and barbed briars snared her again and she groaned in frustration and despair as she tugged her leg free leaving newly latticed lines of blood beneath her shredded trousers. She rested briefly with her back against a tree and taking her hand away from her side she inspected the bloody mess that the Adren arrow had made in her flesh. She thought back to when she had been hit in the first few seconds of the Adren ambush and winced at the memory of the glancing force of the arrow that had spun her around and sent her crashing to the ground. She thought that she must have taken a blow to her head as she fell because the next thing she could remember was awakening to the deafening drone of the nearby flies that were already busy on the bodies of the dead around her. There had been no Adren soldiers and no warriors in the clearing, at least none that were alive, and she had slowly sat up amazed that the chaos of the ambush had given way to such calm.

Her head nodded violently and she realised she had almost slipped into sleep. She pushed herself away from the tree and wished fervently that she had some water to drink; her throat was parched dry and she was beginning to feel faint. She inspected the wound in her side again and was relieved to see that her hurried bandaging seemed to have stopped the bleeding.

Suddenly the woodland erupted into life and she dropped to one knee cringing against the tree for cover as hundreds of crows flew overhead in dense squadrons screaming out their panic. She instinctively reached for her sword but realised for the first time that she must have left it back in the clearing when they had been ambushed. All around her deer were weaving through the trees and springing effortlessly over the trailing traps that had dogged her progress.

Just as suddenly the wood was silent again and Morveren peered around the trunk she was hiding behind already knowing what she would see. She had first seen it many hours ago when she had tried to make her way westwards through the Winter Wood in an effort to get to the point where the war band had left their horses. She guessed that Arthur and some of the others had managed to get away from the trap for two reasons; they were not among the dead and the Adren must have given pursuit. The latter was the only reason she could think of to explain why she was still alive. But her progress had been checked by the same thing she saw now; smoke was spreading across the forest floor and reaching out to her. She could hear the distant low roar of the forest fire as the wood smoke curled about her, stinging her eyes and parching her dry throat further.

With a grunt of effort she forced herself to her feet and once again began to fight her way northwards through the undergrowth. With growing panic she realised the woodland to her left was becoming more and more obscured by the thickening smoke and the occasional glowing ember was now drifting across her path. It was becoming harder to breath and she veered ever more eastward in an effort to outdistance the fires.

After an hour of frantic struggling, and as she was beginning to feel the race could only be lost, she found herself abruptly free of the clamping undergrowth and into more open woodland. Resisting the urge to rest she began to run hoping that the wound in her side would not open again.

She almost tripped over the first corpse and if she had then she would have landed on the second. All around her lay the jetsam of battle; bloodied bodies, cast aside weapons and spent arrows. Most of the bodies were Adren soldiers but as she followed the line of battle she began to find Uathach warriors among the dead. The strewn bodies seemed to show the tidemark of a familiar sequence where the dead marked each successive rearguard of the Uathach's fighting retreat through the Winter Wood.

Morveren wondered whether it was Gwyna's or Ruraidh's band she was following but in either case she knew the trail could only end in one of two ways, either she would meet up with the surviving Uathach or come across the last stand where the Adren tide had finally overwhelmed them. She did not lessen her pace but ran on as cautiously as she could while constantly scanning the trees ahead of her and listening for any sounds of battle.

She saw that one of the dead warriors had a water skin attached to his belt and she stooped down praying that it was full with clean water. It was not full but it contained enough to swill the taste of the smoke from the back of her throat and she drank it greedily and gratefully.

She put the empty skin back down beside the dead man and closed his eyes with a brush of her hand then scanned the trees to her left to gauge if the smoke was getting any thicker. She was about to get up and continue when her eyes were drawn back to the haze between the trees. There was someone there.

She crouched down by the dead warrior and stared into the shifting strands of smoke. Just when she thought she must have been mistaken she caught another glimpse of the figure moving through the trees. She watched as the indistinct outline faded into the spiralling smoke, heading in the same direction she had been previously taking. Without taking her eyes from the place where the figure had disappeared she felt on the ground for the dead warrior's sword that she had absently noted when she had taken his water flask. Gradually she got to her feet and, with a swift look around her to make sure the advancing fire was not outflanking her, she set off after the lone figure.

The climbing sun sent broad shafts of opaque light slanting through the drifting smoke and Morveren hurried between the tall birch and oak trees that dominated this part of the woodland. She moved over the forest floor as quietly as she could with one hand pressed to the wound in her side and the other gripping her newly acquired sword.

A stronger gust of wind cleared some of the smoke ahead of her and she saw the figure once again. She stopped abruptly and swept aside her long hair that had fallen across her face, not daring to hope that the figure seventy or so yards ahead of her was who she thought it to be. Her heart raced as she watched the old man wrap his dark cloak around himself and pick his way through the woodland with the aid of a long staff clutched in his right hand.

It had to be Merdynn and she was drawing breath to cry out his name when suddenly more figures emerged from the haze beyond him. They were warriors and they were heading straight towards him but Morveren knew immediately that they were not Uathach or warriors from the southern tribes; no warrior she had ever seen carried two swords. She stared through the haze and realised with a shock that the warriors were Cithol. Somehow Merdynn had arrived with Cithol warriors.

More of them were appearing from out of the smoke and it dawned on Morveren that she had never heard any mention that the Cithol had warriors, in fact quite the opposite; she was sure the Veiled City had no warriors to defend it. Filled with contradicting certainties she dropped to the ground and crawled towards a nearby ditch. When she felt she was safely concealed from those ahead of her she risked a look. There were fifty or more of the strange warriors and they were kneeling before the old man who was beckoning with his staff for them to stand once more. One of them approached him and pointed back the way they had come clearly reporting something to him.

Morveren's previous conviction that it had been Merdynn was rapidly evaporating. He looked like Merdynn from where she was positioned but something felt very wrong to her. Indeed everything felt wrong and her heart was beating faster for a very different reason now. She resisted the almost overwhelming urge to crawl away and steadied herself to continue watching.

The warrior had finished his report and the old man was now giving him his instructions. When he had finished the Cithol bowed and turned away leading his men back into the haze of the forest. The old man moved off at his own pace and as he walked through a sunlit shaft of smoke Morveren saw that the dark cloak he was wearing was of a deep blue and not the brown she had imagined only moments before.

Just as she was thinking that she had only ever seen Merdynn wearing his worn brown cloak the old man stopped and turned around. He seemed to be staring straight at her and she stopped breathing and remained absolutely still, sure that the slightest movement would give her away. She shut her eyes and willed herself to resist the urge to squirm deeper into the debris of the forest floor. In an effort to deflect her fear she forced herself to remember her brothers and their families and started to reel off the names of the children from her village in Wessex. After long minutes she opened her eyes, terrified she might find the old man standing over her, but there was no one in sight just the thickening smoke and the surrounding haze.

She lay there for several minutes steadying her breathing and trying to convince herself that the only thing to fear was the fire, and that could only be getting nearer. She got to her feet slowly, continually checking to make sure that there was no one else in sight. When she was sure that she was quite alone she took stock of her position trying to decide what she should do next. The fire was somewhere to her west so she could not go that way and the way east was just as suicidal as that led back to the main body of the Adren army. She could not face going back the way she had come and she felt that even if she tried then the fires would surely trap her. Which left the path she been following; the way the battling Uathach had retreated and the same way that the old man and his Cithol warriors had taken.

Morveren looked around in desperation as if seeking an inspirational alternative to the option she must take but she knew there was none and with a sense of deep foreboding she headed once more for the northern fringes of the Winter Wood.

For hours she hurried on through the woods intensely aware of both the fire burning in the West and the less definable but just as real fear of what may lay ahead of her. Her thirst returned and grew worse with each passing hour but none of the corpses she occasionally came across had been carrying any water and it was with an immense sense of relief that she saw a stream cutting across her path a little way ahead of her.

The stream ran quickly between narrow banks and she knelt by its side scooping up handfuls of water to her dry lips. She realised she had made a mistake in not taking the dead Uathach's water flask and in an effort to compensate she drank long after her immediate thirst was slaked. She drank until her head ached from the coldness of the icy water and when she felt it was impossible to drink any more she rinsed the blood from her bandages and sat back on a tumble of moss-covered masonry to inspect her wound. The arrow had scoured a groove through her flesh but as much as it hurt and as ugly as it looked she knew she had been fortunate. She knelt by the stream again feeling the sodden earth through the knees of her tattered trousers and gingerly dabbed the wet bandages against the raw gash in her side.

When she had washed the wound as best as she could she scrapped some moss from the stone blocks around her and after a brief hesitation packed it around her side and covered it with the tightly strapped bandages. She had seen Ceinwen use moss on deep cuts before but she still felt unsure if she had done the right thing.

She shrugged her uncertainty aside and took stock once more of her surroundings. The woods were still hazed by the smoke from the fires but there did not seem to be any signs of immediate danger and her thoughts drifted to Morgund and the others and she wondered anxiously if they had got to safety yet or if they were somewhere underground attempting to defend the Veiled City. She thought the latter was unlikely; at best they might have escaped the Adren trap and got to where the horses were picketed and thence to safety.

Her musings were interrupted by her stomach loudly protesting the long absence of any food and she added the need to find something to eat to her growing list of urgent requirements. She got to her feet and absently brushed away the grit and moss from the damp seat of her trousers. As she bent to retrieve her sword her skin prickled and she shot a glance to the North where the unmistakable sound of battle drifted through the woodland.

She grabbed the sword and set off at a steady run with one hand pressed firmly against her bandaged side and her eyes scanning the trees ahead of her. She gauged the battle to be no more than a mile or two ahead but it was difficult to be sure as the woods alternatively dampened and echoed the sound of clashing steel.

The trees rapidly thinned to either side of her and she realised she must have reached the very northern fringes of the Winter Wood. The ground started to rise and suddenly she could see the battle taking place on the slopes of the hillside ahead of her.

Her first impulse was to rush towards the group of Uathach warriors who were about halfway up the gentle slope of the sparsely wooded hill but they were already surrounded by several hundred Adren. Instead she ran towards a straggling clutch of young sycamore trees that were growing around a head-high pile of the ubiquitous rubble that littered the expanse of the Winter Wood.

She scrambled through the ancient masonry until she had an

unobstructed view of the unfolding battle. The fifty or so Uathach had gathered into a tight group but the encircling Adren seemed to be keeping their distance content to deny their enemy any escape. Morveren guessed that the Uathach bowmen must have spent their arrows sometime during the long retreat through the Winter Wood as none were now flying from their ranks.

She felt a surge of guilt and had to check herself once again from leaving her cover and racing towards the Uathach. Her guilt was deepened by the knowledge that without the northern warriors' intervention at the Causeway her own people would never have escaped from the Adren trap but she knew there was nothing she could do other than throw away her life in a futile gesture, and she had no stomach for heroic suicide. She cursed in self-reproach and scanned the fringes of the wood in the wild and desperate hope that some help might be at hand. It was then that she noticed the old man and his strange warriors making their way towards the stalemate on the hillside. They must have passed within a few hundred yards of her position and she squirmed deeper into the gap between the crumbling blocks and the leaning trunk of the tree where she was hiding.

She reflected bitterly that if she had her short bow and just one arrow she might well be able to bring down the impostor who so closely resembled Merdynn but even as the thought crossed her mind it was chased by the doubt that she would be able to hold her aim steady on the figure who had so scared her.

She watched as the old man covered the ground to the penned Uathach. His warriors followed behind him in a loose phalanx and as they approached their trapped enemy the Adren soldiers parted before them. Morveren shifted her position and looked on, puzzled by what was happening on the hillside. The Adren still remained on three sides of the Uathach but they had drawn away to make room for the strange warriors who had halted and were now standing only thirty yards from the Uathach line.

The old man advanced a few paces and seemed to be addressing the Uathach. Even at this distance Morveren could see and sense the unsettling affect that his words were having on the northern warriors. Their line was wavering and many of them kept casting glances behind them as if they were looking for reassurance from their own leader. Finally a figure emerged from the Uathach line to face the old man and Morveren instantly recognised the red-haired Gwyna.

She groaned in frustration and despair. The Uathach were heavily outnumbered and had nowhere left to retreat to; they were doomed and it would fall to her to bring the news of Gwyna's death to Arthur. She cursed the Adren for taunting the Uathach before falling upon them.

'Take the bastards with you...' she muttered under her breath and gripped her sword tightly.

What happened next surprised her. She had expected the Adren to rush the Uathach from all sides making the most use of their greater numbers but if anything they seemed to draw further back. Only the old man's warriors advanced on the Uathach line and they numbered no more than Gwyna's band. She watched as they charged into the Uathach and seconds later the frantic clash of battle rolled down the hillside to her.

The battle was ferocious, short-lived and shocking; the Uathach had been slaughtered in less than a few minutes. Morveren stared in opened-mouth disbelief as the old man's warriors stepped back to make way for their master. She counted them as best she could from her position and reckoned the fifty Uathach had killed no more than ten of these new Adren warriors.

She felt sick and was about to turn away from the massacre on the hill when she saw that the parting warriors had revealed one surviving Uathach who was weaponless and down on one knee as if injured.

Gwyna's dazed stare came back into focus and she gazed at the carnage around her. She had managed to keep her band together during the ambush that their Cithol guides had led them into and somehow she had kept them together as they had fought their way out of the trap. They had fought rearguard after rearguard during their long retreat through the Winter Wood and always the Adren had paid dearly for each of her fallen Uathach warriors. Until now. She stared uncomprehendingly at the bloody death all around her and finally she brought her eyes to the enemy who had so quickly overwhelmed them.

Her head was still ringing from the blow she had taken and blood flowed from her scalp and down one side of her face. She tried to wipe it from her cheek and neck with the palm of one hand but only succeeded in smearing it further across her pale skin. She felt for the knife tucked into her belt and drew it as she staggered back to her feet. She lurched forward and only just stopped herself from pitching headlong to the ground. A figure was moving towards her and she turned to face him with her knife before her.

The old man looked her in the eyes and levelled his staff at her. He slowly lowered the staff until it was pointing to the ground at her feet and Gwyna sagged to her knees. The knife fell from her limp hand and she knelt in the long grass looking up at the old man with an equal mixture of hate and fear.

'You will deliver a message to Arthur.' The old man's lips had not moved but the voice filled her head and she cowered before him. 'The old fool he sent east has failed and his warriors are slain. In return for destroying what was mine in the Cithol City I will destroy this feeble land and every living creature in it. His people and every trace of their existence shall be wiped clean from the history of this Island. My shadow guard will hunt down Arthur and his warriors and slaughter them as they slaughtered those around you. That is the price of standing against me. Take this message to Arthur.'

She managed to raise her head but the old man had gone and with a swift glance to either side she could she that the Adren soldiers were already filing away. Most of the old man's guard were leaving with their master but five remained standing before her. Gwyna looked at them and knew immediately what they intended to do. She grabbed for the knife but as she picked it up it was kicked from her grasp. She leapt to her feet but another foot slammed into her stomach and she doubled over gasping for breath. She was kicked from behind and she crashed to the ground. Two of the warriors grabbed her by the wrists and held her facedown in the grass where she struggled fiercely as her trousers were cut away.

Morveren watched the nightmare with tears of anger and shame running silently down her face. She kept telling herself that had they been ordinary Adren soldiers then she would have raced headlong into them but she had seen these warriors fight and knew she was no match for five of them. With her short bow she would have stood a good chance of killing them before they could cover the distance to her but with just her sword she knew she was no match for them. Part of her urged her to go to Gwyna's aid anyway; it was the right thing to do and she would have expected Gwyna to do the same if their positions were reversed. The same part of her argued that even death was better than witnessing this while cowering under cover. She knew for certain that neither Arthur nor Morgund would stay hidden no matter what odds faced them and she tried to reason to herself that at least they might be able to overcome the five on the hillside but she suspected that none of the war band would do as she was doing now; even the diminutive Ceinwen would fling herself at Gwyna's attackers. But whatever it took to do what she felt was right, in spite of personal cost, she realised she did not have it and the shameful tears of that acknowledgement burned her eyes.

She desperately wanted to leave the terrible scene behind her and strike out for the West but she felt compelled to stay until they finally ended Gwyna's nightmare by killing her and so she watched while they each took their turn before leaving the still figure lying in the grass alongside her dead companions.

When they had left the hillside and disappeared after the others Morveren got slowly to her feet and trudged towards where the Uathach had been massacred. Each step was more reluctant than the last and she came to a stop twenty yards from the prone figure of Gwyna. She could not bring herself to go straight to her and instead she wandered among the fallen Uathach to make sure that none were still alive. She soon realised that the Adren had already made sure of that and instead she counted the dead from the old man's guard. Eight. Fifty odd Uathach warriors had only managed to kill eight of the Adren warriors. She felt a streak of justification in not intervening in Gwyna's death and despised herself for it. In that moment she realised that she would never tell anyone that she had witnessed it all and done nothing; and she despised herself for that too.

Finally she turned to where Gwyna lay and was shocked to see her crawling towards one of her dead warriors. She raced across to her and Gwyna turned to face her with a look of terror on her battered and bloody face.

'Gwyna! It's me, Morveren, it's all right.'

But nothing was right at all and Gwyna stared at her with a look of pure hatred. Morveren knelt down beside her and much to Morveren's surprise Gwyna pushed her weakly away. Morveren stared at her in confusion as she hauled herself the last yard to the sprawled warrior and with one hand clamped between her bruised and bloody legs she tried to unfasten the belt of the dead man's trousers. Morveren saw what she was doing and helped her pull the woollen trousers from the dead warrior and handed them to her.

Gwyna took them, unable to meet Morveren's eyes, and painfully pulled them on over her legs. Morveren had no idea what to say and no idea why the Adren had left Gwyna alive. She watched helplessly as Gwyna finally belted the trousers around her waist. She tried to stand but was unable to do so and she turned fiercely to Morveren, 'Help me up.'

When she was standing she gripped Morveren's tunic and brought her face close to Morveren's.

'If you say a word of what happened here to anyone then I'll make you wish it had been you here and not me.'

Morveren stepped back in shock and Gwyna nearly tumbled to the ground without her support. She reached out a hand and Gwyna grabbed at it to steady herself.

'Get me my sword,' she said pointing to where it fallen.

Morveren took her arm from Gwyna's clutch half expecting her to collapse but Gwyna remained on her feet swaying slightly and clenched in pain with the same look of loathing on her face. Morveren fetched her sword and told her there was a stream nearby.

With Morveren's arms around her they gradually made their way down the hill. With every painful step Morveren could sense Gwyna's resentment and anger towards her. It was not until they reached the stream and Gwyna was washing away the blood that she realised that Gwyna would despise her for the rest of her life; not because she had hidden and watched, she had no way of knowing that, but because she alone knew what happened, and that shamed and humiliated the Uathach girl beyond endurance.

With a half-muttered explanation Morveren left Gwyna at the stream and hurried back to the carnage on the hillside to see what she could scavenge for their journey westwards. To her surprise she found that the Adren warriors had left behind the swords of their dead comrades and she picked one up to study it. She hesitated over whether or not to take them with her but they were far finer than most she had seen so she bundled them up in a cloak together with two spare water flasks and heaved it over her shoulder to carry back down the hill. She stopped for a moment and looked out over the Winter Wood. The fires had encroached to the heart of the forest and a pall of smoke stretched for miles as it tumbled upwards reaching out for the East.

As she made her way towards the stream she tried to fathom Gwyna's attitude towards her. She could understand Gwyna's fear, anger, humiliation and guilt at having lost a battle in which her warriors were all killed and understood that those feelings would be compounded by the nightmare that had followed, but she could not understand why her hatred should be directed at her. She concluded that it must be because Gwyna had lived when she would rather have died and having to face Morveren was the inescapable proof of that. She was still puzzled why the old man had let Gwyna live. That in itself was perversely the greatest humiliation for her. She dreaded the journey back to Caer Cadarn with Gwyna and dreaded equally her first meeting with Arthur when she would have to lie to him about what exactly happened here and the passive part that she had played in it.

Ceinwen stood at the exit of the tunnel with Elwyn, the Anglian boat captain. The long journey through the maze of tunnels under the Winter Wood had been a personal nightmare for him; for one used to the open horizons of the sea, the dark and narrow passageways underground had been a sore trial but if nothing else Elwyn was bloody-minded and doggedly persistent and he would rather have plummeted into an unexpected and unseen abyss than voice the fears he had felt.

Several times during the long hours underground the world about them had shaken bringing rocks and earth cascading down around them and several times they found themselves backtracking to seek alternative routes. Once they had come to an exit but fires had been raging through that part of the forest and they had been forced to turn back and seek another route. Had it not been for the Cithol, who they were technically escorting, then they would have soon become hopelessly lost and almost certainly would have died in the endless underground mazes. Thankfully and much to Elwyn's relief the last few miles had been through a relatively large and straight tunnel. They now stood at the exit to this tunnel surveying the ruined landscape before them. Behind them and resting in a line against the wall were Terrill and Seren together with the several Cithol they had come across who were also fleeing the devastation of the Veiled City.

'Looks like the fires have passed,' Elwyn said, staring at the charred stumps and scorched earth of the Winter Wood.

Ceinwen detected the note of relief in his voice and wondered if it was because the fires had swept on eastwards or whether he was just glad to be rid of the claustrophobic tunnels. She cast a glance at him and guessed it to be the latter. He was not all that much taller than she was but there any similarity abruptly ended; he was broad and strong and his cropped fair hair and pugnacious features matched his truculent and stubborn nature.

'Glad to be out of the tunnels are you?' Ceinwen asked half-smiling at him.

'Tunnels are for rats,' he replied just as Terrill joined them. He just stared unrepentantly at the Cithol.

Terrill still looked shocked from the events back in the Veiled City and his first view of the fire-ravaged woodland did nothing to improve his state of mind. He just stood and gazed blankly at the desolation before him as if he were unwilling or unable to accept the terrible transformation of the Winter Wood.

Ceinwen felt a surge of sympathy for him. He had been one of the few to go against Lord Venning's decision not to defend the city from Lazure and he had witnessed the terrible repercussions of his Lord's decision. Any satisfaction Terrill may have felt from being wholly vindicated had been entirely lost when he witnessed how his city and people had been ravaged by the Adren invaders. To make matters even worse the very person he had put his faith in to defend the city had ultimately destroyed it. He had no idea what Seren must be feeling as she had gone through even more including having to watch while Arthur coldly killed her father. Terrill had been unable to bring himself to talk to her during the long journey underground and in any case they had needed all their remaining strength and will just to carry on moving. As he looked out on the smoking wreckage of the Winter Wood he felt the last vestiges of that strength and will drain away from him. He sat down heavily and with a finality that clearly suggested he could go no further.

'Terrill, we have to go on,' Ceinwen said gently, recognising the obvious signs of defeat in his slumped form and vacant stare.

'No,' he replied. He said it without any trace of defiance. He was just stating a simple fact.

Ceinwen looked to Elwyn who shrugged. Arthur had asked her to escort Seren and Terrill to Caer Cadarn but they had picked up more than twenty Cithol during their escape from the city and she knew it would be difficult to force them all to follow her. She knelt down by Terrill and spoke to him quietly and reasonably. 'You have to come with us. You can't stay here. Where would you live? What would you eat?'

'It doesn't matter.'

Ceinwen realised he no longer cared about what happened to him so she changed her tack, 'The Adren will find you eventually. Seren's in a bad way already. She may lose the child if we can't get her to some proper shelter where she can rest safely. And what do you think will happen to her if the Adren find her?'

This seemed to elicit some response from him but Ceinwen feared it had only deepened his despair further as he bowed his head to his knees hiding his face. She pressed on, 'The others will look to you now. You're a captain and they'll expect you to make the decisions for them. Our horses aren't far from here so Seren won't have to walk for long and then we can all get to safety.'

She had no idea how near they were to their horses and she feared that safety was still far from guaranteed but she knew that Terrill did not need to hear either of these facts just now. One thing was obvious to her; they could not stay here at the mouth of the tunnel and she had to convince Terrill about that.

'Your horses aren't far from here?'

'Less than an hour's walk,' Ceinwen said, ignoring Elwyn's sceptical glance.

'And you have wains to carry us in?'

Ceinwen confirmed that they did but she had forgotten that the Cithol had never ridden horses and she was certain that there would be no carts or wains to carry them. She put the issue of transport to one side, determined to face only one problem at a time.

'Where would we go?' Terrill asked now looking at her.

'Caer Cadarn or Caer Sulis. Perhaps on to the Haven.'

Terrill seemed to lose interest again and he returned to staring at the ground. After a minute or two of silence he said quietly, 'Why? We won't be welcome there. We betrayed the Britons. There's nothing for us there.'

'There's nothing for you here either – except death at the hands of the Adren!' Ceinwen was beginning to lose patience despite her sympathy for him. Terrill shrugged as if he did not care about his own fate.

Elwyn was a practical man and his unbending attitude when he knew he was right had earned him a certain respect among the southern war bands. Not many people had flatly refused to do Arthur's bidding but he had done just that during the storm at the cove on the Shadow Land coast when he had refused to put the longboats to sea despite the Adren closing in on their position. But he was not a patient man and Terrill's attitude infuriated him.

Before Ceinwen could stop him he bent down and lifted the Cithol to his feet. 'Listen to me. You didn't betray us so you've nothing to fear by coming west with us. If you don't care about your own life what about your wife's and her unborn child?'

Terrill gazed at him blankly. Ceinwen stared at him too. Elwyn swore in frustration and nodded to Seren as she approached them, 'What about her?'

Terrill looked from Elwyn to Seren and back to the warrior holding him before finally saying, 'Her?'

'Yes!'

'She's not his wife,' Ceinwen said, understanding his mistake and laying a hand on Elwyn's arm.

'And it's not my child,' Terrill added, shaking himself free from the Anglian's grip.

'She's not your wife?' Elwyn echoed as he let the Cithol from his grasp.

'And the child I carry is Arthur's.'

They both stared at Seren as Terrill took a step away from them.

'Did you know that?' Elwyn asked turning to Ceinwen.

'No. No, I didn't.'

'Bloody hell, no wonder he wants us to get her to Caer Cadarn.'

'I'm standing right in front of you,' Seren pointed out reasonably and for a moment the haunted look left her face and something about the tilt of her chin and the hint of playful reproach in her voice reminded Ceinwen of the girl she had first met in the Winter Wood; the girl who had taken Arthur's arm to show him the Winter Garden.

'I'm sorry. We had no idea that, well, it's Arthur's child that you carry,' Ceinwen gabbled at a loss for the proper words.

'Well, that decides it then,' Elwyn said and walked back into the tunnel. He was addressing the Cithol there in a clear voice that was loud enough for them all to hear.

'We're going to be pushing on for Caer Cadarn straight away and Seren's coming with us. We want you to come with us too. There's food and proper shelter there and you'll be welcome to it. Stay and face the Adren if you prefer and you're welcome to that too. We're leaving now.'

Ceinwen smiled as he returned, 'You and Balor ought to get together for a drink.'

Elwyn ignored her and walked up to Terrill to give him the same ultimatum.

Balor was drinking with Morgund. They were toasting the dead; one mug of ale for every name they could recall. They were hopelessly drunk and were having difficulty remembering who they had already remembered. Not for the first time Morgund raised his beer to Morveren's memory and Balor once again cursed him for tempting fate and reminded him that they had agreed to drink to only those they had seen fall or who they knew for certain were dead.

It was supposed to have been a celebration for the bravery of dead warriors but too many of their friends were missing; Ceinwen was still out there somewhere escorting Seren back to Caer Cadarn, Mar'h was now at the Haven, Morveren had not been seen since the ambush and the rest, well, the rest were dead. To make matters worse the rumoured death of Cei and his warriors, together with Trevenna and Merdynn, had spread throughout Caer Cadarn and with it the hope that the Adren would have to turn back had begun to fade. The invading army that had broken through on the Causeway and swept them from the Winter Wood would soon be coming west. In fact, after their fifth drink they had come to the realisation that there really wasn't much to celebrate at all and the drinking had become morose and soon they were drinking to forget the dead rather than to remember them.

Gereint recognised some serious drinking when he saw it and strolled across the grass and mud of the compound to join them. He had met up with Ruraidh's band of Uathach on the Westway and together they had arrived back at Caer Cadarn a day ahead of Arthur. Ruraidh had lost almost half his warriors to the Cithol inspired ambushes but Gereint's band had fared much better thanks mainly to his inherent distrust of anything and anyone not Mercian. He had never trusted the Cithol and his wariness had kept most of his war band alive.

Of the fourth band, Gwyna's, there had been no news and Gereint cast his eyes towards the wall where Arthur stood looking out to the East. His attitude towards Arthur had changed over the last few days. After the immediate grief of losing his brother, Glore, he had been able to look back on the defence of the Causeway more objectively and he acknowledged to himself what he had always known; that Arthur had defended the Causeway better and longer than anyone else could have done. The Adren had paid in their thousands for their first foothold in Britain and according to what he heard they had paid in their thousands for taking the Veiled City too. Arthur's response to being betrayed by the Cithol had gone a long way to restoring his leadership in Gereint's eyes. The Cithol had lost their entire city and Arthur had managed to engineer it so that its fall took a hefty toll on the Adren too.

The last reason he had for believing once more in Arthur was a more personal one, and one that gave him no pride. According to the rumours circulating through Caer Cadarn, Trevenna had died in the Shadow Lands on a mission that Arthur had sent her on. If Arthur was responsible for Glore's death then by the same token he was responsible for his own sister's and that responsibility was no more and no less than any other leader who took his warriors into battle.

He drained his beer and remembered a line from one of the irritating Wessex drinking songs about how fishermen fished, farmers farmed and warriors died and if he needed any more evidence of the latter then the two he was drinking with were certainly providing it. To his annoyance he found himself singing the tune in his head but he smiled despite himself when he came to the line about what Cornish girls did.

Balor swore at him. He had been grinning as Balor was reciting the heroic eating feats of Cael and clearly he had taken exception to what he drunkenly thought was an inappropriate response. Balor was trying to stand up to make the point more physically but just as he found his balance Morgund pushed him back down again. He seemed to instantly forget what had upset him and the three of them raised their beers to Cael's memory.

Arthur watched them briefly from the wall thinking that the drinking might spill into a brawl. He could ill afford to lose any of his warriors through some drunken argument and he watched them until they were sat down once more.

Aelfric, the young Anglian, was passing just below him with a clutch of swords to be sharpened and he called down to him. 'Aelfric! Take some food to Balor and Morgund and tell them they'll be on the next patrol.'

Aelfric looked across to the warriors and back to Arthur with some trepidation.

'Just tell them it comes from me.'

The boy nodded but remained standing where he was looking up at Arthur plainly weighing up the dangers of asking a question. Arthur studied him for a moment then put him out of his misery, 'I don't know about Cei and the others. If you believe in the gods then pray they are still alive. And if you don't trust in them then trust in those swords and make them as sharp as you can.'

Arthur turned away without waiting for any reaction from him and scanned the land for any returning patrols. His hopes that Gwyna's Uathach would still make it to Whitehorse Hill were diminishing with every passing hour. Without them he would have less than one hundred and eighty warriors. He scanned the wooden palisade that encircled the hill fort and came to the same conclusion that he had already reached a dozen times; he did not have enough warriors to defend Caer Cadarn. The same conclusion prompted the same question; if he could not defend Caer Cadarn how could he hope to defend Britain?

He began pacing the wooden terracing that ran around the inside of the walls and, although he did not know it, many eyes followed his progress and those eyes also held the same question. He tried to keep away the encroaching thoughts about his sister's fate and about Fin Seren who he now knew carried his child. Both deserved serious consideration but he could afford to give them no more time other than how they bore upon the immediate situation.

The first thing he had done when he reached Whitehorse Hill was to send out several patrols. Two were sent eastwards back towards the Winter Wood to look for any surviving members of the war band and to go further on and report back on the Adren movements. Others were sent to make sure Caer Sulis and the surrounding countryside had been evacuated. His orders had been quite clear; take everything that could be carried to the Haven and to burn whatever was left behind. Over the last day or two the country to the West of their base had sprouted smoking pyres in an ever-widening semi-circle as the word passed from village to village.

Some thought that if the Veiled City had been the Adren's main reason for invading Britain then perhaps, now that it was destroyed, they might turn back to where they had come from, but Arthur's orders to burn the land clearly showed he did not hold the same view. Those who had delayed their departure for the Haven had watched with increasing anxiety as others packed up what they could and left, and when the Uathach villagers started arriving from the North their anxiety grew to fear.

Those who had stayed up to this point greeted the warriors as heroes even though they had come to tell them to leave their homes. As the news reached them that first the Causeway had fallen and then the Winter Wood so too had the news of the overwhelming Adren numbers and they were proud of the warriors who had fought the enemy and killed so many. For most of the villagers the evacuation of their homes was not a harrowing experience as they had done so every year with the onset of winter for the journey to the Western Lands; they had absolute faith in their warlord, Arthur, and felt the hurried departure for the Haven was only a temporary one. The fear they felt and expressed to one another was always quelled by the same argument; Arthur had kept Wessex safe and in peace for over twenty years and he would defeat these Adren from the Shadow Lands. But few stopped to tally up the numbers and those that had were the first to leave for the Haven.

Chapter Four

Arthur paced along the walls of Caer Cadarn. He watched as stragglers from the battle in the Winter Wood made their way up the winding road that climbed the slopes of Whitehorse Hill. They arrived in one's and two's having been separated from their main groups during the ambushes and Arthur questioned each of them as they entered the gates. None reported having seen any Adren during their journey from the woods and none could say they had seen anything of Gwyna's Uathach.

Arthur waited impatiently for the returning patrols, desperate to know what the enemy position was. Almost a third of his warriors were now out on various reconnaissance missions and he had to fight the impulse not to ride out eastwards to see for himself. He knew he had to stay in the one place where all the patrols would report to but he despised the waiting while the enemy was free to roam his land.

During those first few days those that knew him tried to avoid igniting his simmering anger knowing that while he was at his best when in the thick of things his temper was equally at its worst when events were unfolding without his influence. It was too soon to reasonably expect any of the patrols to be returning yet but every day that passed without any certain news ratcheted everyone's anxiety one notch further.

In one ill-advised moment Laethrig, the war band's blacksmith, pointed out that the lack of any news could only mean that the Adren were not yet coming this way. His well-meant efforts were rewarded by a scathing condemnation of the meagre amount of arrows and new weapons that he had been able to produce. Laethrig had been ready to justifiably point out that he had little in the way of raw materials and only children to help him but he knew the danger signals in his warlord as well as any of the other warriors did and he quickly made himself scarce. He took some satisfaction from the exchange when many of the warriors still at the camp turned up to see if they could help him.

Everyone was relieved when Ceinwen arrived later that same day and not just because she and Elwyn had made it safely out of the Veiled City; she was one of the few who seemed to have any success in communicating with Arthur during times like these. They were less pleased that she arrived at the head of three wains filled with Cithol refugees from the underground tunnels of the city.

Despite Elwyn's scepticism they had found their picketed horses with relative ease. Arthur had left three warriors there to guard the spare horses for those yet to escape the woods and much to Ceinwen's surprise there had been a number of carts and wains there too. Whether they had been used to ferry the wounded from the Causeway or whether they were the surplus from the Cithol supply line to Caer Sulis she neither cared nor asked. She had told the Cithol that there would be transport and she quietly thanked the gods that she was not proved a liar so early in the journey. She had a lot less confidence in how the Cithol would be received at Caer Cadarn.

They were received in stony silence. The warriors throughout Caer Cadarn stopped what they were doing and stared at the Cithol in the wains. Ceinwen released the reins and clambered down from her seat ignoring the staring warriors around her, many of whom now had their hands on their weapons. Some of them were casting glances at Arthur as if awaiting his reaction before acting themselves.

Arthur was at his customary place on the wall. He had watched the progress of the approaching wains and now he too stared at the newcomers. The Cithol could sense the surrounding hostility and one by one they followed the glances of the warriors and turned to face Arthur. Only Seren kept her eyes on the wooden floor of the cart.

The warriors stirred as Arthur finally made his way down the steps and crossed the short distance to the Cithol. Ceinwen stopped her unnecessary fiddling with the harnesses and took a tentative step to intercept Arthur but he strode straight to the wain carrying Seren.

No one was sure what would happen next; all of them thought of the Cithol as their enemy because of the betrayal in the Winter Wood but these were unarmed men, women and children who were clearly no more than refugees seeking shelter. The warriors tensed as Arthur slapped the pins free that held the tailgate in place.

'Are any of you members of Venning's council?'

Unsurprisingly the Cithol shook their heads in denial.

'Did any of you have any part to play in the ambushes in the Winter

Wood?'

The shaking of heads was more vehement but still none of them dared to speak. Arthur searched their faces and returned his gaze to Seren.

'Fin Seren?'

She finally brought her eyes up to meet the man who was both the father of her child and the killer of her own father. He was standing there with his hand held out to help her down from the wain. With an appalling and sickening realisation she knew she still loved him.

She lurched to her feet and picked her way through those around her before lowering herself to the tailgate. Arthur lifted her down to the ground.

'See they get food and shelter,' he said to Ceinwen as he led Seren towards the main hall.

She allowed herself to be guided into the hall. Conflicting emotions were sweeping through her; blind rage at the death of her father, bitter anger at the destruction of her city, guilt for the betrayal of the Britons, relief to be safe at last and overlying all of these the accountable pleasure at the touch of Arthur's hand as he guided her down the length of the hall.

Arthur led her to a room that was set off to one side near the top of the hall. It was his private quarters and he indicated a low chair padded by furs for her to sit in as he crossed to the open window and closed the wooden shutters. The bright sunlight from outside was closed off immediately and in the semi-darkness she watched him as he lit two long tallow candles and placed them on a simple table. In the soft mix of filtered sunshine and candlelight she surveyed the room and her eyes strayed to the corner where a large bed dominated the small chamber. Her thoughts flicked involuntarily to the red haired girl on the cliffs above the Causeway and she looked at Arthur with uncertainty. He saw the reproach and fear in her eyes but he said nothing as he poured her a beaker of clear, cold water. He handed it to her and their fingers brushed as she took it.

Arthur sat on the floor opposite her with the low table between them. They held each other's gaze through the flickering light but neither said a word. Seren wanted to say so much; so many questions, so many recriminations. Long hours had been spent preparing for this moment but now that it had come she realised there was just too much to say and she had no idea where to even start. Nine months ago she had only known the man opposite her as the warrior who had accompanied Merdynn on rare visits to her city. And now, now she was overwhelmed with the magnitude of all that had happened in those few months; her love for Arthur, her child, Arthur's marriage to one of his own kind, her father's betrayal of the Britons, the Adren invasion of her city, the killing of her father, Arthur's destruction of the Veiled City and all of this while Britain shuddered under the shadow of the unstoppable Adren armies. Even Merdynn was said to be dead. Nothing was as it had been and nothing was as it should be. She had gained and lost everything. Arthur poured himself some water and finally broke the heavy silence.

'There was a time when I considered turning my back on everything just to be in the Winter Garden once again.'

'With me.'

'Yes, with you,' Arthur replied, holding her gaze.

'But not now?'

'No.'

Seren looked away and lowered her head, 'No. Now there is no Winter Garden, no Veiled City, nowhere for my people, nowhere for me and nowhere for us.'

'You can stay here.'

'For how long? You saw how your warriors looked at us. We betrayed you all.'

'You didn't, Terrill didn't.'

'Only because we thought you were going to protect us. We thought you would defend the Veiled City,' Seren replied, anger now edging her voice.

'I had no other choice.'

'And murdering my father?'

Arthur's expression hardened, 'He's the reason why I had no other choice. He would have murdered Britain. He betrayed Britain.'

'And marrying Gwyna?'

'Without that marriage there would have been no Uathach and without the Uathach Britain would have died on the Causeway.'

'Your Britain, not necessarily ours!'

'It's one and the same.'

'Tell that to the dead!'

'It's the living that concern me.'

'You betrayed us!'

'I betrayed no one.'

'You betrayed me!'

'I loved you.'

Seren stared at him as his words permeated through her anger.

'What did you say?'

'I loved you, Fin Seren.'

'And now?' she asked, unable to keep her voice steady.

'Now is not the time for love.'

She grasped at the implication that once the war was over there would be time for them to be together but her hope quickly drained as the reality of the war overwhelmed her. Somewhere in the hall, or perhaps outside in the village, she heard the hour bell being rung and its dull clanging sounded ominously to her.

'You're going to fight on?'

'Of course.'

'How can you hope to win against so many?'

'Even without hope we would fight on.'

'Your people will die like mine have.'

'No, if necessary then they'll sail for the West.'

'Then why not go to the West now? We could all escape the enemy.' Seren leaned forward as she implored him.

'And how long would we be safe in the West? How long before we have to flee again? No. This is our land. This is our home. It's your home and it's our child's home. This is where we stand against the Adren.'

As Arthur spoke Seren could almost believe that it was possible for the Britons to defeat the Adren but then the horrifying images of the last hours of the Veiled City flooded back to her and she recalled the sight from the cliffs above the Causeway and knew that Britain was doomed.

'It would be safer for you and the child to go to the Haven and wait there.'

Seren nodded in silence unable to bring herself to mention Gwyna again. She had not seen her among the warriors when they had entered

Caer Cadarn but she knew that this was Gwyna's place and time and not hers. She looked around the darkened room thinking that this was Gwyna's room too and she glanced involuntarily at the bed. She saw that Arthur had followed her gaze but his face betrayed nothing of what he was thinking. With a feeling of utter emptiness she asked, 'When do you want me to leave?'

'I don't want you to leave. I need you to leave. We each have to do what we must, not what we wish.'

'Must I go immediately?'

'When you've had food and rested,' he replied and they both stood up. He took a step towards her and for a heart-stopping moment she thought he was going to embrace her but he reached beyond her and opened the door onto the main hall. She stopped in the doorway and looked into his face wondering if they would ever be alone again. There was still so much left unsaid, so many questions she needed answering and yet somehow none of it seemed relevant any longer.

As she walked out into the hall she heard him quietly say, 'Look after our child, Seren, keep her safe.'

The other Cithol were already seated at one of the long tables with various foods laid out before them. Few seemed to be eating and she went and sat by Terrill. She had no appetite for food either.

The Cithol left for the Haven several hours later after they had rested and once again sat and stared for long minutes at the food the Britons had provided for them. Arthur sent a small escort with them to make sure they were quartered safely at the Haven. He suggested to the guard that they stay at the harbour master's house as it was large enough to house the Cithol group and far enough from most of the villagers and any potential confrontations.

Arthur said no further farewells to Seren but in the bright sunshine he watched until her wain had disappeared from view on its way to the Westway where it would join all the other Briton and Uathach refugees on their journeys to the Haven.

He returned to his vigil on the wall and while many had noted his meeting with Seren none of them questioned him about it and few even mentioned it among themselves. Ceinwen and Elwyn thought they were the only ones who knew that the child Seren carried was Arthur's but Ruraidh of the Uathach also knew and he had watched with interest when Arthur took her from the cart and led her into the hall.

As the days passed the Uathach warriors began to give up hope for Gwyna's band and they naturally accepted Ruraidh as their leader in her prolonged absence. The common assumption was that they must have been unable to escape from one of the Adren ambushes; most of them were still counting their good fortune at their own escapes.

When the first returning patrol was spotted on the road to Caer Cadarn word quickly spread that Gwyna and Morveren were with them and both the Uathach and Wessex warriors gathered at the gate to welcome back two more they thought they had lost.

It was Morgund's patrol and he rode into Caer Cadarn laughing with Morveren who rode between him and a grinning Balor. Gwyna was just behind them with the other warriors but her face was grim and still carried the bruised weal from the sword blow that had stunned her. Once through the gates they were met by their respective groups and while the Wessex were jubilant at Morveren's return the Uathach greeted Gwyna in a far more subdued manner; relief at her safety being overridden by the certainty that her warriors were dead.

Ceinwen was the first to greet Morveren as she awkwardly dismounted and she held out a hand to steady the younger woman as she landed heavily on her feet.

'Are you injured?'

'Just a cut on my side,' Morveren answered, gesturing to the bandages under her tunic.

'Let me take a look at that,' Ceinwen replied automatically then grinned at her, 'Thought you'd got yourself lost in the woods!'

'Lost? You lot abandoned me and left me for dead!'

Morgund winced at the tone that suggested more than a trace of genuine reproach but Ceinwen shrugged it aside with a laugh and said, 'You should have listened to your brothers and married a farmer - and stayed out of the woods!'

'You should stay out of woods, that's a fact. And avoid horses too come to that,' Balor added, rubbing his saddle-sore behind and looking around for something to drink.

'Better let me take a look at that cut.'

'I think our warlord wants a word first,' Morveren replied, nodding to Arthur who was standing at the doors to the main hall and watching them impatiently.

Gwyna seemed to have got the same message and they made their way to the hall. Arthur stood aside and as they went inside he called out for Morgund who looked wistfully at the mugs of beer that Balor was carrying before turning to the hall.

'Don't worry, I'll see it goes to a good home!' Balor called after him.

Morgund need not have worried as there was a flagon of beer waiting for them on the table at the top of the hall and he poured himself a drink before passing it on to the others. He drank it gratefully, glad to be out of the sun and enjoying the coolness inside the hall.

The wooden shutters were propped open down both sides of the long hall and the sounds of Caer Cadarn mingled reassuringly with the familiar smells of wood smoke and cooking. He looked across the table at Morveren and smiled, just glad to be alive and glad to be home. Somewhere just below his conscious thoughts he knew that neither were likely to remain true but it only seemed to heighten the simple pleasure he took in being where he was and he recalled the typically erudite Anglian saying; 'summer brings heat and winter the snow' - what would happen would happen, but for now he could sit in the cool and smile at Morveren when only a few days ago he had thought that he would never be able to do so again.

'There's no immediate threat to us from the Adren?' Arthur asked him.

'Not immediate, no.'

'Good.' Arthur turned his attention to Morveren, 'What happened?'

Morveren shifted in her chair to ease the ache in her side before replying, 'I got hit by an arrow in the first moments of the ambush then got bashed on the head. The next thing I remember is waking up with no one around. Except the dead of course. I searched among them and soon realised that most of you must have escaped.'

Arthur asked her who she had seen in the clearing and when she had given him the names of the dead he left them to give the information to a messenger to take on to the Haven where all the warriors' families were now quartered. The three of them sat in silence waiting for Arthur to return and Morgund puzzled over Gwyna's attitude. She had been completely withdrawn from the first moment the patrol had come across them and he had initially put her reticence down to the loss of the warriors under her command but during the journey to Caer Cadarn he had noticed how she avoided even looking at Morveren. He looked at them both now and although they were sitting side by side there was a wide gulf between them.

Arthur came striding back up the hall to the table and poured himself a drink indicating for Morveren to continue.

'Well, after checking the bodies I tried to head west to where we left the horses but the fires forced me to turn more and more to the North and that's when I started to come across the trail of the Uathach rearguard.' She hesitated as Gwyna stiffened beside her but whether it was because she had used the word 'Uathach' or whether it was just the recollection of the battle she could not tell so she hurried on to the part of her tale that she had not yet told to Morgund. 'That's when I thought I saw Merdynn.'

'Merdynn?'

'That's what I thought, at first. He looked a lot like him, even down to the cloak and staff but then these Cithol warriors appeared out of the smoke and haze and bowed to him.' She sensed Gwyna recoil again, this time at the mention of the warriors, and once again she hurried on now wanting to finish as quickly as possible and get away from the hall. 'I can't describe it but there was something about the old man that, well, made me afraid.'

Arthur nodded, 'Lazure Ulan. The Adren Master. Venning told us he commands the Shadow Land City and the Adren armies. Somehow he's linked to Merdynn but I don't know how yet. Who were these warriors?'

'Cithol, definitely, but unlike the Cithol of the Veiled City. These were warriors, very dangerous, much more so than the Adren soldiers.' Morveren stopped abruptly, hoping that Gwyna would now pick up the tale. She felt Arthur staring at her and she willed Gwyna to start talking. She did.

'It was those Cithol who finally overcame my warriors. We had fought the Adren in running battles from the first ambush right through the wood until we had made it to the northern fringes. We fought long and hard but they had us surrounded on a hillside. Then this Lazure you speak of arrived with his Cithol warriors. As many of them died as my own warriors but there were too many of them. We fell one by one until I was the only one left.' For the first time since she started speaking she dropped her eyes from Arthur's and stared at the drink in front of her.

Arthur knew she was lying and briefly glanced to Morveren who was looking intently at her hands.

'Gwyna, if these are new warriors to us and they surround Lazure then we need to know the truth about them.' Arthur spoke quietly but there was no mistaking the command in his tone.

The strength seemed to drain from Gwyna and she replied in a flat voice devoid of emotion. 'They were Cithol. They each wielded two swords and they numbered the same as my warriors. We were no match for them. They slaughtered us in minutes. Lazure left me alive so I could deliver his message to you.'

Morveren risked a glance at Arthur to see if he realised that Gwyna had omitted her own ordeal and was shocked to see the barely controlled rage on his face.

'What was his message?'

Gwyna was silent for a moment, a slight frown creasing her forehead as if she were trying to remember exactly what Lazure had said. She blinked and her eyes appeared to glaze over as once again she spoke in that eerie, lifeless tone.

'The old fool you sent east has failed and his warriors are slain. In return for destroying what was mine in the Cithol City I will destroy this feeble land and every living creature in it. Your people and every trace of their existence shall be wiped clean from the history of this Island. My shadow guard will hunt down you and your warriors and slaughter you just as they slaughtered the Uathach warriors. This is the price of standing against me and this is the price you shall pay.'

Morgund and Morveren listened horrified by her tone; it was as if her will had been taken over by another who was talking through her. They were no less appalled by the message itself. Morgund felt despair wash over him and he was powerless to resist it; Cei and his Anglians dead,

Merdynn, who was older than Britain, slain by Lazure. He felt what little hope remained being slowly extinguished and realised now that it was only a matter of time before darkness fell on Britain forever.

Morveren was staring blankly at Gwyna but she was seeing Cei as he cheerily waved them good-bye when he left them in the Shadow Lands. Trevenna, Leah, Cerdic and Ethain all dead. All the others, some she hardly knew, others good friends. It was as if the full effect of all the lost friends had finally sunk home and her chin dropped to her chest. She had been able to bear the loss of those close to her but the loss of hope emptied her soul and the despair she had kept at bay for so long finally overwhelmed her.

Arthur laughed out loud.

'Empty words from an old man too frail to fight his own battles. He's nothing but a pale shadow of Merdynn. All he can do is slink from shadow to shadow, whining like a toothless wolf too old to attack anything without his scavenging pack around him. He's going to destroy Britain is he? Wipe away the history of our peoples? He'll rue the day he ever heard of Britain. He'll lament ever seeing the Causeway and our white cliffs. He wants a war of annihilation? Then so be it. We'll destroy his armies and lay waste to his city and we'll add that to our history. He will never destroy Britain, never destroy us. All he'll find here is his own ruin.'

As Arthur mocked him, the hopelessness was plucked from their hearts and the spell of despair was broken.

'This shadow guard ...' Morveren began but Morgund interrupted her,

'We'll take his shadow guard and shove it up his arse!' he said, raising his beer and grinning at her.

Only Gwyna remained seated with her head still bowed. Arthur stooped down and lifted her onto her feet and turned to Morveren, 'Get a sleeping draught from Ceinwen for her, she's been through too much. And Morgund, bring in Hengest, Gereint and the captains to hear your report.'

He half-carried the unresisting girl to his quarters and laid her on the bed. Morveren came in some minutes later with some leaf-wrapped powders and Arthur emptied them into a drink which he handed to Gwyna. When she had drank it they left the small room and Arthur turned to Morveren.

'Was there anything else you wanted to say about your escape before I hear Morgund's report?'

Morveren looked up at Arthur wishing she could lie to him.

'Yes. Yes, there is...'

'Good. I know what happened. Lazure used Gwyna to deliver more than one message and there was nothing you could have done to stop him. I wanted to give you the chance to tell me. Now go and get Ceinwen to look at your side.'

Morveren left feeling a great weight had been lifted from her shoulders. She passed Morgund in the doorway as he was coming in with the others and she flashed a bright smile at him. Elwyn saw the smile and for a brief second felt a stabbing jealousy before he forced it from his mind as he joined the others gathering around the table.

Arthur indicated for Morgund to start his report and he quickly glanced at those now seated around the table. The two Anglians, Hengest and Elwyn, were opposite him along with Ruraidh of the Uathach. Gereint and his new second-in-command, Dystran, had taken seats to his right and were waiting patiently for him to begin. In contrast to the two Anglians, who were both in their mid to late twenties, the Mercian commanders were a good twenty years older and they both looked it. Dystran was of the same height and build as Morgund both being broad across the shoulders and standing at over six-feet but whereas Morgund shaved his head Dystran's hair had receded to the point of baldness. As if to compensate for this he had a series of interlinked tattoos stretching from his forehead to the back of his neck, which matched the tattoos that covered his arms, and despite his ready smile he looked to Morgund like a man not to cross lightly. He had one of those granite faces, Morgund thought, that looked like punching it would only hurt your hand. In fact, he looked like a man not to cross at all. Morgund had heard someone say that he came from the valleys in West Mercia and that explained the tattoos which were more or less an obligatory custom in that part of the country. It also explained why you felt like he was looking for a fight even when he was smiling at you.

Taking his eyes away from Dystran's tattoos Morgund cleared his throat and started, 'First of all we saw no sign of the Adren anywhere west of the Winter Wood. One of the other patrols we met up with said they weren't southward either. We pushed right through the Winter Wood following the course of the Isis until we saw their camp just beyond the eastern edge of the woodland. Obviously we couldn't get too close but it seems they're set to stay there for a while.'

'Which side of the river are they?' Gereint asked.

'South. But the odd thing was that they had built a bridge, supported by rafts, across to the North side. At the time we had no idea why. We were on the North bank ourselves so we doubled back and swam our horses across. Nearly lost Balor doing that – he's useless on a horse.'

The others chuckled at the thought of Balor on horseback in the water. Aelfric, who had been standing close by the whole time, took the opportunity to bring across the food he had been asked to serve. Once he had put the plates on the table he returned to the nearby fire and pretended to look busy. Out of the corner of his eye he watched the warlords and listened to every word they said.

As they helped themselves to the food Morgund continued, 'We skirted the camp as best as we could trying to get some idea of their numbers and what they were up to. It seemed that most of their supplies had been brought up from the cliffs above the Causeway to this new camp. After watching the camp for a day we rode in a loop down to the Causeway and sure enough, there's only about a hundred stationed there now.

'What we couldn't understand was why there only seemed to be about ten thousand of them in the new camp. Now, we know they lost thousands crossing the Causeway and possibly thousands more in the destruction of the Veiled City but that would still leave half their force unaccounted for. So we went back to the camp on the edge of the Winter Wood and tried to get a more accurate count but each of us came up with more or less the same number. There were over ten thousand Adren missing.'

'Would they have gone back east?' Hengest asked.

'That's what Balor thought.'

'North! They've gone north!' Ruraidh said, slamming his hands down on the table.

'We came to the same conclusion and it explained why they had built the bridge. So we crossed the Isis upstream and rode north looking for them. We found them after a day's hard riding then we made straight for

Caer Cadarn.'

'Have your people all left for the Haven yet?' Gereint asked Ruraidh.

'Most have. Some wouldn't have. Gods, they'll be slaughtered, Arthur, we must ride to help them!'

'They were given the same warning that the Anglians, Mercians and Wessex were given: make for the Haven. They were told to evacuate because we couldn't guarantee their safety,' Arthur replied.

'We rode to your help!' Ruraidh crashed his fist down on the table as he spoke.

'And we've given your people sanctuary! It was more than we could do for Eald and Branque and the Belgae. Once we've destroyed the enemy all our peoples can go back to their homes.'

'How are we going to destroy them if we won't face them!' Ruraidh said, shooting to his feet.

'That's what we're here to discuss. Now, sit down,' Arthur replied evenly.

Ruraidh stared into the gray eyes and slowly sat back down.

'Good. As soon as we're finished here send four riders north to shadow the Adren army. They can give a last warning to any of your people who have chosen to stay. They can give the same message to the other northern chieftains, Benoc and Hund. My offer of sanctuary still stands should they wish, and still be able, to accept it. We'll be relying on those four warriors to give us warning when the Adren army turns south so pick them well. We'll face that army later.

'The enemy seeks to destroy our land completely and to destroy all our peoples too. It seems he's sent half his force northwards for that purpose. In six to eight weeks time we can expect that force to come at us from the North while the other half of his armies push westwards towards us.'

'Twenty thousand Adren,' Elwyn said, shaking his head, 'It could've been worse but still, twenty thousand.'

'But the Adren Master has split his forces. He's confident that either force is large enough to destroy us. He saw how many of us escaped the Causeway and he believes that's all we have. After the ambushes in the Winter Wood he'll think there's even less of us now. But he doesn't know about Mar'h or our own army and he's split his forces. We don't have to face twenty thousand Adren in battle - just ten thousand, and with Mar'h's army the odds will only be three to one. We'll have surprise on our side and a battle of our choosing in a place of our choosing at a time of our choosing. And that is all we need to destroy them. Now, was Lazure with the northern or southern force?'

'He was with the northern one...'

Aelfric sat by the fire chewing on some dry bread openly watching the warlords as they concentrated on Arthur's battle plan and he listened avidly to each suggestion, counter proposal and each new strategy. When Arthur left the hall some hours later Aelfric stayed where he was and listened to the others as they laboriously discussed the logistics of Arthur's plan.

Arthur sought out Morveren. She was still with Ceinwen and they were sitting and chatting on the grass slopes beyond the walls. Arthur joined them.

'How's her side?' he asked Ceinwen.

'It'll heal nicely. Scarred but then she had too few of those for a proper warrior.'

'Pity your jaw healed so quickly,' Morveren replied, then turned to Arthur, 'It's only a scratch really but it's something to impress my brothers with when I next see them.'

'Are they at the Haven?' Arthur asked lying back in the long grass.

'Should be by now. They went to the village first then they were due to sail their boats around the coast to the Haven so they should be there by now.'

Arthur nodded in reply and they lapsed into silence.

'Beautiful, isn't it?' Ceinwen said a few minutes later, idly gesturing to the country laid out before them.

The other two gazed out over the fields and woods that stretched away into the distant summer haze. The sun beat down from a blue-white sky highlighting the summer colours of bright wild flowers strewn throughout the rolling grasslands before them; the yellow and blue of buttercups and harebells punctuated by the deep reds of the taller poppies. The woods and copses that dotted the landscape and lined the banks of streams and rivers were now fully in leaf and the cries of the migrant birds that inhabited them carried far on the soft wind.

Morveren couldn't help contrasting the scene before them with the recent horrors of battle, 'Bastards. How dare they invade our land.'

At another time Ceinwen would have laughed at the righteous indignation in Morveren's voice but she had been thinking exactly the same thing. So had Arthur.

'They'll never take this land from us,' Ceinwen said with uncharacteristic ferocity, 'Never.'

'Lazure has split his forces and that arrogance will be his undoing.' The other two looked at Arthur who continued, 'Morveren, if you're fit enough I want you to ride to the Haven and tell Mar'h to bring his new army here as quickly as possible. He'll need as much in the way of supplies as the Haven can spare.'

'We're going to take the fight to the Adren?' Morveren asked with enthusiasm and Arthur explained to them what he had outlined to the others in the hall. When he had finished they both grinned to each other.

'It will work!' Morveren said clenching her fists.

'If it goes to plan and if Mar'h's army is steady enough,' Ceinwen replied more cautiously.

Arthur shrugged, 'Battles never go exactly to plan and it's then that we'll find out if Mar'h's army is steady enough. But we'll never get another chance to fight them on anything like even terms.'

'I wouldn't call those terms exactly even,' Ceinwen said looking out over the sunlit countryside once again.

Morveren got up intending to ride for the Haven straight away. She prodded Ceinwen with her foot, 'You're getting cautious old girl. Three to one, we'll slaughter the bastards!'

Before Ceinwen could reply she had turned and ran off towards the gate.

'Cheeky cow,' she said, wondering for the thousandth time if Morveren really was Arthur's daughter. That thought led her naturally to Seren. She assumed that Arthur knew that Seren carried his child but she wanted him to know that she knew too. She thought for a few minutes about how best to broach the subject and then gave up and just came out and said it, 'I know Seren's child is yours.'

Arthur just studied her and she wondered if she had made a bad mistake in bringing up the topic, 'And Elwyn knows too.'

Arthur continued to gaze at her. She felt he was gazing into her and rather than listen to the silence she continued onwards, 'No one else does as far I know. Only us two. And he won't say anything. I told him it was none of our business. It was between the two of you and nothing to do with anyone else.' She realised she was beginning to babble and ended lamely, 'So he won't say anything.'

She stared out over the distant fields feeling his eyes still on her and she felt a slight panic rising inside her. She hated Arthur when he was like this, she had no idea whether he would laugh, strike her or just keep silent and stare at her. The second of those would have been unthinkable only a year ago and was still extremely unlikely but over the last few months, ever since the attack on Branque, she had found it increasingly difficult to predict his responses. It seemed that his violence simmered constantly just below the surface; it was not likely to manifest itself in angry or vicious outbursts but if the cold rage did surface then blood was quickly spilt. To her surprise he broke the anxious silence with a quiet voice as if he were talking more to himself than to her.

'Fin Seren is different to any other woman I've known. She is completely unreadable to me and I never thought to find someone like her. I would have given up almost anything to be with her and considered it to be a good trade. But I found her at the wrong time, or the Adren found us at the wrong time, either way she can be nothing to me while this land is threatened by the Shadow Lands.'

Ceinwen listened in silence thinking back to the time she was with Arthur all those years ago and wondering if what he had just said in someway explained why they had never got back together when she had returned from her season in the Western Lands. She had certainly wanted to. Perhaps he was explaining to her why he had not sought her out again. Her confusion inevitably led to thoughts of Andala, her dead husband and her brother, Ruadan, one of Arthur's oldest friends, and equal waves of grief and guilt surged through her.

'Andala was a good man, he loved you and you never let him down.'

Ceinwen was not even surprised that Arthur had guessed where her thoughts had led her.

'I miss him, and Caja. And Ruadan too.'

'And we'll miss many others before the end comes.' Arthur told her about the message from Lazure and how he had said that Cei and the others were dead.

'Do you think they are?' she asked, unable to keep the dread from her voice.

'I don't know.'

Arthur got to his feet and without another word walked back to Caer Cadarn. She watched him go once again feeling warmth and sympathy for him. If Trevenna, Cei and Merdynn were dead then Arthur would have lost those closest to him and Britain's peril would be all the greater for the loss.

Arthur went straight to his private quarters where Gwyna was still sleeping. He joined her and still half-asleep she clung to him desperate for his acceptance to wash away the violation and humiliation she felt.

Ceinwen sat on the grass slope letting the hours drift by lost in the memory of her dead family. She was eventually brought out of her long reverie by the thundering of hooves as Hengest and the Anglians rode from Caer Cadarn. Tagging along behind them was Laethrig and a very unhappy looking Balor.

So, she thought, it's time to take the fight to the enemy.

Chapter Five

Mar'h arrived at Whitehorse Hill eight days later. At Arthur's instigation the warriors at Caer Cadarn lined the Ridgeway to honour those who had chosen to fight alongside them. They watched with mixed emotions as the long procession marched past them. They all felt proud that so many of their people were prepared to fight to defend their land but they also felt varying shades of uneasiness; it had been their responsibility to keep these people safe from attack and although they knew that no one could accuse them of not giving their all still they had failed in their prime responsibility.

Arthur felt none of these conflicting emotions. He stood on the wall above the gate watching as the freshly trained army filed through beneath him. They were a fairly even mix of Wessex, Anglian and Mercian with a smaller contingent of Uathach villagers. It was understandable there should be less from the northern tribes as they had arrived at Caer Sulis and the Haven much later than most of the southern villagers and Mar'h would have had little time to organise them into a fighting force. As far as Arthur was concerned this was a war of annihilation and he expected every single Briton to fight for their survival.

The warriors were as encouraged by the numbers that Mar'h brought with him as they were by the cartloads of supplies that followed behind the marching army. There was enough food to last them for the next two to three months and several carts held thousands of arrows. The army itself marched through the gate proud to be standing alongside their warriors and desperate to prove themselves to the warlord who stood and watched them.

Once inside the walls of Caer Cadarn the captains of the war band started to organise the newcomers; tents were set up, supplies stored and quarters assigned. The process would take several hours and Arthur left it to Gereint to manage the whole chaotic business; as the king's warlord it had been his responsibility to organise the yearly departure from the Haven so he was more than capable of dealing with this influx. Gereint, in turn, left the stocking of weapons to Morgund.

Arthur summoned Mar'h to report on the readiness of the new army and he reluctantly left the raucous reunion with his friends and made his way to the main hall. Like Morgund before him he was glad to be out of the glaring sunshine and he poured himself a beer holding the flagon awkwardly in his damaged hand.

'It hasn't got any better?' Arthur asked gesturing to Mar'h's hand.

'Good as it's going to get. Sounds like you've given the Adren a good beating on the Causeway and in the Veiled City.'

'And yet here we are.'

'Yes.'

Mar'h took his eyes away from Arthur not wanting to bring up the rumour of Cei and Merdynn's deaths, or the deaths of any of the others either.

'Did the Cithol arrive safely at the Haven?'

'Yes. I garrisoned them at the harbour master's place, like you suggested.'

'Did Unna complain?' Arthur asked with a half smile, thinking about the harbour master and her intolerance of disorder.

'Actually she's leading one of the cohorts so she's been too busy to think about her home or its new occupants.'

'Cohorts?'

'Well, they aren't really warriors and they certainly don't belong to any war band so I based the structure on one of Merdynn's unlikely stories. Remember how he used to talk about the legions and ancient battles?'

'Made up nonsense to wile away the long dark winters,' Arthur replied, thinking how even Mar'h was talking about Merdynn as if he were dead.

'Well, it gave me a structure to work on and a sense of identity for the would-be warriors so I saw no harm in it.'

'So, how many of these would-be warriors have you trained to stand against the Adren?'

'Three and half thousand.' Mar'h looked towards one of the nearby shutters and the noisy activity outside, 'There's more out there but two hundred or so are just acting as cooks, blacksmiths, wagon drivers and so on.'

'How good are they?'

'I didn't have all that long to train them and most of them had no idea to start with. Some I had to coerce but more volunteered than I had expected. Some were too old or too young and we still need people to till and fish of course so others I had to turn down.'

Arthur was looking at him with growing impatience but Mar'h had been away from the war band for too long and he was unaware of Arthur's shortening temper.

'How good are they?'

'Well, none of them could use a longbow to save their lives which was hardly surprising but there's five hundred of them who can now fire a short bow with a fair chance of putting nine out of ten arrows in a ten yard circle on the ground at a hundred paces. Good enough for arrow storms but they're a lot worse at one to one targets unless it's at less than fifty paces.'

'How fast can they fire?' Arthur asked.

'With that accuracy? About half our speed – ten a minute. Faster if you widen the target circle to fifty yards.'

'That's good enough.'

'We also received about five hundred of those crossbows from the Veiled City before the supplies stopped so there's five hundred trained up to use those though the killing range on those things is only about twenty to thirty yards. Their rate of fire is about five a minute and you can double that if it's just a storm that's required. Both those cohorts are trained to fight with a spear as well but I put the smaller and weaker ones in the crossbow cohort for obvious reasons so they wouldn't be very effective in close fighting.'

'There's five hundred in each of your cohorts?'

'Yes, there or thereabouts. Four others have been trained with sword and shield. I've tried to keep those from the same villages together as much as possible. When the fighting starts it'll help them to have their own people alongside them.'

'And how good are they?'

'They've learnt what we were taught as children. Simple block, cut, parry, thrust. They aren't warriors, Arthur. Perhaps some of them might be, if they can live long enough to learn by experience. Despite that I think two of those cohorts could stand up to the Adren and be a match for them. The other two I'm less convinced about, for a start we don't have enough swords for them all so a lot of them are equipped with just scythes and sickles and the like. It would help if the warriors here could give them some training in smaller groups than we were able to do, if there's time.'

'There may not be. What about the last cohort?'

'I got together over four hundred who could ride horses and set about training them how to use a spear on horseback. Trouble is we don't have enough horses for them.'

'We have spare horses,' Arthur replied, and Mar'h nodded having already heard from Morveren about the ambushes in the Winter Wood.

Arthur went on to outline the plan he had for attacking the Adren.

'Will your legion be able to play their part?' he asked once he had finished.

'Yes, as long as it's drilled into them exactly what they have to do.'

'That'll be your responsibility. I want you to lead the legion into battle and I want the warriors who helped you to train them to lead each of the cohorts.'

'I've already put Unna in charge of one cohort,' Mar'h pointed out.

'I want battle-experienced warriors to lead each cohort. Unna doesn't have that. Make her one of your commanders and keep her close. She can learn from you. You'll need riders who can take orders across a battlefield too. Communication will be as much a problem as their inexperience. The legion will need to react as quickly as if it were a war band or its size will be a disadvantage. Bring your captains here as soon as there's some semblance of order outside. I want to make sure they know exactly what is expected of them. And tell them not to make themselves at home here as we'll be heading west as soon as we get word from Hengest that he's ready.'

Ruraidh was telling Gwyna about the detailed plan that Arthur had laid out for the attack upon the Adren. They were walking unhurriedly along the Ridgeway path that led to Delbaeth Gofannon. Behind them Caer Cadarn was in constant upheaval despite Gereint's organisation of the new arrivals and both were glad to leave the teeming compound behind them for an hour or two.

'So what do you think?' Ruraidh asked when he finished.

Gwyna's mind had been elsewhere and she had only half-listened as Ruraidh outlined the proposed attack on the Adren.

'Sounds too complicated. The best plans are the simplest,' she replied not committing herself.

'That's what I thought. It relies too heavily on this new legion or whatever they call themselves.'

'What do you think of them?'

'You can't put weapons in the hands of villagers and call them warriors, that's what I think.'

Gwyna lacked the energy to reply. Ruraidh turned his head to look at her just as she stumbled, turning her ankle in one of the deep ruts that had been baked stone-hard by the summer sun. For an alarming second Ruraidh thought she was going to burst out crying but she quickly composed herself and suggested they sit in the shade of a ring of trees that was over to their right.

Ruraidh hesitated as they entered the grove, 'It looks like a burial mound.'

'Afraid of the dead?' Gwyna answered with a sneer.

Ruraidh relaxed, glad to hear the more familiar tone and thinking he must have imagined her immediate reaction to her stumble, but he could not entirely shake the thought that there was something wrong with her and had been ever since she returned from the Winter Wood. They sat in the shade of the trees and looked out over the fields.

'It's good country here,' Gwyna said quietly.

'Do you think Arthur will keep his word and let our people settle down here?'

'He will if he's able to. But not here, too close to Caer Cadarn.'

'You don't think the other chieftains will overrule him once the Adren are no longer a threat?'

Gwyna laughed scornfully, 'Arthur will be the king of the southern tribes so it won't matter what the chieftains think or say. Either that or there won't be anything to be king of.'

'Which do you think is more likely?' Ruraidh asked carefully.

'If it was anyone but Arthur I'd say we were as good as dead. We may have a chance but then I've seen their leader too and he's worse than

Merdynn. Far worse. And I've seen his shadow guard too. Steer clear of them both, Ruraidh. Steer well clear.'

Again Ruraidh was troubled; it was unlike Gwyna to give cautions or act as if she were intimidated by someone. He decided not to explore yet why she was acting in such a strange manner.

'You still have your aim set on being the queen of the southern tribes?' he asked her in an attempt to bring back the more familiar, avaricious Gwyna that he knew and could trust.

'Of course. And Arthur won't live forever, he's more than twice my age so the time will come when I will rule the North and South. If not directly then through our children. Gods give us children!'

Ruraidh stared off into the distance weighing up whether he should tell Gwyna what he and Ablach had found out about the Cithol girl. He needed the old Gwyna back, the Gwyna who had taken control of the tribe by killing her father. More importantly the northern warriors needed the old Gwyna back so he decided to push her.

'He has bastards strewn across southern Britain if half the stories are true,' Ruraidh said, testing the water.

'They're true all right but he cares nothing for them or their mothers. None of them could claim to be an heir before our children. If we have any.'

'The Cithol witch, the one with the green eyes, she survived the carnage of the Veiled City.'

'The one who was at the cliffs?' she asked, slightly puzzled as to why Ruraidh would mention her.

'Yes.'

Gwyna stared at him and asked after a moment's pause, 'The pregnant one?'

'Yes.'

'Why do you talk of her, Ruraidh?' she asked with narrowed eyes.

'Arthur met her at Caer Cadarn. He took her to his chamber, the one off the main hall. Your chamber.'

'Arthur knows her?'

'He detailed Ceinwen and Elwyn to bring her and a few of the others out of the Veiled City.'

'Why did he do that, Ruraidh?' she asked in a studied level tone.

Ruraidh shrugged half wanting her to come to the obvious conclusion and half wanting to be the one to tell her. He was relieved to see that her aloofness of the last few days had entirely dissipated; so much so that he prepared himself in case she should launch herself at him. He found himself unable to resist one further taunt, 'Perhaps he cares for her.'

He was not prepared well enough. No sooner had he finished speaking then Gwyna had flung herself at him, grabbing his hair with one hand and forcing his head back into the turf while whipping her knife free and placing it beneath his chin with the other hand.

'This Cithol girl is pregnant, he saves her and he cares for her. Why don't you say what's on your mind?' Her snarling face was inches from his and as he tried to free himself he felt the knife draw blood.

'Well?'

'Seren is carrying Arthur's child!'

Gwyna slowly withdrew the knife and released her grip on his hair. He burst free from under her and put a few feet between them as quickly as he could. Gwyna was still toying with her knife; still contemplating murder.

'Gods Gwyna, I thought you were going to kill me!'

'Perhaps I should have done. The next time you choose to test my patience with taunts I will kill you. And I'll do it patiently with taunts.'

'You've been around Arthur too long!' Ruraidh said rubbing the trickle of blood from his throat.

'You forget that I killed people long before I met Arthur and long before I became your chieftain, which is something you also seemed to have forgotten. Best not to forget these things. Best not to forget anything.'

Gwyna stood up and slipped her knife back into her belt. Ruraidh could see the stark difference in her; whatever dark cave her thoughts had been roaming in had been left behind now and despite the risks it had carried he was relieved he had brought her back to her old self.

'This Cithol witch carries his child, does she? When is she due to give birth to this bastard?'

'I don't know but it can't be more than a month or two away.'

'She probably means nothing to him. What use is a Cithol witch to him? Probably nothing now that the Veiled City is destroyed. Still, these are dark times and no one is safe from harm, are they Ruraidh?' she said, turning her eyes to him. He rubbed his throat again and silently agreed that indeed they were not.

Arthur was asleep in his private chamber. The normal routine for the summer months in Caer Cadarn was for most of the camp to sleep for the four hours following the twentieth bell. This was the usual practice throughout the southern tribes and during these hours a restrained peace would fall over the villages and towns as people slept in the coolest places they could find. In contrast the winter months were far more conducive to sleep and most settlements would remain quiet for up to twelve hours following the twelfth bell. The arrival of the legion from the Haven had thrown any such semblance of order to the four winds and the constant activity around the camp made it almost impossible to get any proper rest.

Gwyna looked across at Arthur and wondered how he could possibly sleep with so much noise in the hall and outside in the compound; the door and shutters gave them some privacy from the eyes of others but no protection whatsoever against the barrage of noise that was being created.

She shook her head in disbelief and went back to rubbing the ointment she had got from Ceinwen into the bruises on her abdomen and thighs. Ceinwen had given her a small pot of the colourless paste to treat the weal that still marked the side of her face but she had other bruises that needed soothing too. Arthur had said nothing about the marks on her body and she had not volunteered any explanations. She felt fairly certain that Arthur knew anyway as the signs were all obvious enough but as long as neither of them talked about it then she did not have to confront the truth again and with it the accompanying shame and humiliation.

She looked up as someone knocked on the door. She waited a moment thinking it was probably just someone knocking against the wooden door by mistake as they carted things back and forth from the hall but the same knock came again. She scowled and eased her trousers back over her hips and tucked her tunic back in as she crossed to the door and opened it.

Morveren was standing there and they stared at one another both surprised to see the other. Gwyna recovered the quickest and glared at the intruder who was the very last person she wanted to see.

'What do you want?'

'Is Arthur here?'

'Yes, he's sleeping. Come back later,' Gwyna said and began closing the door on her. Morveren held out a hand and stopped the door. They stared at each other and Morveren felt herself recoiling from the loathing on Gwyna's face.

Nonetheless she held the door open and said in a steady voice, 'I don't think this can wait. There's something he needs to know.'

Gwyna looked beyond Morveren for the first time and saw three men standing behind her. Two were both in their mid to late thirties and the other looked about ten years older; they all looked very much like the nervous villagers they were.

'Are these the messengers?' Gwyna asked indicating the three behind her with clear disdain.

'Yes. It's important.'

'Village news is never important. Come back later,' Gwyna replied and again started to close the door. To her surprise Morveren pushed back and placed herself inside the doorway.

'These are my brothers and they have news for Arthur.'

'Oh, your brothers? Yes, I can see the resemblance now that you mention it. Well, if your pig's sick then you better see him straight away. But you can have the pleasure of waking him.' Gwyna opened the door wide with sneering courtesy and once Morveren was inside the room she barged her way between the three nerve-stricken brothers and went out into the hall thinking she was leaving behind some overblown domestic village squabble.

Morveren glared after her, furious that she should be so contemptuous of her brothers. 'You weren't so high and bloody mighty with your face in the dirt were you?' she muttered under her breath at the departing figure then added in a louder voice, 'You three stay here for a moment.'

She closed the door quietly and looked around at Arthur who still lay on the bed dead to the world. She was surprised he was still asleep even though both she and Gwyna had kept their voices down during their brief exchange. She took a step towards the bed but, now that it came to it, she was uncertain how to wake him. She moved around the room hoping that he would just wake up by himself but he did not stir. Seeing a beaker of water she had a mad impulse to throw it in his face but she quickly buried the suicidal idea and decided to open the shutters instead and let the light stream into the room.

She turned to see if it had woken him and started when she saw his blank eyes staring right at her. The same sightless gaze that had so unnerved Caja several months ago back in Branque had the same affect on her and she took a step backwards, clattering into the small table and sending the beaker of water skittering across the surface and rolling onto the floor. She quickly glanced back to Arthur and was relieved to see his eyes blink and the life come back into them as he raised himself on one elbow.

'What are you doing here, Morveren?' he asked yawning.

'Oh. It's my brothers, they have a message for you.'

Arthur swung his legs off the bed and stood up. 'Your brothers?' he asked through another cavernous yawn.

She looked up at him feeling dwarfed by his height in such a small room. 'Yes. A message, a message from Merdynn.'

Suddenly the atmosphere in the room changed as Arthur came abruptly and fully awake. He took her by the elbows and almost lifted her from the floor. 'A message from Merdynn? When? What message?'

'I, I don't know. My brothers are outside, they just said they had a message for you from Merdynn. They wouldn't tell me more so I brought them straight here.'

Arthur wrenched the door open and Morveren's brothers jumped back in comic unison. They were not timid men and each of them carried in their faces the evidence of a hard life spent at sea but standing before the warlord in his hall in Caer Cadarn they found themselves truly out of their depth for the first time in their lives.

Arthur stepped back from the doorway for the three men to enter but they stood outside hesitating and only shuffled forward when Morveren told them to come in. She introduced them as they filed into the small room and Arthur indicated for two of them to sit on the bed and for the third to take the only chair. Morveren leaned against the wall feeling claustrophobic in the suddenly crowded room while Arthur stood by the open shutters his expression unreadable with the bright sunlight behind him. The fishermen were unwilling to speak first and the silence stretched as Arthur studied each one in turn.

'You've seen Merdynn?' he finally said, directing the question at the eldest brother who sat in the chair. He immediately got up to answer and Arthur told him to sit back down.

'Just answer the warlord's questions directly, Sal,' Morveren gently said trying to calm his nerves.

'We saw him at our village, Lord.'

'Arthur will do. When was this?'

'Dawn, at the time of Imbolc. Not that we got to celebrate...'

'Imbolc! Why have you waited so long before bringing the message?' Morveren cried, aghast that so much time had passed.

'Well, we had to sail our boats from the village round to the Haven and then we got caught up in this war business and joined Mar'h's legion. That was your order that was, Lord, taking the boats to the Haven. We've been puzzling about that. If you don't mind me asking, why would you want our boats there and not at the village?'

Morveren brought her hands to her head in anguish. Arthur remained unmoved beside the open shutters.

'Was there no way you could bring the message to us quicker?' Morveren asked once she had regained her voice.

'Didn't seem to be much of a hurry what with us being too late to save the others and Merdynn dead and all.'

The room became absolutely silent and the din from outside suddenly seemed very far away. Morveren felt sick. Sal was squinting at Arthur wondering why the questions had stopped and thinking that perhaps he should fill the silence.

'Tell me exactly what happened from the first moment you saw Merdynn to the last,' Arthur said without any trace of emotion.

'Well, it was little Kea, Keir's daughter.' Sal started gesturing to one of his brothers, 'She was playing down by the breakwater when she heard a commotion out in the shallow water. She clambered across to investigate and saw a man with a staff held in one hand splashing through the water like the Uathach raiders were after him.'

'Merdynn?' Morveren asked hastily.

'Morveren,' Arthur curtly admonished her for interrupting.

'No, it weren't Merdynn. Don't know who that was.' Sal frowned for a few seconds then looked up, 'Where was I?'

'Kea,' Arthur prompted him.

'Kea, yes, she heard a wail from the boat and went and fetched Keir here.' Sal gestured unnecessarily to his brother again who nodded his agreement with the story so far. 'Keir fetched us two, that's me and Garwin here.' Again Sal gestured to indicate who he meant and Morveren suppressed a groan, sure that Arthur's impatience would break upon her brothers.

'I know who you all are. We've met before and I remember you well,' Arthur said evenly.

'Right. Of course,' Sal said, thinking back to the times that Arthur had visited their village, and more particularly their mother. He hadn't expected him to remember them though.

'Go on,' Arthur prompted him.

'Well, we fetched the boat into shore, it was only a skiff really. Wouldn't catch me making a journey like that in a boat like that. Merdynn was lying in the boat in a bad way but not as bad as the other poor bugger though. He was deader than King Maldred. If you don't mind me putting it like that...' he added hurriedly having momentarily forgotten just who he was talking to.

'Who was deader than, ah, dead?' Morveren asked shooting a quick glance towards Arthur. She had heard the expression recently but was unsure if Arthur had and she was equally unsure how he might take it.

'Anglian warrior. Cythwin or something like that, Merdynn did tell us. What was the bugger's name?' Sal asked turning to his brothers for enlightenment.

'Cuthwin?' Garwin offered.

'That's it. Anyway he was dead. Blood everywhere. Recently butchered too. No sight for young Kea to see at any rate. We took Merdynn inside and we treated his stomach wound as best as we could, which weren't much. Though we wasn't sure it was Merdynn until he woke up a couple of days later. He put us straight about who he was and demanded that we take him to the Breton coast where the others were trapped by some army or other. None of us took much to that plan as we didn't have any idea where this Breton place was and we certainly weren't keener for going if there was an army there. He convinced us it would be for the best and that you'd be thankful if we took one of our boats across there,' Sal stopped and looked at Arthur as if expecting that gratitude. Arthur just stared at him. After another moments pause Sal continued, 'Well, we thought that if they could make the journey in that little skiff then we could do it in one of our boats easily enough and if there was an army there and it all looked a bit nasty then we didn't have to put in to shore. Not that we told Merdynn that.

'But we needn't have worried though. The battle was over by the time we got there. We searched around the headland but there weren't any bodies or anything so we decided to head back to the village. Merdynn wouldn't come with us. We pleaded with him but he just flatly refused to leave the place. We made him comfortable and left him to die as peacefully as he could.'

'You saw him die?' Morveren asked quietly.

'Can't say that we did but no one gets up and walks away in that state.'

'Cei, Trevenna, the others?' she asked, unable to keep the despair from her voice.

'I don't know them but there weren't any bodies on the headland or by the wall,' Sal replied gently, understanding at last that they were his sister's friends that he was talking about.

'You said Merdynn had given you a message?' Arthur asked from his place by the open window.

'Yes. He said it was important that I remember it exactly but it was some time ago now and, well, we've been caught up in this legion thing. It was along the lines of tasks being unfinished, that they all died and that someone called Ethain was to blame for it all.' Sal finished and shrugged as if to suggest that was as close as he was ever going to remember it.

Arthur stared at him in silence for a long minute and then said, 'Did the message go like this: 'Just tell him that I did what I could and it wasn't enough. Arthur must stand against the Adren, he must stand against the tide. My task is unfinished and we shall not meet again. We died. We all died. Ethain betrayed us but the blame is mine. Tell Arthur to look for him. Arthur must find him.'?'

Sal stared at the face he could not see. He shuddered and quickly made the sign to ward off evil.

'Was that the message?' Arthur asked again.

'Gods, yes, that was it exactly. How...?'

'Tell no one of this.'

Arthur turned his glance towards Morveren and she quickly ushered her brothers out of the room. They were glad to get out. She came back in and sat down heavily before quietly saying, 'So they're all dead. All of them. Even Merdynn.'

Arthur crossed the small room and strapped his sword on without replying. As he left his place by the open shutters Morveren could at last see the expression on his face and a shaft of fear coursed through her.

'They didn't see Merdynn die and Merdynn didn't see the others fall,' she spoke quickly, the words tumbling out onto one another in her haste.

Arthur ignored her and took a step towards the door. With one violent kick he tore it from its hinges and sent it flying into the hall.

'Where's Ceinwen?' he roared in the sudden silence. Ethain was still alive and somewhere in Britain and he needed someone to find him and find him quickly.

The warriors in the hall remained frozen in their places as the dust settled around the door. Arthur took a step towards them and as he scanned their faces looking for Ceinwen he spotted Aelfric racing out of the main doors to find her.

'Mar'h!'

Mar'h stepped forward and cast a glance towards Morveren who stood in the doorway to Arthur's chamber wondering what on earth had prompted Arthur's rage.

'I want your legion assembled before the main gates within the hour!' Arthur turned away from Mar'h and addressed the rest of the warriors in the hall.

'Merdynn's quest east has failed. It is down to us and us alone to defeat the Adren. Your captains know the plan so get ready what you need and prepare to leave immediately.'

The warriors sprang to life and the hall suddenly filled with noise again. Mar'h collided with Ceinwen as he dashed from the hall.

'What's going on?' she asked him.

'Morveren took her brothers to see Arthur and now he's telling us that

Merdynn and the others have failed!'

'They're dead?' Ceinwen asked horrified by the news.

'Don't know. Ask Morveren, but don't ask Arthur! I've got to get the legion ready to move within the hour!'

'Impossible!'

'I know,' Mar'h said over his shoulder as he ran out into the sunshine.

Ceinwen stepped inside the doorway to make room for those dashing out and took a second to survey the frantic activity in the hall. She stopped Gwyna as she was barging her way out. 'Do you know any more about all this?'

'I know as much as you do,' Gwyna replied bitterly, regretting now that she had left Arthur's chamber when Morveren had brought the message.

Ceinwen stared across the hall and saw Arthur standing outside his chamber. With a deep breath she made her way across to him and her feeling of trepidation doubled when she saw the door to his chamber lying in the dust on the ground.

'What's happened Arthur?' she said looking up at him.

He turned and entered the small room and she followed. Morveren was still there and she exchanged a wary glance with her.

'I want you to find Ethain and I want you to bring him here,' Arthur said coldly.

'Ethain? How? He's in the Shadow Lands. Isn't he?' Ceinwen looked quickly between Arthur and Morveren, confused by his request and scared that her confusion would enrage him further.

'Explain it!' Arthur barked at Morveren and strode from the room. Morveren grimaced and sat down on the bed.

'What's going on, Morveren? People are saying that Cei and Merdynn are dead. Is it true?'

'We don't know that. Or about the others. Not for certain anyway.'

'What *do* we know then?' Ceinwen asked exasperated.

'Merdynn turned up at my village around the time of Imbolc...'

'But that's months ago!' Ceinwen interrupted.

'My stupid brothers followed the orders they'd been given and decided to take the boats around to the Haven first and then join Mar'h's legion before getting the message to Arthur.'

'Gods!'

'I know, I thought Arthur was going to kill them with his bare hands. Perhaps he should have.'

'What was Merdynn doing at your village?'

'He arrived in a small boat with Cuthwin and Ethain. It seems that Ethain attacked them both, killing Cuthwin and injuring Merdynn before running for it.'

Ceinwen sat down heavily on the only chair in the room shocked by what Morveren was telling her.

'Ethain attacked them?'

'Again, we don't know for sure. It's possible they were attacked before they set sail but part of Merdynn's message was that Ethain had betrayed them and for Arthur to look for him.'

'But why would he do that? What about the others?'

'The others were trapped on the Breton coast by an Adren army. That's why Merdynn sailed to Wessex, to get help or at least to get boats to rescue them.'

Ceinwen just sat staring at Morveren in shock so she continued, 'My brothers took Merdynn back to the coast but when they got there the battle was over and neither Cei's lot nor the Adren were anywhere to be seen. Merdynn was convinced they had been overwhelmed.'

'Oh gods, Cei? Trevenna? All of them?'

'And Merdynn too. He demanded to be left there so my brothers sailed back without him.'

'Could they have escaped somehow?'

'I told Arthur that no one had seen Cei or his sister fall and my brothers don't know for sure that Merdynn died either but, well, you saw him. Part of Merdynn's message was that the quest east had failed and that they had all died and Arthur certainly seems to believe it.'

'Everyone but Ethain?'

'And that's why Arthur wants you to find him. None of it seems possible does it?'

'Why would Ethain attack Cuthwin and Merdynn? It just doesn't make any sense. How am I going to find him? He could be anywhere in Britain by now!'

'I don't know, Ceinwen, but I wouldn't say that to Arthur if I were you.'

'So I've got to go traipsing round Wessex trying to find one person, who could be anywhere, while everyone else launches an attack upon the Adren?'

'Yes,' Arthur said from the open doorway. They both jumped at the sound of his voice and turned to look at him as he continued, 'And I want you to find him quickly. Take Morveren with you. Tell no one of Ethain. Pack some food and go now.'

He stepped aside to make room for them to leave and they both left without a further word. Arthur packed the few things he needed into a small saddlebag and returned to the frantic scenes of preparation in the compound. He spent the next hour overseeing the packing of provisions for what he estimated to be a three-week campaign. Mar'h had told him that his legion could cover twenty to twenty-five miles a day and while the mounted warriors could cover more ground than that Arthur had based his estimates on the slowest of his forces.

Long after the hour had passed Mar'h came up to Arthur and told him that the legion was assembled before the main gate. Arthur left the final storing of weapons and food to Gereint and climbed the steps to the parapet by the gates. The walls of Caer Cadarn were encircled by a deep and broad ditch and over three thousand of Mar'h's legion were now standing crowded together on the banks of this ditch and looking at their warlord who stood before them.

Arthur surveyed them in silence for a minute then his voice roared out to them, 'You've had to leave your families behind. You've had to abandon your villages. You've had to abandon your fields and your boats. Why? Because of the Adren.

'We've stood against them on the Causeway. They fell in their thousands. We've fought them in the Winter Wood. Their corpses lie forever buried in the Veiled City. Now you, the peoples of Britain, have come to join the battle. Anglians, Wessex, Mercians and those from the North have come together to join the battle. We will never abandon each other. We will never abandon the fight. We will never abandon our land, our Britain.

'The enemy were many. They thought to slaughter us like they had the other kingdoms to the East. Half of their number are now dead. Together we will destroy the remaining half. You have nothing to fear from the

Adren. Every single one of you is more than a match for them. Trust your captains. Trust your training. Trust each other and never forget what it is you're fighting for. You fight for the person next to you. You fight for your homes and families. You're warriors of Britain and you fight for Britain. We fight for Britain!'

Over three thousand voices echoed the cry.

Within a few hours Caer Cadarn stood almost deserted; only a handful of elders remained to feed the remaining livestock and look after the youngest of the warriors' children. They found the sudden peace more unsettling than the preceding chaos and they went about their business with an unnatural quiet long after the raised dust on the Ridgeway had drifted away. The children were too young to understand what was being undertaken and the adults were lost in their own memories of battles that they had lived through and each of them privately recalled the names and faces of those who had been denied old age.

While the war band and the legion made for the Westway, Arthur headed straight for the village on the Isis where Hengest and the Anglians had gone. He travelled alone and kept his horse at a steady walking pace. The journey through the rolling downs and on into the Isis valley would take a good ten hours and with the comparatively slow pace of the legion on the Westway he knew there was little to be gained by hurrying so he used the time to rein in his anger. Now that his battle plan was in operation, the violent rage that Merdynn's message had precipitated had channelled itself into a cold, seething fury.

The sky was cloudless and the overhead sun was already beginning to brown the long grass that reached up to his stirrups. Small clouds of dust rose from the baked and cracked earth about his horse's hooves and everywhere the deep greens of spring were fading as the summer gradually burned the colour from the landscape.

The hours and miles slipped by and both man and beast sweated freely in the breezeless heat. He stopped in a grove of oak trees that grew on either side of a small brook whose banks had been undercut by the faster running waters of early spring. He refilled his water flask while his horse lowered its head to drink lengthily from the swirling water.

His thoughts had alternated between Seren, and their unborn child, to the fates of Merdynn and Cei. His mind had gone back to the time when as a young child he had taken his baby sister and hid them both from an Uathach raid in the village well. That was when Merdynn had first found him and taken him to Caer Cadarn and it was not long after that he first met Cei who had come to the hill fort as one of the children of a visiting group of Anglian warriors. The same question kept repeating itself; were they all dead? He knew that if they were then it was he who had sent them to their deaths.

His fury ebbed and flowed and he dragged his horse across the stream and continued on to the Isis trying to force his thoughts onto the plan for the coming battle but the soporific heat dulled his thoughts and he found himself once again dwelling on Seren and the child. Thoughts of her spiked his anger towards the Adren and Lazure and once again he set his mind to the coming battle.

The first part of the plan relied heavily on each section of his army doing exactly what they were supposed to do, and doing so exactly when they were supposed to do it. If it worked then the second part should be simple enough and if it did not work then they were unlikely to need the second part of the plan. His impatience to be at the Isis forced him to kick his horse into a canter for the last few miles across the valley floor.

He could hear the echoing of hammers and axes from half a mile away and he urged his horse onwards. The village sprawled along the bank of the Isis for about a thousand yards. It had no defensive wall and the wooden and thatch dwellings all stood on stilts set firmly into the earth to avoid the floodwaters of early spring. Dug-out canoes and small boats lined the bank but the fields were untended and the livestock pens empty; the villagers had long since left for the Haven.

Hengest had spotted Arthur riding across the valley and one by one the Anglian warriors stopped their work and watched as he approached. The plan had been for them to send word to Arthur once they had finished so they were puzzled and a little anxious to see him riding so hastily towards them.

The Anglians were dismayed to hear the message that Merdynn had sent to Arthur. Some of them held on to the belief that Cei had somehow managed to escape from the Breton fortress but most of them accepted what they had long held as inevitable. Arthur did not tell them about the part that Ethain had played and he had asked Morveren and Ceinwen to keep Merdynn's accusation of betrayal to themselves, at least until they had brought Ethain before him.

They were angry too; like the Wessex warriors they had lost most of their war band to the Adren soldiers but unlike the Wessex they had lost their warlord too and they wanted revenge on those who had invaded their tribal lands to the East. They knew Arthur would be feeling the same way; Cei had been like a brother to him and if Cei was lost then so was Arthur's sister, Trevenna. They wanted vengeance and they listened avidly as Arthur outlined his battle plan to them and told them more about Mar'h's legion and their battle readiness.

When he had finished he told them to make ready to leave while Hengest showed him what they had been working on. The two of them walked down to the river's edge where two jetties stood out into the eddying current.

'We've only had time to build six of them,' Hengest said with an apologetic shrug.

'Six will be enough. Are they ready?' Arthur asked surveying the barges tied alongside the jetties.

'They're a shame to Anglian craftsmanship. They aren't even watertight yet but if we have to leave now then, well, they won't keep your feet dry but they'll stay afloat.'

'Good. And they can each carry twenty or so people and still stay afloat?'

'Yes,' Hengest replied reluctantly as he eyed the barges which were little more than rafts with sides.

'You can continue the work as we head down river.'

Hengest nodded unhappily, still feeling ashamed to be associated with such rudimentary craftwork. Arthur left him to organise the final preparation of the barges and went to find Laethrig. When he found him he took him to one side and talked to him for twenty minutes explaining exactly what it was he needed him to do. As Laethrig rode back to the Haven the Anglians led their horses onto the barges in readiness for departure. Arthur's horse required some convincing and refused to step onto the leaky barge until the last of the Anglian horses was led aboard.

Finally they were ready and the barges were pushed away from the wharves and rowed out to the faster currents in midstream. The horses were in the barges steered by Aylydd, Lissa and the giant Saewulf; each of which was being towed by one of the other boats that were manned by the rest of the Anglian warriors. The Isis was flowing fast enough to carry the boats downstream without much need for rowing, except when the extra momentum was needed for steerage, and the miles slipped effortlessly by.

Balor and Arthur stood at the front of the leading barge with the cool river water slopping back and forth over their feet. The boats had proved to be as leaky as Hengest had feared but the Anglians' were in no mood to put up with any criticism as Balor had quickly found out when he complained about the amount of water they were shipping; he had been told in terms that left little to be misunderstood that he was welcome to swim if he preferred. He had the good sense to keep his reply of 'might as well be' to a low mutter that only Arthur could hear.

Neither Arthur nor Balor had much to do during the journey as the Anglians had hastily taken the rowing benches, not trusting the Wessex warriors to be any use whatsoever on water, even on a sedate river. Most of them remembered the sea crossing back from the Shadow Lands when Balor had been persistently seasick and Arthur had stood at the prow hurling abuse at the storm-wracked seas and their respective performances had only confirmed to the Anglians what they had always thought; the Wessex warriors should keep their feet dry and leave the seas to themselves.

Balor left his place at the bow and splashed his way back to the stores. The Anglians watched him warily as he selected some food and returned to his place by Arthur. He handed him an apple and some hard cheese, which Arthur took without any acknowledgement. Balor followed his gaze and together they watched a hawk hovering high over the reeds and long grasses that stretched along the bank to their left. The hawk slipped the current and dropped fifty-feet before settling once again to its patient hunting of the reeds. They turned to carry on watching as the boat slipped onwards and the hawk suddenly bent its wings and arrowed straight down into the reeds. It emerged in a graceless flurry of beating wings and flew away without its prey.

'That's a bad omen for us,' one of the Anglians muttered. Arthur stared at him scathingly and he refrained from uttering any further opinions.

The country they passed through was open grassland and gently rolling hills much of which was often obscured by the tall reeds that grew along either bank. Occasionally they would pass the remains of a stone buttress on one bank with similar remains mirrored on the opposing bank and these were usually accompanied by clusters of overgrown stone ruins to either side of the river. Balor and some of the Anglians would make the sign to ward off the evil spirits that were known to haunt such ruins and the oars would dip into the water to speed them past the unseen danger.

Halfway through the journey Arthur ordered the barge to moor at the next open stretch of land. Elwyn shouted the order to the boat behind and the message was passed back down the line. Once they were tied up to the bank the horses were given a canter to stretch their legs and ease their restlessness and Arthur ordered a three-man patrol to range ahead on each bank to make sure the country was free of the enemy.

When the second patrol had been set down on the far bank they rowed the barges back into midstream and resumed their unhurried journey towards the Winter Wood. The sky was still cloudless and the overhead sun glared off the rippling bow wakes and shone on the clouds of insects that hung above the water like swirling dust motes. The warriors not manning the oars sporadically dozed in the heat and slapped at the biting insects.

The patrols intermittently reported back and called the all clear from the banks and the barges continued on their way to the rendezvous point to the West of the Winter Wood and despite their unhurried progress they reached the ford several hours before the rest of the war band arrived.

They tied the barges up to the northern bank and Hengest resumed his work on them while Arthur sent one of the patrols across the ford to gauge the progress of the main army. The river had been widened at this point and hundreds of blocks of stone that had been scavenged from the ruins lying on the outskirts of the nearby Winter Wood had been dropped to the riverbed to provide a causeway across the Isis. At this time of year it was still covered by four-feet of slow moving water but as the summer wore on the stone causeway would eventually surface as the water level dropped. Gaps had been left in the base of the causeway to allow the river to flow on and in more peaceful times it was one of the tasks of the war band to ensure the underwater arches remained free of obstruction. The days of maintaining the roads and fords seemed a long time ago to the Anglian warriors who were setting up their camp two hundred yards upstream.

Arthur took Saewulf and Lissa and they rode across the sparsely wooded river meadows towards the Winter Wood. Smoke still hung in the sky drifting slowly across a pale half moon setting in the East. As they pushed onwards the evidence of the forest fires soon became apparent to them; great swathes of fire-blackened earth spiked by the charred remains of tree trunks stretched out for miles before them. In places the fires had cut mile-wide avenues through the woodland but left the trees and undergrowth to either side completely untouched. The acrid smell of burnt earth and wood still clung to the air and the ash still lay hot underfoot. The fires had stripped away the forest cloak to reveal the endless tumbled remnants of the ancient city that once stood there. The devastation of the woodland and the immensity of the revealed ruins stopped the three riders in their tracks and they stared at the desolation for long silent minutes.

Saewulf eventually broke it as he reined in his nervous horse, 'The legion won't march through this. The Winter Wood was bad enough as it was but this...'

Arthur silently agreed and brought his horse around to ride back to the ford. They had seen no sign of any Adren activity and when they returned to their temporary camp the other patrols reported likewise. The Adren based on the South bank of the Isis on the other side of the Winter Wood seemed content to guard their camp and await the command to move west on Caer Cadarn.

The Uathach were the first of the main army to arrive at the ford and Gwyna and Ruraidh made their way straight to Arthur's tent. It was little more than canvas sails draped over a wooden frame but it offered welcome shade from the constant sun.

'Are the others far behind you?' Arthur asked without looking up.

'Only a few hours. Will we camp here?' Ruraidh asked as he watched

Arthur who was leaning over a makeshift table and concentrating on a square piece of cloth.

'Yes. Ten hours for the legion to rest, sleep and eat, but no fires. It's unlikely that any Adren will see the smoke but we won't risk it.'

The two Uathach watched Arthur, filled with curiosity at what he was doing. Gwyna took a step closer to get a better view of what Arthur was studying and finally asked, 'What are you doing?'

Arthur looked up at them for the first time and noticed that the bruising on his wife's face was beginning to fade to a dull yellow.

'Are your warriors concerned about the Adren army in the North?'

'Of course but their families are safe at the Haven – they all made sure they got the message. They saw the Adren army on the Causeway remember?'

'And what of Benoc and Hund?' Arthur wondered if the Uathach had heard any news of the other two northern chieftains.

Ruraidh stepped forward and glanced at the cloth that Arthur had been working on before he answered, 'Hopefully they'll gather what's left of the northern tribes and make straight for the Haven.'

'What is this, Arthur?' Gwyna said gesturing to the white cloth.

'The battle plan. Merdynn taught me long ago how to represent a battle on cloth. With this I can explain exactly what I expect every captain to do and when I expect them to do it. If everyone does as they are ordered to, and when they are ordered to, then we will win.'

'And if not?' Gwyna asked.

'Then it'll end up a bloody battle between the war band and ten thousand Adren.' None of them were in any doubt about how such a battle would end.

The rest of the war band and the legion arrived at the ford over the next few hours and they spread out over the meadows on the northern bank to rest. Food and drink were brought to them by the small army of cooks and helpers that had travelled with them.

Arthur summoned all the captains to his headquarters and they sat on the cool ground or stood against the walls of the tent as he went through every detail of the battle plan once again. They listened silently in the crowded tent. Morgund and Balor were there from the Wessex, Gwyna and Ruraidh from the Uathach, Gereint and Dystran from the

Mercians, Hengest, Elwyn and Saewulf from the Anglians and Mar'h with his captains from the seven cohorts. Arthur appointed Elwyn to lead the cohort of five hundred archers with its current captain acting as his second-in-command. Morgund was assigned the four hundred strong mounted cohort, once again with its acting captain as his number two. Mar'h was in overall charge of the legion and had direct control over the four cohorts trained to use sword and shield. Arthur told him to use the crossbow cohort directly behind the shield wall; their weapons would be ideal close quarter support for the defensive line.

When he had finished he asked if there were any questions. Gwyna pointed out that Mar'h could pick up more weapons for his two ill-equipped cohorts from the battle the Uathach had fought on the hillside. Arthur reiterated to Mar'h the need for mounted messengers to take his orders quickly to the other cohorts during the battle; Mar'h had already assigned two riders for each cohort.

Finally Arthur called them forward in smaller groups and used the battle map to go through the sequence once again. When it came to Saewulf's turn he explained precisely what he was to do with the barges he was to take downstream.

When he was sure everyone knew their part and when all the questions had been answered he dismissed them to go and rest. In five hours time the legion would begin its march around the northern side of the Winter Wood.

Chapter Six

Ceinwen and Morveren decided to make their first stop at the standing stones on the upland plain to the southwest of Caer Cadarn. They let their horses roam off to feed on the yellowing grass and set about fixing a wide blanket from the tumbled pile of massive stones to create some shade. Ceinwen insisted that Morveren change her bandages and while she was gingerly unwinding the cloth from around her waist Ceinwen started to get some food ready. She realised that she had left some of the supplies in one of the saddlebags and called across to her horse. Her horse looked up and studied her for a moment before taking a few steps further away and lowering its head once again to resume its leisurely grazing; Ceinwen trudged off through the long grass muttering under her breath.

She retrieved the necessary food and they ate their meal in companionable silence. When they had finished they sat in the shade with their backs against the cool stone watching their horses forage some distance away.

'Merdynn said this was a place of great significance long ago,' Ceinwen said, running her hand over the weathered surface of the stone they were leaning against.

'I can't believe they're dead. It's like I've forgotten something then suddenly I remember that Cei and the others are dead and then I discount it again as just impossible,' Morveren said, gently shaking her head.

'Merdynn's disappeared for years before so I wouldn't raise a funeral pyre for him just yet.'

'Maybe not, but the others?'

'I don't know, Morveren, none of us do.'

'But you think they're dead?'

Ceinwen sighed before answering, 'I thought they were dead from the moment they left us in the Shadow Lands. I still hope I'm wrong. We have our own worries now.'

Morveren looked away unhappily and started absently plucking at the long grass to her side. Ceinwen tried to change the subject, 'It seems daft us wandering around Wessex looking for just one person.'

'Especially as the others are riding to battle.'

117

'You'd have thought Arthur would need every single one of us if he plans to face the Adren in open battle,' Ceinwen said.

'They won't miss me much. I'm good with a short bow but in a battle? I'd have thought you would have been indispensable though.'

'He's got the Anglian healer, Henna.'

Morveren thought for a moment trying to place a face to the name before saying, 'I don't think I know her.'

'Short dumpy woman. Always looks grumpy.'

'Good at healing then?' Morveren said, half-smiling at Ceinwen's tone. Ceinwen just snorted in response.

'She'd better be good,' Morveren said more seriously.

'You don't need to worry about Morgund,' Ceinwen replied, mistaking her anxious tone.

'Oh, I'm not worried about him. The big lump can more than look after himself.'

'What are you worried about then?'

'My idiot big brothers. How on earth did they get themselves involved in Mar'h's legion? They don't know the first thing about fighting the Adren. Stupid.'

'They're not stupid, Morveren, everyone's as involved as we are – or would be if we weren't hunting the sickle in the hayfield. Surely you're proud of them, aren't you?'

Morveren hung her head and her long hair fell around her face hiding her expression from Ceinwen.

'Aren't you?' Ceinwen asked again.

'I was ashamed of them,' she replied in a quiet voice.

'For fighting alongside us?' Ceinwen asked incredulously.

'No, of course not. I was ashamed of them when I took them to Arthur,' she said miserably.

'Because you thought Arthur would rail at them for taking so long over the message?' Ceinwen asked puzzled.

'No, no. That was idiotic and exasperating but I'd never be ashamed of them in front of Arthur, or you, or any of the others come to that.'

'Well, who then?'

'Gwyna. The way she looked at them and just brushed them aside as if they were irritating dogs or goats or something.'

Ceinwen snorted dismissively, 'I wouldn't pay that girl too much mind. Gods know what gives her the right to act so high and mighty.'

'Especially as...' Morveren stopped herself abruptly and looked away.

'Especially as what?' Ceinwen asked.

'Well, being just another Uathach girl from another Uathach dunghill village. I mean, I know she's Arthur's wife but she's still Uathach.'

Ceinwen studied her for a few seconds before saying, 'That wasn't what you were going to say was it? What were you going to say?'

Morveren felt the burning need to explain to someone why she had done nothing while Gwyna was being raped. She felt far more ashamed of herself than she did her brothers and she needed someone to tell her that she had acted in the only way possible; and so she told Ceinwen what happened on the hillside to the North of the Winter Wood.

When she had finished Ceinwen took her eyes away from Morveren and stared out over the plain. 'Gods know that I don't much like the girl, I'm not sure I even trust her that much, but I wouldn't wish that on anyone,' Ceinwen said quietly.

'I should have gone to help her,' Morveren said, fearing that Ceinwen would agree with her.

'Well, that shadow guard of Lazure's seem like skilled warriors. The Uathach only killed eight of them?'

Morveren nodded in reply.

'It sounds like if you'd gone to help her then you wouldn't be feeling guilty about it now. You'd be dead. Look, Morveren, you weren't with her when she was attacked so you didn't abandon her or run away. You'd only have been throwing your life away if you'd tried to intervene. I was near Ruadan when he fell to the Adren and the others stopped me throwing my life away in a futile gesture. They did the right thing – I didn't think so at the time but, well, I'd be dead now if they hadn't. Arthur did much the same at Branque where I saw my husband butchered.'

Morveren remained silent, glad on the one hand to have Ceinwen's support and horrified on the other to have brought up the memories of the deaths of Andala, Caja and Ruadan. Seeing the pain in her friend's eyes she resolved anew never to tell Ceinwen of the true circumstances of her daughter's death.

Ceinwen got to her feet and began to dismantle their shelter saying, 'It's too hot to sleep here. We'll move on and sleep when we get to some woodland beyond the plain.'

'I'm sorry, Ceinwen, I didn't mean to...'

'Don't worry about it,' Ceinwen said, folding the cloth that had sheltered them from the sun, 'What I was trying to say was that the others didn't think it was worth me throwing my life away trying to save Ruadan when he was already beyond help. If Ruadan, or Andala and Caja weren't worth the gesture then Gwyna certainly isn't.'

'That's true. I suppose I felt more guilty because she's Arthur's wife.'

'He should have married Seren,' Ceinwen said, more to herself than her companion.

'The Cithol girl?' Morveren asked in surprise.

'Yes.'

'The pregnant one?' Morveren asked staring at her.

Ceinwen just looked at her then called out to her horse. It ignored her again and her mood darkened when Morveren called hers and it came dutifully trotting towards her with Ceinwen's following on after it.

They mounted their horses and looked out across the shimmering haze of the plain.

'How on earth are we going to find him?' Morveren asked as she settled her eager horse.

'Perhaps it won't be as hard as we think. Everyone should be at the Haven now so any signs of life will probably be him. We'll try your village first as that was where he was last seen.'

'And after that?'

'We'll try his village,' Ceinwen answered and spurred her horse to head deeper into Wessex.

'I almost hope we don't find him,' Morveren said quietly and followed after Ceinwen.

Arthur waited patiently on his horse. Around him were just under two hundred mounted warriors; all that remained of the combined war bands of the South and the warriors from the North. The Adren camp was five miles to the North of them and they waited patiently under the burning sun.

Arthur glanced across to Hengest who dismounted and took two objects from his saddlebag. He squatted down and put them both on the ground. The first object was his lodestone and he carefully aligned it then positioned his sundial next to it. The sundial was a circular piece of metal about a foot across with finely engraved notches running around its circumference. He unfolded the thin indicator from the centre and bent over the instrument to be exactly sure where the shadow fell. He nodded to himself and stood up, packing his precious instruments back into his saddlebag.

'It's time,' he said, looking up at Arthur.

Arthur looked around slowly at the warriors surrounding him, many of whom carried long spears, and without a word he turned to the North and set his horse to a casual walk. Behind him the war band settled their nervous horses and followed after him in a wide jagged line.

Mar'h was on the other side of the Isis with his legion concealed in the outskirts of the Winter Wood about a mile from the Adren bridge. He turned to Morgund, 'You'd better be getting back to your horsemen. Arthur's attack will begin soon.'

'Glad to be back where the action is?' Morgund asked as he jumped up onto his horse.

'Wouldn't miss it for anything,' Mar'h replied sourly and with a very dry mouth.

'Just be sure to bring your cohorts forward at the right time!'

'And when would that be again?'

Morgund laughed, 'As soon as I'm in trouble!'

'Just bugger off,' Mar'h replied and Morgund grinned as he kicked his heels in and rode off to join his new cavalry cohort.

Mar'h called over one of his riders and sent him ahead to Elwyn with the unnecessary message to prepare his archers. He then sent the young Anglian, Aelfric, the two hundred yards down to the riverbank where Saewulf waited by the barges. Having sent two messages that he knew were redundant he finally turned to the nearby tall tree and climbed the rope ladder to the hastily erected platform set a hundred-feet above the ground. The messengers came back and reported that everyone was ready and Mar'h settled himself on the platform watching the Adren camp through the heat haze that wavered across the simmering land. Before long he saw a dust cloud rising to the South of the river.

When Balor saw the sprawling Adren encampment his first instinct was to turn his horse away and ride back the way he had just come. It stretched for over a mile along the southern bank of the Isis and its sheer size appalled him. He immediately thought that the reports must have been mistaken; it looked to him that the whole Adren army was camped out before them, all twenty thousand of them. He glanced to his left and right and the sight of two hundred mounted warriors suddenly looked a lot less formidable. He reckoned they were outnumbered two hundred to one and to make matters worse Arthur was about to shout out the order to charge at the enemy. He fidgeted in his saddle and broke wind noisily. His horse responded by tossing its head from side to side possibly in reproof, possibly in agreement, but perhaps only to rid itself of the flies that crawled around its eyes. Dystran, who was to his right, laughed loudly.

'You'll scare the horses,' he said and leant across to slap the neck of Balor's horse.

Balor just grunted in response to the Mercian and took his axe from his belt before putting it back once again to leave both hands free to manage the reins. He waited impatiently for Arthur to give the command to advance but it never came. Instead Arthur just spurred his horse into a canter and the long line of warriors started after him. Balor gritted his teeth and did likewise.

When they were half a mile from the enemy camp the canter turned into a charging gallop and Balor hung on, grimly urging his horse to keep up with the line that was pulling slightly ahead of him. All around him clods of dry earth were being thrown up from the horses in front and dust billowed about him and stung his eyes. He was not even aware of the sporadic arrows that fell amongst them until a horse crashed to the ground in front of him and his own horse instinctively jumped the sprawling tangle.

At the last possible moment he freed his axe from his belt just as they tore into the edge of the enemy camp and any reservation or consideration of the Adren numbers immediately left him.

Arthur's plan was to hit the side of the Adren camp nearest to the bridge spanning the Isis, stay long enough to inflict the maximum damage then draw the Adren after them as they crossed the bridge. Balor knew the plan as well as anyone but in the first few minutes of battle he never thought of it once. The Adren camp was in complete chaos; from the first sighting of the mounted warriors to the moment they hit only a minute had passed and they were utterly unprepared when the horses crashed into their rambling encampment.

Balor found himself fighting his horse more then the Adren as he tried to force it in tight turns to get at the scattering enemy. The more accomplished riders around him were creating havoc as they rode down the hated invaders. Finally he managed to goad his mount towards two Adren who were scrambling out of their shelter but Gwyna reached them first leaving her spear in one and cutting down the other with her slashing sword. Before he could even swear at her she was spurring her horse on towards a knot of Adren who were already beset by two Wessex warriors.

Balor had little idea whether seconds or minutes had passed but as he searched for likely targets he realised that the marauding riders were inadvertently pushing deeper into the camp in their pursuit of the enemy.

Arthur had noticed the same thing but the Adren were still completely disorganised and his warriors were slaughtering hundreds of them so he led the attack deeper into the Adren camp.

Mar'h had watched the charge with Unna, the harbour master from the Haven, from the platform in the trees across the river.

'Can you see what's happening?' she asked him.

'They're fighting in the camp still and it looks like they're pushing further in.'

'The plan was to get across the bridge! Why are they going further into the camp?'

'I don't know,' Mar'h replied, staring at the chaotic turmoil in the distance.

'Gods! Look!' Unna shouted pointing towards the much smaller Adren camp on their side of the bridge.

'What?'

'They're blocking the bridge!'

Mar'h stared intently at the activity on the North side of the bridge. It was difficult to tell exactly what they were doing but it seemed that the Adren on the North side were preparing to defend the bridge to stop Arthur's warriors from crossing it. Mar'h felt a moment of panic, no one had expected the Adren to form a defence on the bridge; the general feeling had been that they would probably cross the bridge to join in the battle. The Adren could not have known that Arthur planned to cross the bridge; why should he when he had all the country to the South for an easy escape?

'What are we going to do? We can't let them set up a defence on the bridge, the war band won't be able to get across!' Unna cried.

Mar'h's mind raced. The plan had been for Arthur to draw several thousand of the Adren across the bridge and for Morgund's horsemen, who waited below in the wood, to charge into the flank of the pursuing Adren. If the Adren managed to defend the bridge against Arthur then the war band would be caught on the bridge between the two Adren forces, but if Mar'h released Morgund's horsemen to clear the North bank then he would be showing his hand too soon and the Adren would evade the waiting trap. Uncertainty gripped him as he considered the options. He crossed to the far edge of the platform and shouted down to Aelfric who came clambering up the rope ladder as fast as he could.

When he was twenty-feet from the top Mar'h leaned over the edge and shouted down to him, 'Tell Morgund to move his horsemen into position but not to break cover until I order it. Tell him they may have to clear the North side of the bridge so that the war band can get across!'

Aelfric repeated the message back to Mar'h to be sure he had it absolutely correct before sliding back down to the ground and sprinting off through the woods to where Morgund waited with his cavalry cohort.

Mar'h turned back to Unna and they stared at each other as they both heard the faint blowing of a hunting horn; the signal for the war band to abandon the battle in the Adren camp and make for the North bank.

Arthur wheeled his horse around and roared out the command to retreat across the bridge. Dystran sounded the hunting horn once more and Balor kicked his horse into following the other riders who were turning back through the havoc they had wreaked on the western edge of the Adren camp. Balor saw hundreds of dead and wounded Adren and wondered how it was possible that he had failed to strike at a single one of the enemy. He did not have long to wonder; within a minute his horse's hooves were slipping and sliding as they fought for purchase on the wooden planks of the bridge.

Arthur was ahead of him with a cluster of warriors from Wessex and they blocked his view of the far end of the bridge so he had no idea why those ahead of him suddenly slowed. Arthur had seen the problem as soon as he had turned for the bridge and he rued letting his bloodlust get the better of his judgement in deciding to continue the slaughter in the enemy camp; it had allowed the Adren time to construct a makeshift barricade on the North side of the bridge and man it with archers.

He had hoped to reach the far side before the Adren could get emplaced but once on the bridge he realised he was too late. Behind him he knew that the rest of the war band would be piling onto the bridge and he realised he had no other choice now but to charge the barricade. He roared out the order for shields and the horsemen tried to check their headlong flight to unfasten their shields. He glanced about to see that those around him had their shields ready and without waiting to check those behind him he crouched behind his shield and spurred his horse forward towards the barricade.

He heard the arrows tearing through the air around him as his horse thundered over the dry wood of the bridge. Someone behind and to his left screamed as they were plucked from their horse and trampled by those charging after Arthur. He felt an arrow smack into his shield and glance away. Another flew past the side of his face and he heard the soft hiss of the feathers as it fled past. Then his horse jolted and he felt its pace slacken immediately. He glanced above his shield and saw he was almost at the barricade then his horse was pitching forward, crumpling as its own momentum sent it crashing into the base of the line of carts that blocked the bridge. He threw himself off to one side and at the last second tried to use his shield to protect himself from the impact. All around him other horses were leaping the barrier or smashing into it and he lay curled on the ground with his mind reeling from the force of the crash.

He forced his limbs into action and he crawled towards the near side of the barrier with the ringing in his ears loud enough to drown out the sound of the battle erupting all along the barricade. He wiped the blood from his eyes in time to see an Adren only yards away and bearing down on him with his sword drawn. He stumbled to his feet and swayed as he drew his own sword but as he tried to focus on his attacker the Adren was lifted bodily from his feet by a spear as a rider swept by.

His blurred vision was coming back into focus and he glanced quickly about; other Adren were converging on him. His shield had been splintered by the impact of his fall so he gripped his sword with both hands as he desperately looked for a spare horse to take him from the chaos of the North bank. He saw neither a spare horse nor any other riders from the war band. The plan had been to get across the bridge and, if the Adren from the main camp were following them, then to keep on going. His warriors had kept on going so that meant more Adren must be storming across the bridge behind him.

He looked at the Adren soldiers charging towards him and thought of Cei and Trevenna and he wondered briefly how they had fallen at the last; they would have fallen with pride and courage so he let the rage at their deaths fill him and he charged into the oncoming Adren.

Mar'h stared out towards the North side of the river from the elevated platform. 'Gods! They're turning round and heading back!' he shouted as he pointed at the riders who were wheeling their horses around and charging back to the bridge.

'Why? They've only just got away from them! And the main army's pouring across the bridge! It's suicide! Turn back you fools!' Unna, normally so self-controlled, was screaming at the warriors who were the best part of a mile away.

'Arthur,' Mar'h said quietly.

'Turn back you idiots!'

'It's Arthur,' Mar'h said just as softly.

'What?' Unna asked turning to face him.

'Arthur must have fallen at the bridge.'

Unna stared at him appalled at the possibility.

'It's the only reason they would turn back. If Arthur was still with them they would have continued onwards to draw the Adren onto the flood plain.'

Unna turned back to the unfolding battle, her face drained of colour. The riders had nearly reached the bridge once again and more Adren were charging across from the far side.

'Arthur's dead?' she asked bewildered.

'And we're about to lose the war band as well,' Mar'h turned quickly away and yelled to the ground below, 'Aelfric! Tell Morgund to ride! The war band's in trouble on the North side of the bridge!'

A hundred-feet below him, Aelfric leapt onto a horse and sped off to where Morgund waited with his four hundred horsemen.

Morgund saw the young Anglian tearing through the trees and knew that something had gone wrong.

'You're to ride! The war band's in trouble – this side of the bridge!' Aelfric shouted as he neared him.

Morgund turned his horse away and rode to the front of the mounted cohort. He stood in his stirrups and shouted out at the top of his voice, 'Close order! Two ranks!'

The horsemen followed him out of the trees and formed up into two ranks. They set out at a canter at first then, as they fell into position, they urged their horses onwards and the pace quickened until it reached a flat out gallop. They charged along the North bank of the river with thirty yards between the two ranks and with only a yard or two between each rider. The thunderous drumming of four hundred horses charging across the hard earth was deep and deafening. They closed the distance within two minutes and as they neared the wheeling melee by the bridge their spear tips came down in a uniform wave and they crashed into the Adren forces that were spilling onto the flood plain.

Mar'h watched the charge from his platform and then began his one-handed descent down the rope ladder. When he reached the ground Aelfric helped him strap his shield onto his arm.

Elwyn, who was commanding both the archer and crossbow cohorts, strode across to them, 'Our turn now?'

Mar'h nodded at the shorter man, taking heart in his assured confidence, 'We'll keep to the plan. We'll advance along the riverbank. Shield wall first, crossbows behind them with the archers covering our left flank.'

'Right you are then,' Elwyn replied and turned to organise his cohorts.

Aelfric finished fastening Mar'h's shield.

'The battle's just starting isn't it?' he asked.

Mar'h took a deep breath, 'Yes, yes it is. Tell Saewulf it's time.'

Saewulf grunted in response to Aelfric's message and heaved his massive frame from the fallen tree trunk he had been sitting on. He strode to the fire and used it to light the already prepared torch then hastened to where two barges were tied up against the bank. Aelfric followed him and to his surprise the young Anglian held out his hand. Saewulf engulfed the small hand in his own broad grip, 'Watch the battle from the platform but if it goes against us then ride like hell for the Haven.'

'I will. It's what Arthur told me to do as well.'

'Then make sure you do.'

'I will. Good luck, Saewulf.'

'You too lad,' Saewulf resisted the urge to ruffle the boy's hair; something in his manner made him older than his years and Saewulf realised the gesture would have been oddly out of place. He strode to one of the boats thinking that even their boys and girls had to act like adults now days. Well, he thought to himself, that's why we're fighting.

He settled himself in the upright wooden box that Hengest had constructed in the middle of the barge and placed the burning brand in a holder by his feet. Aelfric pushed the barge away from the bank then ran back to the second boat to untie it from its moorings. Saewulf slotted the oars into the open slats and flexing his broad shoulders he hauled on the long oars and the two boats gradually slid away from the bank and out into the river. The wooden housing around him was open sided to the rear and he watched as Aelfric held up his hand one last time before disappearing back into the trees of the wooded riverbank.

Saewulf strained on the oars as he hauled the two barges towards the middle of the river where the current would carry them down to the pontoon bridge that spanned the Isis. Both barges were stacked with brushwood and dry branches, and oil had been slopped generously over the heaped tangles of wood. Hengest had used the time at the ford to improve the hulls of the barges and they were far more watertight now than they had been on the first leg of the journey.

The current of the wide river began to sweep the boats along and Saewulf used the oars to hold a course equidistant from both banks. He could hear the thundering charge of Morgund's four hundred horsemen and he had to force himself to resist the temptation to lean around the safety of his wooden cubicle to watch as they crashed into the Adren ranks. He wondered what had happened that made Mar'h send in the horsemen before they were supposed to be unleashed.

Such thoughts were banished when the first of the arrows thumped into his crude cabin and flicked into the water around him. He knew he must be nearing the bridge and he guided his boat to one side then dug the oars hard into the water to bring the towed boat alongside. An arrow crashed into the barrel of spirit at his feet and he watched horrified as a wide crack split down one side. As the precious fluid gushed out he hurriedly leant forwards and tipped it onto its side with the splintered tear pointing upwards.

More arrows were sniping around him and he risked a glance around the side of the cabin and saw that the bridge was only fifty yards away. He was heading more or less for the middle of it and it was packed with Adren trying to cross to join in the battle raging on the North bank. He lit a second brand and tossed it onto the jumbled brushwood packed into the second barge that was now alongside him. He hauled on the oars once more to urge the two boats onwards then lobbed his brand onto the wood piled at the back of his own boat. The oil immediately caught alight and in the bright sunlight the air rippled as the invisible flames spread across the branches.

The fires in both barges quickly took hold and Saewulf felt a moment's panic that he had lit them too soon but seconds later he felt a jar as his boat rammed into the bridge and began to swing sideways. He hefted the barrel of spirit over his head to throw onto the bridge and prayed that the smoke from the burning oil would cover him. It didn't. An arrow tore into his thigh and he staggered. Another smashed into his shoulder and he dropped the barrel as he was half spun around. Two more thumped into his chest and he slumped to his knees, crouched over the emptying barrel as the fire burned all around him. Blood frothed up his throat and he found it impossible to breathe. He reached down and cradled the barrel in both arms and he forced himself to his feet. He staggered into a tottering run and crashed the barrel against the edge of the bridge. It split apart and the flames rushed forward to embrace the dry wood of the Adren bridge.

Sal tightened his grip on the shield and stole a quick glance at his two brothers who stood either side of him; like himself they were sweating profusely. They had left the shade and cover of the trees and were now steadily advancing towards the battle milling around the North side of the bridge.

Mar'h had arranged the foot cohorts into five ranks of five hundred with the best-equipped and best-trained cohort at the fore and the crossbow cohort immediately behind them. They were advancing across the floodplain with the river tight to their right flank and Elwyn's archers positioned on their left. Three thousand Britons were marching towards the invaders but only a handful of them had ever seen battle before and they were relying entirely upon the two battle manoeuvres that had been drilled into them.

Sal checked the strapping on his large rectangular shield once again.

'Don't fancy that poor bugger's chances.'

'Whose chances?' Garwin asked staring straight ahead and spitting on his shield.

Sal nodded his head towards the middle of the bridge where the burning barges were sending a column of smoke high into the still air.

'Who took the boats in?' Keir asked from his other side.

'Some big Anglian bastard,' Sal answered, looking towards the spreading flames again.

'Don't fancy his chances much,' Garwin chipped in.

'That's what I just said.'

'Well, you'd be right then.'

Sal looked at his brother and saw the streaks of sweat on his face and decided it didn't matter if he was cheeking him or not. The chaotic battle was only two hundred yards ahead of them and they heard Mar'h shouting somewhere to their left and near to the centre of the line. The order was relayed by the cohort captains and they stopped to readjust their positions in the line.

Sal's throat was too dry to swallow and he offered a quick prayer to his sea gods wondering if they would have any sway over matters on the land. Beside him Garwin was urinating against his shield and Sal stared at him in disbelief.

'If I don't go now I'll only want to go later,' Garwin answered with an unapologetic shrug. Sal shook his head while Keir laughed and then the order came down the line to advance and they started to close the distance to the enemy.

Mar'h was in the centre of the line and he looked anxiously to his left and right to reassure himself that the legion had followed out his command. He was relieved to see that the cohorts had adjusted their formation; the previously straight line now resembled the cutting edge of a saw with the triangular teeth pointing towards the enemy.

Mar'h knew that the next hour would tell whether his training of the legion had been good enough and whether Merdynn's tales of ancient battle tactics were based on experience or merely the dreams of an old man. Mar'h felt reasonably confident for even though the battle had not gone to plan they had still achieved their main objective in splitting the Adren into two roughly equal forces. The centre of the bridge was now blazing fiercely, effectively isolating half of the Adren soldiers on the southern bank.

Mar'h could see that more of the Adren were now turning away from the battle with the mounted warriors near the bridge to face this new and unexpected assault on their flank.

'Keep advancing!' he shouted out to those around him just as the first

Adren charged into their jagged ranks.

Aelfric held his breath as he watched Mar's legion advance into the battle on the riverbank. He had listened to Arthur's captains as they had discussed the tactics and strategies for this battle. Like Mar'h, he knew that events had not gone exactly as they had planned but he also remembered Arthur saying that battle plans rarely worked as they were supposed to and that the key to winning was to be able to adjust to new situations quicker than the enemy could.

He feared for Saewulf who was supposed to have dived clear of the burning barges and make for the northern bank. One of the reasons why he had been chosen for the task was because he was one of the strongest swimmers among the Anglians. Another reason was because he was strong enough to manoeuvre both barges to the centre of the bridge but the overriding reason had been because he absolutely refused to let anyone else undertake the task. He had been among the last to give up hope on Cei and the others but when he had finally accepted that they must have died on the Breton headland then he burned for vengeance. Aelfric had the sickening feeling that he had done just that.

He watched the progress of Mar'h's legion as they slowly advanced into the Adren mass. As far as he could tell from where he watched, the numbers on each side seemed roughly equal although he suspected that the Adren had probably lost several hundred already. He had no way of knowing if the battle formation was working as they had thought it would; it was designed so that as the cohorts advanced, and as the Adren pressed to get at them, the enemy would be channelled into the teeth of the saw where the large shields would prevent them from getting at the Britons. As more Adren forced themselves forward the enemy would become packed into the indented spaces of the saw and unable to wield their weapons freely whereas the slowly advancing Britons would still be able to stab from between their shields with their shorter swords while the crossbows in the second line would fire their darts over the top of the shields into the massed enemy. The tactic relied upon two elements essentially; the cohort's ability to hold their jagged line and the enemies' overwhelming urge to get at the Britons.

Aelfric was sure about the second of those elements and it seemed that the first was holding true too. As he watched he saw that the mounted warriors were beginning to disengage themselves from the melee by the bridge and he wondered fearfully if Arthur was still among them or if he had fallen as Mar'h seemed to think he had. The five hundred odd horsemen were reforming some distance from the battle and, just as Mar'h had predicted they would, the Adren, unable to use their left flank because of the river, tried to outflank the Britons on the open side. Elwyn's five hundred archers were waiting for them and Aelfric could see volley after volley fly into the Adren ranks.

The bridge finally separated in the middle and the burnt ends began to swing down current like a huge gate slowly opening. The fire was still spreading down the length of each arm of the remaining sections and Aelfric realised a benefit they had not expected; the smoke was obscuring much of the battle from the Adren stranded on the South side of the river.

Aelfric could see that despite the devastating volley fire of Elwyn's archers the Adren were still intent on closing around the legion's left flank. He knew the battle would be won or lost on whether or not the Adren could get around the side of the advancing cohorts and that it would be won or lost within the next hour. Without waiting any longer he turned away from the battle and clattered down the ladder as fast as he dared. If he had stayed a few seconds longer he would have seen the mounted warriors gather and charge the Adren force that was threatening the legion's flank.

When he reached the ground he raced to the man in charge of the miscellaneous wagon drivers, cooks and metal smiths who had travelled with the legion. He suggested that they immediately start the journey back to the ford on the far side of the Winter Wood. They started to ready the wagons straight away, not because he had ordered it but because it made good sense; if the Adren won then they would have a vital head start in the flight to the Haven and if the Britons won then they would need to be at the ford anyway. Aelfric also suggested that the wagons of arrows and the war band's longbows should be kept nearby and that he would stay with them.

When the last wagon had lumbered off through the trees Aelfric lit a brand from the same fire that Saewulf had used and placed it in the ground near to the wagons that contained the arrows. If the Adren won the battle they would not be getting the war band's stockpile of arrows; not that he thought it would make much difference by then if they did.

Sal grunted with the effort it took to keep the shield before him, straining to resist the press of bodies that were pushing against it. For minutes now it had been all that he and those around him could do to keep from being forced back; any forward momentum was impossible.

He swore as his footing slipped on the bloody grass and his shield wavered against the weight bearing on it. The woman behind him immediately fired a crossbow bolt into the sudden gap of shields and then leant her shoulder into his back and helped to push him back into line. The resisting force gave momentarily and he pushed forward stepping over the squirming body now at his feet. Someone else behind him, he had no idea who, thrust their spear into the body at his feet and it stopped thrashing as the spear was ripped free. 'Another bastard down,' he thought grimly then ducked as a flailing sword bit into the top of his shield. It was wrenched free and came hacking down again. He yelled out for help, unable to take his right hand away from the shield to unsheathe his own sword. The sword came down again and was stopped a bare inch from his shoulder. He shouted out desperately for help and an arm appeared reaching over him and holding a crossbow. He heard the thud as it fired and the attacking sword was gone. Again he heaved against the press of bodies and gradually the line was moving forward once more. His throat burned with thirst, his arms were almost numbed with fatigue and any moment could bring death but he had never felt so alive. He understood finally why his sister, Morveren, had chosen to become a warrior. He turned his head to grin at Keir but Keir was no longer standing next to him.

Elwyn shouted out the order to cease-fire then stormed along the front of the line as arrows kept flying from the ranks of his archers. He had heard the charge of the horsemen long before he had seen the first of them burst through the ranks of the attacking Adren. The combined horse of the war band and Morgund's cohort shredded the Adren flanking attack and those that survived the initial charge sought to regain the safety of their main force.

The horsemen wheeled away and Elwyn could see what they planned to do; charge into the rear of the Adren force that was attacking the legion. He also saw what he had to do and turned the Adren's flanking attack against them as he advanced his archers beyond the left arm of the legion. Despite having the Adren force exposed before him he shouted out for his archers to aim only at the rear of the enemy. Five hundred archers rained volley after volley down upon the Adren and only ceased when the mounted warriors charged once more into them.

The Adren were trapped on three sides with the river on their fourth and they fought on for another hour but they were doomed and they knew it. When only a hundred remained the horsemen and legion pulled back and Elwyn's archers slaughtered those that remained standing. The first part of the battle had been won but not without its cost.

Chapter Seven

Morveren reined in her horse and turned to look back at her village. She had seen it deserted before but only in the darkness of winter and somehow it seemed emptier with the bright sun shining down on the empty homes and the lifeless main thoroughfare. The village should be echoing to the sounds of life; a boat returning with its catch, children chatting as they mended nets, a dog barking at an inquisitive piglet but the only sounds were the low hum of insects as they danced among the wild flowers and the ceaseless background noise of waves crashing on the shingle beech. The village seemed dead and she was reluctant to leave it to rest in peace.

Ceinwen watched her patiently for a minute or two then nudged her horse closer and said, 'You'll see it again.'

Morveren stirred from her reverie and brought her horse back onto the path. They took the coastal road that dipped along the cliffs and bays as they headed further west.

'You will,' Ceinwen said again some time later.

Morveren shrugged, 'It's a dung heap really. I wouldn't much mind if I never saw it again.'

'What's bothering you then?'

'I was wondering if my daft brothers will ever see it again. Or any of the others come to that.'

'Of course they will,' Ceinwen answered and Morveren smiled at the weak platitude.

'How long do you think it'd last if no one ever came back to it?'

'The village?'

'Yes.'

'Not long I suppose. Certainly not as long as the ruins in the Winter Wood have lasted.'

'We haven't left much behind to be remembered by have we?'

Ceinwen looked at her and frowned, 'What's put you in such a cheery mood?'

'Well, this,' Morveren replied, gesturing vaguely with her hands.

'This what?'

'Us, wasting our time. Riding around a deserted land looking for someone who probably isn't here.'

'If you're happy to tell Arthur that then we'll head back now.'

Morveren sighed in resignation and carried on riding westward towards their next destination; Ethain's home village.

'Did Arthur used to be more...' Morveren's voice trailed off as she sought for the right word. The subject had been gnawing at her for some time but now that she had the chance to talk about it she was finding it difficult to articulate exactly what she felt.

'More what?'

'Well, less harsh? Most of the time people seem almost afraid to even approach him.'

Ceinwen thought about the question and wondered how she should answer it. She wondered who was asking it; a warrior in the Wessex war band or Arthur's daughter.

'Well?' Morveren prompted as the silence lengthened.

'I'm thinking.'

'It's a straight forward question,' Morveren said, correctly guessing why Ceinwen was deliberating over the answer and feeling angry about it.

'The question may be but the answer isn't.'

'Well, take your time!' Morveren snapped and rode on ahead. She hated the ever-present undercurrent whenever she talked to someone about Arthur. She knew full well it was inevitably brought on by the unspoken question of whether or not she was his daughter but it made it no easier to bear.

Ceinwen bit back a retort and watched as Morveren cantered off down the path wondering what had made her so irritable. She knew the heat of summer and the difficulty of finding an adequate place to sleep while travelling could shorten a person's temper considerably but she felt it was more likely to be the thought of her brothers involved in the battle far to the East that was preying on her mind. She could understand why she would be worried about that and she could understand too why Morveren would be worried about actually finding Ethain, he had been her friend after all.

She caught up with Morveren some hours later. She had stopped by a river that ran down to the sea and this was where they would leave the coastal path and head inland towards Ethain's village. Morveren had taken the opportunity to bathe in the river although the water level was so low there was barely enough to submerge herself in.

They greeted each other with a politeness that showed neither was entirely comfortable. Ceinwen led her horse into the shallows and as it lowered its head to drink she hauled the saddle off and carried it back to the grassy riverbank. She followed Morveren's example and let the gently flowing water wash the sweat and dirt from her skin while Morveren prepared some food. When she felt the cool water beginning to cramp her muscles she dragged herself onto the bank and used her tunic to towel her hair dry.

'How far is it to Ethain's village from here?' Morveren asked, already knowing the answer but wanting to fill the silence between them.

'Four, maybe five hours,' Ceinwen replied and helped herself to some of the food that Morveren had picked out from her own saddlebag. That annoyed Morveren further and she struggled to hide her irritation. They ate without speaking and when they had finished the meal they re-saddled their horses and set off along the path that followed the course of the river.

After a few miles of studied silence Ceinwen turned to her companion, 'Do you know the story of how Merdynn found Arthur?'

'What's that got to do with Arthur ignoring me?'

'I'm trying to explain it to you, you stupid girl!' snapped Ceinwen, thoroughly fed up with Morveren's attitude. Morveren was taken aback by Ceinwen's uncharacteristic outburst and just stared at her.

'And he doesn't ignore you. The last time we were together we were sitting and talking on the bank outside Caer Cadarn.'

'He was telling us the battle plan! Besides, I mean more generally than that,' Morveren replied angrily.

Ceinwen waited a few seconds to calm herself before repeating her earlier question, 'Do you know the story?'

'He hid in a well with his baby sister when his village was raided,' Morveren replied, looking straight ahead.

'No. He hid his sister in the well *before* the raiders arrived.'

'Well? What's the difference?' she replied truculently.

'He knew what was going to happen and he saved who he could.'

'What's that got to do with him hating me?'

'He doesn't hate you. Try being less self-obsessed.'

'I still don't see what you're trying to stay.'

'Ever since then Arthur's motives and actions can be summed up by one word.'

'Vicious? Murderous? Power-crazed-insanity?'

Ceinwen reined in her horse and glared at the younger woman in fury, 'Is that what you think? That he's just more vicious than anyone else and that's why he's the warlord?'

Morveren was unable to meet her glare and replied more quietly, 'No. No, I don't but it is what some of the people from my village say.'

'Then they're idiots. They have no idea what they're talking about or who they're talking about!'

They started off along the path once again and Morveren stayed silent unsure how angry Ceinwen might still be.

Eventually it was Ceinwen who broke the silence, 'Protection.'

'What...?'

'Shut up and listen.'

Morveren bridled at the rebuke but she shut up and Ceinwen continued, 'More or less everything that Arthur's done since that raid on his village has been about protection. If he could have saved his village then he would have done, but he knew that if he told them that the raiders were only minutes away then his parents would have tried to protect both him and his sister; and failed. He did what he could and saved all he could. He's been doing the same ever since. I could list hundreds of examples but I'll give just two. He took control of the Wessex war band because back in those days they were a bigger threat to the people of Wessex than the Uathach were and once he had control of the war band, and changed it to what it is now, then he could protect Wessex properly from the northern raiders!' Ceinwen took a deep breath trying to dissipate her anger.

'And the second?' Morveren asked.

'Now. Trying to save Britain and everyone who lives on this island from the Adren invaders. In a sense he's trying to protect everyone he was unable to when the raiders came to his village. And once again he's finding he can't.'

'He can't?'

'Of course he can't.'

'We'll lose?' Morveren asked shocked at Ceinwen's words.

'Of course we'll bloody lose! How in all the gods' names can Arthur or anyone else save us from an invading army that numbers as much or more than our entire population? How desperate do you think Arthur would have to be to send Cei, and the sister he saved as an infant, on a mission that could only end in their deaths? And you sulk because you think he's ignoring you. He's got more on his mind than just your feelings. I don't know if you're his daughter or not but you need to stop acting like a child and open your eyes.'

'That's not fair!' Morveren retorted hurt by her friend's words, 'I've done my share of the fighting and seen my share of death. I fought in the Shadow Lands, on the Causeway and in the Winter Wood! I've seen Talan and Tamsyn die, and Elowen and Tomas! I've stood against the enemy and watched my friends die and even now my brothers are fighting the enemy! You can't call me a child!' But despite her words tears were running down her cheeks, 'I just wanted him to accept me!' She dug her heels into her horse's flanks and sped away from Ceinwen.

Ceinwen watched her go and added, 'And now we're hunting the last of your friends.'

Heavy-hearted and feeling sick of it all she coaxed her horse forward to a walking pace and followed on after Morveren. She saw no sign of her for the next four hours and when she did finally see her she was standing by her horse on the brow of the hill that overlooked Ethain's home village.

Ceinwen dismounted and walked her horse up to where she stood. Morveren didn't say a word but just pointed down into the village. Ceinwen followed the outstretched finger and just caught sight of a hooded figure disappearing into one of the wooden huts. She looked at Morveren and raised her eyebrows in question. Morveren shrugged in reply and together they led their horses down into the village.

They stabled their horses and Ceinwen waited while Morveren fetched them some water from the well. When they had filled the water trough they made their way to the hut that they had seen the figure enter. They hesitated outside the door both hoping in a strange way that it was not Ethain inside.

Finally Ceinwen put her hand on the door and pushed it open. Sunlight flooded into the hut as they stood in the doorway.

'Well, you took your time getting here.'

The voice from the shadows startled them both and they stared at the corner it had come from.

'Ethain?' Morveren said uncertainly.

The figure shifted and a slant of sunlight momentarily crossed his chest. Ceinwen pushed the door open wider and dust danced in the light that streamed into the room.

'Merdynn?' Ceinwen asked, taking a hesitant half step towards the figure sitting in the shadows.

'Here we go again,' Garwin said and spat on his shield.

'Gods protect us,' Sal replied trying to steady his breathing.

Once again they found themselves in the front shield wall of the jagged formation that Mar'h had employed for the battle on the North bank; now they were on the South side of the river and advancing towards the Adren army who were standing in ranks before their camp.

The legion had lost just under a third of its number in the first battle; almost a thousand Britons lay dead and unburied on the North side of the river. Morgund's mounted cohort had lost about a hundred and fifty riders and the rest of the casualties had been in the front ranks of the shield wall and their places had been filled by the two less able cohorts. They had slaughtered every last Adren in the first battle but now they faced twice their own number and this time the Adren were prepared for battle.

Arthur had already led the war band in a wide loop south of the Adren camp to a position behind the enemy. It had been Gereint who had first realised that Arthur was no longer with them after they had crossed the bridge and fought their way free of the barricade. Without hesitation he had thrown away the battle plan and led the charge back to the bridge where they had found Arthur and four others fighting with their backs against the river. By the time they had hacked their way through to the surrounded Britons only Arthur remained standing and they were only able to get clear once Morgund's charge tore into the Adren ranks. By the time the battle was over the war band had lost forty warriors and they counted themselves fortunate not to have lost more.

Sal heard Mar'h shouting out the command to stop and the advancing Britons came to a halt less than two hundred yards from the waiting Adren ranks. The dust gradually settled in the still air and for a minute or two both armies faced each other silently in the searing heat. Sal just wanted it to start. Fight and live or fight and die; he just didn't want to have to wait to find out which it was going to be.

Suddenly five hundred arrows rose into the air like a startled flock of birds and arced overhead towards the Adren ranks. As the first volley fell into the enemy the second volley left the bows of Elwyn's archers; the battle for the South side of the river had begun.

The Adren seemed to have been waiting for the archers' onslaught and their ranks immediately came together with shields raised. Sal watched as the third and fourth flights of arrows fell amongst the enemy. He shifted nervously and glanced across to where Mar'h was at the centre to see if he had seen what he was seeing; the Adren were forming up into what seemed like a tight-packed wedge shape with those deeper in the formation holding their shields above their heads to provide protection from the arrows raining down on them. The wedge started to move towards them, slowly at first but gradually picking up speed.

Mar'h watched as the Adren spearhead charged straight towards his position. He knew that he needed to fold his right flank immediately behind his left and double the strength of his line to withstand the oncoming attack but he also knew that his inexperienced legion would never react in time and to even try it would only result in his force being hit while in neither one formation nor the other. He also knew that he and those around him were about to die. In desperation and in the few seconds remaining he shouted out for the left flank to form a square and roared out the commands for the right flank to do likewise but even as the legion began to withdraw into the new formation the Adren spearhead crashed into the centre of the shield wall.

For a few seconds Mar'h thought that the line had withstood the impact but then the combined momentum of those within the Adren wedge carried it forward and the centre of the shield wall buckled and then collapsed. Mar'h and those around him were pushed backwards and hacked down as the four thousand Adren drove their wedge into the centre of the Briton force dividing it into two.

Elwyn, who was stationed behind the shield wall with his archers, had seen Mar'h's frantic attempts to reorganise his forces and now understood what he had been trying to do; if the legion became divided then their best defence would be in two tight squares. He could see that in the chaos of the Adren breakthrough the left flank of the legion was beginning to close ranks but the right side of the shield wall was in complete disarray and the Adren wedge was already breaking up to overrun them. He knew there was no way to get his archers through the Adren and into the square forming on the left and he could not fire at the Adren attacking the disintegrating right flank without hitting his own people.

He only had a minute or two before the Adren pressed their advantage and charged his cohort and at this distance they would be quickly overrun and massacred. He did the only thing he could and ordered his command to retreat three hundred yards and reform.

As they sprinted away from the turmoil of the shattered shield wall Elwyn cursed the war band, unable to understand why they had not entered the fray but the Adren captains had seen the havoc caused by the mounted warriors when they had charged through the encampment and they had kept back a body of fifteen hundred soldiers to meet the horsemen when they appeared. The war band and Morgund's cohort were embroiled in their own battle half a mile from the dying legion.

He ordered his archers into three ranks and tried to make sense of what was happening in the battle. To the right was carnage; the legion on that flank had been unable to form into a defensive square and what was left of the several hundred Britons from that side of the shield wall were now fighting individual battles against overwhelming odds. Elwyn knew they were lost and guessed that Mar'h too must have fallen as he had been in the centre where the Adren spearhead had smashed through. That left the river flank of the legion as the sole effective survivors. The battle there seemed to be more concentrated and he prayed it was because someone had managed to form the Britons into an ordered defence, but they had nowhere to retreat to and it seemed that their only option was to put the river to their backs so that they could concentrate their defensive lines. It was how the last of the Adren had died on the North bank.

Elwyn had a choice; he could try to retreat from the battlefield altogether and possibly save his five hundred archers or he could continue the fight without a shield wall and risk being completely overrun. The thought of retreat sickened him but he refused to let his pride rule his judgement. Arthur had decided to take the war to the Adren and had engineered it so that each battle on either side of the river was fought with roughly even numbers or at least without a massive imbalance. Elwyn realised that if the Britons could not win this battle then they could not win the war; he had to stand and fight.

As he made his decision he felt the ground drumming to the sound of horses. The mounted warriors had broken through the Adren cordon and Elwyn watched as they tore into the unequal battle on the right. It was too late to save the legion on that flank but the Adren were dispersed and ideal targets for the lances and swords of Morgund's cohort. Other horsemen seemed to be bypassing the battle and riding around to join the archers. Elwyn could see that Arthur was leading them and realised that while Morgund had led his cohort into the mess of the right flank, Arthur was leading the war band to support his own archers. He felt a surge of hope and returned his attention to the situation immediately before him.

Some of the Adren were already turning away from the fighting on the right flank and mustering to charge Elwyn's cohort. Elwyn chose not to wait for the inevitable charge and ordered his first row of archers to aim at the fringe of the battle that had spilled closer to their position.

'Two hundred yards!' he roared out the distance to his archers and they fitted arrows to their strings, 'Draw!' A hundred and fifty bows bent and pointed skywards, 'Fire!' The arrows flew into the blue sky, arced then sped down into the enemy.

'Second rank! Draw! Fire!' Another cloud of arrows flashed into the sky and before they landed Elwyn was calling out the orders for the third rank to fire.

The Adren that had destroyed the entire right flank of the legion were now being hammered by Morgund's riders and many of them were seeking a more even battle; some joined in the fighting bunched near the river, others turned on the archers. There was no cohesive charge but they came at Elwyn's cohort first in small knots sprinting forward with their shields raised, then scores came in more ordered charges and finally they turned on the archers in their hundreds.

At two hundred yards the arrows caused some damage among the Adren but their shields provided adequate protection. At a hundred yards they were taking serious casualties but they still charged onwards. Less than a hundred yards it was either death for the attackers or Elwyn's archers. Despite the continual barrage of missiles more of the Adren were reaching the critical distance and closing it. They knew that if they could get among the archers then they would slaughter them.

The war band pulled up their horses behind the archers and grabbed their arrows and longbows from the lengthways strapping of their saddles and sprinted through the three ranks and formed a new front row. Elwyn continued shouting out for the ranks to fire while the war band strung their bows.

The Adren had closed the distance to fifty yards when the longbows of the war band fired their first volley. At such a short distance the Adren shields provided no protection from the more powerful longbows and the leading edge of the onrushing Adren tide was flung backwards as another volley smashed after the first. Every few seconds another hail from the longbows crashed into their ranks and all the while the archers of the cohort were sending a constant rain of arrows down upon the Adren.

The enemy charge faltered as they sought shelter behind their shields and the war band heard Arthur's voice roaring out behind them, 'Ten paces forward! Archers follow!' He shouted out the command as he sprinted between warriors and the archers and the lines rippled forward as he passed. The ferocious storm of arrows continued as the lines began to advance upon the enemy who were being forced backwards towards the tightening battle on the riverfront.

As the two battles came together Arthur strode once more between the lines, 'Cohort! Spears! Two of you to every warrior. Stay behind them, one to each side!' Again the order was repeated as he crossed the length of the first rank.

Arthur's advance had taken them close to the river edge of the battle that was raging around what remained of the legion and his warriors could see that his intent was to free one side of the beleaguered square.

The war band flung aside their longbows and unstrapped their shields from their backs, and freeing their weapons advanced upon the enemy with Elwyn's cohort now wielding spears following close behind.

Those in the nearest edge of the Legion's square could sense the confusion of the enemy as Arthur's war band cut into the rear ranks of the Adren and word was shouted back to the commander of the Britons. Unna had been on the left flank of the legion when she had heard Mar'h's last desperate orders to form up into a square. Along with the jagged shield wall it had been the only formation that had been drilled into the legion. Forming up in a field outside the Haven had been relatively easy but to do so under the pressure of the Adren attack was almost impossible and so it had proved for the right flank. It was no small measure of her leadership that she had been able to salvage enough of the left side to form a square and then edge them towards the river.

When she heard that the Adren to the West were under attack from behind she decided to throw her reserves into that side of the square and put the Adren under more pressure. It might have worked had the legion been more experienced in keeping tight battle order but as they forced the Adren back the square that had held so well up until that point finally broke apart.

Two things saved the legion from being completely destroyed in those next few minutes; Arthur's war band reaching the square as it broke and the arrival of Morgund's cohort that had reformed after the battle on the right and then charged into the Adren on the river-side of the battle. Elwyn's archers, now wielding their spears, rushed into the scattered, formless battle and attempted to pair up with those from the legion's shield wall as their training had taught them to do.

The Adren still had more soldiers in the field than the Britons but Morgund's cavalry were continually narrowing the difference as they cut back and forth through the thronging enemy. It was no longer an ordered battle of flanks and formations but a desperate and bloody fight to the end; the victors would be whoever was left standing when there was no one left to fight. Only the experienced warriors of the war band managed to stay close to each other and even they broke up into smaller groups. Gereint and Dystran led the Mercian warriors into the thick of the fighting. The Uathach fought alongside Gwyna and Ruraidh while Arthur and Hengest took the remnants of the Wessex and Anglian war bands into the heart of the battle. Elwyn stayed with his spearmen and fought with the Britons of Mar'h's legion.

Under the searing heat of the summer sun the battle gradually turned in the Britons' favour but no Adren backed away or tried to flee the battlefield. Over two more exhausting and bloody hours the Adren fought and died until they were finally defeated; the southern half of Lazure's army lay dead on both banks of the Isis. Arthur's war band and Mar'h's legion were victorious but Arthur had less than a hundred warriors still able to fight and the legion was effectively destroyed as an army. Lazure still had ten thousand soldiers in the North.

Sal sat on the dry grass of the riverbank and gazed sightlessly over the water. The incessant sun was over his right shoulder and he could feel its heat burning the back of his neck and drying his sweat-soaked clothes. His stare shifted as his eyes caught some movement out on the water; another section of the burnt bridge detached itself from the shortened stump jutting out into the water and began drifting downstream on the slow current. He wondered absently where it would end up and tried to imagine its journey down the Isis. He supposed it would end up in the Channel Marshes that he had heard of but never seen. He clung to the thought afraid that once he let it go he would have to face the horror of the last few hours.

As the drifting section disappeared into the glaring reflections of sunlight he searched the far bank for further distractions but the only movement across the river came from the thousands of crows that had been drawn from the Winter Wood by the bountiful feast left by the battle. It only served to remind him of what he had been trying to put from his mind; his brothers, Garwin and Keir, had both died in the battles on the Isis.

He tore his eyes away from the triumphant feasting and stared at his blood-caked hands; hands that were scarred by a lifetime of fighting the capricious nature of the western seas. He was unable to stop them from shaking. He was also unable to stop the silent tears that dropped from his face and fell onto his hands bringing the dried blood back to life. First it had been the fear, then the fatigue and now it was the shock; he was exhausted and sickened by all he had experienced and underneath these raw feelings there lurked the inescapable sense of relief that he had survived and that sickened him further. He thought of little Kea, his brother's daughter, and bowed his head and cried.

In the aftermath of the battle Arthur had gathered together the surviving leaders of the war band. The warriors that had lived through the battle congregated nearby, their jubilation at having defeated the Adren tempered by their own losses.

Arthur looked around at those surrounding him, some standing and some squatting down, and immediately put their victory into perspective, 'That's half the battle won.'

Everyone knew that neither battle had gone entirely to plan but equally they also knew that they had defeated an army nearly three times their size.

'The second half will be harder.'

Had there been only one Adren army loose in Britain then it wouldn't have ultimately mattered how slim this victory was - it still would have meant a complete victory. As it was they now had only a few hundred left with which to face the Adren who were currently somewhere in the North.

'Mar'h?' Arthur addressed the question to Elwyn who just shook his head.

'Who held the square together on the river side?' Arthur asked, scanning the weary faces before him.

Again it was Elwyn who replied, 'I think it was Unna, the harbour master.'

'Did she survive?'

Elwyn looked towards the small group assembling by the river, all that was left of Mar'h's legion, and shrugged.

Arthur turned to Morgund, 'How many of your mounted cohort are left?'

'Thirty, perhaps forty.' Between the two battles he had lost nine tenths of his command and most of those had perished in the final two hours of the fighting.

'And your archers?' Arthur asked returning his attention to Elwyn.

'Less than fifty probably. Haven't done a head count yet.' Something in Elwyn's tone betrayed his anger at the questions and Arthur stared at him until he looked away.

'Get your mounted cohort together and saddle the freshest horses,' Arthur said directly to Morgund.

'Now?' Morgund asked trying to keep the surprise from his voice.

'Yes. Now. They're riding with us to the Causeway. I want those Adren dead too before we turn to the West.'

Morgund nodded and left to round up what remained of his exhausted cohort. Arthur turned his attention back to Elwyn. 'You'll stay here. Organise the legion to collect our wounded. Find Henna and see to them as best as you can. She will have to decide who we take back on the wains and who we leave here...'

'Henna's dead,' Elwyn interrupted him.

'Then find someone else to tend to the wounded. Or do it yourself.'

Again they stared at each other and again Elwyn broke away to look at the ground. Arthur continued, 'Bring the carts up and load them with the Adren supplies. Kill the Adren wounded and burn our dead. Once you've done that then send the wounded and the surplus supplies back to Whitehorse Hill and then make for the Causeway with every able person still here.'

Elwyn trudged away and Arthur watched him in silence. Hengest cleared his throat and gestured to Gereint and Gwyna as he said, 'Shall we get the war band ready to ride?'

Arthur took his eyes away from the departing Elwyn, 'Yes. Collect the longbows and arrows. Get the horses watered and make sure everyone takes enough provisions for a few days. As soon as Morgund's ready we'll ride to the Causeway. Hengest, collect or fashion as many digging tools as you can then bring them with us.'

Arthur turned away from them and strode off to the riverside where the legion's survivors were gathering. He walked among them and stopped to talk with each small group of legionnaires praising them for their victory and listening to their accounts of the battle. As he made his way along the riverbank he recognised Sal sitting by the water's edge. He called out to him and Sal looked around and lumbered to his feet as Arthur approached.

'Your brothers?'

'They're dead. Both dead.' Sal looked surprised by his own words, as if an unspoken fear had been made real by voicing it.

'Then Garwin and Keir died to protect Kea and all the others like her back at the Haven. There's no better reason to have to fight. There's no better cause to have to die for. It's the only reason, the only cause, the only justification for today. Together you've kept those at the Haven safe for that bit longer. Your brothers have played their part and now it's up to you to carry it on.'

Sal nodded at Arthur's words but he had been so surprised by Arthur remembering their names that he had hardly heard any of what followed.

'Do you know if Unna survived?'

'No, she died too.'

'Sal, I need to talk to you about Merdynn. I want you to remember everything you can about what he said to you. I need to know if he talked about the battle against the Adren at the fortress, about what happened on the sea crossing and if he said anymore concerning Ethain.'

'I don't remember much of anything right now.'

Arthur rested a hand on his shoulder, 'Try to remember. You'll be joining us at the Causeway in a few days and I'll speak to you then.'

Arthur returned to the mustering war band and Sal made his way across to where Elwyn was organising the legion. But he wouldn't be speaking to Arthur at the Causeway; Sal died an hour later, killed by a wounded Adren.

Hengest rode at the front of the column that was making its way along the Westway at walking pace. The hundred odd riders were stretched out in a line that covered almost a mile with Morgund's cohort bringing up the rear. The horses were as tired as the warriors and as quickly as Arthur wanted the destruction of the small Adren camp on the cliffs above the Causeway he had left orders not to push on too hard. Morgund's cohort had lost almost as many horses as it had riders during the second battle when they had been enmeshed in the heart of the fighting but enough of the riderless horses from the charges of the first battle had been rounded up to make sure each of the warriors had a mount. Arthur had ridden ahead with a small patrol to reconnoitre the Adren camp.

Hengest looked around at the surviving members of the Anglian war band that rode with him. Less than fifteen were left. He looked further back down the line to where the Wessex warriors were; they seemed to number about the same. He would have given anything to have Cei back leading the Anglians, and to have his father, Aelfhelm riding by his side. He thought of the others who had gone east never to return; the experienced Herewulf, Cerdic whom many had thought would lead the war band after Cei, Leah and Roswitha both good warriors, stubborn Leofrun, reliable Cuthwin – so many gone, so many warriors they desperately needed now. He was so lost in his thoughts that he did not notice that Aylydd had brought her horse alongside his until she spoke to him, 'Did Saewulf get away from the bridge?'

Hengest looked at the reins in his hands for a moment before replying thinking that there was another warrior who was lost, 'I haven't seen him. If he got away he'd have swum to the bank and probably joined in the fighting. I'm sorry Aylydd but I don't think he can still be alive.'

She turned in her saddle and asked the same question to the other Anglian warriors. Some shrugged and others averted their eyes. No one had seen him since he had steered the fire boats into the bridge.

Lissa was the only one to reply to her question, 'He must have died at the bridge and if I ever get another beer before me he'll be the first one I drink to, without him we'd never have divided the Adren and we'd have lost.'

Those around him voiced their agreement.

'If it hadn't been for Arthur's plan we'd never have won the day,' Hengest added.

'If it hadn't been for the plan then Saewulf might still have been alive,' someone replied.

'Saewulf knew what he was doing, he wanted the job of firing the bridge,' another voice answered.

'I heard that Mar'h died,' Aylydd said dropping back to Lissa and leaving the others to their weary discussion. Lissa had sailed to the West with Mar'h during the previous winter and they had formed a firm friendship during the journey.

'Yes. Elwyn was saying he went down when the Adren drove their spearhead into the centre of his shield wall. He was a good man.'

'He was a bastard. He got what was coming to him.' Ruraidh spat over his horse's neck to emphasise the point; he and Gwyna were also talking of Mar'h's death.

'He led the legion well,' Gwyna replied and turned her face away from her companion so that he could not see that she was merely antagonising him.

'Led the legion well? He raped your mother during some cursed Wessex raid! I'd have thought you of all people would be dancing on his dead body.'

Gwyna took the smile from her face and turned once more to him, 'I liked him. You did too before Esa made her claims – besides my father decided she must have been mistaken.'

'Well the bastard's dead now, pity the Adren got the pleasure.'

Gwyna tired of her game and tugged at the neck of her leather battle tunic in an attempt to loosen it and relieve the uncomfortable chaffing it was causing. The sun had already passed its zenith and begun its long slide into the East but it had not yet lost any of its strength and the scorched land lay suffocating in the oppressive heat.

The thirty Uathach warriors were riding in the middle of the strung-out column with Gereint's Mercians bringing up the rear some way back. Gwyna did a quick tally of the surviving warriors and came up with about a hundred.

'Bastard or not we could have done without him or his legion dying,' Gwyna said. She gave up on her efforts to loosen her collar and instead untied the fastenings running down the side of the tunic and took it off altogether. She breathed deeply and sighed with relief as the constraining tightness around her chest was released. Ruraidh watched as she plucked at the linen undershirt that was plastered to her skin with sweat.

'My husband may not approve of your obvious attention,' she said without looking at him.

'Ah, but I know that you do,' Ruraidh replied and they both laughed.

'Where is the madman?' Ruraidh asked finally looking away from her.

'Madman?'

'He's a bloody lunatic. Did you see him by the bridge?'

'He probably killed more Adren there than we managed together all day.'

'I don't doubt it. I wasn't sure who his fury was more aimed at – the Adren, or us for coming back for him,' Ruraidh said, then added grudgingly, 'I'll give him one thing though, he planned the two battles well and won them both against greater numbers.'

'It's little wonder we had no success against the Wessex bastards.'

'Has he gone on ahead?' Ruraidh repeated his question.

'Yes, to scout the Adren camp above the Causeway,' Gwyna replied between taking thirsty mouthfuls of water from her canteen. She passed it across to Ruraidh who did likewise.

'If there's only a hundred or so there then it'll be short work,' he said, handing back the empty canteen.

'And that just leaves Lazure's ten thousand sacking the North.'

'Do you think Benoc and Hund will stand against him?'

'Yes and they'll be slaughtered but with any luck they'll dent his force.'

'And what about our people?' Ruraidh asked, angry that she should be so casual about her own peoples' destruction.

'They aren't our people, they're Hund's and Benoc's. Anyone who counts to us is already at the Haven. The others had their chance and more fool them for staying.'

'We'll be next. I don't see how even Arthur can win with a few hundred against Lazure's army.'

'He can't, not now.'

'So that's how your glorious plans end – dying in some doomed battle or hiding in some deserted village?'

Gwyna looked coldly at him before replying, 'I don't plan to die and I don't intend abandoning any of my plans.'

'How can you have any share in the rule of this land when there'll be nothing and no one left to rule?'

'Because, you fool, I don't intend to stay in this land.'

Chapter Eight

The huddled figure gradually stood up using the two walls of the corner as support and stepped out from the shadows. Ceinwen stared in disbelief and Morveren took an involuntary step backwards.

'You wouldn't happen to have anything more interesting to eat than wild berries by any chance? Some cheese perhaps?'

'Gods,' Ceinwen muttered under her breath.

'Flattered, but no.'

'But, you're dead...' Morveren said still in shock.

'Less flattered but again, no. I could eat some cheese if you want proof of that. Don't have any do you?'

'How did you...?' Morveren stuttered.

'Ah.'

'When?'

'Well.' Merdynn smiled at them both, delighted by their ashen faces and shocked expressions.

'Clearly none of us are at our best so why don't you fetch whatever food you have in your saddle-bags, Morveren, while Ceinwen here clears a table and finds some chairs then we can put our thoughts and questions into some semblance of order. And eat. We could even eat first.'

Morveren laughed aloud and stopping at the doorway to look back and make sure her eyes had not deceived her she went to fetch the requested food.

'She hasn't laughed for a while has she?' Merdynn asked.

Ceinwen went to embrace him but he looked so frail and thin that she took his hands in hers instead. 'I don't know how you're still alive, or how you're here but this is the best thing that's happened since I first set eyes on the bloody Adren. Wait until Arthur sees you!'

'Fetch the chairs, Ceinwen, and make some room on that table.'

Ceinwen's smile was checked by Merdynn's quiet response and as she prepared the table some of the happiness that had swept over her began to ebb away.

Morveren entered the hut almost dancing despite the saddlebags over each shoulder and the flask of water and a skin of wine under each arm. She ignored the chairs and knelt by the table as she pulled various foods from the bags and piled them in front of Merdynn. With a final flourish she produced a small square of cheese and placed it before him. He took it almost reverentially in both hands and raised it to his nose.

'It's a bit old, it's gone a bit crumbly with the salt,' Morveren said apologetically.

'It's a blessed delight and possibly the single best reason to live forever.'

Morveren grinned at him in relief and poured three cups of wine. Merdynn diluted his with water and held up a hand for them both to be silent as he alternatively took nibbles of cheese then sips of wine.

'Talking of living forever...?' Ceinwen asked tentatively when the cheese had eventually disappeared.

'Figure of speech,' Merdynn said quickly and concentrated on slicing an apple into pieces with a small knife.

'My brothers left you on the Breton coast. They said you must have died there from your wounds,' Morveren prompted, watching the old man's crooked fingers as he cut up the apple.

'Redoubtable fellows but obviously mistaken.'

Ceinwen leaned forward, 'What happened Merdynn?'

Merdynn sighed and sat back in his chair leaving the apple cuts on the table. 'I died. At least I thought I died. I wanted to die. I was weary, soul-weary. It's been so many years, so many seasons, so many generations have come and gone and I've watched them all from birth to death, and I wanted to join them finally. I wanted peace but I was sent back. It was not my time to rest, not yet. The task is never finished. It's endless, cycle after cycle, and someone has to stand through it always guiding, protecting, fashioning. Time is terrible, ruthless and relentless, and nothing can weigh heavier on a soul. I yearned for rest but I was denied it. The burden continues.'

'Then you've returned to help us defeat the Adren?' Ceinwen asked, unsure what he meant by his talk of tasks and burdens.

'No. It has never been my role to stand directly against the enemy. Others have had that role in the past but they're gone, long gone. No, it's my responsibility to guide and counsel those who would stand in the storm – to prepare them for their part in the endless cycle.'

'You're talking of Arthur, but he still needs you.'

'I can teach him nothing now. He no longer needs any guidance – if he ever did. No he doesn't need me any longer. He'll need you though, both of you. You must trust him absolutely if anything of Britain is to survive.'

'Then our survival is possible?' Morveren asked remembering Ceinwen's words to the contrary.

'So much still hangs in the balance. The enemy is still greater in number and stronger too. Lazure is more powerful than any who might stand against him and yet he is merely a lieutenant of the one who sent him.'

'Then how can we survive?' Morveren asked in despair.

'Arthur.'

'Is there nothing you can do to help him?' Ceinwen pleaded.

'I shall help, though perhaps not directly. I have to look now to the next cycle.'

In the silence that followed Merdynn resumed his interest in the food and began eating the apple pieces one by one as he watched the faces of the two women. They both reached for their wine cups and drank without realising they were a mirror image of each other. Merdynn smiled and raised his own cup to them both, 'Thirsty work, eh?'

'What is?' Morveren asked.

'Explaining things.'

'You haven't explained anything!' Morveren said exasperated.

Merdynn looked offended and finished the apple grumbling to himself.

'What happened on the Breton coast? What about Cei and Trevenna and the others?' Ceinwen asked.

Merdynn sighed heavily, 'Hasn't Ethain explained it all to you?'

They exchanged glances before Ceinwen replied, 'We haven't found Ethain yet.'

'What?'

'We're still searching for Ethain,' she repeated.

'What, still?'

'Um, yes.'

Merdynn frowned.

'What happened at the fortress?' Morveren persisted with the same question.

Again Merdynn sighed. 'You want to hear how they all escaped don't you? How the others found some caves and hid there. Or how a boat from further up the coast came to their rescue. Or how they magically fought their way out, a handful against an army. Or how I came to their rescue with a boat from Wessex. Well, I didn't. I was too late to save them and so they died. They put their faith in me and I failed them. This is the way of the world, there's no unlikely ending to Cei's tale. This isn't one of my glorious stories of the past.' He brought his eyes up to look at them and he immediately regretted letting his guilt lace his tone with spite; they looked distraught at his words.

'But you lived. Perhaps they got away somehow too?' Morveren said.

'Yes, I lived. But then I *am* from the old tales and if you'd been listening you'd know we're notoriously reluctant to die. I've seen so much but I never want to see another barren ground where friends have died waiting for me; died because I failed them. I didn't want to see anything anymore but the choice was not mine and so here I am when others have gone. They're dead. I'd give anything for it not to be so.' Merdynn sighed deeply, 'And yet you'll still hope they lived somehow. Hope is always the last to die.' He stood up and crossed to his scant possessions piled in one corner of the small hut. He returned and placed two items on the table; a war axe and a strange pendant hanging on a leather cord.

'I found them on the Breton headland long after Sal had left. When the life returned to my body I searched for any sign of what had befallen our friends. This was all I found.'

'Cei's war axe!' Morveren cried suddenly recognising the design of the longboat on the iron head.

Ceinwen had recognised the axe and she added quietly, 'And that's Arthur's pendant, the one the Cithol girl gave him...'

'...And which Arthur gave to Trevenna when they parted in the Shadow Lands,' Merdynn finished and sat back down.

In the heavy silence that followed Merdynn poured them all another cup of wine, once again adding water to his. 'Surely Sal told you about the fallen fortress months ago?' he asked softly.

'I haven't had much of a chance to talk to him about it,' Morveren admitted quietly.

'Why ever not?'

'Him and the other two joined Mar'h's legion at the Haven.'

'Mar'h's formed a legion, eh? Perhaps I wasn't wasting my breath after all.'

'So Arthur's not long had the message you sent via them,' Morveren added cautiously.

'So you've only just started to look for Ethain?' Merdynn said incredulously.

'Well, yes.'

'Gods boil them alive!' Merdynn erupted sending a mouthful of wine flying to the dirt of the floor.

'Who?' Morveren asked, alarmed by the outburst.

'Your fool brothers, that's who!'

'If they're still alive to boil,' Morveren answered under her breath.

'What do you mean?'

'They're with the legion fighting the Adren in the East.'

'They're in the Shadow Lands?' Merdynn cried, shooting to his feet and knocking over his chair behind him.

'No! The other side of the Winter Wood!' Ceinwen replied quickly at last taking her eyes from the axe that lay on the table.

Merdynn composed himself, picked up his chair and sat back down, 'Good, good. So Lazure hasn't reached the Veiled City yet,' Merdynn said to himself as he weighed the situation.

'You've only just returned to Britain haven't you?' Ceinwen asked guardedly.

'Yes. I presume Arthur's gathered the people at Caer Sulis or the Haven?' Despite the question it was clear that Merdynn was mulling over other thoughts.

'Merdynn?' Morveren said, fearing his reaction.

'Yes?' he answered absently, his mind still clearly elsewhere.

Morveren took a deep breath and glanced quickly at Ceinwen, 'The Veiled City is destroyed.'

Merdynn stared at her.

'The Cithol turned against us and threw their lot in with Lazure. At least Venning and Commander Kane did.'

Merdynn continued to stare dumbly at her. Morveren took a deep breath and continued, 'So Arthur destroyed the whole city – at least what was left after the Adren sacked it. And most of the Winter Wood. And presumably most of the surviving Cithol too.'

Merdynn looked panic-stricken. He stared at Morveren with wide eyes and gripped the edge of the table with a strength that belied Ceinwen's earlier opinion of his frailty.

'What of Seren? What's happened to Fin Seren?' Merdynn almost whispered the question.

'Seren?' Morveren asked nonplussed.

Ceinwen flinched at the imminent outburst. Merdynn shot to his feet knocking over his chair for the second time and cried out the question again. Morveren flinched backwards as if she had been physically struck. With her heart racing Ceinwen stood up with deliberate slowness and held her hands up before Merdynn who now looked far from frail or absent-minded.

'She's safe, Merdynn, she's safe. She's at the Haven.'

'And the child?'

'You know she's pregnant?' Ceinwen asked in confusion, then seeing the danger in the old man's eyes quickly added, 'I don't think she's had the child yet...'

Merdynn strode to the doorway brushing her effortlessly aside. He stared up towards the sun gauging its position and then he seemed to sag against the doorway. When he turned back to them Ceinwen saw the dawning relief on his face. 'Of course, it's not her time yet. Soon, but not yet. But there's no time to lose. I shan't be late again.' Merdynn was mumbling to himself as he sought about the hut gathering together his few possessions.

'Quickly, tell me everything's that happened since we parted in the Shadow Lands!'

'Well, the king's dead and Arthur's forged an alliance with the Uathach...' Ceinwen said fully expecting another fit of outrage.

'Yes, yes, I heard that from Sal. Tell me everything else!'

Ceinwen started by telling him that Ruadan, her brother, had died at the Causeway then hurriedly backtracked and recounted the events from the beginning with Morveren adding parts as she left them out. Merdynn collected the food from the table then sat down impatiently as they continued their tale.

It took some time for them both to recount all the events that had led them to their search for Ethain and contrary to Ceinwen's fears Merdynn seemed to become more patient as the story unfolded; at first he interrupted them with constant questions or demands for clarification but gradually his interjections gave way to nods or shakes of his head depending on how he took each new turn of events.

When they finished Merdynn sat in silence for a long time. Ceinwen would not have thought it possible but he somehow looked both relieved and worried at the same time; the furrowed lines had left his face and his posture was more relaxed but his eyes spoke of a deeper anxiety.

When he broke his silence he asked them further questions getting them to elaborate on certain aspects of what had happened and his questions always returned to Gwyna. He had never met her, even though she was the daughter of Ablach, and his ignorance of her appeared to worry him more than anything else did. Ceinwen was all too ready to admit that she held Arthur's wife in little regard but she was nonetheless puzzled by Merdynn's concentration on her and she chose her words carefully when he directly asked her what she thought of the Uathach girl.

'She's just a girl from an Uathach village. It's a harsh life in those lands and it wouldn't necessarily have been any easier for being the daughter of Ablach. There's nothing remarkable about her except perhaps her ability to grab an excellent opportunity when one presents itself. She probably can't believe her good luck in marrying the ruler of Britain – even if it's all bound up with the Adren invasion. She won't let much stand in the way of what she wants, she killed her father after all. I get the impression she'd rather have the chance of glory, despite the danger of losing everything, than have lived a safe life as a gift-wife for one of Ablach's warriors.'

Merdynn's frown returned at Ceinwen's opinion and he asked Morveren if she felt the same way about her.

'I don't know about all that. Without her killing Ablach and taking charge of the Uathach then we'd have died on the Causeway so I don't know about her motives, I know I don't like her much but then I doubt many women do – most men would though, if you see what I mean.'

Ceinwen wondered if Morveren was inferring that she was jealous.

Morveren was not even born when Ceinwen had been with Arthur but she had no doubt heard from Morgund or Mar'h about the time when she was.

She wondered uncertainly if she was in fact jealous and added, 'It's just an impression I got at the marriage feast. She just looked too delighted and smug considering she was marrying a stranger and she was furious when her father initiated the challenge through that Uathach warrior.'

'Ablach was behind that?' Morveren asked genuinely surprised. Ceinwen just looked at her as if she were simple.

To hide her embarrassment Morveren turned to Merdynn and took the subject away from Gwyna and back to Ethain, 'What happened on the boat Merdynn? Your message said that Ethain betrayed you. How?'

Merdynn looked sharply at her, 'Who else knows that?'

'Just us two, and Sal of course, Arthur asked us to keep it quiet until he questioned him.'

'Good. Tell no one.'

'Were you and Cuthwin injured escaping from the Breton coast?' Morveren asked, loath to admit her fears that Ethain had attacked his companions.

Merdynn sighed, clearly unwilling to answer the question. Morveren looked at him almost imploring him to deny her fears.

'It's best not to ask such questions,' he finally said.

'Why? Arthur will know when he talks to him,' Ceinwen pointed out.

'Yes he will and you must stay his hand. It's desperately important that Ethain remains unharmed! Or at least that no further harm befalls him. Everything may hinge on the unhinged.'

'Are you saying he's gone mad?' Morveren asked hoping that if he had indeed attacked Merdynn and Cuthwin then at least he may not be entirely responsible for his actions.

'Mad or not, Arthur won't stay his hand if he believes Ethain betrayed Cei and Trevenna.'

'He must not harm him! Ethain and I are linked now and Britain's fate may rest on that connection. Swear to me on your lives that you'll not let Arthur kill him!'

Such was Merdynn's anguish that they both swore to protect Ethain although neither knew what they would be able to do to stay Arthur's wrath.

Ceinwen tried one more time, 'Come back with us to Caer Cadarn – you'll be able to stop Arthur if Ethain's so important.'

'Ethain is so important because I *can't* go back with you. Even I cannot be in two places at the same time and my path now takes me away from Arthur. Whether Arthur saves Britain or not I still have my own task to fulfil. This is Arthur's time, his destiny and I must look to another time, another destiny. I cannot go with you.'

'Then where are you going?' Morveren asked, only really understanding that Merdynn was saying goodbye.

Merdynn looked at them both sadly wishing it were otherwise. 'The Haven, eventually. There is much to do and I must leave now.'

'You're going into the West!' Ceinwen cried, appalled that Merdynn would leave Britain to its fate.

'You must find Ethain soon,' Merdynn said, averting his eyes and checking the food he had already packed away.

'How? He could be anywhere!' Morveren cried.

'Can't you help us? You said you had some connection to him,' Ceinwen said, still shocked that Merdynn would leave Britain to its fate.

Merdynn stopped his rooting around in the saddlebag and looked intently at Ceinwen. 'Yes. Perhaps. Possibly. Yes, I believe I can. Give me a few moments silence.' He lowered his head and closed his eyes.

He remained motionless for so long that Ceinwen wondered if he had fallen asleep and she bent down to look into the old man's face. She could see his eyes moving behind his eyelids. She straightened up and shrugged in reply to Morveren's inquisitive look.

'If he can tell where Ethain is then why didn't he know that we hadn't found him yet?' Morveren whispered quietly.

'Because, young Morveren, I'd rather assumed that a few months were enough for your idiot brothers to have delivered the message to their idiot sister and for their idiot sister to have found the simpleton,' Merdynn replied without looking up.

'So you're awake then?' Morveren answered smiling.

'Oh course I'm bloody awake! I'm searching for Ethain!'

'Any luck?' Morveren asked not put out by his chiding.

Merdynn laughed and raised his head, 'He's stowed himself away in a gorge a few miles to the West of here. He's been coming and going between there and this village, at least he was until I turned up here. Do you think your legendary tracking skills will be able to unearth him, Ceinwen?'

'As you well know old man, I can track a ghost.'

'Good, because you will be. Now, when you find him you must return to Caer Cadarn immediately. You must arrive there before Arthur returns. And, other than Arthur, tell no one that you've seen me – not even Ethain! And tell Arthur that no matter how far the Adren advance, he must stand against the tide!'

Merdynn stood up to leave and the two women got to their feet. They watched him as he crossed to the brightly lit doorway and he stopped as if to say something more but after a moment's pause he just smiled and left. They hurried to the doorway and Ceinwen called out after the departing figure,

'Do you want to take one of our horses?'

'No need! I'll find a pony – I'm uncommonly good with animals!' he replied with a wave of his hand and without looking back.

Merdynn's voice echoed and died in the deserted village and they watched him as he strode down the pathway and towards the wooded valley with their plundered food tied in a bundle and slung over his shoulder. They both felt sure they would never see him again.

Without speaking they saddled their horses and stowed away their gear. Ceinwen secured Cei's axe to her horse's flanks and placed the Elk Stone safely in one of her pockets.

Whatever growing antipathy they had felt towards each other before arriving at the village had been completely annulled by their meeting with Merdynn. It was Ceinwen who summed up what they both felt some hours later as they made their way over the rolling hills towards the gorge, 'I've never felt so happy and yet so sad. Just seeing Merdynn alive has given me new hope but I still can't believe he's abandoning Arthur.'

'Has he always talked in such riddles? What could be more important than helping Arthur against the Adren?'

'I've no idea what he's implying most of the time but clearly he feels that his presence would make no difference to whether we'll stand or fall. Presumably his presence will make a difference elsewhere.'

'I still can't believe Ethain turned against the others or how he can have any crucial role in the battle against the Adren. It's not as if he's ever been a great warrior or anything.' Morveren was still desperate to believe that Ethain was somehow innocent of her suspicions.

'Remember to keep what Merdynn said to yourself! If the Anglians even suspect that Ethain somehow betrayed Cei then he's as good as dead.'

'How on earth are we going to stop Arthur cutting his throat?' Morveren asked hopelessly.

'I'll talk to him.'

Morveren snorted in response.

'Fair enough,' Ceinwen conceded then added quietly, 'If it comes to it then I'll stand in his way.'

'Then he'll kill you too.'

Their talk of Arthur reminded them both of their previous argument.

'He won't kill me,' Ceinwen said with conviction.

'How can you be so sure? Oh. You still love him, don't you?' Morveren asked looking across at her friend.

'I've been married to Andala for twenty years!' Ceinwen said defensively then corrected herself, 'Was married.'

'I'm not judging or criticising,' Morveren said hastily.

Ceinwen kept her eyes on the path ahead both horrified that her friend had so casually voiced the thought she had kept private for so long and yet longing to admit it aloud.

Morveren waited a while before asking, 'Why didn't you stay together?'

Ceinwen shrugged, 'It was a long time ago. We were young. We spent a winter apart and by the time the sun returned he was with,' she hesitated, 'someone else.'

Morveren knew instinctively why she had hesitated.

'He was with my mother wasn't he?'

Ceinwen nodded.

'She must have been a good deal older than him,' Morveren said attempting to sound matter of fact.

Ceinwen sighed, 'He was about your age, she mine.'

'That's what I mean.'

Ceinwen smiled, acknowledging the attempt to lighten what was undoubtedly an awkward moment, while Morveren fell silent uncertain what to feel and having to re-evaluate some of her previous judgements. She thought about her feelings for Morgund and wondered if perhaps her mother and Arthur had felt the same way about each other; if the future was so uncertain then perhaps you lived with little regard for it. If tomorrow could bring your death then perhaps you lived only for today. Morveren glanced across at her friend trying to imagine how she would have looked at her own age and then tried to imagine a younger Arthur. She found it easier to picture Ceinwen as a teenager than Arthur; she simply could not imagine Arthur was ever a young man. Perhaps, she thought, no one could envisage their parents as being young and she turned to Ceinwen to finally ask the question she had never voiced, 'Is Arthur my father?'

Ceinwen had often wondered how she would answer the question but now that it was asked she suddenly felt unready to reply. She delayed by asking, 'Has no one in your family ever mentioned it?'

'No,' Morveren replied looking mortified that she had actually brought up the subject so directly.

'Has Arthur ever spoken to you about it?'

'No,' Morveren replied in an even smaller voice.

'Then how can I know or say?'

'Of course, I'm sorry... it's just, well I thought as you were close to Arthur...' Morveren's voice trailed off in misery.

Ceinwen frowned. She felt sorry for the girl but she was also irritated that Morveren was unable to recognise that it was because she had been so close to Arthur that the subject was difficult for her too. She looked at Morveren and her obvious vulnerability disarmed her.

'I don't know Morveren, I honestly don't, but if you're asking me what I think then I think you are Arthur's daughter.'

Morveren stared at her unable to put words to her emotions.

'Sometimes there's a certain resemblance,' Ceinwen said then added even more lamely, 'the timings were right.'

'He's never acknowledged it or shown any sign,' Morveren said, hoping Ceinwen could provide some more convincing evidence.

'Perhaps not but when you were growing up he certainly paid more attention to your village than was necessary.'

'How do you mean?'

Ceinwen thought for a minute before replying, 'Did you never question why your family had its own horse?'

'But that belonged to the village – we just looked after it,' Morveren said, trying to remember where the horse had come from and wondering for the first time who it had actually belonged to.

'Or why you had a proper bow when the other children had striplings and twine?'

Morveren shrugged.

'Or when the Anglians came to repair your brothers' fishing boat after it came in barely afloat after a storm? Did you think the Anglian war band went around mending every Wessex boat?'

Morveren looked nonplussed. Ceinwen carried on asking similar questions for several minutes and gradually the extent of Arthur's influence in her village and over her early life began to dawn on Morveren.

'When Sal and the others abandoned their attempts to get me to marry the farmer?' she asked and Ceinwen nodded.

'But Arthur was rarely in our village, how could he have known I was so against the proposal? I think I only saw him once during that time and I certainly didn't speak to him about it!'

'You know the answer to that as well as I do,' Ceinwen said and Morveren looked away uncomfortably, recalling the times when Arthur had seemed to read her thoughts and feelings.

'How do you know all this about my village? Weren't you in Branque by then?' Morveren asked.

'Ruadan told me. He was always convinced you were Arthur's daughter.'

Morveren fell silent, she had already said far more than she had intended to but she steeled herself to ask one last question knowing that if she did not ask it now then she probably never would.

'Do you think Arthur only accepted me into the war band because I'm his daughter?'

Ceinwen had wondered if Morveren would so openly expose one of her insecurities and she was glad she had asked it as it gave her the opportunity to say what she had wanted to say for some time, 'You're an excellent rider – the quickest and most skilled in the war band and you're good with a bow so, no, you're not in the war band just because you're his daughter. You're with us because you're good enough to be with us. But I do think he always intended you to be eventually at Whitehorse Hill – hence the horse and bow when you were a young child. I think he wanted to have you nearby.'

Ceinwen pushed her horse on ahead leaving her friend to ponder this new information. She had always imagined that revealing to someone else how she felt about Arthur would have come as a relief but if she felt anything it was a low undercurrent of panic. She was afraid that Morveren would mistake what she had said; her idea of love was very different from that of the young Morveren's, and worse, she might actually tell someone else. She regretted saying it now and wondered how she could either explain it or dilute it enough to take away any significance. Ceinwen doubted that Morveren would have understood the implication of her acknowledgement that Arthur had left her for Morveren's mother. Arthur had wanted a child, so in a sense, Morveren had been the reason why Arthur had left her all those years ago. She knew that Morveren was not to blame for any of what happened but she was still finding it difficult to forgive her.

She ducked under a low hanging bough welcoming the dappled shade and cooler air as the path wound across a wooded hillside. The well-worn pathway led around the side of the hill and, if her memory served her correctly, to the head of the gorge. Merdynn had once told her that all roads lead to home and she supposed he was right in a typical Merdynn way; this path led to both Ethain's old home and, in the opposite direction, to his new one in the gorge.

Her thoughts switched to wondering how the battle against the Adren had gone; any day now either the victorious legion would return to Caer Cadarn or the fleeing survivors would ride into view heralding the end of Britain's defence against the invaders.

She felt oddly removed from those events and her thoughts strayed to why Ethain would have betrayed Cei and what his connection to Merdynn could be. She also puzzled over why Seren and her child should be so important to Merdynn when they did not seem to carry the same importance with Arthur. Ceinwen had no doubt that Arthur loved the Cithol girl with an intensity he had never felt for her, or that he would ever feel for Gwyna, and yet even that was not enough to prevent him from turning his back on her too. She wondered if there was anyone or anything he was not prepared to sacrifice in the defence of Britain and the thought left her cold.

The path veered around the head of the ravine and then carried on across the rolling hills towards the Westway so Ceinwen dismounted and waited for Morveren to catch up with her. Ceinwen heard her before she saw her; she was whistling one of the war band's songs, the words of which would undoubtedly have made her brothers blush, and the clear notes carried through the woodland. Nearby a bird answered with its own song and Ceinwen listened as one countered the other and thought how far away the war seemed.

Morveren came into sight through the trees and her whistling stopped as she grinned at Ceinwen. The bird's song faltered in the absence of a companion and Ceinwen heard it take off from a branch somewhere overhead.

'You've made a friend there,' Ceinwen said as Morveren slid easily from her horse.

'I make friends wherever I go, I'm just that kind of girl,' she answered with a bright smile.

'Well one of your friends is down there somewhere so let's find him.' Ceinwen regretted saying it as Morveren's smile wavered and the trepidation returned to her eyes, but something about the younger woman's high spirits had irked her and the words were out before she could stop them.

Feeling mean she looped her horse's reins loosely around a tangle of thin branches and set off along the path peering into the dense undergrowth between them and the ravine.

Morveren just let her horse wander off and she sat back on the trunk of a fallen tree waiting for Ceinwen to find what she was looking for. She found it half an hour later and some way back down the path. Morveren joined her and she stared at the seemingly impassable lattice of branches and trailing roots that Ceinwen stood before.

'Are you sure?' Morveren asked.

'Do I tell you how to ride a horse?'

'I just mean it barely looks like a boar run.'

'Nonetheless,' Ceinwen answered and dropped to her knees. Morveren followed suit and soon they were inching and crawling their way through the thick brambles and bushes. It reminded her of the Winter Wood and just as she was beginning to feel uncomfortably claustrophobic the undergrowth thinned and she joined Ceinwen on an outcrop of moss-covered rock.

The ground dropped sharply away before them and Morveren leaned forward to try to see down the length of the wooded ravine. Somewhere below them they could hear the tumbling of water.

'This isn't going to be easy,' Morveren said, peering down and trying to gauge what their route should be.

'Do you want to go first?'

'Afraid I'm going to fall on you?' Morveren replied with a smile.

Ceinwen was thinking exactly that but taking a deep breath said, 'Just follow me and try to watch where I put my hands and feet. We'll make for the ledge down there.'

Morveren nodded her agreement but had no inkling how she would be able to watch her as she backed down the steep slope. It turned out to be a lot less difficult than she had imagined; footholds or secure roots seemed to present themselves just when she needed them and although it took her longer she joined Ceinwen on the ledge unscathed. She was brushing the dirt from her hands when Ceinwen put a hand on her arm. She looked up to see Ceinwen staring at the entrance to a cave and indicating for her to go first.

Morveren edged around her on the narrow ledge and ducked into the darkness. Once inside she stood up and leant against the smooth wall of the entrance waiting for her eyes to adjust to the blackness. The faint smell of wood smoke lingered like a memory in the darkness and as her eyes became accustomed to the dimness she could make out a small circle of stones and the remains of a fire in the centre of the uneven floor.

She crossed to the fire and knelt beside it. Behind her she heard Ceinwen come in and squat down inside the entrance as she too waited for her winter vision. She put her hand over the dead fire and not feeling any heat she sank her fingers into the ash and raked them through the remains.

'Old?' Ceinwen asked quietly from behind her.

'Only three or four hours. Not long.'

They looked around the cave and saw that it was fairly small, smaller than a room in a village hut. There was a pile of old straw against one wall and a few items that must have been taken from the village; a bucket lying on its side, a cooking pot half filled with water and a small trough that held a few apples and a cluster of berries.

Ceinwen led the way back out and they sat on the ledge overlooking the ravine.

'Well there's definitely someone living here. It must be Ethain,' Morveren said. She looked across at her friend to see her staring below them. She followed her gaze to the swirling river at the bottom of the gorge and stared in silence for a minute or two at the figure kneeling by the water's edge. He was scrubbing furiously at his hands with a stone.

Seren was sitting at the end of a tumble of rocks that formed a natural quay jutting out into the sea. All around her the restless waves surged back and forth slapping against the rocks and sending broken arches of rainbow-spanned spray high up into the air. She could taste the salt water on her lips and feel its coolness on her bare feet as it welled over the smooth boulder she was sitting on.

She heard her name being shouted and she stood up and turned to look back at the cliffs that rose behind her. A figure was standing at the top waving his arms and she guessed it must be Terrill. The brighter light in the East hurt her eyes and raising her arm in acknowledgement she turned back to the sea. She hoped Terrill would not make his way out to her but knew that he would. She did not resent the probable intrusion but she treasured these moments away from the town and the close confines of the harbour master's house, which was now home to the few Cithol who had escaped from the Veiled City.

Pressing her hands to the small of her back in an effort to alleviate the constant ache there she stared once more to the western horizon filled with wonder that such an expanse could contain such ceaseless motion. She had heard tales of the oceans when she was in the Veiled City but nothing had prepared her for its mesmerising nature or the sheer wonderment that captured her every time she stood on the shore.

She stared out to the distant horizon where towering clouds billowed skywards like vast columns of smoke and wondered if the gentle breeze blowing in from the sea would carry the imposing towers landwards. High above her a skeletal full moon hung like a pale ghost of winter in the faded blue sky and she longed once more to see the myriad stars strung out across the heavens above the Winter Wood. The sea enthralled her but she yearned to leave the Haven with its accompanying crowds, noise and overwhelming smells, all of which constantly assaulted her senses and disoriented her. She desperately wanted to return to a home that no longer existed.

Terrill watched her lone figure from the beach. She had been spending more and more of her time in the same spot at the edge of the sea and he was growing increasingly concerned for her. He still wanted to think of her as the spoilt and mischievous young daughter of Lord Venning, playfully mocking and light-hearted, but that girl had long since gone and the woman standing among the waves now had a sadness about her that was evident in her every expression. She still chatted and smiled with the other Cithol and she made great efforts to befriend all the Britons they came into contact with but underlying every smile and every pleasant exchange there was the constant sadness that she masked from the others but was unable to conceal from him.

He knew why she came to this place; she needed to escape and to be alone. The Britons, while not openly hostile, were clearly deeply suspicious of the Cithol and Terrill could hardly blame them after the alliance that Lord Venning that forged with Lazure. Seren's problem was that the other Cithol quietly blamed her for her father's part in what led to the destruction of their city; that and the harsh truth that Arthur had abandoned her. Terrill understood that only here, at the edge of the sea, could Seren escape the isolation she felt everywhere else; that being alone was the only way to escape her sense of loneliness.

He also understood that her time for being alone was rapidly running out; she was due to give birth in just a few short weeks and that was why he was concerned for her. By an unfortunate turn of fate none of the Cithol at the Haven had either had children or been present at a birth and it was one of the Britons who was reluctantly acting as the midwife. The situation pleased no one and only added to Seren's natural worries about her delivery.

Terrill uncomfortably eyed the narrow finger of rocks that led out to the sea and to Seren's precarious position at the very end. He had told her dozens of times that it simply was not safe but she evidently did not share the sense of disquiet he felt every time he stood before the wild sea. Overcoming his nervousness he stepped onto the rocks and began to carefully make his way out to where Seren stood.

Seren sensed rather than heard his cautious approach and sighed to herself. She knew he only had her safety in mind and she also knew that he was perhaps the only friend she had left in this harshly lit world and so she refused to let his intrusion irritate her. She turned her back to the rolling seas and started towards the shore.

Terrill had not gone far when he saw her walking back across the uneven rocks and he abandoned his clumsy clambering and began inching his way back to the beach.

'You make it look easy,' he said as Seren stepped lightly onto the beach.

'Nothing feels easy at the moment,' she replied as she gently lowered herself to sit on the shingle. Terrill leant forward and took some of her weight as she ungracefully plumped herself down. She laughed at her undignified efforts.

'It's impossible to find any position that can stay comfortable!'

'Unless it's sitting or standing for ages with waves pounding all around you,' Terrill said, sitting down beside her.

'Please, Terrill, don't start again,' she replied, putting a hand on his arm.

'It fascinates you, doesn't it?' he asked, gesturing inadequately at the immensity before them.

'Back in the Veiled City when the poets spoke of the ocean I always imagined it to be just a larger version of our lake. I had no idea how alive it could be. Imagine how beautiful it would look under a winter moon with the stars stretching from horizon to horizon!'

Terrill grimaced at the thought as Seren continued, 'It would be like the Winter Wood in a gale – a whole turbulent landscape swaying under the cold stars!'

'I think the sun's got to you. You should have stayed inside more like the rest of us.'

They were distracted by some shouting further down the beach. Two children were playing in the shallows, splashing and screaming at each other while a dog bounded around them barking frantically but largely being ignored. They watched as the children drew nearer, too caught up in their game to have noticed the two Cithol. Unsurprisingly it was the dog that first realised they were there and its playful barking changed instantly. The two children stopped their game and stood and stared at the two strangers.

Seren waved at them and they turned and fled. The dog, reluctant to leave unfinished business behind and delivering a final volley of barks, eventually followed after them.

'They'll never accept us. This is their world, not ours, and we're not welcome,' Terrill said sadly.

'Give them time,' she replied, thinking that he was right.

'I don't think any amount of time will be enough.' Terrill stood up and offered her his hand. As he hauled her up she suddenly let go of her grip on his hand and landed back down with a thump. She gasped, as much in surprise as pain, and doubled over. Terrill stared at her. She regained her breath and smiled up at him.

'Are you all right?'

But before she could answer him she bent over again groaning and gasping. 'I think it's my time,' she managed breathlessly.

'But it can't be!'

'I think it can be.'

'But it's weeks away yet!'

'Oh no it isn't!'

Terrill helped Seren to her feet and half carried her back to town. Her labour had begun.

Chapter Nine

Balor jumped down from the cart and walked around to the back. Morgund joined him and together they lowered the tailgate. A seagull swooped down and Balor batted it away, 'Wait your bloody turn!' he shouted after it.

He grabbed an arm of one the topmost corpses and heaved it from the cart. It landed in a cloud of dust at his feet and he bent down to grip it by the ankles. With a grunt of effort he hauled it to the precipice and levered it over the cliff edge with his foot. Beside him Morgund was doing the same and as his corpse tumbled and bounced down the long drop he swore after it and added, 'And don't be coming back.'

Balor laughed and trudged back to the cart to haul another Adren from the pile. He grabbed at an arm and tugged fiercely at it but there was no resistance and he wheeled backwards to land in the dirt. He lay there looking confused and staring at the arm he was holding with Morgund's laughter ringing in his ears. He scrambled to his feet with his face going red and with a string of curses threw the arm high over the cliff. Amazingly a seagull tried to intercept it in flight and then dove after its escaping prize. Balor glared at Morgund who was still laughing and struggling for breath. He stamped back to the cart and grabbed at a leg sticking out from the pile but this time he tested to make sure it was still attached to a body.

'Give us a hand here...' Morgund said breathlessly and immediately lapsed back into another fit of hysteria. Balor smiled despite himself then started chuckling as Morgund wheezed some more unintelligible advice towards him. No one thought it particularly odd that the two Wessex warriors were laughing like children as they hurled Adren bodies over the cliff.

They had overcome the Adren with relative ease by riding right up to the edge of the small camp and picking their enemy off with arrows. It was impossible to get a full draw on the longbow while on horseback but at such a close range even a half-draw on the powerful weapon was more than enough to kill. The Adren had been slaughtered quickly and without the Britons taking any further casualties.

Another cart trundled up to the cliff as Balor and Morgund heaved the last of their corpses off the edge.

Aylydd climbed down and she called out to them, 'This is the last of them. Want to give us a hand?'

Morgund began laughing and that started Balor off again. Aylydd and Lissa exchanged uncertain looks and started to unload the bodies. Morgund climbed onto the cart to have a look around and see if they were needed anywhere else. Arthur was still studying the Causeway below them with Gereint while Gwyna and the Uathach were loading wains with whatever Adren supplies they could use.

Balor was still chuckling to himself as he hauled a body from the Anglians' cart. For some reason Lissa thought their laughter was directed at him and Aylydd.

'I'd have thought you two would be among the last to be laughing,' he said, obliquely referring to Mar'h's death.

It had the desired affect and the two Wessex warriors stopped laughing. Neither looked at the other. They had searched for Mar'h's body among the fallen and eventually found his bloody corpse buried under friend and foe alike. They had burnt his body in silence and neither of them yet felt willing or able to dwell on the fact that another of their circle had fallen fighting the Adren.

Morgund dropped the corpse he was dragging and looked at Lissa, 'Mar'h's all right. The big nosed bastard is probably swilling beer with Cael and Cei and having a good laugh at us still stuck here.'

'The bugger's probably drinking our share of the beer,' Balor added, looking like he wanted to attack Lissa.

'We'll leave this lot for you then,' Morgund said, pointing at the cart-full of bodies before turning away and walking off towards Arthur and Gereint. Balor followed after him with his fists clenched and his jaw set.

When he caught up with Morgund he asked, 'So, who's going to tell Della and his children, you or me?'

'Neither. We'll let Ceinwen tell her.'

'And who's going to tell Ceinwen?' Balor asked but Morgund had no answer for that.

They approached Arthur at the same time as Gwyna was reporting on the Adren supplies.

'Two wains loaded up with potatoes, rice and smoked meat.' She saw the look on Morgund's face and remembered the stories she had heard about Branque and added hastily, 'Venison haunches, shoulders of ham and the like.'

'Good. Send it on to Caer Cadarn immediately and set up a relay of messengers between here and there in case word arrives about the Adren in the North.'

Gwyna nodded then looked questioningly at Arthur, 'We're staying here?'

Arthur turned to face the Channel Marshes laid out below them and spoke with his back to them, 'When Elwyn arrives with what remains of the legion we'll have over three hundred people. I want to level the last mile of the Causeway and let the marsh reclaim it. I don't think the Adren have any more soldiers to send but if they do then I don't want them walking straight into Britain. They'll have to bring timber and rocks the length of the Causeway if they want to bridge the last mile and that'll at least buy us time. When we're finished here we'll leave someone to keep watch.'

No one had the courage to point out that they would be effectively locking in the ten thousand strong Adren army that was already in Britain.

Ethain had no idea that anyone was watching him as he climbed the steep slope back up to the cave. Morveren watched him with a growing sense of anxiety; she felt that everything she feared to be true was about to be confirmed.

Ceinwen was afraid that the shock of seeing them might make him lose his balance on the rocky climb up to the ledge and signalled Morveren that they should withdraw into the cave. Morveren took a last look at the ascending figure before retreating back into the dimness of the small cavern.

They heard him scrambling up the last of the slope and onto the outcrop, and then the noises outside ceased. Morveren could imagine him squatting outside on the ledge sensing that other people were nearby and staring out into the wooded ravine searching for the intruders.

Nothing happened for several minutes. It was as silent outside the cave as it was inside and Morveren became convinced that he must have detected their presence somehow. She was about to move when Ceinwen held up a hand to still her and at the same moment Ethain darted inside the entrance. Ceinwen immediately moved to block the exit and Ethain spun around before springing across the dead fire to put his back to the wall.

'Ethain, it's all right! It's me, Morveren, and Ceinwen. Friends.'

Ethain stared from one to the other and Morveren could see the horror dawning on his face. 'Friends,' she said again, 'We've come to take you home, back to Caer Cadarn.'

A panicked look crossed his face and he remained tensed against the wall, half-crouching, one hand moving to the hilt of a knife tucked into his belt. Ceinwen saw the movement and laid her hand on her own knife hilt. Morveren watched them in alarm, 'We're friends, you're safe now. There's no enemies here, no Adren.'

Ethain's eyes fixed on Ceinwen's knife hand and he slowly spread his fingers and moved his hand away from his side. Even in the dark of the cave Morveren could see that his hands were rubbed raw by his scouring.

'How did you find...' His voice was croaky and his tongue flicked across his lips, 'How did you know I made it back to Britain?'

'Kea, my brother's daughter, she saw you come ashore near my village,' Morveren said gently.

Ethain's eyes were continually flicking between Morveren and Ceinwen's knife hand.

'Someone saw me? And recovered the boat?'

'Yes, with Merdynn and Cuthwin in it,' Ceinwen said speaking for the first time in the exchange.

'There was nothing I could do for them!' Ethain's voice was thin and high and he stared at Ceinwen waiting for her to either reveal more of what she knew or come at him with her knife.

'Ethain, you're in shock at seeing us so unexpectedly. Relax. After everything that must have happened in the Shadow Lands, then coming back to an almost deserted Wessex, it's no wonder...'

His eyes fixed on Morveren and he blinked repeatedly as if trying to clear his thoughts. 'That's right! I'd thought the Adren had overcome you all – the villages were empty!'

'Sit down. We've brought a little food. I'll get the fire going,' Morveren said and Ethain began to relax a little. He sat against the wall while Morveren lit the fire but he kept his eyes on Ceinwen and his hand near his knife.

The wood was tinder dry and within minutes a small blaze lit the cave and Morveren started to boil some water. As she added some leaves and roots to make a drink she surreptitiously studied Ethain. He was about the same height as her but she reckoned he now weighed a good deal less than her; she was fairly lithe but Ethain had become terribly thin. His clothes were torn and stained and his hands seemed to be the only part of him not caked in grime and dirt. She remembered his black hair as being unruly and spiky but it now lay in long, lank strands, plastered across his forehead and down the back of his neck.

Despite the dryness of the wood a thin blue smoke soon filled the cave and Ethain edged closer to the fire, drawn by the aroma of the stewing beverage.

'Do you have a cup?' Morveren asked looking around the dirt of the floor.

Ethain shook his head.

'We'll just have to drink from the pot then,' she said smiling at him.

Ethain reached out his raw hands to take the cooking pot from the fire. Morveren's hand shot out to prevent him from burning himself and he jerked backwards once more reaching for his knife.

'Ethain! Wait, you'll scald yourself!' Morveren cried, shocked by his reaction and the intensity of his flickering eyes. He settled back and sat cross-legged on the floor staring at the cooling pot.

'You're starving, aren't you?' Morveren asked gently.

Ethain nodded now dividing his attention between the sweet smelling drink and Ceinwen.

'Why didn't you make for Caer Cadarn?' Ceinwen asked.

'I, I thought the Adren had taken control. I hid, yes, I hid from them. I didn't think anyone else could be left alive so I hid here. Hiding here was the only thing I could do. What else could I do?'

'What happened, Ethain?'

'I hid.'

'No, what happened in the Shadow Lands? What happened to the others?' Ceinwen persisted and there was no trace of Morveren's gentleness in her voice.

Morveren watched the exchange between them and was shocked by the change in Ethain; not only was he starved to the point of emaciation but he seemed to be wavering on the brink of madness. Everything from his nervous edginess to his darting eyes was deeply unsettling her. There was a wary, feral quality about him that was more akin to a wild dog than a person and his nature now seemed just as unpredictable.

'What happened, Ethain?' Ceinwen repeated coldly.

A slight tremor passed over Ethain and he glanced towards a far corner of the cave where a jumble of possessions lay against the wall as if he were seeking reassurance.

'We died. One by one. From the city of ruins to the Breton fortress. Hunted through ice storms. Hunted through the darkness. And one by one we died. Some of us made it to the fortress and we defended the walls and cliffs. All winter long. But we couldn't stop them.' His eyes had glazed and he shuddered as if remembering the horrors of the Shadow Lands.

Morveren pushed the cooler drink towards him and his eyes blinked back into focus. As he took the drink his gaze flicked once more towards the bundle against the far wall then returned to watching Ceinwen over the rim of the pot.

'Cei? Trevenna?'

Ethain slurped hungrily from the pot still watching Ceinwen but not answering her.

'Did they die at the fortress?' Morveren asked quietly.

Without taking his eyes from Ceinwen or lowering his drink he nodded slowly.

'How?' Ceinwen asked abruptly.

Ethain lowered his drink and held it tightly in both hands, 'As heroes. The Adren breached the wall and Cei and Trevenna held them off as we scrambled aboard the only boat. Aelfhelm too.'

'And Merdynn and Cuthwin?'

'Both injured. Wounded as we fought away from the dock. Cuthwin died on the journey.'

'Merdynn?'

Ethain's eyes broke contact with Ceinwen and he raised the drink to his lips once more before replying. 'I don't know if Merdynn was alive or not. Dead I think. We had no food or water on the boat. He lost his senses. I thought he was dead. I just remember stumbling ashore.'

'Merdynn lived long enough to return to the Breton coast to rescue the others. Why would he do that if they were already dead?' Ceinwen asked without emotion.

Ethain's eyes narrowed then he placed the pot on the floor and kept his head lowered, 'Lived long enough? So, he died?'

Ceinwen glanced at Morveren before replying, 'The fishermen of the village took him to the Breton coast but there was no one left there. They left him to die on the headland.'

Ethain wanted to laugh out loud. He wanted to hug them both. If Merdynn was dead and none of the others had survived then there was no one left who knew the truth. He sighed and raised his head. Morveren could see his eyes glistening with tears. 'Mad. He must have gone mad with the pain. He was injured before the final battle and we carried him unconscious onto the boat. He was rambling on the crossing. Confused. We had to drink salt water.' A tear spilled down the grime on his cheek, 'All of them dead?'

'All of them except for you,' Ceinwen replied fighting to quell the sickness she felt as the tears fell freely from his eyes.

Morveren's heart went out to her friend. She knew he was lying about some of his story but she was unsure how much of what he said was lies; if it had indeed been Ethain who had attacked Merdynn and Cuthwin in the boat then why had Merdynn not said so himself? And if the fortress had already fallen then why would he attack them? Indeed, even if the fortress was still standing why would he attack them, what purpose would it serve? His story certainly didn't tally with Merdynn's but how much of what he said was lies or merely the product of his deranged state was difficult to discern. She still wanted to believe Ethain, to find a truth that could explain away her doubts and uncertain feelings. Ceinwen had no such doubts and she clung to Merdynn's words about keeping Ethain safe in an effort to control the rage she felt.

'Finish the drink, Ethain, then we'll head back to Caer Cadarn,'

Morveren said softly.

Ethain nodded and tilted up the pot as he drained the remains of the drink. Ceinwen left the cave and stood outside on the ledge breathing deeply with her eyes closed.

Ethain crossed to his bundled possessions and looked over his shoulder at Morveren who was watching him.

'You don't need any of that now. We have everything we need on our horses,' Morveren said.

'One thing,' he said, bending down and retrieving a stout staff, 'I'm still weak. It helps me walk.'

They joined Ceinwen on the ledge and she signalled Morveren to lead the ascent back up the slope. As Ethain passed her she snatched the knife from his belt saying, 'You won't be needing this.'

Ethain glared at her as she tossed the knife down into the ravine.

'We'll protect you now,' she said staring into his shifting eyes.

Despite Ceinwen being the more diminutive of the two women Ethain shared Morveren's horse. Ceinwen had pointed out that Morveren's horse was the stronger but the real reason was that she could not stomach the thought of Ethain being so close to her.

The journey took them four days. When they found shaded, cooler places to sleep Ceinwen insisted that either Morveren or herself should keep guard claiming that Ethain was in no fit state to stand watch.

They took the road to the deserted Caer Sulis and then along the Westway to where it met the Isis. They followed the river upstream to the foot of the Downs before ascending up to the Ridgeway. The sun still burned down from a cloudless sky but their shadows were already noticeably beginning to lengthen as the summer edged on.

They could see the blue haze of smoke from the cooking fires hanging in the still air above Caer Cadarn from several miles away and guessed that those who remained there must be curing haunches of meat; either that or the war band had returned. They re-tallied the time they had been away on their search for Ethain and reckoned the latter to be unlikely. They had not seen another living person, except for Merdynn and Ethain, in the whole time they had been away and it felt strange to be returning back to the unmistakable signs of habitation.

Ceinwen stopped her horse and it took the opportunity to wander to the verge of the path and taste the tall, yellowed grass that flanked the Ridgeway. Ethain slipped from behind Morveren and disappeared behind some nearby bushes, the unfamiliar abundance of relatively rich food was causing him some discomfort.

Morveren turned her horse and nudged it towards her companion. 'It feels odd coming back, doesn't it?' she said ruffling her horse's mane.

Ceinwen nodded, 'The others have been fighting the Adren while we've been wandering around an empty Wessex.'

'Not quite empty,' Morveren corrected, trying to keep her mind from worrying about Morgund and the others.

'We can't mention anything about Merdynn or what he said about Ethain,' Ceinwen reiterated.

'I know but I still don't understand why – Merdynn still being alive would be good news for everyone.'

'And then they would ask where he is and why he isn't with us now that we need him the most.'

'Well, we do need him and they are good questions,' Morveren pointed out.

'He has his own reasons but the warriors would see it as a bad sign. They would feel he's abandoned them and Arthur.'

'So we say nothing?'

'That's right. Apart from reporting it all to Arthur. To everyone else we say nothing about Merdynn, nothing about what he said of Ethain, nothing about Cei and nothing about the other things we talked of,' Ceinwen said, alluding to the more personal matters they had voiced.

Morveren readily nodded her agreement and took a deep breath before saying, 'Let's go and see if the war band's at home then.'

But it would be another month before the war band returned to Caer Cadarn. The wounded from the two battles on the Isis started to arrive in the first few days of their return to Whitehorse Hill and Ceinwen spent endless hours overseeing their treatment. Despite her tireless efforts and skill she was unable to save over half of those who returned laden on the back of the legion's carts and wains.

Ethain spent the majority of his time secluded in one of the huts where he spent long hours listening to Morveren as she related all that had happened in his absence, but the only times he talked about his own tale was when he paced across the dusty floor talking to himself.

News of the great victory was sent on to the Haven but any sense of renewed hope the Britons might have felt was negated by the legion's appalling losses; only one in ten had survived the battles against the Adren and when the rumours spread through the crowded town of the Adren army loose in the North then what little hope that remained turned to a sense of impending doom. They had thrown all they had at the Adren in the East and although they had won the battles against the more numerous enemy they now had nothing left with which to face the army in the North.

The councils of the three tribes argued what the best course of action was but knowing that they could neither surrender nor fight they eventually settled on the only option open to them; to wait for the return of the warlord and what remained of his war band.

Arthur stood with his captains on the flats below the white cliffs and surveyed the work that had taken four weeks to complete. Aelfric passed amongst them with a flagon of water and some dried bread.

Just over a mile of the Causeway had been completely levelled and great ramparts of earth now edged the flats. The last half mile of the tunnel that the Adren had used to get behind the Britons had been collapsed where possible and filled with the excavated earth of the Causeway where necessary. The marshes were at their lowest ebb and had yet to reclaim the scarred line where the Causeway had stood but the autumn rains would soon swell the waters and Britain's link to the rest of Middangeard would be severed.

Under the searing sun and plagued by insects it had been miserable and exhausting work for those digging and carting the earth and rocks away. They had worked in long shifts with the minimum of time to rest and eat but everyone had done their share and complaints had been few. With the task now completed everyone was taking an extended rest before starting the journey back to Caer Cadarn.

'At least we made the bastards pay dearly for crossing it.'

Arthur took his eyes away from the marshland and glanced at Balor who had spoken.

'And ever since. The Veiled City, the twin battles on the Isis,' Morgund added.

'We've paid our own price too,' Hengest said, quietly thinking of his father, Aelfhelm, lost in the Shadow Lands with Cei. They all thought of those close to them who had been lost since the war began.

'We won't be able to trade now with the other tribes on the far coast,' Aelfric said as he stood by Arthur and passed him the flagon.

'There are no other tribes now and what few survivors there might be won't be trading for many years,' Arthur replied without looking at the youngster.

'Haven't we locked the door after the thief's entered?' Aelfric asked, nodding at the levelled Causeway.

The warriors stared at him and Hengest readied himself to drag Aelfric clear of Arthur's blow but to their surprise Arthur turned and silently studied the fair-haired boy.

'That's exactly what we've done. And now the thief can't leave,' Arthur finally said still staring at the boy.

'Then we have one more battle to fight and victory lies in the West,' Aelfric answered, levelly returning Arthur's stare.

Hengest cringed expecting the youngster's insolence to be violently punished but again the response surprised him.

'Yes, we have one more battle to fight but no, victory can only lie in the East.'

'Then we go east?'

'No, my battle lies in the West with Lazure. Victory in the East will be sought by he who picks up Cei's sword,' Arthur answered and handed back the flagon of water.

Aelfric nodded as he took the flagon then turned and left. The warriors exchanged puzzled looks.

'Prepare everyone for the journey back to Caer Cadarn. We leave within the hour,' Arthur said then added to Elwyn, 'Send Sal to me.'

Elwyn stared at him blankly and Morgund hastily explained Sal was one of three brothers who were with the legion. When he still looked blank Morgund added they were Morveren's brothers.

Recognition dawned on Elwyn's face, 'He died. A dying Adren speared him as he sought amongst the bodies for our wounded. Bled to death, there was nothing anyone could do.'

Arthur turned away without a word and faced the marshes again as if he were reluctant to leave the Causeway behind him.

'That Anglian lad deserves a good hiding,' Balor said to the others as they drifted back towards the makeshift camp. He was annoyed that he had not understood the exchange between Arthur and the boy.

'He's got guts, I'll say that him,' Dystran, the tattooed Mercian replied.

'If he doesn't watch it he'll be strung up by them,' Gereint muttered, wondering how Arthur would have reacted if any of them had spoken to him like that.

Gwyna kept her silence and thoughtfully watched the boy's back as he strode ahead of them towards the resting legion. Morgund lagged behind already dreading the prospect of telling Morveren that her three brothers and Mar'h were all dead.

Ethain was the first to see the war band approaching Caer Cadarn. Morveren had finally persuaded him to leave his darkened refuge and take her horse out to give it a run. Ethain had eventually acquiesced knowing full well that her real reason had more to do with getting him to leave his self-imposed prison.

Over the last few weeks and despite his best efforts he had been unable to avoid speaking to most of the elders and recuperating warriors who were at Whitehorse Hill. They had all wanted to hear his tale of the Shadow Lands but so far he had managed to deflect their inquisitiveness and they seemed to respect his reticence; certainly no one appeared to hold him responsible for what had happened. This surprised him at first but in one of his darkened monologues he explained to himself that no one knew anything of what had happened, he was the only survivor and his was the only tale. The only truth was his.

Despite this realisation he still avoided contact with any of the others at the camp whenever it was possible and when he was cornered he kept his stories vague and understated, always searching his listeners' eyes for any signs of disbelief or any indication that they could sense his guilt. They treated him much like Morveren did; careful to respect the horrors he must have faced and unwilling to force him to confront the tragedy that had clearly unsettled his mind.

Gradually his guilt diminished and his lonely bitter arguments became more one-sided. Behind his downcast eyes and subdued tone Ethain started to laugh at those around him for being so gullible and he began to congratulate himself on his cleverness at escaping the Breton fortress and fooling those at Whitehorse Hill; all of them except Ceinwen whom he suspected did not believe his tales.

His confidence had grown to the point where he felt it was now time to move his prolonged and feigned recovery on to the next stage and so he had taken the reins from Morveren's hand and ridden her horse out onto the Ridgeway. It was time to rejoin the living.

Once clear of the camp he let his mask of composed sadness slip away and turned the horse to face the growing breeze from the West. He smiled contentedly as the soft wind rippled across the hillside and ruffled his scraggy beard. Perhaps he was not as brave as Cerdic or as stout-hearted as Cei but then, he reasoned, they would never again have even the simple pleasure of feeling the wind on their faces; he would.

On the distant horizon he could see the ranks of billowed clouds reaching high into the sky. He turned his borrowed horse and set out at a gentle pace with the declining sun warming his face. It was then that he saw the line of carts and horses in the distance.

He knew immediately it was the returning war band and he stopped and stared at the far line. His easy confidence shredded about him and without realising it his hands had once more begun to twist together, his nails raking each palm in turn.

His eyes flicked to the South and he briefly contemplated digging in his heels and fleeing back to the coast. His mind raced as he weighed the possibilities of surviving in the deserted villages of Wessex. He was tempted and had even turned the horse that way before he realised that fleeing would only undo all that he had already achieved in being accepted back at Caer Cadarn. He told himself that no one there yet doubted his vague version of events on the Breton Coast so why should anyone in the war band think differently? *No one except Ceinwen*, a small voice inside his head reminded him. He felt the familiar surge of panic welling up inside and fought to quell it.

He knew that riding south was not a good option; Ceinwen would only be sent to find him again - if he had not already starved – or the Adren would eventually catch him once they had defeated the Britons. No, he reasoned aloud to himself, the safest place for the time being was with the war band and when they were defeated he would flee along with the other survivors and take his chances then. *And what about Arthur?* His eyes strayed to the South again as he reminded himself about having to face the warlord. Surely he could fool the returning warriors just as he had those at Caer Cadarn? Surely Arthur would be too pre-occupied with the defeat of Britain for him to worry about one unimportant warrior? He was on the verge of convincing himself when the nagging question of Ceinwen resurfaced. *Perhaps you should have already done something about her*, he quietly told himself.

Ceinwen had been seeing to the wounded. She was kneeling by a tub of water with her sleeves rolled up above her elbows scrubbing away at her hands and forearms with a stiff brush when she heard the cry go up from the gates; the war band had been spotted on the Ridgeway. She threw the brush into the tub and sprung to her feet as Morveren raced by her.

As they climbed up to the wall by the East Gate Ethain rode through and made straight for the stables. Ceinwen watched him for a few seconds then joined Morveren who was already scanning the approaching column.

'Gods, there's not many are there?' Ceinwen said softly.

'There he is!' Morveren shouted excitedly pointing to the leading riders and clutching Ceinwen's arm.

'You already knew he was safe,' she said smiling.

'Seeing is knowing!' Morveren replied then started to scan the tail of the column where the foot soldiers walked alongside the carts.

'Can you see them?' she asked anxiously.

Ceinwen knew she meant her brothers but she was searching among the Wessex warriors who were leading the riders.

'Oh no,' she breathed quietly.

'What?'

'Mar'h.'

'He's not there?' Morveren asked switching her gaze to the approaching riders.

'No.'

'Then it must be true, he's dead. And I can't see Sal or the others either,' Morveren said, fear creeping into her voice. She had received no definite word concerning the fate of her brothers; some reports said all three were alive, later reports said they were all dead and the last group to have returned to Caer Cadarn said that only Sal had survived the battles.

It was a poor reception for a returning victorious army; the only ones there to greet them were their own wounded and the few elders who had remained at the camp. Morveren jumped the last few steps and landed lightly as the first of the warriors entered through the gate. She called out greetings to them and briefly clutched Morgund's hand before making her way back down the line towards the foot soldiers of the legion.

Once inside the compound the warriors wearily dismounted; it had been a long journey from the Causeway and they had only properly stopped once to rest. Those from the legion had taken it in turns to ride on the carts with the supplies but even so it had been a tiring journey under the heat of late summer.

Ceinwen embraced Balor then held him at arms length studying his face. Balor could not meet her eyes and it was Morgund who answered her unspoken question, 'He died in the second battle when the Adren broke the legion shield wall.' Morgund shrugged as Ceinwen looked at him sadly. There did not seem to be any more for Morgund to say, the details were not important; another friend had died in the war against the Adren. Morgund gazed out towards the gate where the legion were now filing through.

'Will she find any of them?' Ceinwen asked.

Balor cursed and led his horse away to the stables. Morgund shook his head. 'But we beat the bastards. Ten thousand of them we reckon and they're all crow meat now,' he said still gazing out to the gate.

'It will make a glorious tale,' she replied quietly, thinking about the remaining ten thousand Adren in the North.

'Yes, yes it will,' Morgund said, turning his gaze to her and silently acknowledging the unspoken thought.

'I'll see to your horse. Go after her.'

Morgund nodded his thanks and walked wearily to the gate. He found her sitting on the outer bank of the deep ditch that circled Caer Cadarn.

She was staring out to the East with tears running freely down her face. He sat beside her and drew her close.

'Is it worth it?' she asked quietly.

Morgund remained silent fearing how he would answer the question if it had been Morveren who had died and not her brothers.

Ceinwen stabled Morgund's horse and left Aelfric to see to the feeding and watering while she sought out Arthur in the main hall. He was standing by the raised top table listening to the reports from the elders who had stayed at Caer Cadarn. He saw Ceinwen approaching and signalled her to join them at the table. He dismissed the elders and sat down indicating for Ceinwen to do the same.

'They tell me we've had no news from the patrol shadowing the Adren army in the North for two weeks now,' Arthur said, pouring them both a cup of wine.

'That's not necessarily a worry,' she replied taking a sip from the cup.

Arthur nodded and started to eat from the food that had been hurriedly laid out on the table.

'We lost nine tenths of the legion and half our warriors. Half of their total force has been annihilated,' Arthur said summarising the two battles in the East in two sentences.

'So it's definitely true that Mar'h fell?' Ceinwen asked with sadness.

'Yes. I'm going to put Elwyn in charge of the legion now,' Arthur said tearing some bread and dunking it in his wine.

'Is that all you have to say?' Ceinwen flashed angrily.

Arthur continued eating the bread his gray eyes staring levelly at her.

'He was a friend of yours!' Ceinwen said accusingly.

'And now he's dead,' Arthur replied, not taking his eyes from her.

'You used to care for your warriors, your friends!'

Arthur put down the food he was eating, 'And now?'

'Now we're just pieces to be moved on a board! Victory is all that matters to you!'

'Victory *is* all that matters.'

The hall was beginning to fill with warriors looking for food and drink or a place to rest and some of them were glancing up towards the table at

Ceinwen's raised voice.

'Are you prepared to sacrifice every one of us?' she asked in an undertone of fury.

'Yes,' Arthur replied.

Ceinwen sat back in her chair shocked by Arthur's reply.

'Defeat would be total and Britain would be lost forever. The cost of stopping that is ultimately immaterial even if it takes every warrior's life to do so. You already know this.'

Ceinwen's stare faltered and she dropped her eyes to the table. She felt little connection to the man sitting opposite her, the man she thought she once knew so well. Yet despite her anger she knew he was right; if they wanted to defend Britain from an enemy like the Adren then they had to be prepared to fight to the last warrior to do it. Arthur had continued to stare at Ceinwen and suddenly he leant forwards searching her eyes, 'You found Ethain and...'

'We best go to your chamber,' she answered quickly.

They left the table and Arthur closed the chamber door behind her. She wondered absently who had repaired it since the last time Arthur was here. She sat on the low bed and wondered how and what she was going to say. Taking a deep breath she started, 'We got word two days ago that Seren has given birth to a daughter. It was early and the baby is underweight and sickly but the signs are that she will grow to health.' She looked up at him to see his reaction but he had already turned to face the open window.

'Did Seren survive the childbirth?'

'Yes and she too is apparently recovering.'

Arthur sat down and Ceinwen thought she saw relief on his face.

'Good. And Ethain? You found him?'

'We found more than Ethain. We found Merdynn.'

Chapter Ten

Morveren's long hair fell down across Morgund's face as she leant down to kiss him once more. What had started as a consoling embrace had given way to undeniable passion; it was if they needed to reaffirm both life and love amidst the memories of death and loss. As his hands caressed beneath her light tunic she tilted her head back in pleasure and saw before her the walls of Caer Cadarn. Abruptly she sat back on his thighs and brushed her hair away from her eyes, 'Not here. We're in full view of the walls!' she said placing a hand on his chest and gently pushing him back down.

Morgund laughed and sat up as she climbed off his legs. She wiped away the last vestiges of her tears and stood up offering him her hand.

'I'll stay sitting for a short while,' he replied.

She grinned and sat back down beside him placing her hand on his thigh. He gently lifted the hand and placed it on her own thigh. She laughed out loud and he felt delight at the sound of it. He had to fight the impulse to take her in his arms once more and sought around for a subject to distract him.

'So, while we were massacring the Adren did you enjoy your ride through Wessex with Ceinwen?'

'Gods! I forgot!' Morveren said jumping to her feet, 'Ethain, we found him and...' she stopped herself just in time.

'And what?'

'And he's here! At Caer Cadarn! Arthur will want to see him and I need to be there with Ceinwen!'

Morveren was already racing towards the gate so Morgund struggled to his feet and set off after her unsure which feeling was greater; relief that Ethain was still alive or irritation that clearly his reunion with Morveren would have to wait a little longer.

Morveren went straight to the hut where Ethain had made his home but he was not there. She searched the other dwellings with Morgund trailing around in her wake but Ethain was nowhere to be found.

'He must be here somewhere!' she said in frustration as she stood before the main hall.

Morgund gazed around the compound and shrugged wondering if it might be an appropriate time to remind her of other matters.

'I'd better go and see Arthur,' she said reluctantly and climbed the steps up to the hall.

Morgund resigned himself and followed her into the hall his thoughts now leaning towards a well-earned beer with Balor and Ceinwen. He almost bumped into Morveren who had stopped dead just inside the relative darkness of the hall. He saw immediately why she had stopped so suddenly; Ethain was sitting cross-legged on a table with his back to them surrounded by Anglian and Wessex warriors. He was relating the story of the Shadow Lands and they joined the back of the throng unnoticed by any except Aelfric who acknowledged them with a quick nod of his head. Some of the Anglians were asking Ethain how the others had met their fate.

'Herewulf and Ranulf fell first,' Ethain said, staring at the table's surface as if collecting his thoughts, 'We were making our way through a ruined city. It stretched further than I could see and it took us days to cross it. Ruins everywhere. Stone piled on stone as high as trees but no trees grew there, nothing grew there. Every ditch and vale was covered deep in snow and the wind tore through the ruins. The first we knew we were being watched was when the bells began tolling. Iron clanging on iron, some distant and some much closer. We thought it was the ghosts of the city wailing but it was something worse.' He raised his eyes and stared at the silent faces before him as if he had forgotten they were there. He lowered his head again trying to hide his eyes from the searching gazes. He resumed in a quiet voice and the silence around him deepened as they strained to hear every word.

'Merdynn called them the Irrades. They had lived there from a time before the city crashed in ruins. A host of ruined people poisoned for generations and scavenging a living from whatever they could find – and they had found us.

'They must have formed some alliance with the Adren because together they had set a trap for us in the heart of the city. Cerdic and I charged the Adren shield wall...' He bowed his head lower to avoid their rapt attention.

'In truth my horse bolted but Cerdic stayed by my side and together we smashed their wall. When my horse was killed beneath me Cerdic dragged me up into his saddle and we fought our way clear.'

The warriors murmured their approval both of Cerdic's bravery and Ethain's understatement of his own part in it.

'Herewulf and Ranulf were not so fortunate. They were unhorsed and fought bravely taking down many of the Adren but they were outnumbered. Wolfestan went back to help them but all three were slain. When we got clear we found that his sister, Elfida had been mortally wounded. As she lay dying in Cei's arms Cei told her that her brother was still alive and she died with some comfort even though the rest of us all knew that he too was dead.'

Again the voices of approval sounded around the table.

'But we had not escaped the trap entirely. The Irrades were waiting for us and Leah and I became separated from the others. We fought back-to-back and this time it was Leah who saved my life. She fought like four warriors and held them at bay until Cei could come back for us. As we fought our way clear of the city Osla and Wayland fell to the enemy's arrows.'

The voices grew louder again as Ethain paused in his story and the warriors shouted oaths of vengeance to each other and banged their fists on the table demanding to hear more. As Morveren gazed around at the warriors who were hearing for the first time what had become of Cei's band she saw Ceinwen on the far side of the gathering. She caught her eye and Ceinwen glanced off to her left. Morveren followed her look and saw Arthur standing well back from the throng and staring intently at Ethain. This was the first detailed account that they too had heard from Ethain.

Ethain was staring at his hands as they twisted and rubbed together. The clamour rose around him as the Anglians urged him to tell them more of the tale. Ethain's eyes flicked around them and he began again in a quiet voice. The others immediately fell silent.

'We covered a great distance through the driving snow and frozen shadows but an ice storm fell on us. For days we struggled on but it was impossible. So cold. Always hungry. Leofrun died in the storm. She would not call for rest and nor did she lag behind but the storm was too much for her. If we had not stopped when we did then I too would have died just hours after Leofrun.

'We built a cave in the deep snows and waited for the storm to pass. When it eventually did Cei and Merdynn decided we could go no further into the Shadow Lands, it was just impossible in the depths of winter. We made instead for the Breton coast where Merdynn knew of shelter and friends.

'But the enemy had not given us up and through ice and storm they tracked us, hunting us down. It was impossible to track us through that storm but somehow they did. They caught us on the Breton coast on a headland just by the safety of the fortress. We were so close but they were upon us before we could cross the sea ice. And that's where Cerdic saved my life for the last time.'

Ethain stopped and there was total silence in the hall. Everyone stood staring at him waiting for him to continue and the only movement was the twisting of his hands.

'Three of us, Cerdic, Roswitha and I stood on the headland while the others raced down a cliff path to get to the sea ice. We held the Adren at bay for as long as we could. Roswitha was the first to fall. An Adren spear took her. Cerdic and I fought on. I received a deep cut on my head and Cerdic shouted for me to escape down the path. I was loathe to leave him alone but I could hardly see for the blood and he pushed me back down the path. I'm ashamed to say I followed his order. He stood against the enemy by himself so that he could save me and the others.'

Ethain hung his head as if in shame but the warriors shouted that Cerdic was a hero and there was nothing else that Ethain could have done. In the uproar around the table no one noticed the small smile twitch across Ethain's lips. When the noise began to subside they demanded to hear the rest.

'Further down the path Thruidred and Godhelm were the next line of defence. They too died heroes as they held back the Adren long enough for Cei and the rest of us to reach the safety of the Breton fortress.'

Ethain took a deep breath. His mind was racing ahead to the conclusion of his tale and he was trying desperately to recall the version of events he had repeated over and over to himself.

A bead of sweat trickled from his temple as he continued, 'Together with the Bretons we held the fortress all winter long. The Adren came at us again and again. Sometimes they attacked the high wall and sometimes they came across the ice to launch attacks up the cliff paths. Aelfhelm, Cuthwin, Leah and Trevenna were always in the thick of the fighting and Cei was everywhere. The Bretons were brave but they were just ordinary people, not warriors. They fought well and Cei was proud of them. But the Adren were too many. They were remorseless. Leah was mortally wounded. She and I, we were... I began to lose hope but Merdynn kept us going, kept me going.'

His voice faltered and caught in his throat. The Anglians kept a respectful silence guessing that Leah and Ethain had formed a union. After a pause Ethain collected himself and continued.

'The Adren smashed the Breton boats just as the sea ice was thawing. We only had one small boat left. Merdynn had hoped to use it to get to Wessex to bring back other boats so that we could all escape but it became clear we could hold back the Adren no longer.

'They breached the wall and everyone knew the battle was finally lost. We fought a desperate rearguard back to the one boat. Aelfhelm fell during the chaotic retreat. He must have killed dozens of them during the winter months but they finally brought him down.'

The warriors turned their gaze to Hengest who hung his head at the news of his father's death.

'Cei and Trevenna fell on the steps before the boat, fighting to the last and taking down the enemy even as they fell side by side. Cuthwin and Merdynn were injured as they fought the Adren off the boat and as we pushed out to sea. I did what I could for them but we had no herbs or medicines and no food. I know nothing about healing. I failed them. Somehow Cuthwin directed us to Wessex but he died within sight of the shore. Merdynn was raving and beyond my help.

'I don't know why the gods spared me and me alone. I wish they hadn't. Each and every one of the others were braver, stronger warriors than I, and I least of all deserved to escape the enemy.'

Ethain lowered his head and covered his face with his hands. He knew this was the critical moment when the warriors would either comfort and praise him or when voices would be raised to question his tale. Hands reached out to grasp his shoulders and slap his back. Voices of praise and oaths to honour the dead rang out around him. His shoulders gently shook to the genuine sobs that coursed through his body. The warriors crowding around him thought he cried for the dead but his tears were of relief.

Morgund joined the others pressing around him but Morveren took a faltering step backwards horrified as the realisation sank in. She knew he was lying and that he had been lying all along. Everything he had said had somehow been a twisted truth and each time he had twisted that truth it had jarred in her mind. She was somehow sure that it was he who had murdered Cuthwin in the boat and he who had tried to slay Merdynn, and all in an attempt to save himself from having to face the Adren again. He had condemned Cei and whoever else was left at the fortress to certain death at the hands of the Adren.

The absolute certainty made her feel sick and she stumbled backwards. Arthur caught her in his arms. She looked up at him surprised to find him by her side and tried to voice her certainty.

'I know,' he simply said, his gray eyes emotionless and flat, 'When they finish hailing him as a hero bring him to my chamber.'

Arthur turned his back on the acclamations and returned to his room. He shut the door behind him and stood there resting his forehead against the rough wood.

'One of your lost warriors?'

He turned slowly to see Gwyna lounging on the bed.

'Yes. He was with a band in the Shadow Lands trying to stop the flow of Adren supplies.'

'You don't seem too pleased to see him,' Gwyna said, swinging her legs off the side of the bed and sitting up.

Arthur sat in the low chair without replying, irritated that Gwyna was in the room; the fact that she had every right to be in his room only irritated him further.

'He's the only one to have survived.'

'The sole survivor. He must be a mighty warrior,' she said, handing him a cup of wine and helping herself to one. Her tone of voice clearly implied she thought quite the contrary.

'You don't think he is?'

'There's many reasons why only one should survive of many. He doesn't look like a mighty warrior,' she shrugged and added, 'but then looks can be deceiving.'

They drank their wine without speaking while outside in the hall the noise from the warriors increased as more beer was consumed.

'We've had no news from those shadowing the Adren army,' Gwyna said, glancing at Arthur who nodded silently. 'But you have had news from the Haven I hear.'

Arthur looked at her sharply. She avoided his eyes and sought around for a clasp to tie her hair back. Arthur continued to stare at her while she nonchalantly brushed her long red hair back into one pleat and pinned it in place.

'I hear the Cithol girl gave birth to a child,' she said, still fiddling with her hair and feigning distraction.

'And what else would she give birth to if not a child?' Arthur replied, barely keeping his smouldering anger in check.

'I hear she gave birth to *your* child,' Gwyna said suddenly fixing her eyes on him and sounding far from distracted.

'It is of no concern to you.'

'I'm your wife! Of course it concerns me!' Gwyna spat back now standing before him.

'This happened before we were betrothed.'

'I demand you publicly disown both her and the child!' Gwyna shouted at him.

Arthur shot to his feet forcing her backward. He towered over the furious Uathach girl, 'Seren and the child are not of any concern to you and you demand nothing from me.' His voice was low and even but there was no mistaking the controlled fury underlying the words.

Gwyna glared up at him, her green eyes suddenly filled with hatred, then she turned and stormed from the room. She nearly collided with Ceinwen who was about to knock on the door. They stared at each other for a moment and Gwyna's eyes dropped to the axe that Ceinwen held half-concealed beneath her light cloak. For a second Ceinwen thought she was going to grab the axe from her hands but she tuned away with a curse and strode from the hall.

Ceinwen had already told Arthur everything she could remember about the encounter with Merdynn. The relief and joy that Arthur had felt at hearing the news had gradually ebbed away as she had related everything that Merdynn had said. She knew how Arthur must be feeling because she had felt the same; Merdynn still being alive was the best news any of them had heard for a year but countering that was his conviction that Cei and Trevenna were dead. The quest east had truly failed and even though Merdynn was still alive he seemed convinced he had no further part to play in the defence of Britain.

Much of what Ceinwen had said had puzzled Arthur but of one thing he was absolutely sure; Merdynn's preparation for leaving for the Western Lands could not be true. Arthur knew that Merdynn would no more abandon Britain than he himself would, and yet Merdynn was not going to stand alongside them in the defence of Britain. For the first time since the attack on Branque Arthur truly doubted if Britain could be saved. Despite the numbers facing them and despite the casualties they had already taken Arthur had still believed that victory was possible. He knew that ultimate victory could only be achieved in the East, in the Shadow Lands, but he had believed it possible to whittle down the Adren force that had invaded Britain until it reached a balance where he could finally defeat the enemy. Now he doubted it.

There was still one plan available to him but it relied entirely upon fortune and timing and he could control neither. It was a plan he had discussed with Merdynn and one that they had been desperate not to have to use but there now seemed no other option. If Merdynn was looking towards the future, as Ceinwen had said, then perhaps it was because he had already abandoned the present. If this war was lost then perhaps Merdynn was already looking to salvage something for the future.

Ceinwen hesitated at the open doorway. Arthur was standing by the window with his back to her and his head was bowed as if lost in thought. She looked down at the axe she carried and wondered if she should just turn around and leave him alone.

'No, come in,' Arthur said distractedly as if he were answering an interrupting question.

She felt a shudder go down her spine but she stepped into the room and closed the door firmly behind her. She laid the axe on the table and reached into her pocket to withdraw the Elk Stone pendant. She watched it slowly spin on the twine, rhythmically flashing as it caught the sunlight from outside.

'These are the possessions I told you about. The ones Merdynn gave me,' she said softly.

Arthur turned to her and stared at the turning stone as it alternatively flashed reflected light across their faces. He reached out his hand and she gently lowered it onto his palm. His fist clenched around it and his eyes dropped to the axe lying on the table. He bent down and traced his finger over the design that was deeply etched into the iron blade - a longboat in full sail.

'It is Cei's war axe, isn't it?' Ceinwen asked quietly.

'Yes.'

'And that's the pendant that Seren gave you. The one you gave to Trevenna.'

Arthur nodded in reply. Ceinwen sat down heavily and lowered her face into her hands.

'So it's true then. I knew it was but... they're all dead.' Her words were muffled but Arthur could hear the sad certainty in her voice.

'All except Merdynn,' Arthur replied sitting down opposite her, 'And Ethain.'

Ceinwen took her hands from her face alarmed by Arthur's tone, 'Arthur, Merdynn was adamant that no harm should come to Ethain.'

'And why would Merdynn demand Ethain's safety? You know what he's guilty of.'

'I don't know anything for certain other than he's lying, he's hiding something.'

'He killed Cuthwin. He tried to kill Merdynn. Merdynn was going to bring the Wessex boats to Cei's rescue but Ethain stopped him. Ethain killed Cei. He killed my sister and he killed anyone else who was still alive at the fortress.' Arthur's voice was implacable and Ceinwen knew he meant to kill Ethain.

'Arthur, listen to me, you must listen to me,' Ceinwen felt the panic rising inside her as she leant forwards across the table. Without realising she was doing it she took Arthur's hands in her own, 'Merdynn was insistent that you should not harm him!' Her words spilled quicker as she sought some way to convince him, 'They're linked somehow and Merdynn implied that Ethain was still important to the defence of our land. Why would he say that after Ethain had tried to kill him unless it were true? You must spare him! You must! You must show him mercy!'

'Mercy for the man who killed my sister?'

'The Adren killed Trevenna, not Ethain!'

'Ethain betrayed her and he betrayed Cei.'

'You must show him mercy!'

'There is no mercy for those betrayals.'

Someone rapped loudly on the door and Ceinwen swung her head round dreading it was Ethain and feeling the panic escalating beyond her control.

'If I ever meant anything to you, if Merdynn ever meant anything to you, you must not kill him!' she hissed gripping his hands desperately.

Arthur stood up and Ceinwen rose letting go of his hands and feeling a fresh wave of fear wash over her.

'Open the door and do not stand in my way,' Arthur said coldly.

Feeling herself shaking she crossed to the door and opened it; Morveren stood there looking ashen with Ethain behind her.

'Sorry we took so long. Ethain insisted on going back to his hut first,' Morveren said with a shrug.

They entered the room and the two women stood to one side as Ethain came to stand before Arthur. His face was still flushed from the acclamations and praise of the Anglian warriors but he was shifting nervously and his eyes would not meet Arthur's.

'Sit down, Ethain,' Arthur said indicating for him to take the seat opposite him. Ethain was reassured by Arthur's calm tone and ventured a flicker of a smile. Ceinwen groaned, suddenly fearing she would not have the courage to come between Arthur and his justice.

'I've heard your tale of the Shadow Lands. Is there anything you want to add to it?' Arthur asked and indicated once again for Ethain to sit.

'There's not much to add,' Ethain said hesitantly. He licked his dry lips and added, 'Except how sorry I am about your sister, and Cei. And Merdynn too.'

Arthur stared at him but he still refused to raise his eyes.

'Sit,' Arthur repeated and as Ethain did so Arthur saw for the first time what he had been shielding from him. As Ethain settled himself in the low chair he laid Merdynn's staff across his lap.

As Arthur stared in disbelief at the stout oak staff his gaze flattened and dulled. The silence stretched and Ethain fidgeted uneasily.

'How did you come by that staff?' Arthur finally asked as the life returned to his eyes.

'This?' Ethain said trying to sound casual and failing, 'Merdynn gave it to me on the boat. Perhaps he knew he was dying and...'

Ceinwen and Morveren stared at the staff both shocked that they had not recognised it earlier. Ceinwen started forward convinced that this was some sign from Merdynn.

'Get out!' Arthur suddenly roared at them, 'All of you leave!'

Ethain scrambled to his feet as Arthur snatched up Cei's axe from the table. Ceinwen dashed forward and grabbed Ethain dragging him towards the door that Morveren had wrenched open. As she slammed the door behind them Ceinwen heard the crash as the axe splintered the table.

She pushed Ethain ahead of her as she hurried him out of the hall. When they reached the main doors Ethain turned briefly and Ceinwen saw a triumphant smile flash across his sweating face.

Morveren stood with her back pressed against the door to Arthur's chamber. Her heart was thumping and the blood pounded in her ears as she tried to steady her breathing. The violent destruction in the room behind her ceased as suddenly as it had begun. She looked around the busy hall but none of the warriors seemed to have heard any of Arthur's rage; the Anglian and Wessex warriors had been joined by the Mercians and some of the Uathach and together they were making more than enough noise to have covered the splintering crashes from Arthur's chamber.

Her racing pulse began to steady and she thought through the last few minutes in the room behind her. Clearly Arthur knew Ethain's true role in the events concerning Cei and Merdynn and yet he had refrained from taking his head clean off his shoulders. She knew it had been the sight of Merdynn's staff in Ethain's possession that had spared the miserable wretch but she was puzzled as to why that would make Arthur stay his hand; if anything she thought it would have been enough to assure his quick and bloody departure.

The door flew open behind her and she whirled around to see Arthur standing there with Cei's axe still in his hand.

'Get four fresh horses ready, I'm taking a patrol north to find this Adren army for myself. You, Balor and Morgund are coming with me. Tell Ceinwen to keep a close watch on Ethain and to never let him be more than a hundred paces away from her.'

Arthur strode towards the gathered warriors and Morveren hurried away to prepare the horses and provisions. He saw Aelfric listening to the drinking warriors and made straight for him.

'Aelfric, gather everyone in Caer Cadarn who isn't able to fight in either the war band or the legion and leave for the Haven immediately. That includes you. Whatever orders I send to the Haven must be acted on instantly. Make sure the council understand this, make sure they understand that Britain's future relies upon this.'

Aelfric nodded but stood his ground, 'Can you not send another messenger? I want to stand with the Anglians.'

'No. If I thought you would be more use to me fighting then I would have already told you so. Take this,' Arthur said handing him the Elk Stone, 'and give it to Fin Seren. Tell her it's for our daughter. Make sure they are both safe.'

Aelfric left the hall to begin gathering the others and Arthur called Gereint and Elwyn across to him.

'Gereint, let them celebrate and sleep but from then on make sure the war band is constantly ready to ride to war. Elwyn, the same goes for the legion. I'm riding north to find the Adren army – it's been too long since we've heard from the patrol. Do either of you know where Gwyna is?'

'She left the hall before Ethain began relating his tale but Ruraidh's over there with Dystran,' Elwyn answered, pointing to a far corner of the hall where more of the warriors were drinking.

'Tell him what I've told you. Make sure everyone's prepared to leave at a moment's notice.'

Half an hour later Arthur's patrol rode out of Caer Cadarn heading northwest deep into the Mercian lands. Balor and Morgund were half-drunk and busy going over Ethain's story of the Shadow Lands until Arthur abruptly shut them up. They thought he did so because he had no wish to dwell upon Trevenna and Cei's deaths but the subdued Morveren knew better.

The towering clouds in the West had finally marched inland covering the declining sun and trapping the oppressive heat in a close blanket over the land. The coming storms could be felt in the humid air and the late summer light had taken on a filtered, yellowish quality. Morveren's horse was calm enough but the other three mounts could sense the imminent thunder and showed their nervousness. As the first distant rumbling of the storm echoed across the landscape she thanked the foresight that had told her to pack the oiled capes.

She untied a couple and turned in her saddle to lob them to Balor and Morgund who were dropping back to continue their conversation about Ethain out of Arthur's earshot. She handed one of the capes to Arthur and he wedged it in front of his saddle.

The thunder rolled across the West and as they headed onwards they watched the lightning flick from the heavy clouds ahead.

'We're heading straight for it,' Morveren said and ruffled her horse's mane just as lightning flashed closer to them. The thunder cracked through the air seconds later and Arthur's horse shied sideways in alarm.

'Should we seek some shelter?' she asked.

'The storms could last weeks. We haven't the time.'

'You think the Adren army could be that close?'

'We don't know where the Adren army is. We should and until we do then storms or no storms we'll keep looking for them,' Arthur replied.

'Where are we going to start?'

'We'll head north of the Haven and then cover the land further northwards until we find them.'

Morveren swore and pointed ahead.

'What is it?' Arthur asked.

'Here it comes!' she answered as she reached hurriedly for her cape.

Arthur saw it a good few seconds after Morveren and he too unrolled his cape; it seemed like an impenetrable veil of water was advancing towards them. A gust of wind blew the first of the heavy raindrops at them and then the rainstorm swept across them lashing the parched land with torrential rain.

Morgund urged his horse forward into the stinging rain until he caught up with the two ahead, 'Should we seek some shelter?' he shouted over the noise of the rain. As if to emphasise his question lightning tore through the air followed instantly by a deafening crack of thunder.

Morveren glanced at Arthur before replying, 'No! We're carrying on!'

Morgund could barely hear her but he caught the meaning and waited to give Balor the grim news while the other two pushed on into the storm. The cloudburst only lasted a few minutes and before long the rain had settled to a steady hammering rhythm. Lightning still flicked from the dark, blue-black clouds that stretched from horizon to horizon and the thunder rolled distantly across the land with only the occasional sudden and nerve-jarring crack overhead.

The first of the autumn rains had fallen on parched land and the standing water along the pathways and fields reflected the skies in broken ribbons of silver and black. They were riding their horses in single file and at walking pace taking care not to push their mounts on the slippery and uncertain conditions underfoot.

Morveren eased her horse alongside Arthur's and pulled back the hood of her cloak letting the rain fall on her long, dark hair.

'Are we heading towards the mountains?' she asked.

'That was my plan but on the high ground we'll see nothing in this,' Arthur replied, gesturing at the lowering clouds.

'So, where are we heading?' Morveren asked with her eyes closed and her head tilted up toward the rain.

Arthur glanced at her and watched as the rain splashed on her young face. Something about her half-smile reminded him of Seren and unseen by either her or the two following he smiled at her.

'Don't drown.'

She laughed and opened her eyes to look at him, 'You forget, I was raised by the sea. I doubt there's a better swimmer in the war band.'

The thought crossed both their minds that competition for that particular claim had been drastically reduced over the last few months. 'It's just that I haven't felt the rain on my face for so long,' she added lamely and wishing she hadn't made the boast.

'The best plan is still to cover the ground to the North of the Haven then double back and cover the ground further to the northeast and keep doing so until we find them.'

'Perhaps we should have brought Ceinwen along?'

Arthur shrugged before replying, 'Even we should be able to see signs of ten thousand Adren moving through the land.'

'True,' Morveren conceded before asking, 'Has your eyesight always been poor?'

'Only at distance.'

'Same here.'

They carried on riding side by side in silence and Morveren pulled her hood back over her head as a heavier rain squall swept across the fields. A few miles further on their path took them down into a wooded valley and the extra protection it offered prompted them to take a rest and have some food.

Morveren was uncharacteristically withdrawn during their stop and her unwillingness to engage in conversation continued during the full day's journey that followed. Morgund feared that she was succumbing to the fatalism of their situation and wondered if he would ever again hear the laughter that lightened his heart and fired his soul. Like Arthur before him he cursed the fate that had brought him so close to someone just as they were on the brink of losing everything.

The rain continued to fall. The sky seemed to be covered by one expanse of purposeful black cloud spilling in from the West and the thunder rolled and echoed to the tune of the blinding whips of lightning that lashed through the dim autumn light.

They passed north of the Estuary and continued deeper into the hills and valleys of West Mercia. Arthur wanted to cover at least fifty miles between each of the breaks that they took to rest and eat. And so they pushed on through the storms that covered the entire land. It was miserable travelling. They were utterly soaked despite the capes and had no immediate prospect of ever being dry again. They concentrated on putting the miles behind them and spoke little. Occasionally one of them would ride off to investigate a better view of a valley or climb a nearby vantage point to see what could be seen through the driving rain.

It was during one such excursion that Morveren finally worked up the courage to speak to Arthur about what was on her mind. They were building a lattice of branches and covering it with their capes to provide some shelter from the rain while Balor and Morgund were off exploring a nearby valley. They finished tying the capes in place and sat down under the meagre canopy with the rain dripping in a fringe all around them. They were on the edge of a thickly wooded and narrow valley and, having still not seen any sign of the Adren, Arthur had decided to attempt to light a rare fire.

Morveren watched him as he twisted the small bow around the hardwood fire stick. He placed the tip against the softer wood of the palette and began the drilling that might lead to enough of an ember to light the kindling. Whether the lit kindling would be enough to fire the damp wood was fairly doubtful but they both silently felt it was at least worth trying.

'I wanted to thank you, Arthur.'

Arthur glanced up questioningly before returning his attention to the fire lighting.

Morveren had spent too long working up the courage to broach the subject to now let it go unsaid. 'I wanted to thank you for accepting me into the war band. I know I wasn't one of the best prospects.'

'You're the best rider we have. And I'm including the Anglians and Mercians. You're useful with a bow and better than some with a sword. Why wouldn't I have accepted you?' Arthur spoke with his head bowed over the embryonic fire.

Morveren watched him, carefully trying to gauge any impatience or anger but she saw neither and pressed on, 'And there's everything you did for me and my village too. I wanted to thank you for that as well.'

Arthur shrugged in reply as he eased the glowing ember onto the dry straw kindling and began gently blowing on it.

Morveren glanced around the wood looking for any signs of the other two returning. She could see or hear nothing other than the rain falling through the trees. Arthur was placing small twigs around the flickering straw.

'Arthur, are you...'

'Yes.'

Morveren stared at him unable to finish her question or be sure of his answer. Arthur continued without looking up, 'I am your father. Your mother said I was and at the time I thought it was true. But I wasn't sure until recently. Now I have no doubt.' As he finished speaking he finally looked up at her and smiled before once again returning his attention to the growing but fragile fire.

Morveren looked at him dumbfounded, her mind racing but robbed of speech. She had never once thought she would be able to talk directly to Arthur about this and the fact that he was so casual about the whole matter just confounded all her expectations.

Arthur continued to build the fire, placing the damper logs in a tripod above the flames while feeding more sticks into the fire.

Morveren had no idea where to start so she started at the end, 'Recently?'

Arthur sat back and studied her for a moment. 'You remember back at Caer Cadarn when Ethain was retelling his tale of the Shadow Lands?'

Morveren looked confused and cast around for some connection between the two subjects.

'How did you feel as he related the story?' Arthur asked still studying her.

'Well, at first I was just listening like everyone else; enthralled, horrified but just desperate to find out what had happened.'

'You wanted to know the truth didn't you? Ceinwen doubted Ethain from the first moment she met up with Merdynn again but you were his friend and you desperately wanted to believe him.'

'He was my friend. Ethain, Elowen, Tomas, Talan and Tamsyn – we were a close group and he was part of that. He was the last.'

'But you heard the truth when he spoke in the hall even though he was not speaking the truth.'

'Yes, somehow, yes. He would come to a part of the story and even though he was not lying somehow he was twisting the truth. It felt wrong, something felt wrong. When he came to the end he told straight lies and it screeched through my mind. Like iron scraping down iron – I thought I was going to be sick.' Morveren brought her eyes up to Arthur's.

'That's when you fell and I caught you.'

'You knew I was feeling that?'

'Yes, you're my daughter.'

Morveren stared at him.

'My poor distance sight is not the only sight you've inherited from me.'

'The Gift? The Sight? I can see, into, people?'

Arthur shook his head and looked out into the rain-soaked woodland, 'It's not a gift, Morveren, not at all. It's not strong in you and you should never seek to make it stronger. It's a curse.'

'How can it be a curse? You know when people are lying to you, when they're being truthful!'

'Can you imagine what it's like to have that knowledge? Think about it. You love Morgund don't you?'

Morveren nodded in reply.

'Imagine if he knew every single thought you had about him. Imagine if you knew everything he felt and thought about you. And every thought he had about anyone else. It's not a gift. It's a curse. No matter how close you are to someone, whether they are a friend or a lover, such insight destroys everything.'

Morveren looked aghast. She had never thought about it quite like that before; every thought, every feeling, each small resentment or spark of anger laid bare. There had been times when she had felt like killing Morgund – of course she knew she could never harm him, but the thought had been there.

'How do you keep from going insane?'

'By learning not to use it. By shutting it out. By keeping everyone at a distance.'

Morveren cast her mind back to something Arthur had said some time ago, 'Seren, the Cithol girl, you said you can't read her...'

'That's true, it's true for all the Cithol.'

'That's why you had no idea the Cithol would betray us!'

Arthur nodded.

'And that's why you could not stay with my mother, or stay with Ceinwen, but why you can love Seren?'

'That kind of closeness can only be built on faith, not certainties.'

Morveren felt overwhelmed by the conversation and its revelations. A dozen questions formed in her mind only to be scrambled aside by dozens more. She plucked one out at random, 'Can you read me now?'

Arthur smiled, 'No, not any more. Not since Ethain and the hall. Now I can only read you if you wish me to – not that I need to; you're confused, scared and excited but of all of these you should be most scared. Control it, minimise it, shut it out or it will destroy you and everything you value.'

Morveren knew that Arthur was serious and she made a conscious effort to calm her excitement.

'How did you control it?'

'I was born that way. Even at a very young age I knew I was unlike the others but I had the sense to keep it to myself. Despite that, if it hadn't been for Merdynn's training I doubt I would have survived to see twenty.

Somehow he made it impossible for me to read my sister or Cei.'

'And so they became your closest friends.'

'Without them I would have gone insane.'

Morveren lowered her eyes, 'I'm sorry they're lost, Arthur.'

Arthur took Cei's axe from his belt and ran his finger along the design etched into the iron head. 'I sent them to their deaths. It was a desperate gamble. We've both lost friends, eh?'

They sat in silence for a moment with the rain drumming on the stretched capes above them. Morveren leant forward and poked at the struggling fire. 'And Merdynn? Could you read him?'

Again Arthur smiled, 'He could turn my thoughts aside like brushing away a fly. In fact he threatened to turn me into a fly if I ever tried without his permission.'

'Merdynn's good at scaring children.'

'I was older than you. And still scared enough to take him seriously.'

Morveren laughed aloud but the sullen woods dampened the sound as soon as it left their shelter and neither of their smiles lasted long.

'Ceinwen feels that victory is impossible now,' Morveren said quietly.

'I brought you to the war band so that I could better protect you. Not my only mistake.'

'Is there no way we can win against the Adren now?'

'We can still deny Lazure and the Adren victory.'

Morveren took heart at his words without realising he had not answered her question. They both looked up sharply as Morveren's horse neighed and stamped the ground; Balor and Morgund were hurriedly approaching.

'What should I tell Morgund of all this?' Morveren asked with a slight panic.

Leaving the shelter Arthur stood up and watched the two approaching warriors. As they neared he turned to Morveren and said, 'Tell him nothing, ever.'

Morveren nodded and called out to them, 'What is it?'

'Adren!' Morgund called back.

Arthur cursed and kicked the fire out, 'How many?'

'The whole bloody army!' Balor replied.

Morveren picked up both saddles and started preparing the horses.

'How far?' Arthur asked.

'Seven, eight miles to the North.'

Arthur cursed again. Morveren stopped what she was doing looking horrified, 'Then they're only a hundred miles north of the Haven!'

'And it looks like they're making straight for it,' Morgund added.

Chapter Eleven

W hich way?' Arthur asked. They were standing at the edge of the woodland where they had planned to rest.

'You see the dip in the ridgeline?' Morgund said pointing northwards. 'Beyond that there's a gully that winds down to a broad valley. Their army fills that valley.'

Arthur nodded. He could see the ridgeline that Morgund meant and reasoned he could find the gully easily enough. He looked from Morveren to Morgund weighing up his choice. The Haven had to be warned immediately but all his warriors were at Caer Cadarn and he needed them at the Haven as soon as possible; without them it would be defenceless. Morveren was by far the quickest rider among them with Morgund next in line while Arthur and Balor were a long way behind either.

If he sent Morveren to the Haven, which was much nearer, then they would have the maximum amount of warning but word would get to Caer Cadarn slower and hence the warriors' arrival at the Haven would be later, perhaps too late. Sending Morveren to Caer Cadarn would conversely increase the danger to those at the Haven who would have less time to prepare. Without wasting further time Arthur decided that Morveren's speed would be better used over the greater distance.

'Morveren, ride to Caer Cadarn. Bring the war band to the Haven. Cover the distance as fast as possible. Take the Estuary route on the way back – you'll have to swim the horses across the shifting river and you'll need to choose your ground carefully over the mud flats but it'll be quicker than riding all the way around.

'Morgund, make for the Haven and tell the chieftains to sail for the West immediately. At the most they'll have two days to finish preparing the ships, get the provisions and people on board and leave the harbour. Tell them to use the fishing boats if they have to. I don't care how you get it done or who you have to kill to make it happen but anyone not away by then will be trapped by the Adren.'

'Everyone's to sail for the West?' Morgund asked, shocked that Arthur was effectively ordering Britain to be abandoned.

'Yes. I know it's earlier than normal. I know the winds are from the

West and the journey will be hard. I know there'll barely be room for everyone on the tall ships. I know that the provisions will be tight. But make sure they know that anyone still on land two days after you arrive will be slaughtered. Don't try to organise a defence just get everyone and everything onboard those ships and burn whatever's left behind. The war band should arrive before the Adren. Just. Tell Kenwyn and the others it will be safe to return with the rising sun.'

'We aren't leaving with them?' Balor asked.

'No. Now go.'

Morveren embraced Morgund and said quietly into his ear, 'See that Seren and her child get away safely. And take care.' Then she jumped lightly up into her saddle.

'See you at the Haven!' She waved at them and sped away towards Caer Cadarn.

Arthur turned to look at the distant ridgeline fixing in his mind where Morgund had pointed out the gap.

Balor turned to Morgund, 'Bugger. For a while there I thought we might be sailing west with the others.'

Morgund grinned as he hoisted himself up into the saddle, 'They say the West is nice this time of year.'

'That's what they say.'

Without further words they parted and Morgund turned his horse to the South and set off along the outskirts of the wood.

'We'll trail their army for a while then make for the Haven,' Arthur said and headed towards the far gap that was now obscured by a curtain of rain.

Balor followed on behind him wondering how Arthur could be so confident that it would be safe for the others to return with the dawning sun. It took them an hour to reach the dip in the crest marking the beginning of the steep gully that cut down the far side of the hill and it took another hour for them to struggle down the switchback ravine.

The stream that had gorged its course into the hillside was now swollen with the storm rains and it broiled and tumbled from pool to pool in unheeding haste, forcing Arthur and Balor away from the smooth worn rock and into the tangled undergrowth that grew on the steep banks. They had left their horses at the head of the ravine and despite the arduous terrain and the difficulty of making headway they were glad for the cover it offered them; the Adren would doubtlessly have patrols ranging over the open hill country.

Half-way down, at a point where the stream switched back on itself once more, a narrow ledge offered a view of the valley below. They clambered across to it and lay flat on the smooth, wet surface. The distant storms still rumbled their thunder down the valleys and the clouds stretched from hilltop to hilltop like a low, dark canvas settling over the land.

Their view from the outcrop only provided them with a mile-wide cross section of the valley below but the Adren army filled that entire view; a creeping black stain on the green land. Arthur calculated how long it had been since Balor and Morgund had first seen the army and reckoned it to be at least four hours ago.

'Is this where you two saw them from?' he asked Balor.

'I think so. Enough of the bastards aren't there?'

Four hours and the Adren army was still passing the same point, and they hadn't seen the head or the tail of the snaking beast below them. Two uncomfortable hours later the black mass below them began to break up.

'Tell me what you see,' Arthur said.

'Looks like the tail end of the army. There's a lot of carts and wains bringing up the rear. Supplies I suppose.'

'Are they full or empty?'

Balor shifted trying to improve his view, 'We need Ethain here, he'd be able to tell you.'

'I'm asking you.'

'From what I can see they seem mostly empty,' Balor answered quickly.

'Good,' Arthur replied, edging his way back to the cover of the stunted trees. 'A thousand longbows and we'd slaughter them in these hills,' Arthur said bitterly with one last look back towards the Adren. Balor did not need to point out that they didn't even have a hundred.

Arthur decided to follow the tail of the Adren army for a day to get some idea of how fast the horde was covering the distance to the Haven before he and Balor cut south to intercept the war band. It seemed that those within the column were leap-frogging each other as the captains at the front took their soldiers aside to rest until the rear of the army approached then they would march on until they found themselves once more in the vanguard. In this way the army always appeared to be moving onwards and Arthur guessed they would be covering over twenty miles a day. They would reach the Haven within four or five days, probably two days after Morgund and about the same time as Morveren and the war band – if Morveren could reach Caer Cadarn in just two days.

In all the time they were studying the Adren army they saw no sign of any enemy patrols or flanking riders. Arthur wondered if Lazure's confidence meant he hadn't heard about the fate of his army in the East. No one had seen any Adren escape from those battles and they certainly hadn't left any alive but Arthur felt it unlikely that Lazure would remain ignorant of his eastern army's destruction. If he did know then he probably also knew that the Britons only had a handful of warriors left and that would explain why he was making straight for the Haven where the peoples of Britain were now unprotected.

It was difficult to gauge the size of the Adren army bearing down on the Haven as they were unable to see the whole of the straggling column at any one time. Their best guess put the enemy numbers at between seven and eight thousand which meant that any battles they had fought in the far North against the Uathach bands of Hund and Benoc had not only been decisively won by the Adren but that those victories had not cost them dearly; it also meant that Arthur's war band were now the only warriors left in Britain to stand against Lazure.

Morgund had to cover the last four miles to the Haven on foot; his horse had collapsed from exhaustion but he had made the journey in just under two days. He had left everything behind but his longbow and sword and set off at a steady run to arrive at the Haven soaked by the constant rain and splattered in mud.

He made straight for the better houses that overlooked the safe harbour knowing that was where he would find Kenwyn and Aelle, the Wessex and Anglian chieftains. The paths and thoroughfares were teeming with the peoples of Britain and although the town was designed to accommodate the migratory gatherings, those from the North had swelled the numbers and the Haven had not been designed to accommodate so many for so long. Morgund had seen the hurriedly erected and temporary shelters covering the slopes leading down to the harbour and despite his own exhaustion and haste he had marvelled at how so many people had been crowded into one place. He had also seen the full granaries and took some comfort from the fact that the harvests had been brought in before the rains had begun; without that the people of Britain would starve wherever they were.

As he pushed his way through the crowds some of them recognised him and pointed him out to others and he knew that soon most of the town would know that one of Arthur's warriors had been seen, alone and travel-stained, hastening towards the chieftains' houses and that rumours would spread quicker than summer fires.

When he arrived at the main house he immediately demanded to see Aelle and Kenwyn. His wild appearance and ready weapons terrified the head houseman and Morgund had to physically shake him before he was told that Aelle was in the long hall but Kenwyn was down by the ships. Morgund told him to fetch Kenwyn at once and the man fled to the wharves glad to get away from the wild warrior.

Morgund strode to the long hall and walked straight in. Aelle was talking to Fianna, one of Kenwyn's counsellors, whom Morgund knew from previous dealings in Wessex. She shot to her feet quickly for someone of her age. 'Morgund!' she said in surprise and fear crossed her face.

Aelle, the Anglian chieftain, remained seated and watched warily as the warrior strode towards them.

'What are you doing here? What's wrong?' Fianna asked as he stopped before their table then asked in a quieter voice, 'Where's Arthur?'

'I've sent for Kenwyn. We haven't much time.'

'Much time for what?' she asked still standing.

'Looks like you've had a hard journey,' Aelle said and looked at the water dripping from Morgund's clothes onto the polished floor. 'Surely there's time for you to change and rest, then we can get some food prepared for you.'

'No. There's no time at all.'

'What is it, Morgund? Are we in danger?' Fianna asked again.

Morgund nodded and took a cup of wine from the table. He drank it in one and wiped the back of his hand across his mouth.

'Help yourself,' Aelle said, it was his wine, 'and congratulations on the victory against the Adren army.'

Morgund looked back to the doorway just as Kenwyn hurried through into the hall. He stopped short at the sight of the dishevelled warrior and asked, 'What is it? Where's Arthur? And the war band?'

'There's an Adren army bearing down on the Haven. Arthur's shadowing them and the war band is racing to get here before the Adren do. You have to leave for the Western Lands immediately.'

The three of them stared at him and the only sound was the water dripping from his clothes. Then they all spoke at once, 'Impossible!' cried Aelle.

'How many of them?' Fianna asked.

'Can Arthur stop them?' Kenwyn said joining them around the table.

'There's ten thousand of them. They'll be here in a day's time, perhaps two, and they'll slaughter everyone still in the Haven. If Arthur and the war band arrive first they'll be outnumbered a hundred to one and still the Adren will slaughter everyone in the Haven. You have, at the most, two days to leave the harbour and if that's impossible then the Adren will slaughter whoever's left.'

'Gods,' Kenwyn muttered, sitting down heavily then repeated himself as he contemplated trying to evacuate over fifteen thousand people and all their provisions in just two days.

'But the Western Lands will be in winter by the time we get there! They're already in darkness! And we'll be sailing straight into the westerlies!' Aelle protested.

Fianna's mind was racing through the million things that needed to done in just a few short hours. She looked across to Aelle and said, 'It's that or we all die here.'

'Yes,' Morgund said and drained Fianna's wine too.

Morveren had pushed her horse as hard as she possibly dared knowing that if it came up lame or dropped from exhaustion then she would never reach the war band in time and they, in turn, would never reach the Haven in time. She put her fear of the Haven's impending doom behind her and concentrated solely on riding as well as she knew how, focusing entirely on the horse beneath her and the ground in front of her. She made it to Caer Cadarn just a few hours after Morgund reached the Haven; a feat that would have won her great acclaim had it not been lost in the events that were to follow.

She leapt from the saddle and raced for the main hall shouting out to the gathering warriors for someone to see to her trembling and lathered horse. They ignored her request and followed her into the hall knowing that something had to be gravely amiss for her to have ridden her treasured horse so close to death.

Ceinwen was standing by the doors watching her approaching friend with growing apprehension.

'What is it? What's wrong?' she asked as Morveren tore open the doors and burst into the hall. She followed her with the warriors crowding in behind them.

Gereint and Elwyn had been sitting by one of the fires talking with Gwyna when Morveren raced into the hall. They stood and watched the growing commotion by the doors as Morveren hurried towards them.

'Is everyone ready to leave immediately?' Morveren gasped when she stood before them.

'Yes. That's what Arthur ordered. You found the Adren?' Gereint replied.

'The legion too?' Morveren asked.

'Of course,' Elwyn answered.

'The Adren?' Gereint asked again.

'Yes. Lazure's ten thousand were a hundred miles north of the Haven two days ago. Morgund's gone to warn them. Arthur's shadowing the Adren and he's ordered everyone at the Haven to sail for the West immediately.'

There was uproar in the hall as questions rained down on her.

'We'll never make it!'

'What happened to the Uathach patrol tracking them?' Gwyna asked amidst the shouting.

'Abandon Britain? It's already winter in the West!'

'They'll never evacuate the Haven in the time they have!'

Gereint clambered up onto the table and roared for silence. 'The questions can wait! We leave for the Haven now!'

As the warriors pushed their way out of the hall Morveren turned to Gereint and said above the noise, 'Arthur said to cut across the Estuary. It'll be quicker!'

'What about the tide?' someone shouted out.

'I've been checking that and the winter high tide isn't due for another ten days!' Hengest answered from the crowd.

'Good, but by the gods we'll never get there in time. We leave immediately!' Gereint shouted out above the noise.

Gwyna put a hand on Gereint's arm to get his attention and pitched her voice so only he could hear, 'Ruraidh and I will ride ahead – I'm afraid the people from the North won't want to board the boats. Most of them have never even been on the sea let alone sailed for the Western Lands. I'll be able to convince them.'

Gereint nodded, 'Good luck and don't push your horses too hard, we won't be stopping for anyone!'

Gwyna pushed her way through the warriors to collect Ruraidh and two of her trusted warriors. They were the first to leave Whitehorse Hill.

As they were riding out the gate Ceinwen was standing before Ethain, 'Arthur ordered me to stay close to you - to help you and protect you,' she said, unable to keep her voice from implying the opposite, 'I'm going to the Haven. So are you.'

'But that's where the Adren are heading isn't it?'

'That's why we're going there.'

'We'll never get there before Lazure. Wouldn't we be better trying to defend Caer Cadarn?'

Ceinwen stared at him with disgust.

'Besides the boats would have sailed before either we or the Adren get there,' Ethain lamented.

Ceinwen despised the whining undertone to his words thinking she would have to force him to get on a horse but Ethain was thinking about what he had just said and he added quickly, 'Well, if we're going then let's get going, eh?'

Ceinwen watched him leave the hut uncertain whether to be suspicious or surprised at his sudden change of heart. Her instinct told her to be suspicious and she followed him out into the constant rain.

Within half an hour the war band were racing for the Haven leaving Caer Cadarn empty behind them; Gwyna was already five miles ahead.

Kenwyn stood at the beginning of the stone wharf that led to the anchored tall ships. The crowd in front of him was pushing to break through the cordon and the mass of bodies swayed forward forced onward by those behind.

The first thing he had done after the shock of Morgund's news had subsided was to gather together all the crews of the ships into the long hall. He and Aelle had explained to them the situation and what they intended to do.

The first priority was to ensure that the ships were ready to sail. As the time for the perennial journey was close at hand the twenty sea captains were able to report that little needed to done and, apart from bringing onboard the spare canvas sails and the new ropes, the ships were seaworthy enough to sail straight away.

The second priority was to get all the harvest and livestock onboard. In the time left to them this was going to be extremely difficult but if word got out about the approaching Adren then panic would make this almost impossible so Kenwyn ordered everyone present to keep the news of the Adren army to themselves for now.

The final priority was to get all the people now crowding the Haven onto the ships. Kenwyn stressed that it had to be done in that order. If the people learned of the Adren army then they would understandably panic and force their way onto the ships but if the ships were not seaworthy or if they hadn't been able to load the supplies then they would all die either on the crossing or in the Western Lands.

Keeping the news of the Adren army from the people was crucial to saving them. And also impossible. Inevitably the crews of the ships told their families or kin and Kenwyn had only managed to load half the supplies before chaotic panic gripped the Haven and the dock became besieged with people desperate to board the ships.

If it hadn't been for the narrower approach to the wharves then Kenwyn would have been unable to stop the crowds from spilling onto the half-supplied ships. As it was, it was all the crews could do to hold the populace at bay while Kenwyn alternatively begged and shouted at them trying to make them see reason and allow the provisions to be loaded.

Seren watched the confusion from the stone courtyard of the harbour master's house. She wore a loose cape as protection from the cold squalls of rain blowing in from the sea. Beyond the harbour the white-capped waves raced shoreward, driven by the strengthening westerly wind. Her cape flapped open as a gust whipped across the town and she clutched it tighter about her chest. She glanced down at the Elk Stone clasped in her left hand and smiled sadly to herself. When Aelfric had brought it to her earlier on she had immediately thought it signalled the end to the unspoken hope that she and Arthur may yet share a future. Aelfric had seen the distress in her eyes and had quickly said, 'Arthur told me to tell you it was for your daughter, his daughter.'

He had been relieved to see some of the anguish leave her face as she accepted the pendant. He was standing with her now in the lashing rain and he saw the sad smile cross her face. They both glanced back towards the warmth of the house where the infant was beginning to cry once more.

'Thank you for bringing me the Elk Stone, Aelfric,' she said then hesitated before adding, 'Is Arthur well?'

'Yes.' Aelfric thought back to Caer Cadarn and wondered if he told the truth. With Cei and Trevenna's deaths the mission in the Shadow Lands had failed and, although he did not know exactly what that mission had been, he knew that it had been imperative for victory over the Adren. Despite defeating the Adren on the banks of the Isis and despite the thousands they had killed between the Causeway and the Winter Wood it now looked like nothing could stop Lazure destroying the Haven and what remained of the warriors of Britain. Arthur had ordered the abandonment of Britain and now their final defeat seemed inevitable. And if the chaos below could not be controlled then Arthur would lose those he had sought to protect as well. He noticed that Seren was still looking at him and he shrugged, unwilling to share his thoughts with the stranger from the Veiled City.

'Animals! Stupid animals, look at them! They're condemning themselves to death, and it's no more than they deserve.'

They both turned to look at Terrill who had joined them by the stone wall. He was staring with open distaste at the heaving mob down by the dock.

'Crowds act like animals and this one is panicked but those people don't deserve to die at the hands of the Adren. Nor did your people. If your leaders had trusted Arthur most of them would still be safe and alive – if not in the Veiled City then here.' Aelfric answered calmly.

'And you call this safe?' Terrill laughed bitterly, 'Who is this boy? And what's he doing here?' he asked Seren.

'This is Aelfric of the Anglians. He had a message for me.'

'A panicked animal just needs calming,' Aelfric said and pointed down to the crowd. He smiled briefly to Seren, nodded to Terrill and left them without saying anything further.

'That child's not normal, even by their standards,' Terrill said sourly, not caring if the departing Aelfric overheard him.

'He's more than a child.'

Terrill looked at her and saw the excitement on her face as she stared at the crowds below them.

'It's Arthur,' she said quietly and pointed to the two riders at the back of the milling crowd.

Terrill looked at her with an open and equal mixture of revulsion and despair. 'That bastard killed your father, destroyed our city and left you with a child, and you still love him!'

'I see you're picking up some of the local language, good for you Terrill, perhaps one day we'll fit in after all, eh?'

'He betrayed everything!' Terrill shouted, his face contorted by all the hatred and despair that had festered inside him since the fall of the Veiled City.

Seren's playful charade shattered and she turned on him with a vitriol he had never seen before, 'Enough! My father betrayed my people! How many times do I have to say it? Is it possible that you're as stupid as you are jealous? Kane led my father into the darkness and he followed, the fool. Arthur might not have been able to save my city but he would have tried. He certainly would have saved my people. My father gave him no other choice than to tear everything down and bury as many Adren as possible. And still he fights to give his people and my daughter some hope for a land to live in! What have you done? Well? What have any of us done? Answer me!'

Terrill stared at the girl standing before him; her fists clenched, rage in her voice and hatred on her face.

'Nothing! You've done nothing! Our people's sole contribution to the war against the Adren was to lead the Britons into a trap and betray them! What a fine legacy we've left my daughter! I'm ashamed of my people and I'm ashamed of you! Get out of my sight! You disgust me!'

Terrill stumbled backwards ashen-faced and groped his way back through the doorway leaving the girl who had been his life-long love behind in the rain that still swept across the Haven.

Arthur and Balor pushed their horses deeper into the crowd.

'Get back!' Arthur roared at the crowd and turned his horse to force its way sideways into the throng shouting for Balor to do the same in the opposite direction. Gradually those at the rear began to back further away leaving room for those in the middle to do likewise and the two horsemen pushed their way to the front where Morgund stood with Kenwyn.

'What's going on here?' Arthur shouted to them.

'We've got half the stores loaded but then word got out about the Adren and this lot are demanding to get on the ships!'

Arthur turned and surveyed the crowd who had quietened and were now watching warily to see what would happen next. His horse sensed the danger and Arthur reined it in tightly as he stared at the faces in front of him. The quiet turned to silence.

'We have time!' Arthur roared at them, 'The Adren are coming but we have enough time!'

A wave of fear rippled across the crowd.

'How much time?' A man shouted from two or three rows back.

Arthur focussed on him, 'Enough time to load the supplies and then get everyone aboard!'

'We'll be slaughtered if the Adren get here first!' The same man replied to general shouts of agreement around him.

'If we don't load the supplies first then every one of you will die of starvation wintering in the West!'

'We'll take our chances! It's better than facing the Adren!' The man shouted, more to those around him than to Arthur. They agreed and readied themselves to break through the cordon.

'Where are the war band? They're supposed to protect us! Isn't that why we pay them a share of our crop?' The same man yelled out, emboldened by the support around him. Others took up the shout and the fear-fuelled anger of the crowd increased.

Arthur dismounted and slowly led his horse to Kenwyn and gave him the reins. The crowd watched his every move. He turned and stood facing them. Then he walked towards the man who had already said too much. The crowd parted before him and backed away. He spoke loudly and clearly as he made his way towards the man.

'I will not let you or anyone else dishonour the fallen. The war band have fought and died for a year to keep you safe. Time and again they've faced the Adren. Out-numbered a hundred to one. The legion. People like you. They too faced the Adren. And they too died to protect you.'

Arthur stopped before the outspoken man and his friends.

'They had courage!'

They fell back before his anger knowing that they were all dead men but Arthur took his hand away from his sword hilt and looked into each face before adding, 'I will not let you endanger everyone else. You will do as I say and you will live.'

The man glanced at his friends but they would not meet his eye; they too were quailing before the still simmering violence of the warlord.

'You,' Arthur said directly to him, 'And you four, take that cart through the line to the ships and then come back for the next one.'

They looked at him and Arthur pointed to the nearest loaded cart that was marooned in the crowd. Those around the cart hastily stepped away from it.

'Now!' Arthur roared at them, 'Have you forgotten that the Adren are coming?'

The fear of their immediate danger from the warlord, coupled with the reminder that the Adren were getting nearer every hour, spurred them into action and they hurried over to the cart.

'The rest of you! Kenwyn and his captains will give you orders. Obey them and everyone will get safely to the West!'

The fear and tension in the crowd broke as Kenwyn's men immediately began passing among them shouting various orders and directing people.

Arthur made his way back to Morgund and Balor.

Morgund was unhappily handing his friend a knife with a splendidly carved bone handle. Arthur watched them.

'He bet you were going to kill them,' Balor said, grinning as he slipped the knife into his belt.

'The day isn't over yet,' Arthur replied, 'We'll stay here for a while to make sure the loading continues then we'll ride to the ridge and watch for the war band.'

'And the Adren,' Balor added.

'Do you think there's enough time to get everyone away safely?' Morgund asked cautiously, still nettled he'd lost his favourite knife.

'No,' Arthur replied, 'but without the supplies loaded first even those we do get away will die.'

All around them the loading of the ships had resumed. Arthur looked up through the rain towards the harbour master's house and thought he saw someone standing in the courtyard. He wondered if it was Seren.

Seren saw Arthur looking up towards the courtyard where she stood and raised a hand in greeting but Arthur was already turning away and her greeting went unacknowledged. The rain felt colder and the familiar feeling of emptiness suddenly returned. The rainwater was sweeping across the stone floor, swilling around her feet and spilling out through a small gap in the wall forming a waterfall that fell down to the houses below. She watched it for a while lost in her thoughts then taking a deep breath she turned her face to the leaden skies waiting for the wave of sadness to pass, hoping the rain would somehow wash away the sense of futility that the sadness always brought.

She recalled the way she had spoken to Terrill and cringed inside knowing it was both unfair and cruel to have spoken such about his unsaid feelings for her. The memory of his reaction made her bow her head in shame. She knew she had no right to speak to him in such a manner especially as he had been one of the few to have stood by her over the last year. She also knew that there was no way to take back what had been said; it would change their relationship forever. Something else to feel sad about, she thought, and with a heavy sigh turned back towards the warmth and shelter of the house. She stopped dead staring at the figure in the doorway.

'You look more upset than your baby sounds.'

She ran to him and hugged him, 'Merdynn! We'd heard so many things and knew so little! I had no idea if you were alive or dead!'

'I know the feeling,' he answered with a smile.

'Come inside!'

'Splendid idea,' he replied not having left the shelter of the doorway.

'Have you seen the little one? It's foul out there. Does it always rain so much here?' The questions spilled from her and she reminded him of the child she used to be. He let her ramble as he sought out a warm, dry cloak for her. When they were eventually seated in front of the fire, he with a hot drink and she feeding the infant, Seren finally became more serious, 'The Adren are close, aren't they?'

'Indeed they are.'

'Will we have time to get away?'

Now that Seren had finished feeding the infant Merdynn leant forwards to take a closer look at the baby.

'That seems to be Arthur's plan. Either way I'm here to make sure you're safe,' he said offering the baby his little finger to grasp, 'She has her father's complexion but your eyes,' he said, returning his attention back to Seren.

Seren looked at the child in her arms still somewhat in awe that she had given birth to the life she now held, 'She's part Cithol, part Briton; part me, part Arthur.'

'And ruler of both.'

'Arthur hasn't seen her yet,' Seren said, the sadness stealing its way back in.

'I meant Cithol and Briton.'

'Oh. Well, there's not many left of us to rule is there?'

'More survived the downfall of the Veiled City than you might think.'

'And how many of the Britons will survive?'

Merdynn sat back and the baby squalled its disapproval. Seren swayed her in her arms until she settled once more.

'Have you chosen a name for her yet?'

'You know it's our custom to wait for a year before naming our young.

It was you who named me after all. How can you name a child before you know its nature?'

Merdynn laughed, 'How indeed. It's a very serious business.'

'Don't mock us or our customs,' Seren replied but her smile robbed the words of any reproach.

The baby soon fell asleep and Merdynn suggested he take her to the cot in the other room where Aelfric was endeavouring to cook a last meal before they left for the ships. Seren was surprised by the old man's gentleness as he gently lifted the baby and carried her away.

Seren settled herself in her chair hoping to get some sleep while the baby slept. She wondered when the Britons would come to fetch them to board the boats. At least the packing for the voyage had been easy, she thought; they owned nothing. She opened her eyes and saw Merdynn watching her from the doorway, the baby still in his arms.

'Arthur would have come to see you both if he possibly could, you know that don't you?' he said softly.

'Perhaps when we're safe in the Western Lands, when all this is over.'

Merdynn nodded but neither believed it likely.

Gereint looked back across the mud flats of the Estuary. The rest of the war band were filing past him as they led their horses up the steep path. The sweeping rain hid most of the wide Estuary and he could no longer see the shifting river that cut its way through the flats. On the far southern bank Elwyn had come up to him and told him that he had just discovered that the legion riders were not trained to swim their horses across rivers.

Gereint had been loathe to have them take the long way round; without the legion's riders their numbers would be almost halved and he knew the Haven would need every last one of them. He called Hengest and Ceinwen over and briefly sought their opinion. They decided they would lash the legion horses to their more experienced mounts and rig a rope handrail across the river to help the legion's soldiers to cross.

They knew it would add to their journey time but hoped the extra hour or two was worth their arriving together. The shifting river was wide and the rains had strengthened its current; two of the legion had drowned trying to cross it but Gereint estimated it had only added an hour to their race for the Haven.

As the last of the war band filed past him he turned away from the Estuary believing he had made the right choice despite the loss of life.

Ceinwen felt the same way and as she re-mounted to begin the last leg of the dash for the Haven she wondered how far behind Morveren was. Almost every spare horse from Caer Cadarn had been sent to the Haven and the only mounts not belonging to one of the warriors or legion were two venerable warhorses neither of which were capable of the journey. Morveren had decided to rest her own horse for a day then try to make up the time on those who left before her. Ethain had volunteered to let Morveren take his horse and Ceinwen had been tempted reasoning that it would be much better to have her friend by her side in the coming battle than to have Ethain standing behind her. If it hadn't been for Arthur's order to keep Ethain within her sight she would have gladly left him behind.

She looked around in a sudden panic thinking Ethain might have taken the opportunity to sidle away whilst she had been distracted. He was sitting on his horse a few yards away smiling at her and when the relief showed on her face he laughed out loud. Those around them took heart that he could laugh when they faced such danger but then again, they reasoned, when you've fought your way through the Shadow Lands what else was there left to fear?

He laughed again when he heard their comments and shouted out, 'The Haven!' The cry was taken up around him and once again the mad dash for the Haven resumed. Despite her distaste Ceinwen rode as close to him as she could.

Arthur stood at the crest of the long sloping rise looking back down to the Haven. When he had been sure that the panic of the populace had been channelled into readying the ships he had ridden to the vantage point of the crest taking Morgund and Balor with him. He had then sent the other two onwards to maximise their warning of the approaching Adren army.

He stared at the scattered barns and pens that littered the gentle slope all the way down to the Haven. Most of them were empty now. He studied the town that was mainly comprised of tightly grouped wooden houses radiating out from the wharves where the tall ships were still berthed.

The Haven was impossible to defend. No Uathach raid had ever come this far and it had never been necessary to defend the town and so no defences had ever been built. Even if he had a year Arthur knew that it would be impossible to make the town safe from attack. There were about fifteen thousand sheltering at the Haven but the legion had taken the best of those fit and able to fight and those that now remained would never be able to stand against a ten thousand strong Adren army. The Haven was doomed and it only remained to be seen if the people there were doomed too.

The far end of the Haven was obscured by the grey curtains of rain that were continually pushed shoreward by the fierce wind from the West. The Mercian sea captains had assured Arthur that it would be possible to use rowed barges to tow the ships out to the open sea where their sails could take them away from land, although their first course would have to take them dangerously close to where the flats of the Estuary began. Even though the unseen sun was already setting towards the eastern horizon the journey west would not normally be undertaken for a few more weeks when the gales from the West settled and lost their ferocity. With the winds as they were now it would be a hard, long journey to the Western Lands.

Something caught Arthur's eye and he stared out to the eastern approach to the Haven. He could see horsemen racing towards the town. They were tightly grouped, perhaps four or five of them, and they were pushing their horses hard. He cursed his eyesight and wondered why there should be an advance guard for the war band and how far behind this group the others were.

He turned his attention back to the North and saw Morgund riding hard towards the crest with Balor trailing some way behind. Adrenaline surged through him but he held his ground and waited for Morgund to draw level.

'How far?'

'Fourteen, fifteen miles,' Morgund replied between breaths.

'Tell Kenwyn to cast any unloaded supplies into the sea and finish getting everyone onboard.'

Morgund turned to go and Arthur shouted after him, 'And make sure Seren and the Cithol get aboard one of the ships!'

Without turning Morgund raised a hand to show he had heard and galloped down to the Haven cursing himself for having forgotten Morveren's very same message. As Arthur waited for the labouring Balor he stared to the East looking for some sign of the war band.

Chapter Twelve

Morgund rode straight for the wharves where Kenwyn was still organising the last of the supplies and told him he had two to three hours to get everyone onboard the ships. Kenwyn immediately shouted out the orders for his captains to begin the evacuation. He had fifteen thousand people to embark and only three hours to do it in but he was confident it could be done if people didn't panic.

Morgund left him to it and made his way towards the harbour master's house where the Cithol were quartered. Half-way there he heard hooves and turned around to see Gwyna racing towards him with Ruraidh and two of her warriors following close behind. He waited for them.

'We've been trying to find the Cithol! Do you know where they're billeted?' Gwyna shouted as she approached him.

'They're up at the harbour master's house – I'm just going there. Why?'

'Arthur had given Morveren a message for the Cithol girl, Seren, but she forgot to pass it on,' Gwyna smiled and shrugged and Morgund knew exactly what the shrug implied; Morveren's pretty enough but it was stupid to rely on her for anything. Gwyna knew exactly what she was doing, knowing that the unspoken insult would avert Morgund's attention away from the plausibility of her answer.

'Where's the war band – and Morveren?' Morgund asked trying to hide his dislike of Arthur's wife.

'A few miles behind us. And Arthur?'

'Up on the ridgeline. The Adren are only hours away.'

'Best hurry then,' she replied, indicating Morgund to lead the way onwards.

He nodded and, still smarting from the implied insult to Morveren, led the way up to the harbour master's house with the Uathach following silently in the driving rain. They dismounted in the courtyard and Morgund knocked on the door before pushing it open.

Seren started awake at the sudden intrusion and looked around in alarm. When she saw Morgund she relaxed and sat upright, rubbing the tiredness from her eyes. She looked up wary once again as the others filed into the room behind him.

'Is it time to leave? And do we need so many guards?' she asked, wondering why so many had come to deliver the simple message.

'Yes and no,' Gwyna answered from behind Morgund as she drew a knife from her belt.

Morgund heard the unsuppressed hatred in her voice and was turning to face her when she drove her knife upwards into his back. Blood coughed from his mouth as he cried out. He staggered forwards reaching for the knife he had lost to Balor but Ruraidh hacked him down and he collapsed to his knees. Ruraidh gripped his sword with both hands and plunged it down through Morgund's shoulder. He had to plant his foot on Morgund's back to pull his sword free.

Seren stared at the sudden horror and Gwyna turned to face her, 'Yes it's time for you to leave, but no, where you're going you won't need any guards.'

She took a pace towards Seren who stumbled backwards, 'Why?' she asked, staring from Morgund's prone body to the advancing Gwyna.

'I'll not have you or your bastard whelp stealing from me what's mine.'

'Stealing what?' Seren asked now focused on the danger before her.

'I'm not having you or Arthur's bastard interfering with my right to rule. Now, where is the half-caste whelp?'

Seren was unable to stop her eyes flicking towards the room where her baby lay sleeping.

Gwyna laughed and motioned for Ruraidh to bring the infant to her. There was a struggle in the other room and Ruraidh returned with Terrill at sword point.

'Where's the child?' Gwyna spat at him.

'There's no one in there, just an empty cot and this bastard ghost quivering in a corner.'

'Where's the child?' Gwyna repeated to Seren advancing with her knife poised before her.

Seren's mind panicked, where was her child if not in the next room? Suddenly she realised and she smiled coldly at the Uathach girl, 'You'll never find her, not now. She's safe.'

Gwyna snarled, 'You'll tell me and you'll think childbirth was painless before I finally let you die.'

231

Terrill caught Seren's eye and shouted, 'Run!' At the same instant and with surprising speed he dived forward away from Ruraidh's sword and snatched up a chair. He swung it around in an arc just as Ruraidh rushed at him, catching him full in the face. Seren darted for the doorway. Terrill threw the chair at one of the Uathach warriors and flung himself at Gwyna. She buried her knife in his chest and whipping it free threw it at Seren who was already half-way through the door. It caught her in the base of the skull and she crashed forward, dead before she hit the floor.

Gwyna screamed in rage and kicked out at the dying Terrill.

'Pick him up,' she said, pointing to the unconscious Ruraidh with obvious contempt, disgusted at how easily Terrill had managed to get away from him.

She strode into the other room to make sure that it was indeed empty and kicked over the cot with another howl of rage before leaving for the courtyard. Behind her Aelfric slipped from his hiding place and stepping over the upturned cot he hurried from the room.

Gwyna stood by the courtyard wall where Seren had earlier watched Arthur quell the panicking crowd. The cold wind from the West still drove the lowering clouds landwards and the heavy rain slanted across the thousands now gathering on the wharf. She knew it would be hopeless to search for the infant among so many people but Seren had said the child was safe; it could only mean that she had sent it on ahead of her to the ships. Gwyna smiled to herself, if she couldn't eliminate the threat to her ambitions here then she would have to do so in the West. She went back inside and ordered the others to follow her down to the wharf.

Once he was sure they were gone Aelfric crept back into the room to see if there was anything to be done for Seren and Terrill. He checked Terrill first then knelt by Seren. Both were dead. He drew the knife out and taking the shawl from her shoulders he wiped the blade clean. He put the knife in his belt and the shawl inside his tunic. He gently turned Seren onto her back and, as he closed her staring green eyes, he slipped the Elk Stone from her around her neck and put it in his pocket. He muttered a promise and with a last look at the two lifeless forms he left the harbour master's house and made his way through the crowds down to the wharf.

Arthur and Balor rode down to meet Gereint who was at the head of the approaching war band.

'You made good time!' Arthur called out as he reined in his horse.

'How far away are the bastards?'

'An hour. Perhaps two,' Arthur replied as he looked around at the circling warriors, 'Where's Gwyna?'

'She must be here by now – she and three of her warriors were a few miles ahead of us.'

'And Morveren?' Arthur asked looking at Ceinwen.

'She got to us impossibly quickly but her horse nearly died under her – she's some way behind us.'

'Are we going to face the Adren in open battle?' Hengest asked.

'Not yet. First we'll make sure there's no panic down by the wharf,' Arthur answered and hauling his horse around headed towards the town and the docks.

Gwyna was already at the head of the wharf arguing with Kenwyn, 'Arthur's ordered me to lead the first ship out of the harbour!'

'He never mentioned that to me but we could certainly use the four of you to help row one of the barges that lead the ships out.'

'Fool! Do you know who I am?'

'Yes, Arthur's wife,' he replied, resisting the temptation to elaborate.

'And you think I'm rowing a barge to lead out the first ship?'

'No. That one's already on its way,' Kenwyn replied evenly, looking over his shoulder to where the first of the tall ships was swinging away from the stone wharf, 'But you could help with the second.'

Gwyna was about to loose a poisonous tirade at him when she heard horses forcing their way through the waiting crowd that milled around them.

Arthur urged his horse closer to them and stared at Gwyna. She looked away from him and gesturing at the throngs around them said, 'We thought they might need help controlling the crowd and I might need the rest of my warriors to do so properly – there's thousands here,' she replied ignoring Kenwyn's pointed look at her.

Arthur's attention was diverted as Ruraidh swayed in his saddle. He would have fallen if the warrior by his side hadn't grabbed his arm.

'What happened to him?' Arthur said indicating Ruraidh's bruised and bloody face.

'The fool fell when his horse slipped as we came into town.'

Arthur studied her for a second knowing that she was hiding something but a sudden disturbance distracted him and he swung around to find the source of the fighting.

'Sort them out then,' he said indicting the commotion before adding, 'Have you seen Morgund?'

'He was on his way to deliver a message to the Cithol,' Gwyna called back and hurried away from him taking her warriors with her.

He returned his attention to Kenwyn, 'How long?'

'That's the second ship away now. Maybe two hours before the last one casts off.'

'You might have an hour but don't plan on any more than that.'

The normally mild Kenwyn uttered a foul curse and began shouting at his captains with renewed urgency. Arthur had the uneasy feeling that he had been distracted from something important but having despatched Morgund to see to Seren's safety and with the Uathach now controlling the crowds, Arthur cast his concern aside and turned his attention to the army bearing down on their position. He ordered the war band to make for the brow of the hill overlooking the Haven. As he was leaving he called out to Kenwyn, 'Have you seen Laethrig?'

Kenwyn nodded, the Wessex blacksmith was working in the barges helping to tow the ships out of the harbour, 'He gave me a message for you – he's done what you've asked him to and it's where you asked it to be!'

Arthur raised a hand in acknowledgement and set off after the war band. In the noise and chaos of the crowds he didn't hear Aelfric shouting to him and the young Anglian, unable to force his way through the mass of people, could only watch as Arthur rode from the town.

The rain eased as the warriors lined up along the ridge but the heavy, black clouds out to sea promised it would only be a temporary respite. The ground underfoot was already sodden and rivulets of rainwater coursed through the long grass.

Arthur surveyed the two gentle slopes; one leading back to the frantic Haven, the other gradually falling to the wide valley floor where the Adren army would soon be appearing. Arthur weighed up his options. With their horses they had some mobility but the race from Caer Cadarn had brought every mount close to exhaustion. There were no walls, no towers, no bridges; there was nothing to defend and nothing to offer any cover for the defenders. With Gwyna's Uathach down by the wharf there were less than a hundred warriors lined along the crest and the army approaching them outnumbered them by a hundred to one.

None of this was lost on Ethain. Ceinwen had never let him out of her sight or let him stray too far from her side. He was sick with fear and bitterly angry that he had come so far and done so much to secure his safety only to be finally trapped in open country with his chances of escape diminishing by the second. He looked over his shoulder down to the harbour and saw another ship slip away from the long stone jetties. If he could he would have gladly killed every single person around him just to be on that ship.

Ceinwen watched him twisting his hands together, raking his nails down the back of one hand then across his palm and then repeating the action on the other hand. Perhaps, she thought, he's trying to clean the blood from his hands. She found herself wishing that Arthur had just killed him or let him go, in spite of what Merdynn had said. She was sick of watching over him and even sicker of the continual goodwill expressed to him by the other warriors. If I told them the truth, she thought, he'd be dead in seconds and I could set about preparing myself for the passage to the next life.

Balor's voice brought her back to the present, 'Looking forward to avenging Cei and the others?'

For a disconcerting moment she thought he was talking to her about her wish to be rid of Ethain but Balor was looking at Ethain and clearly addressing his question to him. Ethain swallowed the bile he felt rising at the back of his throat and managed a sickly smile before turning his back on them and staring out to where the Adren army was expected to arrive.

'Where's Morgund?' Ceinwen asked him.

'Still getting Seren and the other Cithol on board the ships. He's taking his bloody time about it too. Bastard's probably sneaking aboard himself.'

Ceinwen smiled, 'He'll be here before the Adren arrive.'

'More fool him,' Ethain said before he could stop himself. Balor mistook the bitterness for jesting and laughed again, thumping Ethain on the back and nearly undoing all the good work that Ethain had just managed by not vomiting.

'And Morveren?' Balor asked.

'Riding to catch us up.'

'They'll miss all the glory if they don't hurry up,' Ethain said, pointing to the valley.

Even Balor caught the sourness in his voice this time but others along the line were shouting out the same news and he stared out to where they pointed.

Arthur looked back to the Haven. A third of the ships still stood along the wharf. Gereint rode up closer to Arthur, 'They'll have to speed things up if they're all to get away!'

'I'll ride down and warn them – and bring the Uathach back!' Ethain offered, pathetically grasping for a chance of salvation.

'We need your courage here,' Ceinwen pointed out. Arthur sent another of the warriors racing down to Kenwyn with the news. Ethain shrugged, desperate to believe that another opportunity would present itself before the last ship sailed for the West.

Arthur adjusted Cei's axe that was tucked into the belts that crossed his back and surveyed the battlefield one last time. He knew that if they attacked the Adren flanks in an attempt to draw the army away from the Haven the enemy would just wheel off one or two thousand soldiers who would form up to meet the flanking threat while the main body marched onwards to the Haven. They had done as much when riders had previously attacked Adren columns.

Neither was there anything to be gained by holding their ground against so many, the sheer weight of the advancing army would just roll over them and they would have achieved nothing. No, for his plan to have any chance of success he needed to keep his war band alive. He decided to use the two of the advantages they had over the Adren; their longbows and horses. They would ride to within three hundred yards of the enemy vanguard, dismount, loose as many arrows as they could before retreating on horseback another three hundred yards and repeating the process. It would hardly slow their advance, the Adren had already proved themselves willing to die to gain ground, but die they would and

Arthur was prepared to settle for that, for now. He called out his orders and the warriors of the South rode down to meet the Adren army.

They reined in their horses three hundred yards from the fore ranks of the Adren and leapt from their saddles. They pegged their horses' reins into the soft ground and strung their bows. Many of them cast apprehensive looks to the dark clouds knowing that if it began raining heavily again their bows would soon be useless.

The scattered vanguard of the Adren were forming up into closer ranks as the first volley flew at them; the second and third were in the air before the first hit home. The arrows from the legions' shorter bows arced higher than those from the longbows and the advancing Adren had to choose whether to hold their shields before them or raised. Their captains urged them onwards up the slope prepared to sacrifice casualties for speed. The Britons had loosed five hundred arrows in the time in took the Adren to cover two hundred yards and before Arthur shouted out to start the first retreat.

Thinking the Britons were fleeing a great roar went up from the Adren and they charged onwards. As they attacked uphill the army spread across the slope and any semblance of order disappeared in their haste to close with the enemy that had killed so many of their soldiers.

The Britons stopped and, without having to string their bows, fired over seven hundred arrows into the attacking mass. Once again they retreated and reformed, now lined along the ridgeline. Hundreds of Adren dead littered the hillside but their bodies were hidden by the swarming horde that now spread across a mile of the grassy slope.

Arthur left it until the last possible second before ordering the warriors to fall back once again; to their left and right the unchecked Adren were already further forward than the Britons' position. Another roar echoed across the land as the enemy gained the ridge and saw the Haven below them.

As Arthur charged back to the next firing line he tried to count how many ships had yet to sail from the Haven.

Gereint was riding close by him and shouting out to him, 'They'll never all get away! We can't even slow the Adren advance!'

With the enemy now almost all around them the warriors fired from their saddles, wheeling about to face their targets, loose their arrows and turn again to put enough distance between themselves and the charging mass.

Aelfric watched Arthur's fighting retreat down the slope towards the Haven from the stern of a tall ship. People were crowded all around him and they too watched the unequal battle. Some were shouting out encouragement but most of the watchers were silent. The hillside was seething, covered by the advancing Adren who were overwhelming the small knot of mounted warriors as they turned, fought and retreated back to the edge of the town.

Aelfric watched the line from a tow barge rise dripping from the harbour water as the rowers took the strain and the bow of another ship turned slowly away from the wharf. He knew it would be the last to leave the Haven. Those around him knew it too and all eyes turned to the desperate crowd on the jetty, their frantic panic to escape being the very thing that would ultimately deny them any possibility of getting away. Behind him their own rowers were clambering onboard and he turned to see Laethrig hastening towards him. Like everyone else on the ship he was unable to resist witnessing the death of the Haven. Overhead the topsail cracked in the fierce wind and the icy rain once again swept shoreward.

The warriors were being pushed back to the wharf. They fought a running battle in the mud-churned roadways of the town. They fought from horseback with swords and axes, having abandoned their bows in the close fighting on the edge of town. The Adren were to either side of them and ahead of them. They fought as their horses were killed underneath them and then they fought on foot. It was impossible to form a defensive line or fight a cohesive battle. Desperate knots of warriors fought vicious skirmishes, whirling, hacking and killing the enemy that seethed around them while being forced ever backwards towards the wharf and the last remaining ships.

Ceinwen was nearly knocked from her saddle by a blow to her back. She hauled herself upright keeping a grip on her sword as Arthur swept past her already having cut down her attacker. She saw Elwyn being dragged from his saddle by a band of Adren and forced her horse towards him. Balor too had seen the unhorsed Anglian and he spurred his horse into them swinging his axe in single-handed, furious arcs that sprayed blood through the air. Dystran, the tattooed Mercian, joined him on foot and together they hacked down the Adren that had killed Elwyn.

Ceinwen turned her horse and saw Ethain trying to force his way towards the wharf and the ships still tied there. The Adren were already on the wharf slaughtering the Britons who were still trying to crowd onto the ships. She urged her horse after him, swinging her sword at the Adren in her way. As she neared him he reined in his horse and turned back towards her. Desperation lined his face as he stood in his stirrups trying to find an escape route from the town. She looked beyond him and saw oil-fuelled flames flicking from the portholes of the hold on the nearest ship. As she watched she saw thick smoke rising from another. Kenwyn was following Arthur's orders and setting fire to the ships that would not make it away from the Haven. The ships were packed with people who were now trying to get away from the fires but the Adren were already storming across the gangplanks.

She heard her name being shouted and looked to see Balor screaming at her and pointing behind him to where Arthur had rallied the remaining warriors, most of whom were now on foot. She dug her heels in and tried to ride down the Adren who got in her way but her horse lurched and stumbled and she leapt clear as its front legs gave way. Ethain sped by her using the gap in the Adren that she had inadvertently created and she grabbed at his stirrup. She was wrenched clear of the Adren who had brought down her horse and she fought to keep clear of the horse's legs as she was half-dragged to the relative safety of Arthur's stand.

Ethain positioned himself in the centre of the warriors and looked back at the burning ships and the slaughter on the quayside. He was more appalled by the former than the latter and struggled to accept the truth that there was now no way to escape Britain; everything he had done had been for nought.

Arthur ordered those around him to begin a withdrawal from the doomed town. There were only twenty-nine of them left, ten from the legion and nineteen from the combined war bands of the South and between them they only had five horses. They moved quickly through the broken town heading towards the Westway that ran from the eastern edge of the Haven all the way to the Causeway and beyond to the villages of Branque and Eald where it had all begun.

The wind shrieked through the town adding its cry to the screams from the massacre at the waterfront. It fanned the flames on the ships where the dry-stored provisions fed the fire and fuelled the thick smoke that was being torn across the Haven. The Adren had turned their attention to the dockside and Arthur's band met little opposition as they fled from the town to regroup on the Westway where the heavy rain had turned the worn track to sucking mud.

They stopped half a mile from the Haven and watched the town die. They formed a straggled group, some standing, some half-kneeling in exhaustion, all of them silent. They watched the last ship clear the harbour and keel to port as the wind filled the unfurling sails. Smoke still spewed from the ships caught on the jetty as they burned down to the waterline. Few fires burned elsewhere but the Haven was being destroyed nonetheless; fire would have been a cleaner death.

Ceinwen finished doing what she could for the wounded among them. Those with more serious injuries had not made it away from the harbour. She went to stand by Arthur. His expression was unreadable. She let the rainwater drip from her hair and run down her face. No one seemed willing or able to speak and Ceinwen felt the bitterness of defeat burn away her strength and rob her of the last vestiges of resilience. It was over. They had fought as long as they could, from the Shadow Lands to the Haven; one long bitter road of retreat, each battle marked by the deaths of friends.

She looked at those around her who had survived to witness the sacking of their Haven. Of the Wessex only she, Arthur, Balor and Ethain had lived to see the last defeat. The irony that Ethain was still alive brought a sour taste to her mouth and she spat into the water pooling on the track-way. She wondered what had happened to Morgund and hoped he had made it onto one of the ships but in her heart she knew he would have died fighting his way to join them. She had not seen Morveren either and held a more realistic hope that she was still trying to get to the Haven.

Of the five Anglian warriors left she knew only Hengest and Lissa, and only Gereint and Dystran of the Mercians. She didn't recognise any of the legion soldiers. Frowning she looked up at Arthur, 'What happened to the Uathach? Gwyna and Ruraidh?'

'Probably died defending the wharf,' Balor said when no answer was forthcoming from Arthur.

Dystran sat on his haunches and without looking at anyone spoke up, 'Cowards jumped on the last boat out. Bastards and whores every last one of them. They bolted for it.'

'Are you sure?' Ceinwen asked turning to face him.

'Saw it myself,' he answered then added, 'Didn't mean any offence, Arthur.'

Arthur just continued to stare at the smoke shredding across the Haven.

'Bastards must have had it planned – that's why Gwyna left immediately from Caer Cadarn,' Gereint said bitterly.

There were a few oaths from the other warriors but no voice held any real conviction; retribution and revenge were beyond their means.

Gereint came to stand by Arthur, 'You did what you could. Most everyone got away and they're in the hands of the sea gods now. We need to get moving – that bastard on the hill will be sending his dog soldiers to finish us off.'

Arthur looked away from the town and studied the ridge above the Haven. 'You can see him up there?'

'There's lots of standards and a close group of warriors, his guard probably, surrounding them. And if we can see him, he can see us.'

'Good. I want him to.'

Gereint looked around at the others worried by what Arthur was implying and said in a measured voice, 'There's no point in us dying here now. We've done what we can and now it's time to get well away from here, eh?'

Ethain was about to add his opinion on the matter but he caught Ceinwen's eye and saw a recklessness there that made him shut his mouth. Arthur eventually turned his back to the Haven and faced the few warriors that Britain had left.

'You've done all that anyone could have asked. You've done enough and more. Some of you have fought all the way from the Shadow Lands, others have done more than their share in the battles that followed. You've done enough. You've earned the chance to escape. There's five horses that still have a few miles left in them and whoever wants them can take them. Neither I nor anyone else will ask or expect you to stay. As your warlord I free you from any responsibility other than to yourself.

'If you accept defeat then go now. The Adren might return to where they came from; they may stay. You might have the whole wide land to roam; you may be hunted down. The others might return from the West and they might find the land empty. They may send a reconnaissance and find Britain garrisoned by the Adren and if so then our people will never return to our land.

'If you believe everything you've fought for has been lost and can't be regained then go now and know you've done everything you could. If you accept defeat then go now.'

The warriors looked at each other, no one willing to be the first to suggest leaving and no one ready to admit aloud that they were finally defeated. Gradually their eyes returned to Arthur.

'You want to carry on the war? Use raiding tactics to get as many of the bastards as we can?' Dystran asked eagerly.

'Or maybe raise and train a new legion in the Western Lands? Then come back and win back what we've lost?' Gereint added.

Arthur remained silent, studying the warriors before him.

'You don't mean any of that do you, Arthur?' Ceinwen said when he did not answer.

'I mean to finish the war. The Adren army and Lazure destroyed before the sun rises in spring. The land free of their stain.'

The warriors stared at him. Ceinwen had forgotten just how compelling his assured authority could be and she found herself believing it was possible despite knowing just how hopeless it actually was. The others were clearly seeing the same thing and what they saw was not a heroically false bravado but hope; faith that leapt beyond what they thought was possible.

'You can do this? We can do this?' Ceinwen asked, smiling despite the circumstances.

'Yes. But anyone who fears risking all to achieve it should leave now,' Arthur replied looking directly at the self-appointed leader of the legion soldiers who did indeed fear risking all and as other eyes turned to him his pride overcame his fear and he kept his silence.

'Well, bugger it, we've lost everything already,' Balor said truculently then laughed out loud adding, 'Just our lives left and we wouldn't be warriors if we held those with any worth.'

Up until that point Ethain had managed to keep alive the flicker of hope that they might come to a sensible conclusion, one which gave him some chance of survival, but as the others joined in laughing with Balor he finally lost control of the charade he had kept up for so long.

'You're insane, stupid, mad! All of you!'

The warriors looked at him uncertainly, unsure whether he was joining in the joke or not.

'Look!' Ethain screamed at Arthur pointing with his staff to the destruction of the Haven, 'I know you're half-blind but trust me, we've lost! There's ten thousand Adren and thousands of our own dead right there if you don't believe me! Lost! Everyone else is dead and now you'll pitch what's left at an army? Mad! Lost! Lost! Lost!' He paced back and forth, stamping in the water and mud, no longer even addressing himself to Arthur, 'It's time to give up. Yes. Run, hide, survive. Better a hunted dog than a dead dog. Survive, run, hide! Now, before it's too late!'

The others either looked at him with pity or turned to hide the shame they felt; madness they felt, however understandable, humiliated everyone.

'Ethain. Calm yourself lad, think back to Cei and Aelfhelm, Cerdic and Cuthwin – they'd have wanted us to fight on to the end, they did,' Hengest said gently.

Ethain laughed shrilly and it unnerved many of the warriors who began to think he must have become possessed.

'Cei? Another madman! Another one unafraid of everyone else dying for his cause. Cei? He's dead! Dead, dead, dead! The others? They're dead too! They can't tell me anything. Why? Because they're dead! They aren't saying anything to anyone. The dead don't talk! They can't talk!'

He laughed again and Hengest took one stride to him and punched him in the face as hard as he could. Ethain flopped backwards and landed with a splash in the mud.

'We'll leave him for the Adren. Where do we head to from here, Arthur?' Hengest said, ignoring Ethain who lay staring up into the rain silently mouthing words through a bloody mouth.

243

'We'll make for the Estuary where the river meets the sea. Laethrig's prepared a longboat for us there.'

'Then we better get moving,' Balor said pointing to the hill above the Haven where Lazure was beginning to organise his army. His shadow guard were already heading towards them.

They turned the spent horses loose and Arthur led the surviving warriors off along the Westway. Ceinwen grabbed Balor's arm as he passed, 'Help me lift him up,' she said, nodding towards Ethain.

'Let the bastard rot here. I don't reckon anything he said about the Shadow Lands was true. Look at him! Leave him for the Adren,' he replied, shaking his arm free of her grip and striding off.

Ceinwen looked at the wretched figure and bent down to help him to his feet. He stood unsteadily and threw an arm around her shoulder saying, 'We've got to get away somehow. We'll die like the others if we don't. I know a hiding place, a cave, it's a good cave, I've spent some time there, you'll like it...'

Everything about him revolted her but at one time he had been a friend so Ceinwen let him ramble and she struggled on to catch up with those ahead.

A cry alerted her and she glanced backwards, the wind whipping her hair across her eyes. The Adren were beginning to form up outside the town and an advance guard were already on the Westway. She looked to the sloping hill and through the curtains of rain she saw that Lazure's warriors were on an intercept course with them. She urged Ethain to hurry and when she finally got through to him that the Adren were only a mile behind he picked up the pace and was able to walk unaided. They caught up with the others who avoided even looking at the young Wessex warrior. They were covering the ground at a shambling run, some fighting the mud of the track-way others splashing through the ankle-deep water that stood in the fields to either side.

'How far is it to the river?' Balor asked her when she jogged up alongside him.

Ceinwen thought back to the race to get to the Haven and tried to picture how far they had to go. 'I think Arthur said the longboat was near the mouth of the river, we cut across further upstream, not sure – two, three miles to the Estuary?' she panted in reply.

Balor grimaced in reply. Everything he wore was soaked through and had been for days. He didn't remember when he had last slept or eaten and the thought of running for another three miles across this terrain sapped his resolve. 'Can't we just fight them here? I'll be, too bloody tired, to fight them later,' he said between laboured breaths.

'Tell Arthur!'

'I would if I could catch the bastard.'

Ceinwen laughed again then wondered how she could laugh at such a time but she wasn't alone it seemed; all around her others were cursing and laughing. Somehow the fear of death and the bitterness of defeat had been erased by the hope that they might yet escape and fight again; and win. She worried briefly for their sanity and then automatically checked to see if Ethain was still with them. He was doggedly bringing up the rear.

The land steadily rose for the last mile to the bank of the Estuary and by the time they reached it they were exhausted. They sank to their knees in the sodden grass or collapsed against the stunted trees that grew along the bank.

Arthur stood in the open and looked back. It seemed that Lazure had mobilised his whole army to ensure the warriors that had fought and cost him so dear would not escape again. His standards flew at the head of the following horde and Arthur wondered if he was in the vanguard. He toyed with the idea of lying in wait then charging forward in an attempt to kill the Adren Master but discarded it quickly as too unsure. He laughed at the absurdity of his dismissal; what he planned to do made the charge seem a guaranteed surety. The others grinned to each other at his laugh.

'Pity we haven't got a Wessex Horse to raise in the bastards' faces,' Balor said, watching the advancing Adren.

'Rather have the Anglian longboat!' Hengest answered.

'You straw-heads and your small boats, it ain't natural. What we need is the dragon flag here,' one of the Mercians countered.

'Look!' Ethain shouted, pointing out to sea.

The others stared through the mist of rain and cheered.

Arthur looked to Ceinwen for an explanation.

'It must be the last of the tall ships that got away. It's still on its landward tack, someone said they had to come this way first because of the gale. I hope those bastards following us see it and know that it's not over, they didn't get us and that we'll return one day.'

'There's the longboat!' someone else cried pointing down to the Estuary flats just before a denser curtain of rain obscured the view.

Everyone set off again, slipping and sliding down the treacherously steep bank careless of the danger in their haste to get to the mud flats. Ceinwen and Arthur were the last to start the descent.

'It's on the wrong side, Arthur.'

Arthur just took a last look toward the Adren.

'Arthur, the longboat's on the other side of the river. How are we going to cross to it?'

Arthur looked into her eyes but did not reply. She stared after him as he clambered down the slope desperate to believe her faith in him was not utterly misplaced. She looked out over the mud and sand of the Estuary. She could no longer see the river but guessed it was another two or three miles away. She suddenly felt certain that Arthur had led them here for no other purpose than to die in a final futile stand.

She fell the last ten yards, tumbling through the reeds and landing painfully on the hard-packed grey mud. Arthur was there offering his hand and he pulled her to her feet. She tested her ankle to see if it would hold her weight, 'You're a bastard to give us hope,' she said as they set off after the others who were once again running to put distance between them and their pursuers.

'The hope's real. It will unfold either as you think or as I hope. We'll know soon enough.'

The running was hard on exhausted legs. Despite the frequent and sometimes deep covering of water the rippled grey mud underneath was as solid as stone and each step jarred their aching joints but a glance backwards showed the Adren already at the bank and so they pushed themselves onwards.

Lissa was the first to reach the edge of the estuary river. The longboat could clearly be seen on the far bank sitting on a low cradle that positioned it levelly with its high prow pointing towards the open sea only a few hundred yards away. Even over the roaring wind he could hear the waves as they crashed against the steep-banked beach. The rain hurtled across the flats and mixed with the spray that was driven from the sea in endless horizontal sheets. Despite the turbulent seas he was confident he could get the boat to open water with Hengest's help, and with everyone else on the oars, but first he had to get to the boat and he cast about the flat bank of the river looking for whatever had been left to assist them. The rest of the warriors began to join him in one's and two's as they covered the flat expanse.

'How do we get across?' Gereint shouted to him.

'I don't know – they must have left some kind or rope-rail or something but I can't find it!'

'Why's it on the other side?' Gereint shouted.

Lissa shrugged in exasperation, 'How should I know? Maybe they thought the Adren would be close behind, we'd cross whatever bridge they left or swim our horses across and leave the Adren on this bank? I don't know!'

'That's no bloody good to us if we can't get across!'

'I know that!' Lissa shouted back at him angrily.

Arthur and Ceinwen brought up the rear and Lissa turned to him, 'There's no rope-rail, no barge to get us across!'

Arthur went to the river's edge. It was two to three hundred yards across to the other side and the heaving river was racing to the sea.

'No one could swim that! Impossible! You'd be carried out to sea in seconds!' Lissa said thinking Arthur might try to swim across.

'If we had horses we might make it but we'd have to go upstream some,' Gereint said.

'We haven't got any bloody horses!' Lissa shouted back. Arthur looked back to the high Estuary bank and others followed his gaze.

It was swarming with the Adren. They stretched along the slopes for a mile or more and the vanguard of the army was already cutting across diagonally and to landward; even if they tried to race back along this side of the river the Adren would cut them off within a mile. They were trapped between the river, the sea and the Adren army.

Ethain sank to his knees and started to cry, the sobs racking his body, but the sound was lost in the wailing wind. Most of the warriors turned to face the still distant but encompassing Adren, accepting that there was no way to get to the longboat and readying their weapons in silence.

Lissa turned to Arthur, 'I'm going to try.'

'You won't get across, not even a horse could swim that.'

'I'll go upstream a few hundred yards and hope the current will carry me to the far bank before it carries me out to sea.'

'And then what?' Hengest asked him.

'Maybe there's rope onboard the boat.'

'And if there is?'

Lissa shrugged, 'Tie one end to the boat, swim back and then at least we'd have a rope-rail,' he shrugged again to acknowledge it was only a slim possibility.

'You don't have a chance, Lissa,' Hengest said trying to dissuade him.

'There's not much chance anyway, is there?' he asked with a look towards the Adren. They too had seen the boat and were covering the distance quickly, intent on denying the Britons any chance of getting away from them again.

Everyone bar Ethain watched as Lissa ran back down the river. He dived in three hundred yards upstream and the Britons roared out their encouragement even though the wind and crashing surf drowned any noise they could make. It seemed he was making good headway at first but by the time he neared the middle of the river he was already level with their position and then the current took him under. The shouting died and they saw him surface a hundred yards further on as he was borne helplessly to the swirling chaos where the river met the sea.

No one said a word. They turned to face the Adren who had stopped their advance half a mile away. They were no longer in a hurry as it was clear the Britons had no way to cross the torrent at their backs. Their ranks filled the flats as they spread out in an arc denying the Britons any escape route. Lazure had spread the word among them that they had the Briton's leader at bay at last and that he wanted his own guard to slay him and those around him.

'What are they waiting for?' one of the legion asked but no one answered him. The levity they had felt during the chase from the Haven had evaporated. Their high-spirited confidence had given way to the cold certainty that they would soon die on the windswept flats of the Estuary.

'Anyone got any food?' Balor asked to a few short laughs, 'No, I'm serious, I hate fighting on an empty gut.'

'You sound like Cael,' Ceinwen replied.

'He would have had some food with him for emergencies like this. Sensible lad.'

They watched as the ranks of Adren parted to let through a new group.

'Who's that?' one of the Anglians asked.

'That'll be Lazure and his personal guard – the lot who took down Gwyna's Uathach. Well, Uathach are one thing but we're another altogether. They're in for a bloody surprise,' Gereint said, hefting his sword.

'No, not there, over by the longboat. Who's that on horseback?' the same Anglian asked.

Everyone turned to see what the Anglian warrior was talking about and they all saw the figure on horseback, arms waving frantically trying to get their attention.

'It's Morveren!' Ceinwen shouted.

'Tell her to check the boat for rope!' Hengest shouted.

'How?'

Hengest moved to one side and began an exaggerated mime for coiling a rope, throwing it and reeling it back in. The rider on the far bank had stopped by the very edge of the swirling river, the horse obviously reluctant to enter the fearsome current. Hengest continued his actions and others pointed toward the longboat.

Morveren appeared to understand what they wanted and hauled herself up the side of the boat. She disappeared from view for a minute and the warriors checked to see how near Lazure's shadow guard were; they were much nearer and closing the remaining distance rapidly.

Morveren came back into view and holding her hands apart she drew them closer together and shook her head; there was rope but nothing long enough to cover the breadth of the river. The warriors cursed.

'Is there any way she can launch the boat by herself?' Arthur asked Hengest.

'No, it'd take three or four people and each stronger than her. Even if she did she'd never get to it to this side of the bank – she'd need double that number to row it across this river.'

'Can't she swim her horse across with what rope there is and we'll take our chances hanging on for the return journey?' Dystran asked.

'Her horse will be exhausted. It'd never make the journey once let alone twice and with us dragging it down there'd be no chance,' Ceinwen replied.

'Is there nothing she can do?' Gereint asked in desperation.

Clearly Morveren felt the same way. She was coaxing her agitated horse into the eddying water but the horse knew it was unable to cross and refused to enter the deeper swells.

'She can save herself,' Ceinwen said.

Arthur moved right to the water's edge and waved his sword above his head. Morveren saw him and steadied her mount. Arthur pointed back the way she had come but she stayed where she was. Arthur gestured again, pointing with his sword, telling her to leave the Estuary and to leave them.

Morveren hung her head and hauled on the reins turning the thankful horse back out of the water. When she was out of the shallows she turned to look at the band of warriors, so desperately few against the backdrop of the Adren army that seemed to fill that side of the Estuary valley. She recognised Ceinwen and Balor and forced herself to return their waves. There was a figure kneeling by the edge of the river but she couldn't make out who it was. Morgund was not with them, she was sure of that; he must have died in whatever battle took place at the Haven. She felt empty and lost, unable to help her friends and unwilling to leave them. She watched Arthur who stood facing her on the far bank and she raised a hand in a final farewell to him and then, with tears in her eyes, she turned and rode away from the Britons' last stand.

They watched her until she was lost from sight in the driving rain and flying spray.

'At least she got away,' Ceinwen said, feeling glad for her. Balor agreed and Morveren's escape from the Adren lifted all their spirits.

Resigned to their fate the warriors formed up in a loose phalanx with their backs to the river, ready to fight to the end and resolved to kill as many of Lazure's guard as they could. Ethain remained on his knees, rocking back and forth and no longer aware of his surroundings; he hadn't even been aware of Morveren on the far bank.

Arthur moved to the fore of the phalanx as Lazure's warriors closed to within fifty-feet. He stood with his sword held ready in one hand and faced the enemy. The wind buffeted them and the icy rain slanted across the ground between the two groups as they waited.

The Adren ranks parted and Lazure walked towards the Britons with his Cithol guard flanking and following him. He stopped five yards in front of Arthur.

'How bitter is your defeat, Arthur of the Britons? Your land laid waste. Your people slaughtered or in exile. And those in exile I'll hunt down and slaughter too. Tell me, how bitter is your defeat?'

The warriors felt the power behind his words and had to fight the overwhelming and sudden urge to throw down their weapons and plead for mercy.

'Merdynn told me all about you, old man. I know your history and who you are. And I know who you serve. But tell me, why did you come to my land?'

'All lands are my Master's and all within those lands belong to my Master. Merdynn was a fool to resist us and now he's dead. You were a fool to resist us and now you'll die too. You should have left the Veiled City for me.'

'It was a mistake for you to come to my land,' Arthur replied calmly.

The old man raised his staff and pointed it at the warriors, 'KNEEL!' he commanded in a voice that drowned the wind and sea.

The warriors behind Arthur dropped involuntarily to their knees and hung their heads. Arthur fought the urge to obey and it was all he could do to remain standing.

Lazure looked at him strangely, 'So you do have some of the old blood. And you have the old sword too. Lay it on the ground and kneel before me. My Master has cause to wish it in his keeping.'

Arthur felt himself bend to put the sword on the ground but gripping it with all his strength he forced himself to straighten up and face Lazure.

'Do it now! You are commanded!' Lazure shouted at him and pointed his staff directly at Arthur.

'No. The sword was never forged for you.'

Arthur wrenched his mind free from Lazure's control and with a final effort hurled the sword away. It arced high, turning end over end and plunged far out into the raging river.

Lazure's face twisted in fury and he was about to command his guard to slay the Britons when a chanting began behind Arthur, barely audible at first but rising to soar above the roaring around them. The incantation was repetitive and clear, and something about the strange language seemed immediately familiar to Arthur; suddenly he was remembering the ancient burial mound of Delbaeth Gofannon and Merdynn standing before the entrance and chanting in the same way.

'Impossible!' Lazure shrieked, echoing Arthur's thoughts, 'You're dead! Gone from this world!'

Lazure was leaning on his staff and staring with incredulity at the chanting figure beyond Arthur. Arthur turned to see Ethain facing the sea and holding out the staff he had taken from Merdynn.

Lazure's horrified attention was fixed on the chanting Ethain. Arthur swiftly freed Cei's war axe from behind him and in one ferocious swing brought it crashing down on Lazure's outstretched arm. It sliced through the wasted muscle and splintered the bone. Lazure stared in disbelief as his staff and forearm dropped into the mud of the Estuary. His eyes shot up to meet Arthur's just as Arthur swung the axe with all his strength up under Lazure's chin snapping his head back and cleaving half his face off. Lazure's dead body slumped to the ground and a thin wail rose above the wind long after it was possible for him to cry out.

The warriors all around Arthur were coming back to their senses and picking up their fallen weapons. They stumbled to their feet just as Lazure's enraged guard charged them.

'Defend Ethain!' Arthur roared out to them, 'Defend Ethain!'

Ethain was still facing the sea, still chanting and oblivious to the desperate defence and the dying warriors around him.

The legion were no match for Lazure's Cithol guard and they were the first to fall to the enemy. The remaining warriors formed a tight ring around the chanting Ethain and fought desperately to keep Lazure's guard from reaching him but they were outnumbered by an enemy who were at least their equal and Arthur knew they only had minutes before they were overwhelmed.

Ceinwen killed two of her attackers but one of them cut her left arm deeply and she was unable to defend herself from the two swords of her third attacker; she died trying to take him with her. Moments later Balor died avenging her. Gereint and Dystran held out for another minute but it was all they could do to protect themselves and Ethain, and they too fell to the inevitable and died within seconds of each other. Hengest and the Anglians blocked the attackers from reaching Ethain but a renewed charge from the enemy sent Anglian and Cithol alike crashing into the river were they traded blow for blow and death for death.

Arthur could feel the river swelling beyond its banks and running over the backs of his legs. He looked towards the sea for a fraction of second and saw a three-foot wave tumbling across the flats and racing towards them but in the time it had taken him to see it one of the guard had cut through his defence and a sword hacked into his ribs. He stumbled and Ethain was immediately scythed down by two of the Cithol. Arthur hewed at one with Cei's axe but even as he killed him another sword crashed down on his shoulder, cutting deeply and breaking bone. The last of the Anglians fell in the water beside him and Arthur advanced on his enemies, swinging the axe single-handedly in wide arcs and keeping them at bay as blood poured from his broken shoulder. He roared and cursed at the enemy surrounding him and with a last shout he dived into them crushing the skull of one with his first blow and disembowelling a second before the blows rained down on him from every side. He fell to his knees and was knocked sideways as the wave engulfed them all. He struggled to the surface with his blood darkening the water around him. The sea was surging in behind the wave and the Adren were floundering in the sudden tide. Arthur saw the longboat ease from its cradle and spin as the river's current fought the tide for possession. He knew that within minutes the Estuary would be swamped by the vicious winter tide. He let Cei's axe slip from his grasp as his world darkened. The surging sea spun him around and the river's current took him as he slid beneath the waves. He died knowing that Ethain had brought in the high winter tide. Merdynn had not abandoned Britain.

Epilogue

The old man moved slowly, picking his path between the snow-laden trees with care. The air was frozen still and his shallow breaths plumed in the starlight. The trees were winter-bare with precarious lines of snow thickening the interlocked branches that stood black against the canopied stars. He paused to rest and leant on his staff. He kept his breathing light knowing it was unwise to do otherwise when the cold was this deep. The forest around him was silent and completely motionless, held fast by winter's peace, but it was not lifeless. He searched the hard snow for the footprints he had been following for the last hour or so and saw them leading on towards the dark shadows ahead. He smiled to himself and resumed his slow pace.

He found her in the clearing ahead and he stopped in the deeper shadows of a once high wall to watch her. She had already set a fire in a snow-covered stone bower that stood in the lee of a lone, magnificent cedar. Her pack lay open beside her and she was selecting food for their meal. She looked over to where he stood and held up a choice of meal in either hand. The old man chuckled to himself and leaving the darker shadows he made his way across to her pointing to the choice in her right hand.

He pulled off his fur mittens and lowered himself onto the blankets that had been doubled on the stone bench and sat with his old hands splayed to the fire's growing warmth.

'You're getting slow, old man. There was a time when it was me who trailed behind you.'

'And you're still far too young to be calling me an old man,' he replied.

She laughed as she placed a pot of water over the fire to boil.

'Besides, I knew you would come straight to this place.'

'Oh?' she enquired.

'It was your mother's favourite place.'

She stopped adding vegetables to the pot and looked around at the frozen clearing as the old man continued, 'She used to call it the Winter Garden and it used to be a place of great beauty.'

'It must have been a very long time ago.' The young girl was clearly unimpressed and she resumed her preparations for their meal.

'It was destroyed thirteen winters ago.'

'So it was Arthur who destroyed it?' she asked feigning disinterest.

'Well, blame's a tricky arrow – it rarely flies straight and it usually lands wide of the mark.'

'Like your answers. One day you'll give a straight answer to a straight question,' she replied half to her herself.

'And you're too young for that tone of voice too.'

She smiled at him and sat back down beside him. 'So then, who was to blame?'

'Some might say Arthur. Others might blame the Adren. Still others would lay the crime at your grandfather's door.'

'And you? Who would you blame?'

'Inevitability.'

'Typically wriggly of you. What about all those lessons about choice and how fate is just superstition?'

'Fate, young lady, is where a person's choices are already chosen for them – usually by some god with a questionable sense of humour. Inevitability, on the other hand, is where a person will ultimately choose to be true to their own nature – thus they follow and make their own inevitable destiny.'

'So fate and a person's nature amount to the same thing then.'

'No, you infuriating child, fate is imposed while nature is grown and developed.'

'Then the gods help me.'

He looked at her warily, 'Why?'

'You've brought me up, you've helped develop my nature.'

'And witness my punishment.'

'But it was inevitable,' she said with a shrug and the old man laughed.

They sat back in companionable silence and the girl sloughed some water from the pot to make them both a hot drink. She held the steaming cup cradled in both hands and blew gently on the surface before taking a cautious first sip. 'So, this was my mother's home was it?'

'No, just her favoured place away from the city. Her home, the Veiled City, that's below us – or what's left of it is.'

'Arthur destroyed that too according to the tales.'

'I refer you to my previous answer.'

The girl took a longer drink from her cup. 'This is where they first met wasn't it?'

'Yes, it's where they first met, at least the first time with both of them as adults.'

'She wasn't much older than me!'

'You're still a child.'

'If you say so, old man.'

She settled herself before the fire and added more ingredients to the bubbling pot, stirring them in while singing softly to herself. The old man watched her with affection. When the meal was ready she doled out equal measures into two bowls and handed one to her companion. They ate quickly and in silence. When they had finished, the girl stoked up the fire and asked if they were going to sleep there. The old man looked around the clearing, staring at the shadows that flicked in the light from the fire.

'Afraid of ghosts from the old days?' she asked watching him.

'Yes,' he answered simply and the girl frowned at him.

'Tell me a tale of the ghosts then, perhaps that will placate them and they'll leave us alone.'

'You've heard all the tales.'

'Then tell me a new one.'

'We haven't written them yet.'

The girl frowned again, it was unlike him to pass up on a chance to re-tell one of the stories and she had hoped it would distract him from what was obviously making him sorrowful. 'You know that last village we visited, the Anglian one?'

'Yes,' he replied, still staring into the darkness of the surrounding wood.

'I heard a new tale there. Or a new ending to one of the old stories.'

He took his gaze away from the darkness and looked at her enquiringly.

'I sneaked back into the hall once you had gone to sleep,' she said partly in apology and yet with a touch of defiance.

'Well?' he asked avoiding the temptation to chide her.

'It was about Arthur's last battle against the Adren.'

'As if any one of them were there to see it,' the old man snorted dismissively.

'Do you want to hear it or not?'

'Go on then,' he replied and settled himself nearer the fire.

'They say that he and some of his warriors managed to escape from the winter tide, and the Adren, by boarding a longboat. The old man telling the story swore it was true because he heard it from someone who was on the last ship that sailed to the West and that person saw a longboat floating from the estuary.'

The old man stared at her and she saw the sadness in his eyes.

'They say that he'll return, with his war band, when Britain's need is at the greatest,' she added with a shrug, hoping to disarm the scorn she thought was coming her way but the old man was looking away into the darkness once again.

'There is nothing new under the sun – or the stars; what has been will be again.'

'Another of your sayings?'

'Belongs to an ancient prophet actually. I forget which one.'

'So there wasn't a longboat, those that claim there was are lying?'

'No, there was a longboat and some may well have seen it from the last ship. Morveren certainly saw it. Laethrig left it there for Arthur but whether he left it on the wrong side of the river or whether Arthur thought he'd still have his horses to get across the river we'll never know. Perhaps Arthur used it merely to get his warriors down on to the estuary flats so that the Adren would follow and fall into the trap set for them. But in any case Arthur and his few warriors never reached it. Arthur died in the Estuary – along with the last of his war band and Lazure, and most of the Adren army.'

'If people want to believe otherwise they will,' she countered.

'Very true, but believing something doesn't make it so.'

'Sometimes belief is the only thing that *can* make something true.'

'And who's being wriggly now?' the old man accused her with a tired smile.

She nodded her guilt and after a few moments silence added, 'The same Anglian also went on to tell how it was Aelfric and his outlaws who first sailed back to Britain, how they met Morveren who had waited at the Haven and how she had lit the beacon before each dawn to guide them back, and how together they had hunted down the remaining Adren - and that it wasn't Queen Gwyna's war band who finally rid the land of the enemy.'

'And that, you know, is the truth.'

'I should like to meet him again.'

'Who?'

'The outlaw, Aelfric, of course.'

The old man sighed and muttered, 'There truly is nothing new under the sun.'

The young girl smiled and added more fuel to the fire before pulling her furs around her and settling down to sleep with a hand clasped around the clear jewel that hung from her neck.

Merdynn stayed awake, lost in his memories and staring out into the darkness.